THE BIG SKY READER

THE BIG SKY READER

EDITED BY

ALLEN JONES AND JEFF WETMORE

ST. MARTIN'S PRESS ❧ NEW YORK

THOMAS DUNNE BOOKS.
An imprint of St. Martin's Press.

Interior illustrations by Russell Chatham

ISBN 0-312-19362-9

First published in the United States by Spring Creek Publishing
and Big Sky Journal

First St. Martin's Press Edition: December 1998

10 9 8 7 6 5 4 3 2 1

CONTENTS

INTRODUCTION

AROUND HERE, WE CALL IT THE PROJECT. Outside the offices of *Big Sky Journal*, it is called "a magazine." But what it is, really, is a collection of voices, a choir of the uncommon, trying to define itself through a place that is larger than any of us. The magazine is a convenient package of delivery, a reflector, providing the best of the place in the form of essay, image, art and fiction. A lot of good stuff blows through this joint, and some of it sticks between the covers. What we have here is the nearly impossible reduction of several years and several thousand pages into a lucid collection of those voices.

The idea for *Big Sky Journal* crossed my mind several years before I was able to escape the demands of an existing career to move the concept toward reality. By 1992, I was able to ask David McCumber, then the talented editor of a Santa Barbara newspaper, if he would help give the magazine its launch. With the confused excitement of a new project, *Big Sky Journal* punched a hole in the sky, bound for who knows where.

For the past few years, the magazine has enjoyed the award-winning editorship of Allen Jones, in whose hands the reigns still lay. Without such hands, there would be, as they say, no ink, no paper. And no anthology. Pleasantly, we have found that there are still a surprising number of serious readers at large. Just when we might think the entire planet has abandoned the printed word for the sirens of the internet and video store, *Big Sky Journal* continues to grow and evolve.

So what is this collection about? To some measure, each of us has that somewhat odd impulse to try and save the unsavable, to freeze the moment: the prom photo; the yearbook; the Christmas video. Some people collect stamps, we collect stories…

But unlike some collectors, we think we might have an idea why we collect these essays, articles and fiction pieces: they make us feel happy and smart and put us in touch with a place that interests us.

They make us respond in a way we can trust. Wallace Stegner said it best: "...the smell of distance...the largeness and clarity take the scales from my eyes, and I respond as unthinkingly as a salmon that swims past a rivermouth and tastes the waters of its birth."

Describing that moment and making it happen are two different things. The pieces in this collection are easy to read. They are hard to write. Ask the best of them: there is nothing automatic about a well-focussed piece of writing, especially when one is wrestling with a subject as vast as the West. It's hard to get your arms around it. Describing his short story *Big Two-Hearted River* in a 1924 letter to Edward O'Brien, even Hemingway admitted the difficulty in delivering a place to the reader: "What I've been doing is trying to do country so you don't remember the words after you read it but actually have Country. It is hard because to do it you have to see the country all complete all the time you write and not just have a romantic feeling about it."

If we have done our job, you will have Country, and, even if it's only for a moment, we will have saved something. To those writers who have so bravely given us their personal reflection of this amazing place, we offer humble thanks.

Jeff Wetmore
Publisher
Big Sky Journal

THE BIG SKY READER

FICTION
AND
ESSAYS

FIRES

By Rick Bass

SOME YEARS THE HEAT COMES IN APRIL. There is always wind in April, but with luck there is warmth, too. There is usually a drought, so that the fields are dry, and the wind is from the south. Everyone in the valley moves their seedlings from the indoors to the outdoors, into their old barns-turned-into-greenhouses. Root crops are what do best up here. The soil is rich from all the many fires, and potatoes from this valley taste like candy. Carrots pull free of the dark earth and taste like crisp sun. I like to cook with onions. Strawberries do well, too, if they're watered.

The snowline has moved up out of the valley by April, up into the woods, and even on up above the woods, disappearing, except for the smallest remote oval patches of it, and the snowshoe hares, gaunt but still white, move down out of the snow as it retreats to get to the gardens' fresh berries, and the green growing grasses; but you can see the rabbits coming a mile away, coming after your berries—hopping through the green and gold sun—filled woods, as white and pure as Persian cats, hopping over brown logs, coming down from the centuries-old game trails of black earth.

The rabbits come straight for my outside garden like zombies, relentless, and I sit on the back porch and sight in on them. But because they are too beautiful to kill in great numbers, I shoot only one every month or so, just to warn them. I clean the one I shoot and fry it in a skillet with onions and half a piece of bacon.

Sometimes at night I'll get up and look out the window and see the rabbits out in the garden, nibbling at whatever's available, but also standing around the greenhouse, all around it, just trying to tunnel in—dirt flying all through the air—while others of them just sit there at the doorway, waiting.

The hares are only snow-white like that for a few weeks, after the snow is gone; then they begin to lose the white fur—rather, they do not lose it, but it begins to turn brown, like leaves decaying, so that they are mottled for a while during the change, but then finally they are com-

3

pletely brown, and safe again, with the snows gone. But for those few weeks when they are still white, the rabbits sit out in my garden like white boulders. I haven't had a woman living with me in a long time now. Whenever one does move in with me, it feels as if I've tricked her, have caught her in a trap: as if the gate has been closed behind her, and she doesn't yet realize it. It's very remote up here.

One summer, my friend Tom's sister came up here to spend the summer with Tom and his wife, Nancy, and to train at altitude. Her name was Glenda, and she was a runner from Washington, and that was all she did, was run. Glenda was very good, and she had run races in Italy, in France, and Switzerland. She told everyone when she got up here that this was the most beautiful place she had ever seen, told all these rough loggers and their hard wives this, and we all believed her. Very few of us had ever been anywhere else to be able to question her.

We would all sit out at the picnic tables in front of the saloon, ten or twelve of us at a time, half of the town, and watch the river. Ducks and geese, heading back north, stopped in our valley to breed, to build nests, and to raise their young. Ravens, with their wings and backs shining greasy in the sun, were always flying across the valley, from one side of the mountains to the other. Anyone who needed to make a little money could always do so in April by planting seedlings for the Forest Service, and it was always a time of relaxation because of that fact, a time of no tempers, only loose happiness. I did not need much money, in April or in any other month, and I would often sit out at the picnic table with Glenda and Tom and Nancy and drink beers. Glenda would never drink more than two. She had yellow hair that was cut short, and lake-blue eyes, a pale face, and a big grin, not unlike Tom's, that belied her seriousness, though now she is gone, I think I remember her always being able to grin because of her seriousness. I certainly don't understand why it seems that way to me now. Like the rest of us, Glenda had no worries, not in April and certainly not later on in the summer. She had only to run.

I never saw Glenda in the fall, which was when she left; I don't know if she ever smiled like that when she got back to Washington or not. She was separated from her boyfriend, who lived in California, and she didn't seem to miss him, didn't ever seem to think about him.

The planters burned the slopes they had cut the previous summer and fall, before planting the seedlings, and in the afternoons there would be a sweet-smelling haze that started about halfway up the valley walls, and rose into the highest mountains, and then spilled over them, moving north into Canada, riding on the south winds. The fires' haze never settled in our valley, but would hang just above us, on the days it was there, turning all the sunlight a beautiful, smoky blue, and making things when seen across the valley—a barn in another pasture, or a fenceline—seem much farther away than they really were. It made things seem softer, too.

There was a long zippered scar on the inside of Glenda's knee that started just above her ankle and went all the way up inside her leg to mid-thigh. She had injured the knee when she was seventeen, long before the days of arthroscopic surgery, and she'd had to have the knee rebuilt the old-fashioned way, with blades and scissors, but the scar only seemed to make her legs, both of them, look even more beautiful, the part that was not scarred, and even the scar had a graceful curve to it as it ran such a long distance up her leg.

Glenda wore green nylon shorts and a small white shirt when she ran, and a headband. Her running shoes were dirty white, the color of the road dust during the drought.

"I'm thirty-two, and have six or seven more good years of running," she said whenever anyone asked her what her plans were, and why she ran so much, and why she had come to our valley to run. Mostly, it was the men who sat around with us in front of the saloon, watching the river, watching the spring winds, and just being glad with the rest of us that winter was over. I do not think the women liked Glenda very much, except for Nancy.

It was not very well understood in the valley what a great runner Glenda was.

I think it gave Glenda pleasure that it wasn't.

"I would like for you to follow Glenda on your bicycle," Tom said the first time I met her. Tom had invited me over for dinner—Glenda had gotten into the valley the day before, though we had all known that she was coming for weeks beforehand, and we had been waiting for her.

"There's money available from her sponsor to pay you for it," Tom said, handing me some money, or trying to, finally putting it in my shirt pocket. He had been drinking, and seemed as happy as I had seen him in a long time. He called her "Glen" instead of "Glenda" sometimes—and after putting the money in my pocket, he put an arm around Nancy, who looked embarrassed for me, and the other arm around Glenda, who did not, and so I had to keep the money, which was not that much, anyway.

"You just ride along behind her, with a pistol"—Tom had a pistol

holstered on his belt, a big pistol, and he took it off and handed it to me—
"and you make sure nothing happens to her, the way it did to that
Ocherson woman."

The Ocherson woman had been visiting friends and had been walking home, but had never made it: a bear had evidently charged out of the
willows along the river road and had dragged her back across the river.
It was in the spring when she disappeared and everyone thought she had
run away, and her husband had even gone around all summer making a
fool out of himself by talking badly about her, and then hunters found her
in the fall, right before the first snow. There were always bear stories in
any valley, but we thought ours was the worst, because it was the most
recent, and because it had been a woman.

"It'll be good exercise for me," I said to Tom, and then I said to Glenda, "Do you run fast?"

It wasn't a bad job. I was able to keep up with her most of the time,
and we started early in the mornings. Some days Glenda would run just
a few miles, very fast, and other days it seemed she was going to run forever. There was hardly ever any traffic—not a single car or truck—and
I'd daydream as I rode along behind her.

We'd leave the meadows out in front of Tom's place, and head up
the South Fork road, up into the woods, toward the summit, going past
my cabin. The sun would be burning brightly by the time we neared the
summit, and we'd be up into the haze from the planting fires, and everything would be foggy and old-looking, as if we had gone back in
time—as if we were living in a time when things had really happened,
when things still mattered, and not everything had been decided yet.

Glenda would be sweating so hard from running the summit that
her shirt and shorts would be drenched, her hair damp and sticking to the
side of her face, and the sweat would wet her socks and even her tennis
shoes. But she was always saying that the people she would be racing
against would be training even harder than she was.

There were lakes up past the summit, and the air was cooler, on the
north slopes the lakes still had thin crusts of ice on them, crusts that
thawed out, just barely, each afternoon, but that froze again, each night—
and what Glenda liked to do after she'd reached the summit, her face as
bright as if sunburned, and her wrists limp and loose, sometimes wavering a little in her stride, finally, so great was the heat and her
exhaustion—was to leave the road and run down the game trail leading
to the lakes—tripping, stumbling, running downhill again; and I would
have to throw the bike down and hurry after her—and pulling her shirt

off, she would run out into the shallows of the first lake, her feet breaking through the thin ice, and then she would sit down in the cold water, like some animal chased there by hounds.

"It feels good," she said, the first time she did that, and she leaned her head back on the ice behind her, the ice she had not broken through, and she spread her arms out across the ice as if she were resting on a crucifix, and she looked up at the haze in the sky with nothing above us, for we were above the treeline.

"Come over here," she said. "Come feel this."

I waded out into the pond, following her trail through the ice, and sat down next to her.

She took my hand and put it on her chest.

What I felt in there was like nothing I had ever imagined; it was like lifting up the hood of a car that is still running, with all the cables and belts and fan blades still running. I wanted to take my hand away; I wanted to get her to a doctor. I wondered if she were going to die, and if I would be responsible. I wanted to pull my hand away, but she made me keep it there, and gradually the drumming slowed, became steadier, and still she made me keep my hand there, until we could both feel the water's coldness. Then we got out—I had to help her up, because her injured knee was stiff—and we lay our clothes out on rocks to dry in the sun, and we laid out on flat rocks ourselves and let the wind and the sun dry us as well. She said that she had come to the mountains to run because it would strengthen her knee. But there was something that made me believe that that was not the reason, and not the truth, though I cannot tell you what other reason there might have been.

We went into the lake every hot day, after her run, and there was always the thinnest sheet of ice, back in the shadows. It felt wonderful; and lying out in the sun afterwards was wonderful, too. After we had dried, our hair smelled like the smoke from the fires in the valley below. Sometimes I thought that Glenda might be dying, and had come here to live her last days, to run in a country of great beauty.

After we were dry, we walked back, and as we went back over the crest of the summit and started down toward the valley, we would slowly come out of the haze, and would be able to see all of the valley below us, green and soft, with the slow wind of the Yaak River crawling through the middle of it, and on the north wall of the valley midway up the slopes, the ragged fires would be burning, with wavering lines and shifting walls of smoke rising from behind the trees, sheets of smoke rising straight into the sky.

The temptation to get on the bike and just coast all the way down was always strong, but I knew what my job was, we both did, and it was the time when bears were coming out of hibernation, when everything was, and the safety of the winter was not to be confused with the seriousness of summer, with the way things were changing.

Sometimes, walking back, we would come across ruffed grouse—males—courting and fanning in the middle of the road, spinning and doing their little dance, their throat-sacs inflated bright and red, pulsing, and the grouse would not want to let us past—they would stamp their feet and spin in mad little circles, trying to block where it was we were going, trying to protect some small certain area they had staked out for themselves. Glenda seemed to stiffen whenever we came upon the fanning males, and shrieked when they rushed at her ankles, trying to peck her, as we tried to hurry around them.

We'd stop back by my cabin for lunch, on the way back into the valley. I'd open all the windows—the sun would have heated all the logs in the house, so that when we came inside there was a rich dusty smell, as it is when you have been away from your house for a long time and first come back—but that smell was always there, in my cabin—and we would sit at the breakfast room table and look out the window, out at the old weedy chicken house I'd never used, but which the people who'd lived in the cabin before me had built, and we'd look at the woods going up onto the mountain behind the chicken house.

I had planted a few wild apple trees in the back yard that spring, and the place that had sold them to me said that these trees would be able to withstand even the coldest winters, though I was not sure I believed it. They were small trees, and it was supposed to be four years before they started bearing fruit, and that sounded to me like such a long time that I had to really think about it before buying them. But I had just bought them without really knowing why I was doing it. I also didn't know what would make a person run as much as Glenda did. But I liked riding with her, and having coffee with her after the runs, and I knew I would be sad to see her leave the valley. I think that was what kept up the distance between us, a nice distance, just the right-sized distance—the fact that each of us knew that she was only going to be there a certain amount of time—that she would be there for the rest of May and June, then she would be gone. We knew what was going to happen, it was certainty, and therefore it seemed to take away any danger, any wildness. There was a wonderful sense of control. She drank her coffee black. We would snack on smoked whitefish that I had caught the previous winter.

I had a couple of dogs in the back yard, Texas hounds that I'd brought up north with me a few years ago, and I kept them in a pen in the winter so that they wouldn't roam and chase and catch deer, but in the spring and summer the sun felt so thin and good and the hounds were so old, that I didn't keep them penned up, but instead just let them lie around in the grass, dozing. There was one thing they would chase, though, in the summer. It lived under the chicken house—I don't know what it was; it was dark, and ran too fast for me to ever get a good look at it—and it's possible that even if I had been able to see it, it would have been some animal that I had never seen before—some rare animal, something from Canada perhaps—maybe something no one had ever seen. Whatever it was—small and dark, with fur, but not shaggy, not a bear cub—it never grew from year to year, but always stayed the same, though it seemed young somehow, as if it might someday grow—anyway, it lived in a burrow under the chicken house, and it excited the dogs terribly. It would come ripping out of the woods, just a fleet dark blur, headed for the burrow, and the old dogs would be up and baying, right on its tail, but the thing always made it into the burrow just ahead of them.

Glenda and I would sit at the window and watch for it every day. But it kept no timetable, and there was no telling when it would come, or even if it would. We called it a hedgehog, because that was the closest thing it might have resembled.

Some nights Glenda would call me on the short-wave radio, would key the mike a few times to make it crackle and wake me up, and then, mysteriously, I would hear her voice in the night, floating in static, as if it were in the night, out with the stars—her voice: "Have you seen the hedgehog?" she would ask, sleepily, but it would be only a radio that was in the dark house with me, not her, not her real voice. "Did you see the hedgehog?" she'd want to know, and I'd wish she were staying with me, I'd wish she were with me at that moment. But it would be no good— Glenda was leaving in August, or September at the latest.

"No," I'd say. "No hedgehog today. Maybe it's gone away," I'd say—though I had thought that again and again, dozens of times, but then I would always see it again, just when I thought I never would.

"How are the dogs?" she'd ask. "How are Homer and Ann?"

"They're asleep."

"Good night," she'd say.

"Good night," I'd say.

On Thursday nights, I would always have Tom and Nancy and Glenda over for dinner. Friday was Glenda's day off from running, so that she could drink, could stay up late, and she did not have to worry about any after-effects the next morning. We would start out drinking at the Dirty Shame, sitting out front watching the river, watching the ducks and geese headed north, and then before dusk we would go back down to my ranch, and Glenda and I would fix dinner while Tom and Nancy sat on the front porch and smoked cigars and watched the elk come out into the dusk in the meadow across the road.

"Where's this famous hedgehog?" Tom would bellow, blowing smoke rings into the night, big perfect Os, and the elk would lift their heads, chewing the summer grass like cattle, the bulls' antlers glowing with velvet.

"In the backyard," Glenda would say, washing the salad, or rinsing off the carrots, or even the trout fillets. "But you can only see him in the daytime."

"Aww, bullshit!" Tom would roar, standing up with his bottle of Jack Daniels, and he'd take off down the steps, stumbling, and we'd all put down what we were doing and get the flashlight and go with him to make sure he was all right, because Tom was a trapper, and it riled him to think there was an animal he did not know, could not trap, could not even see—Tom had tried to trap the hedgehog before, but had never caught anything—and Tom did not believe there was any such animal. Out by the chicken coop, Tom would get down on his hands and knees, breathing hard, and we'd crowd all around and try to shine the flashlight into the deep, dusty hole, to see if there might be a patch of fur, the tip of a snout, or anything—and Tom would be making grunting noises that were, I supposed, designed to make the animal want to come out—but we never saw anything, and it would be cold under all the stars, and we'd be able to see the far-off glows that were the planting fires, burning slowly, even into the night, but which were being held in check by back-fires; they were in control.

We had one of those propane fish fryers, and we'd put it out on the front porch and cut the trout into cubes, roll them around in sweet mustard and flour, then drop them in the hot spattering grease. We'd fix more than a hundred of the trout cubes, and there were never any left over. Glenda had a tremendous appetite, eating almost as many as would Tom, and licking her fingers afterwards, asking if there were any more. We'd take whatever we were drinking up on the roof—Tom, his Jack Daniels, and Glenda and I, rum and cokes, and Nancy, vodka—and we'd sit high on the steep roof of my cabin, above the second-story bedroom dormer—Tom sat out on the end of the dormer as if it were a saddle—and Glenda would sit next to me for warmth, as we'd watch the far-off fires of the burns, a flaming orange color as they sawed their way across the mountainside, raging, but contained. Below us, in the backyard those rabbits that had still not turned brown would begin to come out of the woods, dozens of them, moving in on the greenhouse and then stopping, just lining up all around it, wanting to get into the tender young carrots, and the Simpson lettuce. I had put sheets down on the ground in the backyard to trick them, and we'd laugh as the rabbits moved nervously from sheet to sheet, several of them huddling together on one sheet at a time, thinking they were protected; and all the time, moving in on the greenhouse.

"Turn back, you bastards!" Tom would shout happily, whenever he saw the rabbits start coming out of the woods in the moonlight, and his shouts would wake the ducks down on the pond, and they would begin clucking to themselves, quacking, and it was a reassuring sound. Nancy made Tom tie a rope around his waist and tie the other end around the chimney in case he fell. But Tom said he wasn't afraid of anything, and that he was going to live forever.

Glenda weighed herself before and after each run. I had to remember that I did not want to grow too close to her, as she would be leaving. I only wanted to be her friend. We ran and rode in silence. We never saw any bears. But she was frightened of them, even as the summer went on without us seeing any, and so I always carried the pistol. We had been pale from the long sunless winter, but were beginning to grow brown from lying out by the lake up at the summit. Glenda took long naps after her runs, we both did, Glenda sleeping on my couch, and I'd cover her with a blanket, and lie down on the floor next to her, and the sun would pour in through the windows, and there was no world outside our valley. But I could feel my heart pounding.

It turned drier than ever in August. The loggers were cutting again. It was always dry and windy and the fields and meadows turned to crisp hay. Everyone was terrified of sparks, especially the old people, because they'd seen the big fires rush through the valley in the past, moving through like an army—the big fire in 1901, and then the monstrous one, in 1921, that burned up every tree except for the very luckiest ones, so that for years afterwards the entire valley was barren and scorched, smoldering—and the wind in our faces was hot, and we went down to the saloon in the early afternoons, after we had stopped off at my cabin, and we'd drink beers.

Glenda would lie on her back on top of the picnic table and look up at the clouds. She would be going back to Washington in three weeks, and then down to California, she said. We were both as brown as nuts. Almost all of the men would be off in the woods, logging. We would have the whole valley to ourselves. Tom and Nancy had been calling us "the love-birds" in July, trying to get something going, I think, but they stopped in August. She was running harder than ever, really improving, so that I was having trouble staying up with her near the top of the summit, on the days that Glenda ran it.

There was no ice left anywhere, no snow, not even in the darkest, coolest parts of the forest, but the lakes and ponds and creeks and rivers were still ice-cold when we leaped into them, hot and heart-hammering; and each time, Glenda made me put my hand on her breast, her heart thumping and jumping around as if about to burst out, until I could finally feel it calming, and then almost stopping, as the lake's cold water worked on her.

"Don't you ever leave this place, Joe Barry," she'd say to me as she watched the clouds. "You've got it really good here."

I'd be stroking her knee with my fingers, running them along the inside scar, and the wind would be moving her hair around. She would close her eyes after a while and it was hot, but there would be goose bumps on her brown legs, on her arms.

"No, ma'am, I wouldn't do that," I'd say and take a swig of beer. "Wild horses couldn't take me away from this place."

I'd think about her heart, jumping and flapping around in her small chest like a fish in a footlocker, after those long runs; at the top of the summit, I'd wonder how anything could ever be so alive.

The afternoon that she set fire to the field across the road from my cabin was a still day, windless, and I guess that Glenda thought it was safe, that it would be just a grass fire, and would do no harm—and she was right, though I did not know that. I saw her standing out in the middle of the field, lighting matches, bending down and cupping her hands until a small blaze appeared at her feet. Then she came running across the field toward my cabin.

I loved to watch her run. I did not know why she had set the fire, and I was very afraid that it might cross the road, and burn up my hay barn, even my cabin—but I was not as frightened as I might have been. It was the day before Glenda was going to leave, and mostly I was just delighted to see her.

She came running up the steps, pounded on my door, and then came inside, breathless, having run a dead sprint all the way. The fire was spreading fast, even without a wind, because the grass was so dry, and red-winged blackbirds were leaping up out of the grass ahead of it, and I could see marsh rabbits and mice scurrying across the road, coming into my yard. An elk bounded across the meadow. There was a lot of smoke. It was late in the afternoon, not quite dusk, but soon would be, and Glenda was pulling me by the hand, taking me back outside and down the steps, back out toward the fire, toward the pond on the far side of the field. It was a large pond, large enough to protect us, I hoped, and we ran hard across the field, with a new wind suddenly picking up, a wind made from the flames, and we got to the pond and kicked our shoes off, pulled off our shirts and jeans, and splashed out into the water, and waited for the flames to get to us, and then to work their way around us.

It was just a grassfire. But the heat was intense as it rushed toward us, blasting our faces with the hot winds.

It was terrifying.

We ducked our heads under the water to cool our drying faces, and splashed water on each other's shoulders. Birds were flying past us, and grasshoppers, and small mice were diving into the pond with us, where hungry trout were rising and snapping at them, swallowing them like corn. It was growing dark and there were flames all around us. We could only wait and see if the grass was going to burn itself up as it swept past.

"Please, love," Glenda was saying, and I did not understand at first that she was speaking to me. "Please."

We had moved out into the deepest part of the pond, chest-deep, and kept having to duck beneath the surface because of the heat. Our lips and faces were blistering. Pieces of ash were floating down on the water like snow. It was not until nightfall that the flames died down, just a few orange ones flickering here and there. But all the rest of the small field was black and smoldering, and still too hot to walk across barefooted.

It was cold. It was colder than I had ever been. We held on to each other all night, holding each other tightly, because we were shivering. I thought about luck, about chance. I thought about fears, all the different ones, and the things that could make a person run. She left at daylight, would not let me drive her home, but trotted, instead, heading up the road to Tom's.

That was two years ago. The rabbits have changed, and then changed again: twice.

The hedgehog—I have never seen it again. After all these years, it has left. I wish I knew for sure that was what it had been; I wish I had a name for it.

Will it be back? I do not think so. Why was it here in the first place? I do not know.

Just the tame, predictable ways of rabbits—that is all I have left now.

Is Glenda still alive? Is she still running? It is mid-February. It hurts, to remember her. Things that should have been done. The field across the road lies scorched and black, hidden beneath a blanket of snow.

JACOB DIES

By Allen Jones

IF THERE WAS NOTHING AHEAD OF HIM, it was not an argument for moving on. If there was nothing behind him, it was not an argument for staying. He was through with arguments. He stared at his gloved hand around the coil of barbed wire and it was like he could have been holding a pistol, a knife, a can of oil, anything at all: connections were not being made, names were falling away.

He wondered if he was going crazy. He wondered if it would snow. He decided that he was in fact crazy, that it would in fact snow.

Half a mile away, he watched Laura pull the old Dodge up to the gate down by the creek, drive through, and then not bother to put it back up. The truck chewed its way through the stubble toward him, pushing patterns of ducks out from the steaming, spring-fed ponds.

It had been a cold winter. Of the few things he knew about himself, he was pretty sure he didn't like winter. Even at the age of twenty-eight, his hands cracked in the dry cold and the shoulder that he'd popped out of joint at the age of nine kept him awake at night. His lips sometimes bled after even half a day working in the February wind.

She pulled up beside him and rolled down her window. "Jake," she said.

That was all it took. His name snapped back at him.

He hooked the coil of wire around the post and laid his wire-cutters on top.

"You were just going to let them bulls on the other side waltz on through, I guess." He nodded at the half-dozen angus bulls grazing not three hundred yards from the gate she'd left open.

"It's colder today," she said, smiling lightly. "I thought you might want some coffee."

She was a light boned woman, and pale; smiling under the kind of cheekbones that made you think of folk singers. Her hair had been long and fine until he'd told her it would get in the way of ranch work and she'd let him cut it. Where was she from? Virginia, maybe. She had a southern accent, though not much of one. Who was her father? Did he smoke? Why was her left pinky so crooked? How did she break it?

He stepped forward and took the empty styrofoam cup from her hand, holding it as she reached through the window and poured from the thermos. He sipped at the cup and immediately tossed it to the ground. "It's cold," he said.

She smiled at him disarmingly with that tilt of her head. He made sure he remained expressionless, but her head-tilt just melted him, all the time.

"I must have let it set for a while," she said.

That stood between them until she finally took her arms off the truck door and wrapped them around her waist. "God, it's cold."

"Yesterday was colder, I believe," he said.

"I think I'm going to head into town today," she said, staring past him up into the Absarokas.

When he didn't say anything, she stepped out of the truck and moved over to kiss him. With the wind blowing, the old snow still skimming along the ground, the feel of her lips was like cold steel, taking his skin with it when she pulled away.

"Get me some cigarettes why don't you. I'm almost out." He bent down to pick up his cup and toss it into the back of the truck.

"I may be in there for a day or two. That house gets me a little stir crazy." She stepped away from him.

"Well, hell. I'll go with you. We'll cut up the town and then just be unstirred crazy together."

"I should go by myself," she said. "Jacob."

He went so still inside.

His cheeks were heavy and hung there. He stared up at the sky, at the highest sheaf of clouds, in thin layers not unlike the rough slide of a sand dune, not unlike the deepening wrinkles in his own face. He took a breath.

"Your hands," he finally said, reaching forward to take one, "are the best part of you. They're so thin and white. Your hands give you away before you even start talking."

She stared at him, taking her hand back and slowly rubbing it, as if he had burned her.

Over her shoulder, he saw Mac, his red heeler, come up out of the ditch and shoot toward them, running silently. The woman followed his eyes and was just able to jump back into the truck before the dog reached her. Only then did Mac start barking, crouching down and looking up at her with his thick, muscular head covered with the blood of something small.

"Somebody's going to shoot that dog one of these days," she said, kicking the truck into gear.

He dropped his coat and gloves on the floor, wincing as the gloves peeled away a fresh scab on the back of his hand. He must have scraped through with the barbs. He hadn't felt it.

He stood over the floor vent and held out his hands, glancing around. Her books were gone. A painting she had done, a six foot trout, was gone. The small black and white television with the tin-foil rabbit ears was gone—and that had been his.

So that was it. He walked through the house in his socks, counting up what she had taken. Her books. Her CDs and a few of his—the Hank Williams that she'd liked, the Patsy Cline. She hadn't even bothered to leave him a note. He brought his hand to his mouth and sucked absently at the blood.

He opened the kitchen cabinets. Her vodka was gone, but she'd left him the Jack. He poured a few fingers into a tin measuring cup, shot in a little water from the tap, and continued stalking around the house, speeding up as he felt the booze.

The guns were still there. His .357, .243, and 7mm. His 12 gauge and sawed off 10 that his grandfather had given him when he'd said he wanted to go dove hunting.

So this was what it had come down to. Five years of work for Denton and what did he have? A dog-piss stained couch. A truck that'd just got stole. A horse. How could anybody have lived like this. It suddenly struck him, with greater strength the faster he walked, that this was no game. No movie. This was his life, and Christ, he was screwing it up.

He threw the empty cup across the room, denting the bare wall and sending out a small puff of plaster. He got the 10 gauge out of the cabinet: sweet little thing. It'd been years since he'd shot it. The bluing worn away from the barrel. The stock rough and ridiculous looking where he'd tried to checker it with an ice-pick and hammer.

There were fifteen or so shells in the bottom of the cabinet, their box yellow and crumbling. He broke the gun down and slid two of them in, not caring how old they were, not caring that the barrel was wrapped-wire and just as likely to explode in his face as not. He wanted noise. He wanted destruction.

The couch got it first. Both barrels from ten feet. Blue smoke and threads of polyester floated down. Then the bookshelf. His tattered copies of Hemingway and Capstick turned to black shreds with one barrel, *The Stockman's Handbook* with the other.

After he'd put a round into the wall where her painting had been, he was past hearing the shots and was feeling them only in his chest: a suddenly echoing chamber, an empty network of veins each retaining some measure of the noise, the destruction.

He stopped while he still had a few shells left and stood breathing, the gun loose in his hands. The world was entirely quiet, and his eyes were blurred from smoke. Nothing left but the odor of gunpowder, the odor of slowly smoldering books.

Jacob walked to the window and stared out, the gun like a crossbar in front of him.

Before he left, he filled a bucket half with grain and went out to feed Caballo, slapping him on the neck and combing through the mane with his fingers.

"You'll be all right," he said. "You'll do good."

He led him through the corral and across the tracks and down into the stubble field: the ponds that stayed open, the fringes of missed grain. A good three months of high winter living in that pasture.

He and Mac slept that first night in an old line shack he knew about from working the Pierson place. He left tracks in the floor dust and when he sat on the cot, the bare mattress, there was a quick skittering of mice from the floor to the walls. Cold enough to freeze the breath on his mustache and still there were mice. In the night, one of them ran across his face.

He stood and went to lean against the jamb, smoking and slowly waking up, staring out onto the moon-smoothed land, how it rolled and built and gathered into the white shoulders of the mountains.

If he thought about what he was doing for long, if he stopped to consider it, he knew that he would have to go back. Or not go back, not with the ranch house in that shape, but veer off away from her, pursue some other end. So he stood and smoked and thought about nothing at all, bringing his mind, after three cigarettes, down into that singular nothingness sought by mystics and priests. An hour before dawn, the moon gave off enough light to throw his shadow back into the shack.

She had talked about Helena some. He would go there first. About some motel where she'd stayed. What was it called?

And if he caught up to her. What then? Noise and destruction? Tear-ful apologies? He had no idea.

Behind the glow of his cigarette, he felt like something that had been left behind thirty or forty years before. Most of his life he'd tried for sincerity, for honesty, and when these had failed, had exorcised his frustrations in work: in the patient training of horses and the herding of cattle and the constant smell of his own sweat. He didn't particularly like himself, but then, he liked no one else better. Except, occasionally, for Laura.

Ten years ago, it had still been possible to think of working toward your own place. He had tied on with Denton with the idea of building a herd and finally, somehow, making a downpayment. But then Hollywood had changed everything. Even in eastern Montana, the driest land had gone up to more than a hundred bucks an acre. Hell.

So he had just worked. There was nothing else to do. Bleeding from the lips, bleeding from his hands.

Last year, as he'd been trying to excise a cheek abscess, one of Denton's steers had kicked him in the ribs. He'd taped himself up and went back out to the pasture, finding the profile of the abscess like a buried fist under the skin of the steer's jaw. He rode up to within twenty yards, rested off his knee, and popped the outer edge of the abscess with his .22 magnum. There was the sudden spray of puss and a bawling, bleeding steer, and his own feeling of ridiculousness.

He'd shot a hawk down by the river just to see it fall and bounce off the limbs as it fell. And then, feeling so awful over what he'd done, drove into town to drink and finally get into a fight with the sheriff's son.

Then he'd met Laura. He'd been leaning over the pool table for a shot and she'd put her quarters down. Their eyes met. The jukebox jangled to a stop. The world stopped spinning. All that sort of thing. With her long hair and white sweater over jeans she had been something else. And her cheekbones! She'd smiled and tilted her head. And then ran the first two tables she played. She talked like an Easterner, but he'd never known anybody from the East that could shoot pool like her.

That had been last year.

He came out of the mountains a week later, trailing his dog and carrying his duffel, the shotgun within the duffel: All but the last two shells had been spent on grouse. With a hobo's beard and jacket tattered at the cuffs and collar, the back of his gloves stained with blood from his lips, he seemed less like a cowboy than some wilderness fugitive, some penniless, lawless drifter: which he was.

He walked with a slight smile on his face. It was a fine afternoon, and it seemed that the mountains—being away from all the light and noise—had wrung something out of him. It had begun to snow again. The road in front of him, whatever road it was, was a sliver of ice cut into the hillside.

It was almost dark by the time he reached the road. There were no lights on either side of him until a vehicle topped a rise miles away, rounded a corner, and flickered back into sight.

He sat on the ground with his arms on his knees and his head on his arms, the duffle beside him. Mac hugged up close and shivered. The cold radiated away from the grass. An old blue and white Chevy pickup, a '52 or '53, pulled up next to him, its window already rolled down and the first puff of heat blowing toward him.

"Lookin' for a ride?" Through the window, leaning toward him, Jacob could just make out a Mexican, long black hair braided down out of a worn Steelers cap.

He nodded and stood stiffly to his feet.

"Your dog can ride in back, I guess." The Mexican spoke without an accent.

Jake went around and dropped the tailgate for Mac, then came back to the front to grab his duffle and heave himself in.

"I'm headed up to Great Falls," the Mexican said.

Jake nodded again, and placed the duffle onto the floor between his feet. "Wouldn't have a cigarette on you, would you?"

The Mexican dug into his shirt pocket and gave him an envelope filled with hand-rolled cigarettes. "Take a couple. You look like you been without for a while."

"Appreciate it."

"You much of a talker? We got us a few hours, here."

Jake lit a cigarette with his own lighter and held his red and burning hands out to the truck's heater. "What do you want to talk about?"

"Hell, I don't know. Bosnia. Clinton. Tama Janowitz. Anything. My wife left me a week ago and I ain't said five words since."

"So tell me about your wife." He leaned back and crossed his arms. The fresh heat soaked through his jacket and seemed to take all the strength out of him.

"Oh, God, my wife." The Mexican shook his head, and lit one of his cigarettes. "Pretty. Real pretty. But, Man! The stuff she was into. I could tell you stories…"

Jacob leaned forward and ground out his cigarette in an ashtray overflowing with cigarettes and leaned back to tip has hat over his eyes. He woke up only later—it felt like much later—when they pulled into a gas station.

The red and green light was a wash across his face. In the side mirror, he watched the Mexican twist the cap back on and walked in to pay. It was a simple thing to move over behind the wheel, twist the ignition key, and drive off.

Helena had changed even in the few years since he'd been there. Congress was in session, and that afternoon, after checking into a motel that could have been what she'd mentioned, he took a stroll up the hill, his thumbs in his jeans.

Even the politicians had changed. He watched a pair of them climb up the steps: their bodies lean and trim; their briefcases shiny and new. Democrats, probably. The politicians he voted for still walked a little bowlegged, still had honest beer bellies draping down to hide their belt buckles.

He tried to imagine her in Helena.

It was how he hunted deer in the bottoms: a lot of standing and smoking and imagining where a buck should be. In this way, he found Laura dancing, head thrown back, laughing above the backward curve of her white neck, one hand held high with a drink. Incongruously, there was a pool table in the corner.

So. A bar with a pool table *and* a dance floor.

He didn't know Helena. It had Government. Did Government drink? Did Government dance?

Not with Laura, he was pretty sure.

He drank his way through three bars, tying Mac up outside each one and easing down into a kind of slow, boiling depression. The fourth bar, mostly empty by one o'clock in the morning, had as its only drinkers a pair of dudes dressed as cowboys.

They stood around the pool table, studying the lay of the balls, and when one of them bent to make a shot, a beer sign reflected off the silver on his heel and toe.

"Nice boots," Jake said. "Pretty."

They both straightened and looked at him. The one closest to the door, with sideburns and a bolo tie, shifted his grip on his pool cue.

"Jack Daniels on the rocks," Jake said to the bartender, who reached behind him for the bottle without taking his eyes off Jake.

"So," Jake said, taking his drink and toasting them, "you pretty boys come here often?"

"Buddy," Bolo-tie said, "you are asking to get your ass kicked." And he stepped forward, hefting the cue.

"Not in this bar," the bartender said, picking up a baseball bat from the corner. "Wayne? Craig? If you want to thump him, you take him outside."

The dudes moved forward together, stepping lightly with the practiced ease of dancers, of boxers.

Jacob reached into the duffel hanging from his shoulder and pulled out the ten gauge, dropping the bag and stepping back far enough to cover both the bartender and the dudes.

They all stopped. "No," the bartender said. "Put the gun away, mister. You got no reason."

"I got reason."

"What do you want? Money? Booze."

Jake shook his head, like he was shaking hair out of his eyes, and stepped to the side, narrowing the angle between himself and the back of the bar. With no thought, no consideration to the moment, he fired the first of his two barrels along the rows of bottles, sending a wave of broken glass and booze to the floor.

"What do you want?" The bartender asked again, his face expressionless, caught between anger and fear.

"I want people to stop dressing up like goddamned cowboys!" And he blew off his second barrel at the pool table, just between the two dudes. He scattered the balls, and, from the way they jumped back, put a pellet or two into the dudes.

He stood with the gun at his shoulder, amazed at the emotional purge that one pull of the trigger had given him. A clean feeling, all in a rush. Like coming out of the mountains. He was laughing.

Then the bartender was jumping over the bar with the bat. "Two's all you got," he said, coming at him.

Jake flipped the gun around and ducked under the bartender's first, clumsy swing. It was an easy thing for him to come up out of his crouch and cold-cock him with the butt of the shotgun.

But then one of them caught the shotgun by the barrel and the other, Bolo-tie, caught his arms. He stepped on the arch of his foot, shoved the stock into the face of the other, and made a break for the door.

Outside, he was fumbling to untie Mac when they blind-sided him against the brick wall. They held him upright by the neck and chin. He could feel the punches in his ribs, against his cheeks; but there was no real pain.

Mac darted in between them, taking pieces out of their calves. They kicked at him uselessly, until they finally let Jake drop in order to turn to the dog.

He slumped to the ground, nearly blind with blood and anger. Through the punchy buzz and ring in his ears, he could hear his dog's first, pained yelps. "Mac," he said, struggling back up. "You bastards."

The tip of one of the pretty silver boots caught him below the eye, snapping his head back on a loose pivot, and that was all, for a while.

He woke in stages, tasting blood and the loose change of his broken teeth. It was getting lighter: he could just see out of the alley and onto the street. A bakery truck drove by, its lights still on. He sat up and put his hand down on Mac.

Mac, with old blood pooled around his head and his mouth tensed open against nothing, his legs poised and cold and hard.

Jake slid down against the wall, already smoothing back the clotted fur. He could feel no line of distinction between the sharp, concentrated pain in his mouth and the dull, formless hurt that was suddenly everywhere else. He tugged at Mac's collar, trying to bring him over onto his lap. There was a dull ripping sound as he came off the pavement, like a sheet being torn apart. Mac lay across his legs.

Bastards, he thought, bastards. And he could think nothing else. Wanted to think nothing else.

It had become not so much a question of when he would find Laura as to how long they would let him look, how long could he run before they caught him. There was no question of who *They* were. Skinny politicians. Dog killers. The college professor who had flunked him out of freshman English.

If not Helena, Jake thought that she would go to Missoula. She had talked about how she missed college, how she would have liked to have gone on to graduate school. In fact, she had been mentioning it lately like an accusation.

He drove without consideration, wiping the slow blood away from his nose and lips until the top of the Chevy's wheel grew tacky with it.

He drove and imagined her in Missoula, walking around the campus, stopping to stare into the dorm windows. He imagined her in the library, among the computers and librarians, at a loss.

Before Laura, he had never been in love. Was this how it always went? Was this how it was for everyone? In the last few weeks it had al-most seemed like they had been trying to steal the comfort from each other. He would find a sopping wet towel laying on his side of the bed. She would find her bathwater scalding hot. He thought now that it had all been a way of trying to bring themselves back from the third that had stood between them for a while, that amalgam of love and dependency.

His face was painless. His ribs were painless, although he did find an odd, numbed, restriction there when he tried to breathe. One eye was-n't blinking the way it should and golf-ball sized spots on his face were numb: down by his chin, next to his eye. It was like there was nothing left. He had been filled with leaves, with smoke.

Was it worth it? What was he looking for, after all? Was it still Lau-ra? Laura. Who was Laura?

He laughed around broken teeth.

An inversion had dropped a ceiling of frost down onto Missoula, and as he came into town it was like plowing into snow.

He took a turn around the campus, and then another, thinking he might have missed her on the first pass. But no Laura. This wasn't her, anyway. One thing about Laura, she wasn't full of anything but herself.

He worked his way back through town, across one bridge and then another, finally finding himself in front of an old movie theater open for a matinee. On the tattered marquis, barely lit, were the words *Last Tango in Paris*. And *that* was Laura. Precisely.

He was exultant, slamming the truck up against the curb and jump-ing out to feel the first real stabs of pain. As if the rush of blood had filled and overloaded fist-weakened vessels. His left eye went black and he could feel it drooping in its socket.

But what was an eye, after all? He stumbled through into the theater, covering it with his hand. An old man behind the popcorn machine backed away. "Good God," he said, just loud enough for Jake to hear.

The movie was almost finished, almost empty. He stood waiting for his eye to adjust to the gloom. The few seats with forms in them were oc-cupied by groping college students. He stood there until those nearest him turned to tell him to sit down. A boyfriend almost stood up, but thought better of it.

He stood in the aisle at a loss, finally yelling out into the rows, sure that she was there somewhere, ducking down. "Damnit, Laura! You get out here!"

A voice behind him yelled, "Put your hands up!"

A pair of forms stood silhouetted in the door behind him, crouched blackly in the light from the lobby. Of course, it was no one he would know. No one he would recognize. No sheriff or sheriff's sons. These were young, ambitious silhouettes. Young sports.

It was not what he had imagined for himself: Jail.

He made a motion with his arms, as if he were raising a pistol, and jumped back from the flashes of their barrels. There were screams around him, and a rush toward the exits.

He struggled to join the rush, only aware as he was running that he had been shot, that the squelching in his shoes was neither urine nor coke, and that it was spurting down his leg in an exact rhythm with his steps.

The cops would follow him. They would be smashing him up against a wall.

He made the exit and just managed to duck into a recessed door, standing straight into its shadow. The cops, being too young and sportish, ran right past him, holding their guns awkwardly out in front of them.

It was an easy thing to slip out and run the other way.

But it was only a few steps, a few staggering lurches, before he felt his leg giving out on him. The gray cloud on the periphery of his one good eye seemed to suddenly grow much darker and the horizon around him tilted and spun.

The theater exit had been below street level, and he found himself standing under one of the bridges he had driven over just a few minutes before.

He leaned against a concrete support and slipped to the ground. Under his hands, his leg was entirely numb. The bone seemed sound, but the blood...his blood was still pulsing out onto the ground.

He leaned his head back and let his hands fall away. Let them lay flat on a surface of pigeon shit and blood and broken glass. He tried to laugh a little, but found everything that could have given rise to such laughter gone.

There, the cold concrete of the bridge against his back, the warmth of his own life spreading out under his legs and growing cold, he imagined Laura someplace warm, someplace with a beach. Dying himself, he couldn't imagine her alive. Couldn't imagine her laughing or dancing or crying.

He closed his eyes against the new blood of the world and found a wave rolling up, cresting above the horizon, and behind it another. He found Laura within the waves. A light from behind her, or perhaps beneath her, illuminated her electric spread of hair and naked, broken limbs. As he coughed and slid down to rest his cheek on the ground, he saw her poised there, stiff and askew: like some animal come from the ancient depths only to pause at the new edge, finally uncertain.

LADY

By Ralph Beer

> *The power of the dead is that we think they see us all the time.*
> *The dead have a presence...*
> *They are also in the ground, of course, asleep and crumbling.*
> *Perhaps we are what they dream.*
> — DON DELILLO
> *White Noise*

IN THE UPLAND MEADOW where his ditch met Blanchard Creek, Clayton Horn cranked his headgate open and watched the water churn to foam in the discharge box beneath his feet. The water sped off down his ditch, clearing as it went, to a lucent, glacial green. When the gate was all the way up, Horn leaned his forearms on the iron spokes of the bullwheel and looked out into the swollen race of the upstream channel where an ouzel dipped on a stone. Its mate darted past through the sunlit mist, singing as it flew.

Horn felt clearheaded for what seemed the first time in months. He had walked the four mile length of the Jack Mountain ditch that morning, throwing rocks and windfalls from its bottom, checking talus-slope flumes for leaks, and patching spots where game had worn away the downhill banks. It was a job he'd done since childhood, a trip he looked forward to during the last dark months of winter, a day that usually meant spring had finally come. Yet on the upper reaches of the ditch, in shaded stands of fir, he had stopped several times to shovel paths for his water, through knee-deep drifts of half-rotten snow.

It was an old claim, this water, and although the people who had dug the ditch were gone, in Horn, at least, something of them remained. He was taller and by degree fairer than most of the mixed-bloods thereabouts, yet the Métis features were plain in his face: high cheeks and aquiline nose, strong mouth and mahogany skin. Still, his eyes were grey, and there was that English cleft in his chin.

A drop of sweat fell from his nose to the back of one hand, and Horn straightened to unbutton his blanket coat. For the third time that day he took a postcard from the left breast pocket, unfolded it, and looked at the cover, where a camel stood amid endless dunes, bathed in burnt-orange desert light. Horn smiled. He shook his head. On the other side, in a hand he knew as well as he knew his own, "By the time you get this, I'll be back. Love, V." Horn refolded the card and buttoned it away, wondering just where she was.

In the opening around him, frost-turned timothy shined in the mid-day sun. Thickets of wild rose and dogwood burned various dark shades of red. It was a warm and sheltered place, charmed by the resonance of running water. Upstream, Blanchard Creek swung south into stands of withered spruce. Above the trees, Horn could see part of the Rocky Mountain Front, peaks worn by wind and kerfed by ice rising grey and white against atomic blue.

Horn looked into the high country until his eyes watered, then turned and looked north toward home. Five miles away the plains began. And between that region of stone at his back and the yaw of space ahead, there lay a belt of grassed and wooded hills, and a band of meadowlands and basins, a countryside between extremes, a verdant place, the center of the world.

Horn glanced at the sun. He took one last look around the meadow and noticed that the ouzels had gone. He closed the headgate halfway, picked up his shovel, and walked down the ditchbank until he was ahead of the first flow. He dropped into the ditch itself, a few yards ahead of the advancing foam, swinging along fast, and listening to the whisper of wa-ter as it followed him down the mountain toward his fields.

In openings where the ditch crossed sidehill parks, Horn could see out to the very edge of the Earth, fifty miles to the north, where the Great Plains curved away toward Canada. Dust rose along the horizon there, augering east on twisting winds over saffron strips of dryland wheat. Among the groves of winterbowed aspen, though, with only the faint sound of his spade tapping cadence on the stones ahead, Horn felt ab-solutely alone. But the clarity of April light among the trees—interspersed with glimmers of mountain-shaded grasslands below—was not enough to satisfy him. Light and country and his own company had been for a long time exactly enough. But as he approached forty, Horn was surprised to discover that he was no longer happy with what he had. During the past winter he had struggled to pin down the restlessness that rode him for days at a time, trying to single out what had gone wrong. The closest he could come to an honest answer was to admit he wanted something new, some change that might accelerate his life or elevate his soul.

He had been daydreaming along for a mile when he saw a tan slash of color in the budding trees above him, and he took several steps before he realized that it was a bear, feeding on the move, occupied with what lay in its own immediate path.

Horn stopped. He eased the tip of his shovel into the hillside above him and leaned against the handle for balance. He watched as the animal quartered downhill, rummaging among last year's leaves, casting its broad, dish-faced head for scent. It looked his way, and Horn turned wooden: an alder snag lodged in mud.

The bear rolled a log and dug at the redrot along its bottom, pausing its hunchbacked labor to lick bugs from runnels in the decay. For all its size, it breakfasted with slow grace, seeming at thirty yards almost reserved. Horn waited, the rounded tip of handle pressing against his chest, feathers of wind touching the short hairs on his neck. When the bear sat back on its haunches to scratch, Horn took a long slow breath.

The water caught up to him with a hiss. It hesitated at his boots, deepened, and ran along its course without him. He tucked his chin and watched it ladder up his laces, inching to the frayed cuffs of his pants, darkening the cloth and climbing on to clinch his calves like block ice when it topped the bullhide boots. Horn sucked air through his teeth and watched the hillside above him for cubs.

The bear got up, shook itself, and gazed around near-sightedly, as if waiting for an idea. It rubbed against a tree; it opened its mouth and seemed to yawn. Sometimes, Horn thought, and gave in to the tremors telegraphing through his thighs, you eat the bear. His stomach cramped with adrenaline, and the muscles in his shoulders quivered with chills. He gripped the hardwood handle and clamped his jaw to quiet his teeth. And sometimes...He waited, the water tugging at his legs, the bear lazing toward him through the scrub. By the time the bear smelled the water, Horn's lower legs had gone numb as roots.

It came down through aspen, disappearing into thickets of snow-brush and emerging again in a clatter of dry leaves and sticks, shouldering along, its hump and back silvered by the sun. Fifteen yards from the ditch, a Franklin grouse broke cover. It churned from a clump of juniper at the bear's feet and flew straight at Horn's face, clucking and pounding the air in panic. As the bird passed overhead, its wingwind touching him, Horn found himself locked eye to eye with a timeworn female grizzly that looked to weigh, even all gaunted-out, as much as an average yearling steer.

The bear stood slack-jawed, lower lip sagging from worn front teeth, in an open-mouthed attitude of surprise. She studied him with small umber eyes, and Horn felt that gaze flare in his veins, a flash of fear so hot he looked to the limerock walls of the Front above him, seeking the safety of corniced peaks and cornflower sky. Twin contrails bent west above him, splayed and knotted by wind. He saw that the weather was changing, and he realized that the water around his legs had leveled off at his knees.

The bear heaved herself erect and swayed there, damp forepaws treading air, belly fleece matted with the chaff of her travels, ears perked his way. She seemed at once surprised and provoked to find him watching her, but she waited, her eyes hunting over him, her nose working the air. Her pelt hung slack and balding across her paunch, and Horn imagined her waking on the mountain, snuffling about the cavity where she'd wintered, perplexed at the absence of offspring, at waking old and undone to this last season of life.

A second grouse jumped cover and Horn flinched. The bear dropped to all fours and broke into a shuffling rush toward him, snowbrush and willows discharging around her. She came at him head low, her hollowed hindquarters pumping, and Horn thought to lift the spade but did not. The shovel was holding him up.

She slid to a stop just short of the ditch, reared upright again, and rattled her teeth. Horn smelled the sweet fecal musk of bear, and he saw in the black centers of her sunken eyes the horrific force of her life.

"Hey!" Horn said, his voice surprising them both above the murmur of water at his legs. He tucked his chin and tried to brace for what came next.

The bear dropped to her front quarters, sidled back an uncertain step, and grunted low in her throat, a harsh ripple of sound like the amplified tearing of meat. Sidelong she regarded him with one eye, the white-tipped guardhairs on her meager back stiff as quills. In the gap where the soft, inside pink of her lower lip sagged away, Horn saw her broken teeth.

He guessed he could almost touch her muzzle with the spade if he had the heart to lift it, and he realized that what fired the acid through his belly was not just the bear, but also his nightmarish inability to move. The adrenaline scalding through him had once been like a friend. Now its visceral burn was only a reminder of the man he had been. For years he had endured its power as the addict survives his drug. Horn knew what it was to be out on his feet and stay on his feet to the end of a round. He took a breath and straightened himself a little. "Come on, old bear," he said, his voice rough and distant in his ears, "just walk away."

At the sound of his voice, she bluffed a charge to the edge of the water and lifted one forepaw to slap him. She waited, flexed and malicious, her monstrous head turned up to him as if expecting a kiss.

Don't you move, Horn told himself, not thinking until later how silly that notion was. He held himself and watched her breathe, until, still humped in threat, she turned and slouched stiffly off, stopping twice to peer over her shoulder before wading the ditch and breaking into a grunting downhill run that took her quickly out of sight.

Chickadees slipped through the willows around him. Down the mountain, in the direction the bear had gone, a pine squirrel worked itself into a fit, its frenzied chatter nerving the stillness. Clouds piled over the edge of the Front. The water sucked at Horn's useless legs.

He leaned into the hillside above him until he was on all fours, then kneed his way out of the water and crawled a few feet to a mat of sun-warmed juniper at the base of a fallen tree. He sat against the snag to rest, feeling as if he'd run a long way winded.

Horn listened to the gurgle of water going by, and he listened for sounds of movement in the brush, deciding after several minutes that the bear would not come back. He waited a while longer, then unlaced his sodden boots, pried them off, and wrung out his socks. His hands still shook, and his feet, pale and distant at the ends of his legs, seemed capable only of betrayal. He closed his eyes to slits and listened to rumors of wind on the upper slopes. Wind with weather on it, coming over the mountains from the west.

A woodpecker in the trees behind him tapped soft wood.

Horn felt the last spasms seep away, his terror slowly replaced by exhaustion and sweet relief that nonetheless mingled with a growing premonition of coming trouble, as if the bear had been a sign, a portent of coiled grief or ruin. He opened his eyes and watched two ravens slip and dive, stunting on the wind. The squirrel had stilled; the woods had gone soft and easy again.

He could count the times he'd seen big bears in this country on one hand, yet nothing was ever secure, Horn told himself, no matter how a man safeguarded his life. But that was what had plagued him all winter; that was what he'd been doing these past twelve years, feeding the same sad cows each winter and eating road dust on the county crew every summer while taking a minimum of risks. Twelve years of nights spent alone in a two-room log cabin, twelve years of work and, for release, a few fast rounds on the heavy bag hanging in his barn. A life of rituals without relief, a life without a plan.

Horn looked into the sky, where the first low clouds rushed past, thinking again of the bear. He remembered the electric jolt of fear that had gone right through him like a good punch, and he wondered, Is that it? Is it the fear I miss?

He pulled the red skirts of the blanket coat over his thighs, and reminded perhaps by the quality of light angling through the trees, Horn remembered his father leading him by the hand on the radiant fall morning of his first day at school. They passed a row of overhanging elms and a stone wall capped with coarse cement, his father asking did he know how to catch the bus, and satisfied that he did, walking with him past the white kids smirks and the Blackfeet kids' appraising looks toward the double front doors of that terrible place where at six years old he would be left on his own. And Horn was brave that morning because his father was there and his father was brave. Laramie was just a young jack then with his fast eyes and quick hands, a man proud to have a son in school. Laramie was something in those days, someone you could trust. In a flicker of understanding, Horn saw how much he had leaned on his father that morning, and how, in some secret way he could see but not quite say, he had leaned on him ever since.

Horn let his mind turn back to the man who taught him how to box and the Saturday nights and the gloves like pillows, when his father took him to face other boys in country bars. Nights remembered as circles of men in roaring bright saloons who cheered the other kid. Nights of shame and rage, of pain and fright, that went on until Horn compressed his fear. He found speed because he had to, and power, because, to his surprise, it was there. After a dozen good beatings, he stepped in one night and knocked the other kid down. But through a hundred such fights the fear was always there, driving each jab and combination, putting the jolt in each left hook.

Horn spread his socks beside him to dry and settled back against the stump; he clasped his hands, closed his eyes, and inhaled deeply, grateful for the warmth of sun on his face and the fullness of air in his lungs. Thinking of his father, then the bear, then his father again, Horn drifted away toward sleep where dream and memory bled together, drawing him down into the uncertain safety of his past.

He was a boy again, cutting hay. Heat waves rose before him from the tractor's shimmering hood, distorting the blue-green stand of alfalfa and the mountains above him into bands of light. He could taste gasoline from the siphon hose. He could smell hay sap and hot grease. He was by himself in the field.

Wind-turned clouds topped mountains along the Front, and he watched them build as he drowsed to the rattle of pitman shaft and the sizzle of reciprocal knife. He held to a rear fender with one hand and steered with the other, imagining he could see the stand of hay decline with each round, imagining his father praising him for a job well done when he returned from town, imagining his mother home again. Most clearly, though, he imagined tall glasses of iced water.

The August sky bore down on him with force. He prayed for clouds and fought the urge to sleep by singing songs he'd learned on his mother's radio. He tried Conway Twitty's version of "Only Make-believe," his young voice frogging low notes, then climbing to break on the line, "You are my very soul." He did a couple of teenage car wreck songs and a few of his favorite surfer hits. He rode, sunburned and happy, singing to the precise turning of machinery, singing to himself beneath towers of cloud building toward the sun.

The field seemed to narrow, and he kept on, planning to complete it before anyone returned. He had decided to do this on his own; after all, he was almost a man. If everyone else took off, he'd put up the hay himself. He'd cut it and rake it, bale it and haul the bales home. That's what he was doing alone in the field.

When only a long elliptical swath remained, he stopped, climbed unsteadily down, and with his straw hat, chased two young cottontails and a file of baby grouse from the remaining cover. As he climbed back onto the tractor, he imagined himself sixteen, taking Victoria Pineday to a dance at Augusta in his father's Ford. Victoria Pineday had the best grades in school, and she wore her auburn hair combed over each shoulder to hide her brand new breasts.

A raindrop struck his cheek, and as he engaged the clutch, he saw Laramie coming across the mown field, gunning the Ford over slick mounds of hay. The truck came on fast, a few more drops sliced by, and he sensed that what was about to happen would not be as he'd hoped.

His father got out of the pickup. He was unshaven, and one pearl-buttoned pocket hung torn from his best white shirt. A puffed lip; under one eye, a mouse. He gripped a lug on the rear tractor tire, his careless hand embossed with hard veins and scars; he stared at the field, then at Horn. "What," he said, "are you doing?" his whiskied voice rising to match the wind tossing his hair. "Radio says three days of rain."

Horn switched off the engine. He noticed his younger brother in the truck. Randall, bored by it all, too smart to make a mistake like that.

His father stepped away from the tractor and lit a smoke with trembling hands. He looked at the field and at the cigarette and shook his head.

"Did you find Mom?" Horn asked.

"You cut this all today, didn't you?" his father answered, his voice gone soft, his damp eyes following the first dim sheets of rain drifting off the mountains.

"Dad?" Horn said and woke to find his hands and face wet. Snowflakes the size of nickels fell from a woolen sky, whitening his pants and the juniper boughs around his legs. Horn brushed himself off with his Scotch cap, pulled on his socks, and laced his boots, the down-at-heel loggers wooden on his wet feet. He got up, shook himself, and stood suspended between his dream and the make-believe landscape veiled in storm around him. He saw faces in treeboles under frightwigs of moss, hobgoblins and bogeys in knotholes and sticks. Horn looked full circle, listening to the creak and sigh of the storm. He tipped his head back and caught a snowflake on his tongue. The floating dobs of white seared his uplifted face, tracking down the smile lines around his mouth, and falling in droplets to the exposed vee of his throat. It could have been winter, and, as in his dream, the man a boy again.

Horn laughed at that. He picked up his shovel, jumped the ditch, and set off along the bank path toward home, swinging the spade ahead like a staff and enjoying the apparitions of aspen looming from the storm. He lost his sense of direction as the ditch doubled back in gulches, following the contour of foothills from west to north and around to east, then back to north and west again, going past trees that grew taller the lower he went, until waist-high pitch stumps appeared where the old-time woodhawks had worked.

Horn left the ditch and cut downhill, planning to go on until he found the remnants of rail fence that would guide him quickly home. He let the grade pull him into a trot and went along in zig-zags through clots of limber pine, boot heels and spade kicking up splotches of duff, wind whistling in his throat. On flatter ground he ran, his long legs light and quick, bursts of breath fogging his wake. He strained to see, feeling giddy and young as he picked up speed. His breath came harder, and his sense of lightness increased until he felt like laughing again.

But the fence he found was half a mile from the one he wanted, and he did not laugh as he slowed to a stop at the rectangle of wire around a stand of trees the woodcutters had left. He leaned on the gate at the entrance until he caught his wind, then opened it and went into the place where the Métis lay buried under stones bearing their names. Parenteau, he read. Lepine, Otter, Dumont. Charpentier, Lamere, Fleury, Horn. A row of Horns, the old ones overgrown with wild rose, the rest overgrown with grass. Room for more.

He bent and swept snow from a toppled stone and read the name he'd heard so often as a child, the name of the woman who helped the others to Montana after the Rebellion up north was lost. When Horn was a boy, those who remembered her were children when she died, and now it was possible that he alone remembered what they'd said. This much, in weathered script, was left:

MARGUERITE HORN
Saint Vital, Manitoba, 1806
South Pass, Montana, 1894
MATRIARCH

Horn shuddered and realized that his coat was soaked clear through. He put his hand into his pockets and looked at the row of bloods that included his uncles—men he could remember, if only dimly—his father's older brothers. And there at the end of the line, under the root-bound sod like all the rest, lay his father.

Horn turned away and saw, on an uncommonly large aspen that grew in a sunken, unmarked trough in the ground, a carved heart, bisected by a crude arrow shot between two sets of initials. And he saw how the bark had scarred black where he'd stripped it once to green. He had been green himself that summer, and Victoria a year younger. They had not just gone to dances. They had come here, to this sheltered spot in the woods. Horn felt an unexpected sweetness pass through him as he looked at this holy place where he had learned to love.

He closed the gate, made the sign of the cross, and ran on, following elk trails through the trees.

In a bowl where hillside clay once sloughed and folded to a stop, Horn passed a hot springs pool, celadon and deep. Then Mad Laurent's woodcamp with its tin can dump and rust-gutted stove, a set of bobsled runners and capsized bolsters abandoned where they lay.

Lower on the mountain and nearly free of the timber, he crossed her tracks, padding off into the gloom—an old bear wandering alone in the storm, trudging down the mountain through Garland Pineday's upper pasture. Horn cut west off her track and went on, wanting to check the dams he'd set that morning, anxious to see the stain of water spreading out across his land.

He was almost to open ground and still running, phrases of Twitty's long-ago song echoing like fragments of dream in his mind, when it came to him to wonder—as he might have wondered once as a boy—why the dreams came at all. Had it been dreams and days of childhood that brought him back to a home where so much had been lost? Was it dreams that had held him there, at times against his will? Or had he taken, he wondered, too many shots to the head?

What he wanted, Horn thought, was really not so hard. Just a chance to leave for a while, to take off up north and see some country with folding money in his pocket to unfold and spend. Or south, on the Norton he'd kept all this time in a shed. He'd explain it to Victoria. She'd know what to do.

He vaulted the jackfence at the edge of the timber and crossed a swale overgrown with balsamroot and sage, land he owned in uneasy common trust with the Great Falls lawyer who was his brother.

He crossed the snowline midway down the last bald ridge above his fields and slowed to a walk in misting rain, buoyed to be off the mountain, to be out in the open again, alive.

Horn stopped to catch his wind and ease the ache in his side. He bent to rest, gripping his knees with his hands, and when he lifted his head to flex his neck, he saw a slim white line of smoke rising from the stovepipe at the front of his shack. "Ah, girl," he said. And gladness warmed him, burning like fox fire in his heart.

From where he stood, most of the cabin was hidden by lilacs that grew to its eaves, but in the rain the corrugated tin roof seemed luminous, as if lit from within. Just beyond the cabin, at the edge of a draw wooded with doghair fir, an unpainted frame house stood open to weather, home only to mice and flies. It had been an improvement no one could endure, that house of calamity built by his father, where, during Horn's early manhood, his family had come apart. Below the house, partly hidden by a grove of waning cottonwoods, Horn could see the dormered mow of his log barn and the west end, too, of the pole corrals and sorting pens.

He looked back at his cabin and watched the smoke twist up through pelting rain to pierce the lowering sky. The rain blued the air around him, smudging the first dim greens of grasslands and meadows to muted shades of lifeless grey.

Below the boneyard, the ditch from Blanchard Creek entered a box made of concrete and stone. The water plunged in, dropped a foot, and surged through headgates left and right to smaller ditches contouring the upper lengths of the field. Down each ditch Horn could see the plastic dams he'd set that morning, bellied tight but holding. Water backed by the dams spilled over the banks and slowed to a sheen as it soaked level ground. Above the continuing white sound of rain came the concord of water in motion, undulant and gentle, polyphonic and clear.

A pair of mallards veered from their course along the tule bottoms to inspect Horn's dams. They quacked past craning their necks, and Horn quacked back. He wiped his face with his hands, and rubbed his hands on his jeans, feeling foolish and full of life, a grown man uplifted by the simple physical force of rain. He was wet clear through and growing cold, but he lingered a few moments, letting his anticipation build and listening to the rain accelerate as the light began to fail.

He lifted his face and closed his eyes and let the rain pound his skin. In darkness and rain and lost time he glimpsed again how good that searing spring had been, and he saw how the heat he'd found for a girl, when he was not much more than a boy, was reborn in the way he'd come to love this place.

Victoria had grown up too, and her flaming hair had darkened with time almost to black. After college in Bozeman, where she graduated a structural engineer, she hit the tank town refineries to ride out the boom. From Wyoming she went overseas, and the jobs in the desert kept her away a year or two at a stretch. When Horn quit fighting and came home to stay, she had been gone long enough. He settled in, saw other women when he could, almost talked himself into marriage once. When he least expected it, she would simply reappear.

The last time she'd come home, Horn had driven into his yard after eight numbing hours in a dump truck to find her perched loose-limbed with a tumbler of bourbon in the golden willow out front. He parked the pickup as usual, took his lunch box from the seat, and as he walked toward her, dusted his jeans with his baseball cap. Victoria watched without expression, waiting for his dust to settle before she broke his heart.

Horn slowed in the uncut grass, squinting up into the spangled light of sun and leaves, a hard guy taking his time. He looked from her scuffed-out boots to the jeans worn thin at knee and thigh, then paused with intent on the chambray shirt unbuttoned to the tops of her freckled breasts. Then the flash of teeth and chestnut skin, her cat's eyes, otter brown—a smile quick and certain, ending with a careless toss of her head.

In her husky voice she asked, "And how's my handsome lad?"

Horn remembered how he'd cleared his throat and swayed inside. He had tried for words. "I'm glad to see you." That's what he'd said.

The ducks swung back, making a lower pass, and Horn remembered the aspen in the cemetery that bore their initials, a tree well nourished as it grew through the bones of some poor nameless soul. He put his spade on his shoulder and started off, the rain ringing on the steel blade, the rain ringing in his heart.

At two hundred yards he saw her coming toward him through the dusk, wearing an oilskin slicker and what looked like one of his broken Stetson hats. She carried a bottle by its neck in her gloved right hand and walked looking down, the rain sluicing past her front from the hat's sodden felt.

Horn stepped through the new grass and mud feeling the life inside him rise. In that person he saw the course of his past, and in that person he discovered again a cause for hope. He opened his mouth to call her name, skidded in the cowpath muck, and glanced down. When he looked up, he saw Garland Pineday standing there instead.

"Garland?" Horn said, and in one stride he saw how it could all go wrong.

Pineday stood rigid as a post. He hadn't shaved in a couple of days, and his whiskered chin was white. He did not look drunk, yet he was not the kind of man to fire your stove while you were gone. He handed the bottle of Dickle over, Horn took it and held it to his chest.

"You're cold," Pineday said.

"It's bad?" Horn answered.

Pineday looked past him up the meadows, a small man of almost delicate build, known in that country as a breaker of horses. He cut his eyes back to Horn. "You drink some of that," he said in the voice he used when working colts, "and we'll go on up to the house."

Horn fumbled the cap away and put the bottle to his lips. He drank, then drank again, the whiskey running from his chin as he began to shake. Without speaking again they faced about and walked through the drifting veils of rain toward the sourceless blue light of the shack's tin roof and the hanging fronds of the willow out front, where nothing would ever be new again.

CHINOOK

By Pete Fromm

THERE WAS A FOG AROUND JESSICA AT FIRST, a fog of guys so thick I could barely see her. They thinned out soon enough, though, 'til she did-n't have much of a reputation for friendly. But I knew most of those guys, and if I was her, I wouldn't've been too friendly either. The rumors about her frostiness got around to hide their rejections.

She'd transferred to Montana State from Alabama State, but she wasn't southern. Year before that she'd been at Indiana, year before that Arizona. I knew all that. Even with the rumors people still talked about her. She wasn't your typical centerfold beautiful, but she had something striking hidden in her that turned heads, stopped talk about anything else.

The day I finally got up the guts to talk to her, March by now, she was in the student union, drinking coffee, filling out an application for the University of Alaska. I asked if I could sit down and she shrugged with-out looking up.

I said something like, "Alaska, huh? Where in the world are you from?" I laughed, making it sound like a joke.

She said, "I don't know."

I sat down anyway, saying, "I'm from Chinook."

She looked at me at last and I said, "It's named after a wind. You probably never heard of it."

She didn't answer and I explained, "It's pretty small. Fifteen hun-dred people. Fourteen ninety-nine now, I guess."

I laughed at myself and she set her pen down on her application and turned to really look at me. I was talking way too much.

"A chinook's a wind we get up there, out of the mountains. They say they only come in winter. It can go from ten below right up to fifty or six-ty, all in an hour or two. Melts all the snow, floods the streets. After it blows through, though, the old temperatures come back, freezing every-thing all over again. But people love them. A breath of summer in the middle of winter."

I was babbling, but I couldn't quit. "My personal theory is that chinooks happen year round. It's always windy up there, and if a chinook blew through in August, who could tell?"

"Who could tell?" she repeated, stopping me at last. But she gave me one of the smiles that'd made all those guys chase after her in the first place.

She was an Air Force kid, she told me, traveled all over the world, never staying more than a couple of years in any one place. Said the whole time she was growing up she couldn't wait to stay put, but when she was out on her own she kept on moving, even more than before. "Go figure," she said.

She was a junior, like me, but in her fifth year of school, because she lost credits every time she transferred. "Same as you lose something whenever you move," she said. I must have looked at her funny, because she added, "Books, pictures, underwear, you know."

And I said, "Yeah," like I knew. It wasn't a five hour drive from Chinook to here. I said, "I've been to Canada once," but I said it dopey, as a joke. Chinook's forty miles from the border. Everybody's been to Canada.

She said Canada was the one place she'd never been. I told her where Chinook was and we laughed. I was going up next week to help with calving and I told her I'd take her to Canada if she wanted to go. She said she did.

She didn't go to Alaska that next year. She fell in love with the ranch and the wheat and the scrubby, battered windbreaks and, more gradually, with me. We'd go up to Chinook most weekends, and she was desperate to learn about everything. She helped with the calving and then with the branding and in the fall with the shipping. Once that was done and things slowed down she kept after me to teach her to hunt. I'd never been very excited about hunting, but I took her out for birds and we'd get some partridge and stuff. She said she'd never stopped like this before, never slowed down long enough to really see what was around her. She said she just couldn't get all that wind and sky under her skin fast enough. When she wasn't looking I smiled, seeing her face and hearing the way she'd talk about slowing down and not being able to go fast enough all in the same breath.

We'd see a lot of deer when we were out and she said she wanted to hunt those too. I like deer, like to watch them, but I shot one once and knew I never wanted to do it again. That's what cattle are for, and we always had enough of them frozen that there wasn't any excuse for shooting a deer. I told her that and she stared at me. Then she came across the grass and hugged me and kissed me once. She said, "I really am getting the best of it. Of everything."

I couldn't agree with that out loud, even though I wanted too. I said, "This must all seem pretty hick to you."

What she said was, "Let's get married."

I managed to say, "When?" and she said, "Whenever," which was vague enough I thought she might have been thinking out loud more than meaning anything. We'd known each other for eight months then.

But we did get married that June, a week after school was out, and we took over one of the houses out on the ranch. I started working in town at the elevator, and Jess took a job at the store, so we could ride into work together. But she quit the store after a while and started working with my folks and my sister, running the ranch.

We were all over each other, you know, like newlyweds'll be. She'd come in with shit all over her boots and grass seed blown into that pile of sunny brown hair, and I'd look at her and couldn't believe this had actually happened to me. I'd always wanted to get off the ranch and into town, even if it was only Chinook. I'd had enough of cow shit and wind. But seeing her like that was enough to keep me anyplace.

She'd undress like it was nothing, which always kind of amazed me too. How she could figure she was nothing, no matter what she was doing, was beyond me. I'd lose track of what she was saying sometimes, all lost just staring at her. Once she got so wound up about something she started making dinner and getting ready for a shower at the same time. Finally, she found herself standing at the stove in her underwear and she hit herself on the forehead, saying, "Shower, Jess. That's what you were doing." She turned to me and smiled, saying, "Couldn't you just see Hubert driving up here right now, catching me cooking dinner in the buff." Then she pranced out of sight to the bathroom.

Hubert was my dad, and no, I couldn't see it. When I heard Jess's shower start up, I looked through the kitchen window, up to the big house, realizing I couldn't even picture what went on up there anymore. Everything I knew or wanted was here now, and I felt vaguely sorry for the rest of them, because they'd never know anything this good.

The baby came the next year, a girl, and I wanted to name her Jessica, because I couldn't think of any girl I loved being called anything else. But Jessica wouldn't have any of that junior stuff, and we settled on Katrina. Well, she settled on it anyway. I thought it made her sound like a foreigner; a Russian or a Hutterite or something. But pretty soon she was just Katy anyway, though Jess always took the time to call her Katrina.

Jess spent less time with the ranch and more time at home. She put stencils around the walls in Katy's room and built some shelves and sewed teddy bears and stuff like that. I hadn't known she could do any of that kind of thing and she said she hadn't either. "But," she said, "I guess you can do anything if you think you have to."

I sat down beside her on the bed, the sag of the mattress pushing our shoulders together. I put my arm around her. I was twenty-four then, and the guy who'd run the elevator had just had a heart attack and retired, leaving me in charge. I'd been doing that for a few weeks and was past the stress part. I thought I'd learned the same thing Jess had—that you can do anything you have to.

I wound up locking those moments into my mind, stunned by my own happiness, and even when things began to change, I still had those pictures. Regardless of what was going on around me, I held them up, evidence of how happy we were. I used those pictures as blinders, though of course I didn't realize that until later—until after the pictures had been lost in the move, just like Jess said was bound to happen.

After Jess quit working the ranch I'd sometimes catch her standing at the window for long stretches, holding Katy, the two of them looking out over the fields, toward the rough breaks of the bluff. I'd wonder what she was looking at, since nothing out there ever changed, but it seemed like she was thinking about things, and I was afraid to disturb her.

Once Katy could walk well through the grass and the gopher holes, they took long walks together. Jess hadn't been hunting since she'd had Katy, but she'd come back and tell me of the places they'd been, places I recognized as places I'd shown her when she'd just come up to this country. I wondered why she'd keep going there, but she'd come home breathless, her hair full of seeds and her face aglow, and she'd tell me about all the things they'd seen. Sometimes she asked if I remembered certain times we'd been places together, and of course I'd say I did. Seeing her excited again was enough to convince me that everything was as good as it had always been, and I wasn't about to say I might have forgotten a detail here or there.

This went on until the night of my twenty-seventh birthday. Things like birthdays and holidays always swept Jess away. She was constantly decorating the house for the seasons; putting up balloons and banners and things like that. During the holidays, my folks and sister used to spend more time at our house than up at the big house, which wasn't the same as it was every other day of the year. I was prouder about that than

I realized. And I was counting on all her preparation to cheer her up some, to bring that smile back from wherever it'd gone.

A bunch of the guys in town took me out for a drink after work, and though I wasn't really that fired up about it, I thought I'd keep it quick and get on home. The bartender made a big deal about the birthday, buying a free round, and the guys I was with had to get me a round of their own, and then another, and when I finally called it quits, I took a lot of ribbing. Everybody knew Jess, who only got more of that haunting beauty each year. It was something she couldn't help, and I don't think she'd've looked like that if she had a choice. She didn't much like people noticing her. But her cheeks stood out more and more, still looking smooth and soft all the same. Her skin did that, smooth enough to glow, and seeming to grow brighter by the year, as if something was alight inside her. People couldn't help but notice her. So I got ribbed about running home to my birthday treat.

They'd planned a night of it though and we had ourselves a driver. We all piled into a four-door truck and started for the ranch. I had to leave my car in town, but they said this was part of my present, getting chauffeured around.

When we got to the place on the highway where you can't see town anymore, but you can just make out the ranch—some fence lines and the jutting row of cottonwoods that make up the windbreak for our house— we saw a car sitting on the side of the road, puffing out wreaths of white exhaust, as if the engine was catching its breath.

It was an odd spot to stop and we pulled over and our driver asked if they needed help. Then everyone was laughing and I looked over and saw it was Jess and that the car was our car. I felt kind of foolish, not recognizing it right away. From where I sat I could just see the edge of the car seat and Katy's leg bouncing up and down. I could imagine the tune she was humming, the same one she'd been going over this morning when I'd left for work. She could get a tune stuck in her head and go on with it until you thought you'd scream.

The truck I was in pulled out then and I asked what was going on. I hadn't been able to see Jess's face, just her chest and lap, and her hands, fidgeting on the steering wheel. They were all laughing then, about me rushing to my birthday treat, and my treat rushing in the opposite direction. I twisted around backwards, watching the exhaust thin out and disappear as the car warmed up. Then we turned onto the dirt and I couldn't see her anymore. "What was she doing?" I asked.

"Said she'd forgotten something she needed," the driver told me.

"She was all right?"

"Sure she was all right. Think we'd just leave her?"

That got some more laughs, and I figured she must have pulled over to search for her shopping list or something. She could get awful scatter-brained if something was on her mind. Must've forgotten the balloons, I remember thinking.

They dropped me off at the house, with more hooting, then roared off honking, screaming the happy birthday song at the top of their lungs.

I stood in the driveway, thinking of Jess making the last minute run to town for balloons and I smiled thinking that all those guys knew how I felt about her, and that they thought enough about Jess to envy me being with her. At least enough to tease me about it. They'd all been married as long as I had, some longer, and they seemed tired of each other. Nobody made jokes about any of them with their wives. Some of them were already divorced, and some of them—it was common knowledge in a town the size of Chinook—were already having affairs.

I was still smiling, but Jess's hands, fiddling with the steering wheel, were hard for me to shake. They had that same anxious look that seemed to burn brighter and brighter in Jess, like she was just barely able to keep something inside from bursting into flame. More feverish than excited. It was the look I'd soon realize I was hiding behind my pictures of the happy times, and I wondered what that was all about. But I walked up onto the porch and nearly went inside before I stopped myself.

No matter that she did it every year, Jess always expected me to be surprised by her decorations. And in a way I was, surprised that she could be like that, that she'd take so much time for a bumpkin from Chinook. So I sat down on the porch swing, where we watched the thunderheads roll in from the plains in summer and I waited for her, not wanting to go inside until she said it was all right.

But it was fall again, late fall, heading on into another winter, and I just had my work shirt on and pretty soon I got cold. She should've been back by now, and I walked down the gravel drive, to see if I could see her returning. The wind moaned through the cottonwoods, cold from Canada, and I thought I'd just sneak inside and grab a coat. There was no way she'd know I'd ever been inside.

I ran back to the house, trying to chase away the chill that way, and banged through the door into the living room. I hunched over the radiator for just a second before getting my coat, because I knew she'd be home any second. Then I realized what I'd seen. I turned around and looked at my house and it was just the same as it had been when I left it that morning. There wasn't any preparation for any kind of celebration at all.

I got my coat and put it on, unable to shake the chill, even inside, and I walked around the house. Nothing. Not a crepe paper streamer or a cake or a single thing. I was embarrassed by how disappointed I was and the very first of those pictures I'd been hiding behind slipped away.

I went outside and sat back down on the porch swing, huddled deep in my coat. There was one of those faceless gray fronts easing in from the north, as if hoping no one would notice. Not a cloud line so much as a hazy wave of darkness on the edge of things that really can sneak up on you without you seeing it. The wind was picking up in front of it though, giving the storm away by its keening through the bare, black branches of the cottonwoods.

I shivered inside my coat and waited until it was nearly dark. I wasn't waiting so much, but just sitting there stunned, watching all those pretty, happy pictures falling away, revealing, too late of course, the way Jess had looked after her long, lonely walks. The chill flushed her cheeks, but even so there was that light underneath, showing the inferno working away at her. It'd been there all along for me to see.

It was dusk when my parents' truck pulled down the road and up the drive. I could see the big house from where I sat and I'd heard the engine of the truck start up and I'd seen the lights come on and I'd listened to it crunch the hard packed gravel. Time was they would have walked, but not anymore, not with Dad's hips.

They were coming down for the party. Coming just to see Jess's face lit up with excitement the way it'd get times like these. I knew the dark house behind me would create a big question mark before they even got out of the car. I listened to the doors slam and I heard my sister say, "Maybe they're in town."

"Naw, she always has the party here." That was my dad. I was shocked to hear him add, "Maybe she's just giving him his present a little early." He laughed. "We'll have to knock."

Mom said something like, "Hush yourself," giggling too, and they were all on the porch before they made me out in the dying light.

They stopped then, and no one said anything. Seeing me out there alone in the dark put it beyond something they could joke past. Finally Dad said, "Where's Jessica?"

I said, "I don't know."

"What do you mean you don't know."

When I didn't answer my father hooked the storm door open with his cane and marched into my house, flicking on lights. He hates unknowns. Mom hesitated, then followed. My sister sat down next to me in the porch swing.

"What in the world, Terry?"

"I've got this feeling," was all I said.

She patted her hand on my thigh, which was something Jess had always done. Neither Jess nor I were great talkers, and sometimes, if something was bothering one of us, we'd wind up just touching like that, rather than working it through in words. I wondered now if that was part of what was going on right now.

Then my dad shouted out from the back of the house, the bedroom, "There's a note here." He sounded victorious, as if it had been a treasure hunt.

My sister jumped up and ran for the back of the house. "I'll get him before he reads it," she'd whispered.

A minute later they all came marching out together, slow and dirge-like. My sister eased that note down onto my lap, like if she'd've dropped it, the weight might have broken my bones.

They just kept right on walking, back into the truck, and Mom said, "Come on up to the big house, Terry. We'll all be there."

I flattened that note against my thigh, to keep the wind from taking it away, and I sat there knowing they'd read enough to tell me what it said by the way they'd trooped out of here. I listened to the bang of the car doors up at the big house. With a wind gust, I even heard the screech of the storm door, then its slam.

I stayed out until that sneaky, darkling storm blotted out every little bit of light, even making the yard light at the big house quaver and dim. It started to snow, and I went on inside where my dad had left on all the lights.

I sat down at the kitchen table, an antiquey kind of thing Jess had bought in Great Falls. It was round with great lion paws for feet. Oak probably, and it had once given me a gigantic sliver. I spread the note on it and saw that there was no Dear anybody starting it and I could have just about told you what it said without reading it.

It said: "I started to decorate this morning, but I just couldn't face it. This is a terrible thing to do to you on your birthday. I thought I was miserable here the last year or more, but knowing how this is going to hurt you is really showing me what miserable is. I can't stay to change that thought. My great settling down experiment has failed.

"I always told you I lost something every time I moved, but I didn't even know myself that part of what was lost was inside. I just used this place up, Terry. There's nothing I can do about that. I have to get to something new or I will lose my mind. All the sky, and the wind that never stops, used to be so magic. Now they seem like something I'm disappearing into, being worn down by, same as the hills. I've got to leave before there is nothing left of me.

"You are what I'm losing this time, and I'm sorrier than sorry about this, and about you. You're the goodest person I know."

That was it. Not even signed. But it had so much of Jess in it, I about gave out. Goodest. I could see her working over that before she put it down. Best was the right word, but it wouldn't mean enough; best at what? Good was what she meant, that I was a good person. The best at being good. Wasn't much consolation.

I sat in my little house and suddenly one of Katy's endless tunes snuck into my head. I tried to lose it before it could take hold, panicky that it would repeat within me forever, but the only other sound was the wind rattling the window panes and scraping the cottonwood branches together. I finally thought of Jess locked up here, day after day, talking baby talk to Katy and listening to the wind. I was amazed she'd been able to put that note into paragraphs. If it'd been me, it would've poured out so hard I doubt I'd've remembered periods.

I walked to the front door and stepped outside. The snow was really coming down, though with the wind, I couldn't tell if it was just ground snow blowing or something that'd really amount to something. I tried to remember if I'd put the snow tires on Jess's wagon. I pulled up my collar and walked through the stinging snow, up to the big house and into the tractor barn. The snow tires were gone, and I was glad I had done that much for her. I walked back down to my place and turned off all the lights. Then I turned the porch light back on, just in case. But I knew there wasn't going to be anyone drawn back to that little dot of cold light.

I walked around my darkened house, eventually drawn back to the porch light myself. Through the glass the snow made hard white flashes in the glare. I glanced to the big house, bathed by the yard light but dimmed all the same by the rush of snow, blurred down to the edges.

I felt like moving out onto the porch—sitting down again in the swing, as if by waiting longer she might come back. But that would've been hiding again, behind pictures that hadn't existed in years.

I sat down on the little love seat in the living room and wondered where she would've headed. She had the whole world to pick from, and all I knew was this one corner of nowhere. She'd once told me that's why she loved me.

I saw why that wore out. She'd seen everything in the world but, for a while, she'd thought that I'd seen more, that I'd seen the finer things she'd always rushed past. So she slowed down, thinking it was something she could just choose to do. And maybe she could've. She was awful strong. But she slowed down enough to learn about me too. She learned that my specialty was in not seeing the very things that were in front of my face, crying to be seen.

Sure, I knew where the partridge were likely to blow out of the grass, and I knew what kind of weather different clouds were bringing in, and I knew I didn't like to kill deer, but she'd figured that all added up to something—an inner vision or something. When she found that I really hadn't seen any of this—that she could live with me and have me see not one thing about her desperation—it must have been the biggest disappointment in the world. Like it'd been for Katy when she decided Santa Claus was something I'd personally made up.

All of a sudden I saw Jess and me sitting on our nappy white bedspread, our shoulders and arms touching, down to the elbow. She was holding Katrina, brushing some of her wispy black hair away from her eyes, and looking at me with the smile that probably still haunts some business school graduates. Even then, I'd seen it falling apart, but just looking at Jess's smile made me afraid there'd be a day I couldn't see it anymore. So I hid behind the good times and hoped they would last forever. Who wouldn't have?

I stood up and turned on the lights. I turned them all on. I couldn't stand the darkness. I dragged an old box into the living room and started to wonder what I should pack. I didn't have a clue where I might be headed, but I had an idea Jess'd had no clearer picture. I was guessing Canada, because ever since we'd first met that'd been a joke—Canada, the one world the world traveler had never seen. I thought it might be the place I'd find her.

First thing I put in that box was that old, nappy bed spread, for padding, then I put in all the pictures I had of Jess, and Jess and me, and Jess and me and Katrina. I folded the ends of the spread over the top of the pictures, then put a pillow on top of that, for added protection.

I wandered around the house after that, not at all sure of what else I wanted to take. I put some clothes in and packed the box into the bed of a ranch truck. I felt bad, leaving all those pictures out there in the snow, but I knew well enough that I could never put those blinders back on, though I missed the idea of them already. I wondered if I somehow managed to find Jess what kind of nicks and bruises we'd get without hiding behind any old times. They were bound to make the final picture something not quite as glossy as the first ones.

I turned on the truck, sitting a minute to let it warm up. The snow shot through the headlights like tracers. I was scared, you know, about what that final picture would look like. But, at the same time, I was excited about trying to find Jess and make it all up to her. Whether I found her or not, I couldn't bear the thought of being left behind in the calm, quiet, cold that follows every chinook, and I backed out of the driveway and started off.

PAINTED INTO THE CORNERS OF AMERICA

By Russell Chatham

YEARS AGO, when I mistakenly thought there might be something interesting in the various art journals, I kept running across arguments about what constituted genuine American art, art which had no roots in Europe. Some thought it was Grant Wood, or Grandma Moses, or Jackson Pollock. Not once was the real answer pointed out.

If you take the position, as I do, that America was fully populated before the famous Italian seaman arrived, then surely the presence of Western European style painting has to be seen as a latter day occurrence.

These days wine is made in nearly every state, consensus being that the best ones come from California. Until recently, America consumed relatively little wine, and most of that was imported from France and Italy. It was predominantly the Italians who were responsible for the large number of wineries in California prior to prohibition.

Winemakers, like painters, have their egos, but I don't know of any good ones who are not proud of the history of vinification, and who do not idolize the great vintners who came before.

Likewise, until recently, outside the cities of New York, San Francisco and New Orleans, America was a culinary wasteland. Now there's a serious chef in nearly every burb in the country. Chefs, along with wine makers and artists, also have their egos, but I know of no fine chef who does not respect tradition, and who does not understand the great cuisines of the world from which he borrows and who is not proud to be in the same line of work as Brillat-Savarin.

What is it that allows cooking and wine making in America to be on the highest level ever, while painting is on its lowest? The answer is simple: the former are governed by their respective professional advocates' respect for tradition and by a high level of standards.

In the arts, music seems strongest of all, again because of respect for tradition and very high standards. Literature falls next in line, though it suffers at the hands of a country that turns dials rather than pages. And, while there are many authors who write well and who respect tradition, and who operate with high personal standards, the audience for their work is shrinking by the minute.

At the bottom of the list comes painting, an art which has been totally co-opted by businessmen. Sadly, the reasons are the very opposite of those which stand cooking, winemaking and music in such good stead. Respect for tradition has been replaced by contempt, humility by arrogance, knowledge by ignorance, commitment by ennui, and perhaps most of all, innocence by cynicism.

I'm referring to official art, the academy, or what some have called American Museum Art, art that's reached its place through business manipulation, and for which society pays inappropriately large sums of money.

In 1985 a book was published by the University of California called *Bay Area Art 1956-1980*. In it are listed hundreds of artists including every sort of junior college teacher and housewife. What they all had in common was a professional resumé listing their gallery associations.

I painted and exhibited in the San Francisco Bay area for twelve years starting in 1960. My circle of friends included a number of artists for whom I had, and still have, respect, yet none of them, including myself, is even mentioned in this allegedly definitive book. Why? Because none of us associated with the right businessmen. The censorship had been done in advance of the arrival of the critic.

Recently, I observed a critic claim that beauty in art was no longer valid and relevant, the point being that art should reflect the life we live, and that today, most of us live with chaos, ugliness, meaninglessness, insecurity, even danger.

Norman Mailer had this to say about it, when, in his recent *Esquire* article about Madonna, he observed that Warhol saw the first symptom of modern life in America as being a lack of respect for the human condition, and that as a corollary, "there was going to be a boundless if subterranean lack of respect for art. So Warhol, a mediocre draftsman, a colorist without his own palette, moved into the void. The emptiness of others was the barren field he would seed for a cash crop. He was a magician. Warhol's real claim to fame was not as an artist, but as the philosopher of voids and silences. Warhol could easily have said, if he had been inclined to give his secret away, that 'authority imprinted upon emptiness is money.'"

If the academy is depraved and soulless, as it clearly is, what has happened to the real artist? There are always some, though their numbers are approximately ninety-nine percent lower than our art institutes and universities would have us believe.

The real artist knows that cynicism is death, and that the job of the artist today remains the same as it ever was throughout history, which is to search for truth and beauty. The artist does not simply hold a mirror up to society. If the world now is greedy, the artist must be generous. If there is war and hate, he must be peaceful and loving. If the world is insane he must offer sanity, and if the world is becoming a void, he must fill it with his soul.

Most of the real artists have been backed into the corners of America. It turns out that the spirit of art is being kept alive by any number of what might best be called serious Sunday painters along with the so-called regionalists, anyone in fact, in love with art itself, for its own sake and not for whatever material reward can be squeezed out of it.

In my case, I came to Montana twenty-two years ago seeking an inexpensive, quiet and beautiful place to paint and work. I loved California as it was when I grew up, but I saw the homicide coming. My goal was to improve my craft and nothing more (I wanted to learn to write better as well). I viewed Montana as being thoroughly isolated, never dreaming anyone would discover it. I planned on being poor my whole life and liking it that way.

What I have done and am continuing to do, is develop my own vision based on history, both genetic and otherwise. I inherited an artist's genes from my mother's family. This, combined with the study of European painting, arrived with me in Montana as the tools with which I would interpret the new landscape.

I want to do exactly what the winemakers and chefs are doing, which is to feed people's senses. I want to give them pictures informed with care, dignity, respect for history, love, heart and soul.

I want an expanding universe that includes all people, not just those with education and money. I pointed out once, and have only come to believe it more as time has passed, that great art may be appreciated by all. Shakespeare, for example, is interesting and amusing to the simplest person, while the most learned scholar finds intellectual minutiae in him with which he can engage himself for a lifetime.

Art, like life, is best when it's allowed a certain unruliness, when it's not overly controlled, and certainly not when it's domesticated. Balance is the key, so long as the beam doesn't tip toward timidity, indecision and conservatism.

One of the problems I observed when I arrived in Montana is one shared by the entire American West as far as painting and sculpture is concerned, and this is that artists of the region, or who were from elsewhere but mined the region for its colorful frontier life, universally put in the prose and left out of the poetry. It's understandable to rebel against intellectual snobbishness, but you can't counter it with corn-pone bump-kinism. Art, like the wheel, was a very big invention, and if you want to be a meaningful part of the continuum, you have to understand matters on the other side of your fence line, and not just now, but back across the centuries.

WHERE OUR DREAMS CHOOSE TO LIVE

By William Kittredge

SOME OF US DREAM we are witnessing the birth of a heartland nation in the American West, an empire which runs down the spine of the continent from the blue Canadian Rockies to the cowboy kingdoms of Wyoming and the Colorado plateau, and beyond to the ski-lift highlands above Durango and Santa Fe, at the edge of the southwestern deserts where the Hopi and citizens at Acoma built their cities on the mesa-tops (in the sky) which remind us of how good we could be.

In 1805 one of our first wayfarers in the West, Meriwether Lewis, sat beguiled beside the thunderous falls of the Missouri River (since dammed for hydroelectric power) and told himself this West was not only the great useful place Jefferson had instructed him to discover, a treasure for the republic, but also sublime, by which he likely meant it reeked of obscurity, privation, vacuity, solitude, silence, boundlessness, and thus, of almost infinite possibility. As it still sort of does.

It was a sweet day and I thought, as I drove along the Wind River, of fishing. Autumn is such a fine time to make your careful way across a meadow, along little trails through willows to crouch on the sodded bank just back from the stream, trying to catch a trout on a fly. But over dinner on an outdoor patio in Jackson, Wyoming, a perfect moon hanging amid clusters of stars over the mountains, I heard about the problem with teen-aged suicides on the Wind River Indian Reservation.

The color emptied from perfection in the eye of my mind, glory fading. The West is a candy-apple kingdom if you have meaningful work, if you are economically OK at a reasonable level and secure to enjoy it—which means, as often as not, if your money comes from outside the region.

The West was a place where good people could come to escape the injustices of an old world. The park-like valleys between shining moun-

54

tains, and the wetland enclaves out in the vast sagebrush and lava-rock distances—for some decades they were refuge for enormous migrations of the oppressed from Europe and (despite racism) from Asia. Families could come find communities in which to farm, vote, tend the hardware store, raise children and pray to God. The West was where opportunity lived, and freedom, if you were tough enough.

But the West was also an extraction colony, to be worked, where the strong could grow rich. Fur trappers, miners, ranchers, and loggers came wave after wave, intent on making a killing. They dug holes in the earth, cut the ancient trees for lumber with which to build towns, killed off the wild animals so they could replace them with grazing herds, plowed up prairies, dammed rivers, pumped the aquifers dry, and waged genocidal warfare against the native populations.

Such adventurers were ruthless, driven by greed, and they were the heroes in the mythology of The Western, a racist, sexist legend of conquest designed to reveal violence—poisoning the badger, strapping on guns, building the great dam—as a way of ultimately solving problems.

Our heroes accumulated money and power, and were willing to use everything up and cause any disturbance. Endless ruination was visited on the land, wilderness creatures died out, indigenous people were left to lives of impossible poverty, and the money and power went off to the East. The West was left with stumpage, riparian damage, holes in the ground, aquifers pumped dry. Good people thought it was what you had to do if you wanted to survive; maybe it was.

My people on my father's side fought their way from poverty in the gold mine districts of California; my grandfather on my mother's side started training as a blacksmith, "sharpening steel" (tempering picks and crowbars) for miners in Butte, at the age of fourteen. We made our way, we lived in paradise, and thought we owned it, that it was ours to use any way we wanted; we left a lot of wreckage. Now some of us hope to reinvent the objectives of our society. We think we can do something about reinventing desire; we've had enough with the unforgivable damage.

Until very recently the West was an intellectual colony of the East, defined by a Dime Novel mythology, passive, waiting for some hero from bad literature to come save us.

Since the beginnings of any sort of society in the West, in mining camps like Butte and Leadville, in our rancher towns like Cheyenne, in Utah's Mormon cities, in petroleum towns like Casper, we've had a ruling class that ruled by controlling the economy and notions of local identity. The Anaconda Company called the shots in Montana from their imperial headquarters in Butte for seventy years. All that time they owned every significant newspaper in the state.

The great timberland corporation, Champion, having ravaged the forests, is withdrawing from western Montana just as the international mining corporations got out of Butte. Loggers and millworkers have been beguiled into thinking their futures lie with the company and now they're being betrayed just as the miners were in Butte. The blue-collar culture of the old rough-handed West is dying (for the most part it is dead), but remnants remain powerfully alive in vast sparsely populated rural enclaves like eastern Montana and Wyoming. Politics in those far counties are deeply conservative and protectionist, for good reason. People there think the world is passing them by, and it is.

My grandfather came of age in Butte; he spoke a language learned there, about metal and heat. The Finnish ceramic artist Rudy Autio grew up in Butte, hearing a half-dozen languages on the streets, with no idea he was living in the cowboy West. The West is a variety of cultures— Chicano sugar-beet farmers working the bottom lands outside Red Lodge, ballet dancers in Salt Lake City, and black-tie roulette croupiers in Elko.

But, as traditional industries fail, many of those cultures are being destroyed or absorbed into our increasingly homogenized nation, and we hate it. We hate to see our homeland losing its memories and its languages. We're forgetting how to talk about going down in the mines. We're becoming an out-West dress-up theme park; our children are learning the idiom of television.

Demographics are changing rapidly. Westerners, these days, mostly live in cities—Phoenix, Denver, Tucson, Salt Lake City, Boise, Las Vegas. Most of them grew up outside the region.

Because of our wide-open history we're taken to be a hide-out for right- and left-wing loonies. We draw Aryan Nation fascists, Libertarians, anti-tax nuts, trip-wire Vietnam vets who think purity resides in the vicinity of wilderness, all of them imagining they can find sanctuary in some remnant of the old West (a very bad idea; the old West takes care of its own and mostly despises everyone else with xenophobic glee.)

A fly-fishing friend picked Kalispell, Montana, as the place where he would start his real-estate business. Right off he sold an extremely valuable shoreline acreage on Flathead Lake to a young man who thought he was going to marry a woman who had become well known for acting in the movies—beautiful property for gorgeous people.

Some months later my friend resold that property. Two commissions on the same place in the same year—a good year for my friend, although the romance had fractured. The gorgeous people had gone off separately.

The privileged congregate in their own enclaves, where they talk shop and admire each other. In the mountain West they traditionally cluster in Aspen and Sun Valley, lately in Jackson, and now in the Boulder River country and at the north end of Flathead Lake. They stimulate the local service economy and upscale restaurants, inspire gossip and magazine articles, but otherwise don't amount to much in the social dynamic of the region.

Out-of-state retirees are another deal, multitudinous and disruptive. This round of immigration may be our last; this crowd may fill the country. They've already overwhelmed Oregon and Washington. The major industry in Oregon is not logging, it's health care. The retirees are a last wave, coming our way, looking for places to hide, hoping they'll have the luck to get by without directly encountering the violence resulting from the so perfectly justifiable anger of the disenfranchised in American cities like Los Angeles.

We wish this crop of outlanders would pay their way into our society. Many of the new in-migrants—the rich and the old—don't see why they should have to pay taxes to live in the hinterlands. We can't afford first-rate schools, and they don't care. They sit tight in homogenous enclaves of the dying middle class. "When you get your first walled retirement community," a bitter sociologist told me, "you'll see the end of anything like actual neighborhoods." By actual I suppose he meant settlements where citizens work, raise children, and count on each other for all varieties of help, from picking huckleberries to burying.

We're left with a dying traditional economy, a taxpayers' revolt, and, some think, nothing in the way of a basis for a new economy but tourism. Working people are leaving. They see themselves in the servant business, a sad career servicing tourists. It's a sorry prospect.

Many Westerners understand that we inhabit a national culture dedicated to the creation of false desire (advertising and television constantly urging us to want some damned thing; we can never get enough, so we're miserable). Westerners know from bitter experience that things can't make us happy. It's an old story—some soul starts buying new combines and pickup trucks—it's a sure way to fail in the ranchland West. Most of us, not just schoolteachers and environmentalists but farm hands and timber fallers, yearn for more than hunting weaponry and whale-song CDs.

Westerners are coming to understand we have to give up on eco-

nomic growth as an ideal. We can't continue; the world is used up in so
many ways. We have to center our regional economy around notions of
taking care, and communiality, making better use of what we've already
got.

Brilliant young people from all over America are cropping up in the
northern Rockies, betting their futures on the West. Many come up with
the idea of finding a life in connection to nature in some approximation of
functional shape; they come for the skiing, the fishing, the wolves and
wilderness, but most of all they come because they hope to take part in
the creative life of an open society.

The word is out: The mountain West is a community where you can
participate, and make a difference. We're paying a lot of attention to people with ideas, naturalist/writers like David Quammen and Terry
Tempest Williams, revisionist historians like Patricia Nelson Limrick and
Richard White, legal thinkers like Charles Wilkinson (students from his
University of Colorado Law School classes seem bound to have enormous
influence in the West for several decades), and our philosopher/mayor in
Missoula, Dan Kemmis, whose writing on communiality is at the cutting
edge of our thoughts about the future.

Every college town in the Rockies has an institute concerned with
Western identity and policies, like the Center for the Rocky Mountain
West in Missoula, and the Center of the American West in Boulder.
There's a writer's conference meeting every week in the summer in resort
areas like Aspen or Yellow Bay on Flathead Lake, or McCall, Idaho or
Joseph, Oregon, or Park City, Utah. Ranchers and environmentalists get
together in groups like the Northern Plains Resource Council and the
Wyoming Outdoor Council. Groups ranging from Ross Perot's pop-
ulist/conservative United We Stand to radical environmentalists in the
Alliance for the Wild Rockies and Earth First! are providing centers
around which citizens can organize their thinking about the future. So are
publications like Missoula's *Northern Lights* and Colorado's *High Country
News*.

Our politicians, like politicians, don't seem interested in much beyond some version of business as usual (to see our ruling class at work
protecting the status quo, keep an eye on the current ranchland Senators
from Montana, Wyoming, and Colorado). Even so many citizens in the
West think it's entirely possible to work (plan, think) our way into a
strong regional economy without giving up on social justice or environmental sanity.

I'm a boy who started life on an outback cattle ranch in the deep West of southeastern Oregon, far from the centers of decision-making in my society. So I cannot tell you how much it means to me to find myself in association with people who are so deeply engaged in trying to define the processes of the right life, to encode those processes in their laws, and live with them in an open society.

We struggle to name things we won't relinquish, like compassion or old growth forest or high times on Saturday night; we want to be done with cold-hearted deliberations and the empty-pocket blues; we want transcendent blue-sky mornings, and turkey dinners with our old pals, and sweet singing later on.

My True Companion and I were shuffling through reefs of fallen leaves in luminous October light, heading for our yearly football game in the little stadium at the University of Montana, above the Clark Fork River in Missoula. We exchanged shouts with three writers and some old downtown drinking cronies, and talked shop with Dan Flores, the environmental historian. I rubbed shoulders with a famous rock-and-roll musician in the hot-dog line; it all led me to feel I was at one with a society in which personal realization was more important than success.

Some sweetest times, for me, are warm afternoons when the autumn sky is blue-white and infinite in its distance from our concerns. The needles on the larch in the high country have gone golden, falling like glory on the logging roads. Cottonwood along the rivers bloom huge and pale yellow against the evergreen mountains, and we're untouchable. We will never grow old; our people will never die. No one will break into our house while we're gone. A long winter is coming. We'll embrace it if we have a brain, ski, roll in the snow. (I in my brainless way head south.)

At the football game we rooted for our team, and it won. If my happiness about that seems excessively stupid, and I can understand that it might, I'm not very sorry. When we got home my front door was standing open but nothing was touched. Maybe it was the wind.

In Asia people save themselves from sorrow by meditating on a paradise of their own inventing which they call the Pure Land. Attempting to see each swirl in the river, leaves on the mountainslope, each intricate butterfly in sun, they try to find peace in the creature they are. In spring the purple and white lilac will blossom in enormous clots of splendor along the alleyways in Missoula.

"If the weather holds," I told my True Companion, "we could live forever." Or anyway give it a try. *Momento vivere.*

CONFESSIONS OF
A TIMBER FALLER

By Fred Haefele

> *I can tell that you're a logger,*
> *Not just a common bum,*
> *Because only a logger*
> *stirs his coffee with his thumb.*
> "LOGGER LOVER"—TRAD.

THERE WAS A TIME WHEN the logging woods conjured images of something other than cataclysmic clearcuts, stream pollution, habitat depletion. The logging woods were a place to prove yourself, a rough-and-tumble arena where tiny men manipulated huge trees on a slender hinge of wood. A place where, if you did everything right, there was a good living to be made. And if you did something wrong, it could cost you your life. Thus the logging woods became a kind of headwaters for a stream of American mythologizing, a place that spawned the likes of Paul Bunyan, who felled a hundred trees with the stroke of his axe, or Ken Kesey's only slightly less hyperbolic Hanks Stamper.

Certainly it was this kind of mythos that lured me to the Montana woods. In 1977 I was a New England tree surgeon when a string of hard times—disastrous marriage, the death of a good friend and the subsequent case of survivor's guilt—finally convinced me to try my luck somewhere far away. By the end of that summer I had immigrated to Boulder, Colorado.

In fair weather, I climbed hundred-foot cottonwoods for a local tree service. In winter, I worked as a sawyer, cutting Ponderosa beetle-kill for the Colorado State Forest Service. It was mid-winter, in the arid high country around Nederland, that I first began to hear stories about the great woods of the Northern Rockies. The one that sticks in the mind featured an unusual technique employed by Montana winter loggers: First they shoveled down through six-foot snow drifts to make their felling cuts at ground level. Then, the story went, as the tree began to go over and the trunk began to rise, the faller would grab his saw, leap aboard, ride the tree up out of the snow-well like a giant green bronco. These stories were told by my fellow crew members with perfectly straight faces and I have no reason, even now, to believe they thought them anything less than the Gospel truth.

I know I bought it. Not the tree-bronc business, perhaps, but the accompanying and very potent notion that, wherever you happened to be in the West, the real action was always somewhere else: the next state, the next drainage, the next ridge over.

A year in the East-West Boulder glitz gave these stories time to germinate and finally, the country up range drew me north like a lodestone. North, to where the winters were long and tough. Where the woods were full of grizzlies, the trees thick as culverts. North to Montana, where the *real* action was.

Thus it was that in 1979, I spent a summer east of Lincoln, felling trees for a gyppo I'll call "Bob." I was raring to go, would have signed on with the devil, but even my Job Service counselor puckered with distaste as he handed me the slip with Bob's number on it.

Bob was a relative newcomer to the logging woods, yet simply everyone had heard of him. From all accounts, he was crooked, rapacious, sleazy. In short, he had the credentials of a highly successful logging contractor. Gangly, boyish and sullen-looking, he hailed from Cincinnati, just another guy from back east who had come to Montana for the real action. In that sense, except for the trust fund he used to set himself up, he was probably a good deal more like me than I cared to admit.

We worked a 100-acre sale up Copper Creek, butting the Scapegoat Wilderness to the north. It was a private sale, belonging to an out-of-stater (a term for which I quickly learned the proper disdain). Montana is unique among the timber-producing states in that it has no laws regulating forestry practices on private lands, so basically, the sale was a kind of free-fire zone for a gyppo like Bob.

It was mostly lodgepole with the occasional pocket of old growth fir, what we called "pickles." The ground was easy, the lodgepole were about seventy feet tall, averaging twenty inches in diameter. All in all, not a particularly formidable looking adversary for a man who'd come north to make his mark, wrestling with the giants under the most adverse conditions. But it would do.

In the course of the summer the other fallers came and went and it was mostly just four of us that worked that sale: the loader man, the cat skinner (the loader man's son), me and my sawing partner, a beetle-kill colleague I had persuaded to come up from Colorado. I'll call him "Ron."

To save money, Ron and I lived in a wall tent in a meadow close by. We tried, at first, to stay out of Lincoln, which meant no restaurants, bars, or showers. We stayed out as long as we could stand it, generally three days at a stretch.

It was a rainless summer and we were covered with dust, insect bites, nicks and scratches of various origins. We reeked of saw gas, boot socks, and the sap of conifers. For piquancy and in the belief it would clear a nagging case of dandruff, Ron took to dousing his scalp with vinegar and at night, the tent smelled like a rancid salad.

We ate hundreds of cheese sandwiches. We got so hungry that neither of us had the patience even to open a can. We were paid a flat rate of a dollar a log and on a good day, we'd make a hundred dollars, not bad money at the time.

In the interest of simplicity, we grew to think: There's a tree, there's a buck.

As mere beetle-kill cutters, we were dazzled by the production faller's argot. Expressions like "cat face," "spike-top" and "barber-chair" seemed charged, full of magic.

We were dazzled by the equipment. The intermountain log trucks were diesel semis, not the gas powered straight-jobs we were used to. We noted that the real players felled with 6 cubic-inch saws, not the paltry 4.5 cubic-inchers we were using. Indeed, the notion of the right saw was something we grew increasingly obsessed with. Though we were aware the real players ran a stable of three or four, at $500 per saw, such an investment seemed well beyond our reach. We preferred instead to think that if we each had the right saw, one that didn't need constant tinkering and maintenance, we would somehow get into the *real* action.

In the course of that summer, Ron and I went through three chain saws each. More and more, the right saw seemed merely to be whatever saw some other faller was using. In a remarkably short-sighted move, at the season's outset I traded my faithful Stihl for a .357 pistol. I'd succumbed to the idea that, sawing in the Rockies, at anytime I might have to defend the tent from ravening grizzlies, hell-bent on a cheese sandwich. Ironically, the best use I could have put that pistol to would have been to blow a hole in the mindlessly engineered McCulloch 850 I bought to replace my Stihl.

Except for the ongoing crises with the chain saws, there was little out there to divert us. Nobody tootled on the mouth harp. We never played cards. We were generally too tired. I recall that Ron was reading a novel called *The Thornbirds* that he seemed always to be reading. The truth was, once we got past our brief infatuation with the lingo and the equipment, the actual logging experience was something of a disappointment. Certainly the work was strenuous, but with the undemanding terrain and the smallish, even-aged lodgepole, it soon grew monotonous, even mechanical: There's a tree, there's a buck.

With the arrival of Friday night, we would wait for Bob to show up with our checks (an arrangement which became more haphazard as the summer progressed), then we'd follow the Blackfoot downstream, ninety miles west in my old Dodge pickup, blowing through the bends, driving like Billy BeDamned to arrive back in Missoula in time for Happy Hour. We'd sit, freshly scrubbed and flummoxed in some sad-looking Front Street bar, Ron feeding the juke box quarters while it gradually sank in that most everyone had *left town for the weekend*, that the *real* action was somewhere else.

We tried to live what we thought was a logger's life, but our vision lacked verve and imagination. What we settled for resembled instead, a poorly conceived Bud commercial. We worked hard, we drank hard. Sometimes, after a few beers, we would swagger around Front Street, looking for trouble. We were stud-horse loggers, fresh from the big woods. But nobody much seemed to give a damn.

As the summer wore on, Ron grew less talkative, seemed melancholic and despondent. In the course of six weeks, he claimed to have read *The Thornbirds* four times. Whenever we drove anywhere, Ron would hunch over the tapedeck, play Ry Cooder's "Dark End of the Street," Emmy Lou Harris' "Sorrow in the Wind" and I remember thinking: "Why is this guy so goddamned sad?"

At first such a nuisance, we grew at last to welcome chain saw repairs. They came to mean we could go back to Missoula in mid-week, when there was actually someone else around. I recall a Tuesday night that Robert Cray passed through town, playing at the TopHat. He did a catchy number called "Snap It Back and Hold It," a song that seemed to really speak to Ron and me. I recall the two of us, drenched in sweat, dancing with startling abandon with any woman bold enough to take the floor with us, and finally, in what was surely a dance of madness, with each other.

Lying in that pungent tent, I began to have vivid, disturbing dreams. One night I dreamed of topless seraphim, brandishing flaming chain saws. I was so moved by it, the next evening, we drove back to Missoula and, on the strength of my dream, Ron and I turned in our breakdown prone domestic models for brand new Swedish Johnsereds. They were sleek, flame-red, gloriously light. They were 5.4 cubes, a *player's* saw if we ever beheld one.

Or not. We soon discovered that to save weight, the handles were made of a plastic so flimsy it split at the slightest tug. By noon the next day, I was eating a cheese sandwich, looking over at Ron and his cracked handle. He was looking back at me and my cracked handle and I knew we were thinking the same thing: Our Dream Saws were pieces of crap! We had shelled out a thousand dollars only to fail, once again, to come up with the right saw! Grimly, we jury-rigged the handles with hose clamps and duct tape and kept on working.

A couple of evenings later, Ron and I got up from our evening sandwich and began to saw again, more or less, just for the hell of it. We had already made our hundred dollars for the day but the conversation had grown thin and the Montana twilight lasted well past ten. In a haze of fatigue and indifference, I cut through the boundary of my "strip" (the faller's designated acreage) and followed a thick patch of lodgepole up a hillside that was, in all likelihood, not even on the Copper Creek sale. I did it because the trees were close together, the cutting was easy, the saw running well. Besides, it was common knowledge that Bob stole trees all the time: There's a tree, there's a buck.

It seemed I'd never cut so fast, with such abandon. When I stopped to tank up at the top of the hill I had a peculiar kind of vision. I looked east, over the current of freshly felled trees in my path, then turned west, to the mid-summer sun. It was red, swollen. It seemed to vibrate, wobble on the ridge line. I felt suddenly lightheaded. My skin prickled. I began to laugh and the hackles on my neck rose. I couldn't swear but that my hair didn't stand on end too.

Years later, while reading the *Odyssey*, I thought I recognized that same sensation: It comes at the point where Penelope's suitors are at her table, stuffing themselves on the last of her stores. It's the night before Odysseus reveals himself and the gods bring a giddiness down on their company, a strange laughing fit that confuses and terrifies them. They don't know quite what they're laughing at. But they sense, for the first time, that there will be consequences.

The next morning I saw Ron working off his strip, shock and disbelief on his face. He was packing his brand new Johnsereds out in pieces. The shroud was fractured, cooling fins snapped off, the bar bent double. He'd been cutting, pinned his saw. In a fit of temper, he'd cut through his hinge. (The "holding wood" between the notch and the back-cut, the hinge is the only means of controlling the tree. Cutting through it is the timber faller's cardinal sin.) The tree had narrowly missed Ron, landed on his saw. Instead of feeling relief that he was unhurt, I was furious with him. I was furious with everything. I was tired of Ron and his melancholy, tired of hearing "Sorrow in the Wind." I was so mad at him that within half an hour, I'd done almost exactly the same thing. I cut through my hinge and lost control. Like Ron, I got out of the way but the tree stove in the muffler of my dream saw and before noon, we were back in the truck, driving ninety miles to the saw shop in disgust and defeat.

The second week in August, Bob tried to move us off Copper Creek, on to slimmer pickings and we quit. He looked bemused, then chuckled, wrote us our checks and said, "Ain't that the way? You guys about get to know what you're doing then you're off down the road."

This remark wasn't entirely false, though it could be argued that Bob would probably be the last to know if anyone knew what they were doing or not. Still, we drove away in good spirits, feeling well rid of Bob until Ron tallied the checks and figured out Bob had stiffed us for the night we'd cut beyond our strips. We nearly U-turned to give him a good thrashing. We opted instead to slash his tires at a later date, drove 170 miles to St. Regis, where we signed with an outfit working a sale on Little Joe Mountain.

It was rugged country, skyline, about seven thousand feet elevation and the ground was too steep for a Cat. I looked at Ron. He looked at me. At last! We thought. The *real* action! We were so impressed by the vista, the Hahn 99 line skidder and the boxcar sized de-limbing machine we didn't immediately notice that the trees weren't all that big here, either. In fact, it took another couple of years for me to understand that the big trees, the ones the players cut, were not just a ridgeline over. Or even in the next state. The big trees, as it turned out, were by then mostly gone.

Our next night in Missoula, Ron hocked his saw, went on a bender and nearly drank himself insane. For a while I tried to help him, blamed myself for bringing him up to Montana. But in a week's time, we'd gone our separate ways.

With its panorama of root wads, slash and broken tops, the last time I saw the Copper Creek sale, it looked like the site for some tactical weapons test. Virtually every tree we left standing (anything under fourteen inches in diameter) was broken by the fall of larger trees, scatted or knocked flat by the Cat. The shorter eight-foot logs we cut were routinely left to rot because it was too hard to place them on the load. Whatever else you can say about that summer, we certainly did make our mark.

But the trees left their mark, too. After a season in the logging woods with barely a scratch, that autumn I received a cut requiring seventy-five stitches while bucking firewood. Talk about a vista—my leg gaped open like a plate from *Gray's Anatomy*. Before I passed out I could identify the tibia, patella and various connective tissues.

I was off my feet for a month and I remember thinking, Good, now I have time to *think* about all this, maybe even make sense of it. But all I could come up with was that the summer seemed to bring to the surface whatever already haunted us. And when we'd cut everything down, finally, we'd done nothing so much as to reveal who we were.

Fifteen years later, I see that my falling partner's fits of melancholy might be viewed as a kind of environmental bellwether, that Ron was a man for whom the logging mythology simply no longer worked. Along those lines, this would be a more uplifting story if I were to relate that in time, Ron went through detox, got his head on straight, and left the logging woods forever. Instead, Ron went through detox, bought sixteen-inch caulked boots, a stable of saws and returned to the logging woods with a vengeance and for the next four years, cut timber in Wyoming, Idaho and Montana. Shortly before he finally quit to become a substance abuse counselor, he related an incident where we used to saw. It was Thanksgiving Eve and when his crew stopped for beers on the way home, Ron went in with them to nurse a coke and socialize. The company quickly became rowdy, engaged in an uproarious test of skill: nothing as obvious as arm-wrestling, these jolly timber beasts were taking bets on who could pick up a quarter with his buttocks. Ron finished his story and shook his head. "I don't know, Fred," he said. "Seems like there's a different bunch of guys out there these days."

Summer of '79 was my last season as a timber faller. That autumn, still dragging a leg, I sat in on a fiction workshop at the University of Montana, where I wrote a story about a crazy summer in the logging woods, about disillusionment, about the boundaries of friendship. It was a flawed story about two flawed men, trying to give their lives shape and meaning by living out a myth. In this sense they were fated men, destined instead to live out the axiom that we cannot accomplish the dismantlement of the wild without in some way dismantling ourselves.

MOUNTAINS OF THE IMAGINATION

By Dan Flores

IN THE FOOTHILLS OF THE SAPPHIRE MOUNTAINS that stretch away from my door, snow is falling, and the loop I run—past flowering delphiniums and alpine shooting stars in the spring, through the feathery caress of waving bunchgrasses in the summer, around the glare of a particularly high-saffron chamisa in the autumn—in winter becomes a ski loop, winding the same familiar path, except now the sagebrush is snow-draped, its nasal burn caught in frost crystals. Wily, my wolf-hybrid, rocks joyously along with me, summer or winter, Nikes or Rossignols, makes no difference. With both Alaska and Texas in the background, he's a flexible guy, and Montana seems to capture the spirit of both his past worlds.

Wily takes in these foothills mostly at close range, and mostly with his nose. For me it's different. All the time we run or ski, what I'm most aware of is that mountains are standing visible against the sky. I don't know what the mountain ranges of the Bitterroot Valley mean to a wolf, but to me they seem to encircle my spot on the planet like a tribunal of earthly gods, their heads in the rarified heavens. Godlike, wild as creation itself, they forge the very weather; they're beyond time as I experience it. How does the Taoist phrase it? "The state is shattered; Mountains and rivers remain."

Like most everyone else in the Rocky Mountain West, I'm here in large part because of the mountains, and I watch them ceaselessly. I also wonder why I feel about them the way I do, why the low, rolling Sapphires with their parkland meadows strike me as human-scale and inviting, why it's the high-drama rocky places—the granite canyons and peaks—of the Bitterroots that stun the endless dialogue in my head to silence. In short, why do mountains seize me, and you, the way they do?

I've got a working hunch about this, and it involves our own time's affection for, even re-discovery of, the grand and theatrical western landscape painting. In other words, the kind of Mountain-As-Nature

61

representations done by once-famous adventurer/artists such as Albert Bierstadt and the brothers Thomas and Peter Moran a century ago. Those images may be as critical to us modern westerners as oak trees were to the Druids. They also happen to be a rich and recent example of the way an ancient geometric form has shimmered in our imaginations.

Start with this set of premises, all of which according to current reflection on human nature seem to be true. (More or less.) That humans are a primate animal. That our genesis as forest foragers gave us stereoscopic color vision to measure forest distances and to pick out ripe fruit against the dim background of green. That perhaps pushed out of the ancestral forests by competition with other apes, our ancestors emerged into the bright, expansive world of the grasslands and literally straightened up and blinked into consciousness. That the openness and the essential forms of the place where the experience unfolded—horizontal yellow earth and domed sky in a yin/yang balance, cone-shaped green mountains standing above the intersect plane, even the tree forms of a fire-swept savanna—became genetically internalized as consciousness budded. That this place imprinting in the deep genes has been dancing a slow waltz with radiating culture ever since.

If you've followed all this, and have silently nodded more than a couple of times, then you're already on the downhill of this deductive trail: We avuncular chimps must have come up with a slew of obsessive, imaginative and colorfully entertaining notions about all those ancient visual archetypes of our deep experience. Like, say, mountains. That is what you were thinking?

Of course you were, so it's no great insight to observe that people the world over are obsessed by the power of the simple pyramidal form whose geometry points towards the sky. According to geographer Yi-Fu Tuan, mountain valleys with rivers coiling through them have long functioned as a kind of ideal habitat, literally Eden, in the human imagination. The earliest landscape art known, in fact, is of this kind of setting.

We Americans have had an intense love affair with our mountains, especially so with some of the ranges of the American West, which, via great national preservation schemes, we've made into a peculiarly American form of sacred places. That's no particular insight, either, of course, but on the other hand, the savvy mountain observer of 500 years ago would never have predicted that Americans would invent national parks and the wilderness idea in order to preserve our mountains. What made our journey such a long strange trip were the gymnastics in thinking about mountains that got us from goddesses to Bierstadt, the Morans, and the Wilderness System.

This has much to do with history, so indulge me for a moment. In Europe, a thousand years or so ago, the old ideas about mountains began changing dramatically. The direct cause was the spreading triumph of Christianity over the pagan nature religions. In discrediting both pagan ideas and high country shrines, Christian theologians made a useful discovery: mountains are nowhere mentioned in the Judeo-Christian account of the Creation! This very odd absence appeared to offer proof that mountains, suspiciously, were not part of the divine plan. The mountain's principal role in the Biblical tradition, in fact, is as the setting for the Satanic temptation of Christ in Matthew 4:8. Think about it: A landform that doesn't appear in Genesis, and is Satan's favorite haunt in the New Testament, surely must have had a spin problem among European Christians. Indeed, in a famous seventeenth century book, *Sacred Theory of the Earth*, theologian Thomas Burnet explained mountains as the chaotic residue of the Great Flood, tangible flotsam of Yaweh's punishment that ought to be regarded as warts or carbuncles on the face of the planet. Mountain air and the instinctive euphoria of great panoramas? Just ole Beelzebub again, tempting the unwary back to paganism with sensuous pleasures of the flesh. Avoid, avoid, avoid.

So how did it happen, with these ideas in our recent past, that in today's American West, altitude equals beatitude? That, too, requires explanation, but fortunately not much, since our present mountain aesthetic has been with us only a couple of hundred years. The maturing science of geology, explaining all that chaos of topography, helped. So did experiential immersion with mountains—mountain climbing, in other words—which had the effect of chasing the hobgoblins beneath the scree forever. But it was people like Bierstadt, a German-American landscapist who first portrayed the Wind River Range by accompanying the Lander Expedition westward in 1859, and Thomas Moran, who initially painted the Northern Rockies for the Hayden survey of the Yellowstone Plateau in 1871, who for us Americans effected a final transformation of mountain gloom into mountain glory. Culturally, many of us put the spectacles of Romanticism on then and there, and we've only wiped them a time or two, never removed them, since.

Bierstadt, Moran, even the photographers who often were alongside them in this portrayal of the Mountain West, were shamans of the first rank, as visual translators obsessed by the mystery of the once-forbidden mountain landscape. Their art turned the former warts into scenery, the reflexive human awe at vastness and topographical complexity into a positive emotion they referred to as "The Sublime." And since Romanticism by no means had escaped religion's influence, mountains that once had been Satan's lair now became... wilderness, places unpolluted by the presence of fallen humans. In short, the Romantics had performed the hat trick of entirely inverting the previous idea: mountains were now holy, the freshest example of God's handiwork, and civilized humanity suspect.

Meditate on such art and do an emotion check. In the play of holy western light in a work like Bierstadt's *The Rocky Mountains, Lander's Peak* (1863), the mountain quite literally becomes the face of God—the powerful but benign, looking down on the tiny humans toiling along, as in Thomas Moran's *Beaver Head Canyon, Montana* (1871) and a hundred other last-century scenes like it that are, in effect, pilgrimage art. Or the Rockies are imagined as a majestic, timeless, unspoiled Eden, and that in good part because of our absence (the kernel of the wilderness idea) in a work like Peter Moran's *The Tetons* (1879). Through the eyes of Romantic mountain artists of the last century, the very existence among us of monumental ranges like the Tetons, the Beaverheads and the Winds became testimony to American destiny and moral superiority. As usual, Thoreau got it before almost anyone else when he shrieked, from atop Maine's Mount Ktaadn in 1846, "Contact! Contact!"

So who cares now that Bierstadt mostly made up his canvases of the Wind Rivers from scenes in the Alps and Yosemite, or that Thomas Moran fudged a bit (combining several locations) when he painted that ultimate confirmation of God in America, the Mountain of the Holy Cross in Colorado? Or that American mountain wilderness was mostly myth, since the continent had seen 400 generations of people come and go by the time the painters got there? For most of us, verticality has meant sublimity ever since, and we've fashioned our world in the American West around the idea.

True enough, the desert aesthetic has been gaining ground of late, eating away at the mountain aesthetic's hold on our affections. But mountains have a big lead, and they have the deep internalization thing going for them. After all, the Georgia O'Keefe desert West is a much newer vision than the mountain glory of Bierstadt and the Moran brothers. It may take us a while before we can take a good look at the encircling desert.

RANCHES
AND
RODEOS

A REBIRTH OF WONDER IN THE REGENESIS OF SIGNIFICANT STEEL

By Ralph Beer

ALONG ABOUT CHRISTMAS it started to seem like one of those old-timey winters, like when Cousin Leroy headed for the johnny house out back and was never seen again. Darned if it did not blow—that Alberta Express ripping down through here all the way from Kolymskoje nagorje, just laden with suspect Soviet snow. The cows shuddered around under their individual drifts like miniature haystacks with feet, as we pulled chairs closer to our cherry-red stoves to recount again how Norma Fish, over at the old Flemm place, burned their dinette set and the tires off her Bronco to keep from freezin' while Earl was marooned with a couple dozen of his redneck buddies down at the Badger Hole Saloon. One heck of a deal that was. By the time Earl got home, old Norma was goin' after the front porch with his Husqvarna.

Anyway, it was long past dark and raw out there when I rumbled from the shop on my tracklayer to doze back frozen plow berms that had drifted in, closing our lane to the county road. Kind of pretty, though, going up through the timber, a million flakes all aswirl in the cones of light out front, like when I was small and riding home with my dad on a stormy night—the patterns of snow parting in the low beams, the clinking of tire chains and growl of gears, and the warm certainty of Pop behind the wheel wrapped me in a sense of venturing through a frozen expanse of, say, the Yukon, although eventually, as I stared into the bright lines of whipping snow, my eyelids would droop, and I'd snuggle down into the lining of my old parka and fall asleep. Every single time.

But this year, when I hit the flats beyond the treeline riding that crawler, there was no danger of falling asleep. Even under all those hoods and tanker mittens, with a tarp tucked round my legs and the best felt boots money can buy on my chubby little feet, I felt like I'd been dumped naked and soaking wet into the world's biggest beer cooler. And there I sat, clanking along at one mile an hour into the wind with chunks of ice the size of yearling mammoths sliding down the blade, my arms and legs becoming ever more remote as the hours passed. I felt like someone from another generation, lost and alone, topping drifts with a team and bobsled. In truth, I was just another poor frozen person feeling sorry for himself in the bleak night of Montana.

After listening to me whimper about such nights, my friend, Ronnie Pierson, yawned, scratched, and said, "Hey. Take my Power Wagon and plow with that. Last time I used it the heater still worked."

I have to admit, up front, that I was skeptical. The Power Wagon was, after all, just a glorified pickup truck, a last remnant of what four-wheel-drives once were. But it was such a generous offer—why, Ronnie loves that truck as much as his bird dogs even—that I could not just say "no," and switch the subject.

Of course when Margaret and I went to retrieve this hunk of storied scrap iron, we discovered straight away that the last time Ronnie had actually started the truck was somewhere back in the early '80s. There it sat, a 1947 "Civilian Model" Dodge Power Wagon, attached by means of pipes and pins and cables to a 1930s vintage Montana State Highway Department snowplow, rusting away in a field of tansy among the paintless hulls of other Detroit fossils, all four tires encased in worn truck chains and absolutely flat, dead weeds sprouting from hood and fenders, the box in back overflowing with broken leaf springs and empty Lagoona Lite cans.

I wanted to sneak off, pretend to something more reasonable, like the throne of Portugal. But Ronnie appeared, love for his cherished collection of the ruptured past lifting his beard into a beatific grin. "Okay, okay!" he said. "Let's get started!"

To avoid hurting his feelings, we spent the next six hours trying to start the engine. Somewhere most of the way through the third tractor battery, the mighty straight six snorted, backfired, and, amid a stench of half-burned rotten gasoline fumes spurting from cracks in the exhaust manifold, actually began to run. Mice rifled from the tailpipe into the tumbleweeds thereabouts like furry little musketballs, and the muffler, which the rascals had packed with seeds and grass, caught fire. We removed the muffler on the double with a hacksaw, then lay panting beneath the studded running board.

"Think I'll pass on this one," I said as we extinguished the last embers and struggled to our feet. Ronnie just grinned, a gentle bodhisattva jack of all trades: master builder, machinist, equipment operator, farmer of family dirt.

One evening a week later, Ronnie showed up in our yard with a dump truck and heavy-equipment trailer, to which the Power Wagon was lashed with log chains like some creature recently hacked from glacial ice. Mister Pierson backed the PW from the trailer, collected his chain binders, and left, all the while beaming with secret glee.

Three or four inches of snow fluffed down that night, and the next morning, after feeding cows and cats, I decided to try that baby out. It started, but right off I noticed from the ammeter that juice was disappearing, that the engine was firing on battery reserves alone. Hmm. Broken wires? Dead short? Bad gauge? Worn brushes or zonked armature in generator? All or most of the above? But, heck, it was running, so off I went, up past the tractor shed and around by the old chicken house, waves of snow flying from the plow's curved wing as I mashed those square-cut gears. Emboldened, I made a run for the meadow and "The Big Hill."

Big mistake. Somewhere along the way I met a hidden rock pile and came to a sudden stop, which shattered one of the plow shoes (farmerized from a field disc) into half a dozen pieces.

When I went to lift the blade to back away, the half-inch winch cable broke. As I repaired the cable, I noticed that one of the tires was going flat. There was also a strong odor of antifreeze in the crystalline air. When I crawled under to investigate, I saw that axles, tranny and engine were leaking oil like the Exxon Valdez. Half a mile from home a side chain broke, the cable snapped again, and the battery delivered its final spark to the ignition system. Except for the wind, it sure was quiet.

We drug it home later with the hay truck and left it to settle beside the shop. A week went by. Two. But as I trudged past on my numbing round of chores I discovered that I would slow to cast longing glances at that great tangle of iron. With the speed of an advancing ice shield, ideas for its restoration began to worm their way past my defenses. And, finally, I heard myself think (felt, in fact, my chapped lips move) Okay, okay! Let's get started!

Enter, then, the Holy of Holies: Into the shop she went, right up next to that sheet-iron stove and directly beneath our twelve-ton chain hoist. Since nothing *except* the heater worked, off came the plow, the hood, the tires and wheels, the tail pipe. On went new, tractor-grip, eight-ply recaps, a new muffler and rebuilt generator, and whole spools of bright electrical wire. I discovered that I could solder *upside down!* In with new points and plugs and clean oil; out with rancid filters, Coors cans from the

'60s, and a homemade rear bumper/trailer hitch that hung as if in shame by two, worn 3/8s bolts. I fixed leaks; I tightened or replaced radiator hoses; I threaded in new grease zerks and poured in fresh lube, the joyful scent of Marfac 00 going right to my head.

My hillbilly bro, Leonard Pickett, boilermaker and welder *extraordinaire*, spent a bright, twenty-below afternoon bending and arc welding three-inch angle iron into place to strengthen the plow frame. And, of course, I was visited by dreams and visions.

The PW was no longer just a magnificent hulk of real steel, it joined "Ghost Riders in the Sky" in my mind—a sleek, muscular wraith with a life of its own and the wings of all myth with which to take flight.

That meant a paint job, plain and simple.

Oops. The first coat of "daffodil" industrial enamel made the PW look like a cross between Big Bird and an over-sized bumble bee. But, wait! Shiny black body with Essex green fenders, running boards, and wheels sure did the trick. (Tip: Snatch the wife's crock pot for such projects. Keep your paint thin in four inches of hot water and just slap 'er on with a brush.)

I rebuilt the tire chains, adding a new cross-link between each old one on the rears, and much of the old winch-and-cable-driven plow, welding and grinding, fabricating or replacing missing parts, then priming and painting coat after coat of that hot enamel until the blade and its angle-iron frame shone like new. I added supports to the winch housing and a heavy H-frame to change the cable angle to the plow, then unspooled half the cable until I got past the rotten stuff and hooked 'er all up.

No turning back by then, so I added high-powered spotlights above the doors on the cab and one pointing backwards off the logging-winch boom in the box, all the better to see with at night. Finally, a battery-powered closet light, super-glued to the dash so I could see which of all those levers I was pulling in the dark. And, as a crowning touch, black, fake-fur seat covers bungeed tight over new, second-hand bucket seats.

From then on it was just a matter of tinkering—splicing in new toggles here and there, filling the master cylinder, dropping in new floor mats, all the while watching from a crack in the cross-timbered shop door as the snow came down and cornices lipped from the eves of homestead cabins, and what passes for roads out here faded away in the general whiteout beyond my sanctuary of nuts and bolts. But I had become enlightened through my labors: What I discovered during all those hours of effort, as I bashed my knuckles and set my pants aflame with sparks, was a tactile connection to a not-so-far-off time when things were made to last, when workers and engineers alike took genuine pride in what they made. And, that because of their dedication to detail and function and durability, their creations are to this day not only still in use, but, in rough country like ours, subjects of some serious bragging rights as well. There, in heavy-duty detail, was the most intractable truck ever built, pride of that generation of Americans who drove Power Wagon ambulances and weapons carriers all over North Africa and from Italy to Berlin. Every single component—from axles to leaf springs to frame—had been overbuilt, beefed up to guarantee failure-proof performance, and the result was a vehicle lean as an atlatl and tough as a pine-knot club.

As I turned around in my uncle Ted's yard in the dark soon thereafter and launched back into the veils of white cast through the overhead spots, I felt an old joy riding in that snug cab beside me. The country seemed vast again and rugged, a land of stunted spruce and frozen rivers, perhaps, where Sergeant Preston and Yukon King patrolled with dog team and sled, a northern outback a thousand miles beyond the lights of the first subdivision, where a man could have the dignity of adventuring out on his own.

In vortices of snow rushing from the plow berm, which the Power Wagon so effortlessly rolled back, it seemed possible for the briefest of moments to see old-timers like Robert Beer and Theo Schuele and Grandpa Wallace floundering home on bobsleds behind sweating teams, and in that singular complexity of sound and light, of chains arattle and gears and wind, of driven flakes cutting parabolas through the blackest night, a warm certainty settled about me as I swung down our lane. I turned down the heater, snuggled against fake fur into the warmth of my parka, and as my eyelids grew heavy with dreams and visions, I smiled large, yawned, and headed for home.

HORSE DREAMS
AND LAMENTATIONS

By Kim Zupan

> *Some young foolhardy dweller of the barrow,*
> *To grip his knees around the flanks,*
> *Leaped from a tree and shivered in the air.*
> *Joy clawed inside the bones*
> *And flesh of the rider at the man*
> *Flopping and bounding over the dark banks.*

YOU CAN GET THERE LIKE THIS: north from Great Falls, past lapidary shops and failed implement dealerships, across a fissured mud flat clotted with tumbleweeds—what passes for a lake here. Bear dead north. Measure mileage Montana-wise, in bars beckoning at the highwayside, pass a Japanese grain elevator, at Fort Benton the great taciturn loop of the Missouri, down then to the Marias River bottom where debauched pink tourist "cottages" squat along the stark and muddied bank. Gun your engine up onto the muddied bank. The Bear Paws suddenly loom. Far to the northwest the glaucous domes of the Sweet Grass Hills, to a stranger got here by grave mistake, might seem a thunderhead rolling down from the Alberta Prairie. West, the crenelated line of the Rockies, a blue hope; southeast the Highwoods beyond the great broken sweep of Breaks that embrace their river, wearied to a slow roll. Just north, Box Elder, bleak hub of the Rocky Boy reservation, where Chippewa Crees were exiled from their wanderings.

Seventy-one miles out, hack a right at Big Sandy and within minutes you are as insignificant as a wren sitting on a fencepost. To get where you're going, travel thirty-one miles more of tortuous gravel. Here, among the tribes of forgotten men, the mountains like tumuluses harboring their dead for centuries, even the road seems to lack the courage to go onward into the tilted landscape. Besides four-wire fence, the only signs of man: one house, early on, set into a bluffside; a natural gas pumping station (unmanned); one windmill standing in a coulee bottom like an exposed saurian skeleton. A power line, a ranch house, then nothing. A calving shed, openness. Openness.

Antelope bolt through the shortgrass. A mottled feral cow hunts the fenceline for escape. Magpies descend on a stillborn calf.

Even before I arrive I have begun to mourn.

> *Joy and terror floated on either side*
> *Of rider rearing. The supreme speed*
> *Jerked to a height so spaced and wide*
> *he seemed among the areas of the dead.*

I was just a kid, with the incumbent astigmatisms, and did not tally it up as luck to have come here. Then, it was just another head to get on, another plew, an eight-second lesson at the craft of spurring bucking horses. And I would not ride here again, graduating to the so-called better shows—more trustworthy stock, more money, and the sanctioning of the pro circuit. But wherever you go from here, to even Helmville or Helena, or farther—Calgary, Cheyenne, Houston—you get farther from the heat of rodeo and closer to the circus of it, the pomp and ephemery.

The National Finals Rodeo, the World Series for cowboys, is the culmination of a year—of a career—of riding bucking horses, and something we all dreamed of. We revered the very idea of it, worshipped the possibility. So it was not with derision when a friend of mine said, "Yeah, NFR: 'Nother Fucking Rodeo." He was saying only that even there, under the luminous dome at Vegas or OK City, it's still the same: you get on, you spur wild, you win the prize.

They call them punkin rollins or jackpot rodeos, and besides the dizzying, occasional basketball championship or Fourth of July picnic, they've been the primary celebration of small towns in the West for a sacred century, ever since Saint Bill Pickett bit that first steer's lip. And this one, hell, it's not even a town: no house, no single resident, no bar.

Wherever there's a rodeo, it's still that man against nature thing, that barely fathomable yen that sent Europeans scaling their massifs that represented the last vestiges of wild in all that tamed and sullied geography. Minoans, long-dead Mediterranean swashbucklers, formed a kind of religion around bull vaulting (a fervor most cowboys would understand) in which men and women clasped the horns of rampaging bulls and somersaulted over impalement onto the animal's back. In the volutionous passage of time, this rodeo in this town that isn't a town, never was a town, is about five ticks of the cosmic clock from that obscure century peopled by roughstock zealots immortalized on the pillars of tombs.

Except that contestant and spectators arrived, for the most part, by car and not horse, it was a rodeo unfettered by time. There were no bleachers, not even poles between the posts for revelers to toe-hook their boots. People sat on their car hoods, some of them front-seated it and honked their horns in lieu of clapping. Children hung from the sheep wire like dwarf crucifixion victims as if to embrace some perfidious charge generated by the excitement in the dirt a frail arm's length away. Beyond the combustion engines lining the arena, the only concessions to modern life were the electrical outlets in the concession booth and the announcer's crow's nest. His amplified drone blared from a single rusted trumpet. No chemical toilet, but a two-holer teetering above a trench. Most males, I recall, shunned that dank shack and sought relief just over the hill. No bunting strung on bleachers, no bands. No "Vern's Hi-Fi House" or "Mid-State Tractor Supply" adorning each chute gate. Just men come to ride and folks come down from the hills to watch.

Later I would ride shows whose tawdry accouterments contributed to the awful notion of rodeo as carnival, some quirky western sideshow. Often, a disenfranchised pep band honked and blared frenetically to get in a few bars while horses bucked or doggers wrestled cattle. At one college rodeo the lights went out midway and a woman in clothes tight as skin rolled in on the flatbed of a truck and began to sing, the quavering song notes oddly commingled with the contagious lowing of steers. She had a Spanish-sounding name. She was Tanya Tucker's third-cousin by marriage or something. Anyway, she was famous. She signed my partner's hat. I've seen monkeys herding sheep, grimly gripping tiny hand holds strapped to the backs of dogs. They tipped precariously as their shaggy mounts jibbed around the arena nipping ewes, their tasseled gaucho hats the size of teacups tipped over one eye. And the trained buffalo that, for all the rodeos he was forced to work, seemed ubiquitous as a god. He cantered, wagged his head like a bear, bowed like a Lippizaner, finally dumbly balanced his carpeted bulk on a teeter-totter, on a ball. And always, under the furl of flags, the serpentine pomposity of grand entry and sashed queens saluting two-fingered from the pink brims of their hats.

The music I miss now with a pang is the sound of penned horses and cattle, the colors of dun, sorrel, brindle and the reposeful sense that the commodious world of grassland begins just there, outside the arena's poles.

The flesh was free,
the sky rockless,
clear,
The road beneath
the feet was
pure, the soul
Spun naked to the air
And lanced against a solitary pole
Of cumulus, to curve and roll
With the heave that disdains
Death in the body, stupor in the brains.

I was a kid then. I nosed the Dodge in among the ring of dusty cars propelled by their drivers to this non-town by hearsay and circling an arena which, even then, was cracked and bleached with age, I didn't know a living soul. I lugged my warbag from the trunk and hunted up a stock list, found my name, foreign among all the locals and Weaselheads, Killsontops, Yellowtails. Found my horse, catalogued with the other fierce appellations given probably for just this occasion: Death Trip, Widow Maker, Renegade. I unpacked my gear slowly, assiduously, like a priest at this tabernacle, to settle rampaging nervousness that stopped, I want to remember, just short of fear. I paced. The chew in my mouth went sour. A calf bleated mournfully from its pen and the bulls roared with indignation. Then suddenly the concussive sound of horses being run into their chutes, the snorts, ringing of hooves against lumber. The shouts of men, the slamming of gates. Dust rose over everything and settled with the clangor of pounding hearts.

I found my horse by a peeling hip brand, snagged an Indian kid to hook my cinch. We eyed the eyeball rolling back at us.

"Know anything about him?" I said.

"Naw.

"Can you come back and give me a tug?"

"Yeah."

I stood above the horse in the chute. He craned back his long head, so wild he goggled his eyes in fear to have such a creature astride his back. I took out a knife and cut away nests of burrs in his mane against the possibility of hanging a spur. He began to kick the sliding gate, shooting back hoof and coughing like a brute Tourette's sufferer. I rubbed this neck, felt the thrum of life, as he banged and flinched at this horror of enclosure and the cacophony of alien men and strange horses—more disquietude in those few minutes than he's had in his entire unbridled life—and I as certainly massaged the anxiety and lonesomeness in myself that at that moment flooded through me and pooled where I think my colon is, that jumbled feeling of dread and elation I never lost and which now I miss as I imagine you miss a severed limb.

Someone had dragged a set of discs through the arena, maybe a harrow rake, but still the dirt seemed an anarchy of Pre-Cambrian stones, undersides turned sunward, and judges and timed-eventers who walked across looked like ungainly fishermen trying to negotiate spring runoff. A barrel racer stood scowling, gesturing, and a man with a rake chunked irresolutely at the clods of dirt around a barrel pin.

I had been on less than twenty head by then, just a kid come to rodeo, too late really, but I'd already been conditioned like that Russian's slavering hound. Because when the recorded national anthem crackled, skipped, began again, my heart rattled in its cage and my legs went limber, the music no more than a distant background overture for the symphony of snapped necks and wrenched tendons.

The Cree kid materialized and began to pull my latigoes without a word. A shriek of rusted hinge and the guy ahead of me spurred out a fair horse. I pulled my hand in to the squawk of rosin and a face leered up through the slates of the chute gate, said, "Nod yer face, son. Come on now. Nod yer face."

Yet earth contains
The horse as a remembrancer of the wild
Arenas we avoid.

Now, twenty years later, I stand at the barbed wire fence at the county road and survey the ruins of memory. The hills are a rough amphitheater, across the sky a slash of mare's tail whipped by spring. This is the Montana I love, too beautiful in its barrenness for any film star wealth to threaten. Never having had a population, it is surely not a ghost town, but sprawled there, like the bones of a great beached trawler, it is a ghost rodeo.

I made a break clean. I can't even go to them anymore, a victim of myself for a decade now, of a prejudice harbored for years that if you ain't riding bucking horses, you ain't shit. But now, as I stand in front of that

Babel of fallen chutes and weather-rent posts and poles, I begin to miss what I had forgotten. The memories rush back as they do when you unexpectedly come across the picture of someone you loved who died, or you see an old girlfriend pass through a doorway across the street.

It had an awful hold on me. Maybe this was how another kind of dried-out junkie feels as they watch a user pump Elysium into a ravished vein. I miss the thrill and, as much, the serenity of single-mindedness in a world of confusion and responsibility, that time when nothing mattered at all but horses. I was a craven disciple to the eight-second jolt and the life that framed it. Of course, when done wrong, like Larry Mahan said, it was like grabbing onto a suitcase handle and jumping out a third-story window. But when it was right it was like flying, just you and a greater life feeding you, another huger heart, creating for the briefest time a single life, and surging up through your arm as if through an umbilicus, joy, fear, pain, analgesia. Like a poem, my partner had said, all the emotions of life in a small space.

I duck through the wire, walk to the arena. I stumble on a sign in the dirt, barely legible. ConTestAnTs Only in AreNA. I climb up, straddle a chute. Chokecherry grows up from the dirt, fertilized by generations of bucking horses and bulls penned in the dusty cell. The arena is an irregular ellipsoid, seems almost thrown up in haste. Sage brush grows up along the rusted sheep wire stapled to railroad ties and bull pine posts, some sheared off like greenbough breaks of femurs. Inside the ground is reclaimed so thoroughly by native grass it is nearly impossible to imagine it had ever seen plow or discs. ARCO could learn something here.

A power line snakes through the grass on the perimeter to a downed pole lying like a broken bowsprit, pushed over by worm-infested cattle or some fearsome Canada gale. Nearby, on a bare knob, the remains of the concession stand, its door stove in. Beside the iron bathtub in which beer was iced, I find the tiny frangible jawbone of a rodent. Like an archaeologist, I try to fix the time this place died. I toe out of the dirt a churchkeyed rusted beer can. Littering the ground all around the booth are aluminum pull-tabs not used, I figure, for at least fifteen years. There's a Copenhagen lid smashed flat, a gnawed pocket comb. And from booth to arena, fractured grey-white lumber bristling with nails cascades down the hill like the bones of Custer's dead.

Incredible in this country, there is not a sigh of wind. No pulse. Songbirds are a month south. It is as quiet here under the blue vault of sky as if I stood in the belly of a mausoleum.

For the colts of the dusk rear back their hooves
And paw us down, the mares of the dawn stampede
Across the cobbled hills till the lights are dead.
— JAMES WRIGHT
FROM *THE HORSE*

The good ones' names I remember: Strawberry, Shady, Three Bars, Alright. The one here, all encased rage, rearing with me in the chute and battering the slide gates with head and hooves and bellowing like a Valkyrian warhorse, I forget. When I got out on him, he bucked weakly and ran off, only just slewing his ass around like a strychnined coyote. A race horse, we called them. In eight seconds I might have spurred him a lick or two (I forget most of the poor rides, too) while he toured the whole arena, so fast the pick-up men were losing ground. My tailbone was taking a pounding and I bailed off, as the pick-up horses thundered past in pursuit. From hands and knees in the dirt I watched as he ran flat-out under the ghost of me.

Even now, twelve years since I last got down on one, this scene recurs on the periphery of REM sleep: my horse stands in the chute and I have forgotten my riggin, a standard-issue rodeo dream, I guess, like the universal slumberous embarrassment of being at school without your pants. In the tristful mist of dream, I see his bulging eye between the slats, a wild, white-rimmed world beckoning me backward. I climb down, take a mane hold, call for the gate, spur out into an effulgent arena of possibility. And in the sober mornings I remember nothing more.

I have brought back with me from that place (for my youngest daughter, the one who's horse-crazy like her old man was) a black hank of horse tail that had been caught up in the crack of lumber. She tucks it in the back of her skirt and gallops her boots through the house.

Standing out there among the raw humps of the Bear Paws, it was easy to slide toward the skerries of remorse—that monument to youth, for all its purity and perfection, decaying before me into the greening grass of April. But I am lucky to have had it then, and I am lucky now. It's just as well true that a girl's exuberant bootclops, a mane of ponytail tied up by a mother's hand, is what I saw reflected in the eye of that bronc. I have my fin keel to hold me in that ocean of remembrance.

CITY LIMITS

By Ralph Beer

YOU KNOW HOW IT IS. Along about the middle of March, when a few
warm afternoons have thawed the top couple inches of ranch road to the
consistency of buttermilk, a latent ambiguity overtakes us. We walk our
fields, dig around in the iron pile, take measurements and scratch, only to
find ourselves later, during the vague hours between midnight and
dawn, camped in faithful easy chairs with tomcats, coffee and note pads,
making lists of upcoming spring projects and the materials needed to see
them through. And, as Orion tilts among the spheres off south, we romance again the notion of going to town.

Before we know it, the first warm rays of a Saturday morning sunrise slant among the tablelands to find us striding about in our best jeans
and boots, all business as we shoo our partner into the toasty cab of the
idling pickup. The day ahead is filled with promise—a rosy sky pulsing
as if with the hot blood of youth; the checkbook, substantial after another
lean winter, within easy reach upon the dash. Even the gumbo provides
release as we goose the truck, oversteering to make it frog and fishtail
down the lane.

At the outskirts of the city, we realize we forgot the list, then do the
unthinkable by pulling into Dirty Don's Carwash, where, after several
dollar's worth of high-pressure suds, actual paint appears beneath that
stubborn crust. Mud, pine needles, manure and gobs of cow hair melt into a foul soup that clogs the floor drain as a disgusted Don looks on; what
might have been part of a pack rat eddies toward him atop a raft of straw.
But Don and his puddles are quickly forgotten as we glide off toward the
cloudland of tinted glass and polished steel rising before us.

New buildings have shot up along the Strip, a hurdy-gurdy of
frameworks and naked trusses that will soon be drive-in banks and casi-
nos, where, heck, it don't seem that long ago, was nothin' but gopher
holes and weeds. Cars—manhandled by kids in black leather—cut in
ahead and shimmy to a stop at the next light, where they torque and twist

under the stress of twenty-inch speakers bellowing an endless bass line that makes your fillings hum. OOM BAH OOM! BONKA BONKA BOOM! A fenderless VW Beetle driven by eight or nine high school girls pulls alongside, and, as if juiced by an unseen spark, they begin to bounce and wave to the boys up front. The one hanging from the passenger-side window just below your elbow sports a white Mohawk and a ring in her cheek. Your wife looks from them to you and smiles, "They're so cute at that age, and to think, half of 'em will end up married to ranchers." This from a lady who dropped out of Wharton to sing lead vocals with the heavy metal band, Toxic Coma, whose album, "A Phosgene Kind of Love," went platinum. The light mercifully changes, and, as you pull away feeling like Pa Kettle, you know age has found you out.

The usual stops: swap oxygen and acetylene tanks and pick up fifty pounds of farmer rod at High Country Salvage, then, next door to the elevator, for six hundred pounds of alfalfa seed, ten blocks of cow salt, a bag of calf bands and four dozen ear tags. At the Hide and Fur Depot, you get the yard apes to throw a hundred six-foot steel posts in back and forklift two, twenty-four inch by twenty-four foot steel culverts to the top of the stockrack, which you boom down nice and snug with chains. Next, the John Deere dealer, for stubble sweeps, a three-point top link, and a little haggling on a new gang of drills, followed by the mandatory bull session with the boys who always seem to be hanging around drinking coffee. Darned if you didn't almost forget those twenty sacks of Portland cement at the lumber yard.

By now the pickup handles like a poisoned whale, the culverts overhead thrumming in the gathering wind as if straining for lift off. One of the bags of cement slides out at a six-way stop, and when you try to do the right thing by halting to remove the hazard from the street, drivers blow past in a bedlam of honks, snarls and gestures not meant to gladden your day. The triple-ply cement sack tears neatly in half when you get it belt high, spewing ninety pounds of flour-like powder from hat brim to boots, and you notice a pounding in your ears like the back-seat bass line to all current woes.

That's when your wife reminds you how you'd promised to stop at the mall, where the parking lot is so big, antelope browse among the cars. Low-moving clouds scud past the nearest hills, but, like the good sport you are, you go in with your lovely gal, feeling about as inconspicuous as Edward Scissorhands—the front of you bleached a deathly white, an elbow burst in your favorite shirt, one thumb unaccountably metering fat drops of blood to the brightly tiled floor—only to lurch along caught between a group of oldsters with walkers and the nauseating crush of steaming teens, who no longer seem so cute. After ducking into a novelty shop to catch your breath, you realize that the counter, where you've come to bay, displays edible prophylactics arranged about the base of a Herculean, milk chocolate phallus. About then Maggie or Annie or Susan takes your hand and leads you like a stunned draft horse from the fluorescent horrors therein.

At the city limits, it begins to snow, a radiator hose bursts, and the Highway Patrolman, who stops to make sure everything is okay, writes you up for not having attached red, long-load warning flags to the culverts. The sight, some hours later, of your front gate header is dampened only by the unhappy realization that you forgot to stop at the liquor store, which, when you'll be heading back in on Monday to somehow cover the $700 overdraft on your checking account, will be closed. The foot-deep tracks where you squirreled the truck only this morning have frozen into unavoidable ruts that immediately blow the beads on both rear tires. But at least you're within walking distance of home, where, within a few weeks spring will come again to your part of the country, and you can go forth to dig or plow, to hew and pound to your heart's content, all the while drenching yourself in the smells of loam and sap and honest sweat as you mend from the wishful allurements of town.

HAYING HORSES IN MY MIND

By Wally McRae

I see lathered teams in afternoon sun
Cutting five-foot swaths in yard-high hay.
I smell drying coils that the dump rakes spun
Of alfalfa and blue joint in contoured display.
There's a buckrake skimming the ground, in my mind,
In controlled weavings, to even the load.
Overshot teams plod a monotonous grind:
"Git up. Whoa. Back." on a forty-foot road.

Modern Christmas-hued monsters on diesel fuel race
Faster than oat-powered Belgians I knew.
Freon-cooled air fans the pale driver's face.
Furrowed rubber replaces the hot-forged shoe.
Coming weather is heard on the FM band,
Not read first-hand in the westerly sky.
"Speed" and "Progress" the team now. Not "Classy" or "Sand."
Modern haying's a pleasure, I admit with a sigh.

I see a kid shooing pheasant chicks
From the few final swaths. Or picking clean
The outside rounds; pitching beaver-cut sticks
Crickward, a scout for Dad's mowing machine.
Hell, there's no nostalgia in diesel exhaust.
You don't speak to tractors you step behind.
We've damn sure progressed, but something's been lost
And horses are haying somewhere in my mind.

APOLOGIES TO ED ABBEY

By Ralph Beer

DEAR ED,

It's one of those Saturday mornings that seem to come along about once a year in this part of Montana, a day caught between February and the temptations of spring. An inch of fresh snow is melting on the sunny side of granite under a sky so radiant with light that from our kitchen windows I can't help but see a desert sky over piñon hills and slick-rock canyons.

Today, the never-ending hard work of ranching involves puttering around with coffee while brewing a two-gallon pot of beans on the wood-stove, a satisfying ritual that includes a ham bone the size of my elbow, big red chilies off the wall, and lots of good, old-fashioned molasses. These are genuine Montana ranch beans, which I learned to make years ago in New Mexico. They are not for the ambivalent or the faint of heart.

Today's sky and light have turned my thoughts to you. The first line of *Desert Solitaire* comes to mind and brings a smile: "This is the most beautiful place on earth." Indeed it is, Ed. You were right for both of us.

What a fine book! One that's helped me through some ugly winters with its images and light and warmth, one that's shored my notions about how to conduct myself among the rocks, grasses, trees and creatures who inhabit this family ranch. I can close my eyes right now and see you out there in *your* most beautiful place, sitting against a favorite juniper, engaged in the hard job of watching cloud formations and thinking, maybe taking a note or two. And I can remember deciding, under the influence of your books, that it was all right to love places as if they were beloved friends and lovers, and to resist the forces that would cripple or kill them for a buck.

My smile and good cheer fade, and I find myself going back to those essays you and I published in *Harper's Magazine* during the confusion of the Eighties. It's been more than ten years now, but that snarl of issues and arguments and bad behavior rushes back and hits me like too much adrenaline. It's a lousy feeling, one that's dogged me too damned long.

An early version ("Free Speech: The Cowboy and His Cow") of your essay started out as a kind of performance piece, delivered as an address at the University of Montana. It was wild and playful, good theater some said, and people who were in attendance still laugh, remembering big Ed Abbey waving a .44 Colt while addressing his subject, which was the need to get private cattle off public lands.

Meanwhile, I'd been reading and researching and compiling the ten thousand notes for an essay dealing with what was then being called the "Farm Crisis in America." I talked to dozens of ranchers and farmers and amassed cardboard boxes of information. I read and thought and tried to organize what I had with what I knew, and, as such things go, got lost again and again. But I did it. My big important essay went to *Harper's*, a fine magazine, and I ended up being pretty darned proud of myself, which would have been just fine if I hadn't also started feeling a little self-righteous, too.

Three months later, there was your "Cow" piece in *Harper's!* You'd formalized it, and in doing so turned it into a damned fine piece. Good, grounding anecdotes, lots of current information, a clearly defined problem, and an offering of, well, solutions. All done in your irascible, desert-rat voice.

"Even the Bad Guys Wear White Hats," as it was retitled, was genuinely funny, and it quickly and convincingly put forth some original and quirky assertions: That there were too many cattle on public (BLM and Forest Service) lands, and that they were doing enormous damage. That Americans did not need cattle grazed on public lands out West, because something like ninety-eight percent of our beef is raised elsewhere, on private land. Public lands, you wrote, should not be subject to cattle grazing. And Golly, Mr. Abbey, if that wasn't outrageous enough, you claimed that the owners of lease-holding ranches were little more than welfare parasites, and that it might be a good idea to do away with them and their "slow, stupid, and awkward" cattle, maybe even ranching in general out West. Darned if you didn't even make fun of cowboys and suggest a hunting season on our bovine friends.

The more serious of these ideas have been kicked around so much by now they've lost their edge. But by God, Ed, when I first saw them in that magazine I so admired, I reacted as if somebody had hit me in the back of the head with a shovel, pumped me full of bad drugs and snake venom, called my momma a whore and run off with Penny, the girl I loved in fifth grade. Why, I felt so downright suckerpunched, I might have slapped your hat off if we'd passed on the street.

But why? What was there in "Even Bad Guys" to get me so hugely upset? Our ranch doesn't use public land, hasn't since the 1930s. So I felt no particular kinship with ranchers in Nevada or Utah or Montana who do. Certainly I felt no need to rush right out and defend them.

Instead of doing something reasonable like driving straight through to Moab and getting hold of your shirt and yelling until I wore myself down to the point where we could have a glass of whiskey and talk, I had to sulk and stew and write a reply. I let it get personal and accused you of just about everything but being a gentleman. I said you took cheap shots at us poor bewildered cattlemen, then took several of my own. I accused you of forgetting about the cowboy/rancher heroes in your early books, and worse, of deserting us in favor of newcomers who want to use our rivers and parks and public lands as playgrounds, where cowshit would be considered bad form. Writing all that, to one of my heroes, put me in a hurt. Thinking back on it still does.

I was wrong to respond in the knee-jerk way I did and sensed it at the time. Maybe I was trying to be a smart guy and was out of my league. Maybe I just didn't know how to act right. I've got a feeling, though, that the fear behind my anger came from seeing—as if in one of those bright lights we keep hearing about—the eventual end of an activity and identity I have always aspired to and still love as much as my next breath.

The tending and raising of livestock on open lands will probably decline in the West, as will a way of living and of naming ourselves that depends on it. Marginal operations like ours, especially those close to cities, will continue to back up, fold, and die under the increasing demands for space made by a population growing beyond its means. Agribusiness-type operations, conversely, will keep growing, becoming corporate principalities secured by vicious dogs and armed guards. Guys like me will end up on the night shift. The vastnesses of our West will be measured, quartered, made smaller; our notions about ourselves and the freedoms made possible by the seclusion of open space will be tested, maybe trampled, while our economy will continue to be replaced by other economies too vast and squirrely to comprehend. Environmental issues will become increasingly complex and the driving, usually destructive force of "harvesting our resources" will grow ever greater.

In my family, four generations of Montana tombstones carry inscriptions like: Stockman. Homesteader. Rancher. That's who my people have been, what I have hoped to be. Retreating in a series of holding actions has been terribly hard on people like myself. To just up and quit, to sell the place and drive away, while tempting, might be worse.

I am convinced that honest, careful ranching is good for Montana's lands, and that it's good for the people engaged in it. Since there is no more running off to homestead somewhere else, we're stuck with not only facing the consequences of our actions, but with asking ourselves some questions as well, always coming back to those biggies of how to best act and of who we can be.

If ranching's future in the West is one of decline and accommodation, where will ranchers fit in and how do we learn how to act? Well, we might start by not getting mad and writing angry letters to our heroes and friends. If we want to keep living here, and living sanely, maybe we ought to take a few weeks off on short notice real soon. Call it a respite dedicated to the watching of clouds, during which we have time to reconsider some of our oldest notions and myths. A vacation focused on the voices of coyotes moving in the night and on lizards moving in sand, when some constructive daydreaming about what is possible and necessary for a good life out here is in order.

Large numbers of people are migrating to our open spaces to "escape." Others, convinced they have the right to dig any damned kind of hole they want, are busily harvesting away. Down in your lovely country, the development boys are grading roads into the new Grand Staircase-Escalante National Monument of southern Utah just as fast as they can, hoping the roads will be grounds to exclude the coal-bearing seams beneath them from federal protection. Scars to nowhere, across the belly of God.

Maybe it's age creeping up on me. Such conduct doesn't so much make me burn as make me feel deeply sad and sorry, just as I'm sorry about my conduct during the *Harper's* deal. From where I stand looking out our kitchen window, it's as clear as the sky outside that you were right to have the courage and the character and the wit to stand up and speak for the desert country you loved.

"Even Bad Guys Wear White Hats" is no longer an essay, at least not in my mind. It's one in a series of letters to America from the desert about how we will decide to see ourselves in the last of our open spaces, and what we'll do to preserve or kill them.

It's been my good fortune, lately, to meet some of your young friends, most of whom, like myself, never got the chance to meet you. They're an unruly bunch from all over the country who are trying to find out as much about the world as they can, kids who read and are just as interested in conservation ethics as in their jobs in Alaska or their favorite places to climb. They're always venturing off, it seems, into desert lands or arctic seas and coming back to talk and write about what they found.

In Montana, some of our young ranchers have grown ponytails. They belong to environmental organizations, and take time to study the consequences of their actions before engaging in those iffy enterprises their grandaddies got away with for so long. We might say they're taking a new approach to an old line of work.

The best of these young people are thoughtful wayfarers concerned with learning how to conduct themselves well and sanely in our natural world, people who aren't afraid of the complexities of issues or to adapt, if necessary, in order to protect the health of lands they love.

Sometimes they make me feel a little out of touch and old, but I like 'em anyway, probably because their energy and lack of ambivalence give me hope. They like to cover lots of ground and laugh, tell stories around campfires and watch stars trace dreams across their skies. Maybe they're a new version of cowboys. But I know you'd be proud of 'em, Ed, being as you are, grandfather and pilot to the whole scruffy bunch.

SALOONS

CHARLIE'S BAR

By James Crumley

YO DOGIES! GET ALONG THERE. If you've got a twelve-step hitch in your
get-along, this piece ain't for you. And it's not for you if your heart has
been hardened by the new American middle-class yuppie hopeless desire
to live forever in health, of both physical and mental persuasions; or if
you've never longed for a place "where everybody knows your name"
and it's sure as hell not a family reunion. Not for you or your herd-like
ilk. Maybe it's not for you unless you've gotten a Christmas card at your
"home bar," or a collect call from an old friend in the midwest who has
spent the evening tracking you down from bar to bar. And you accepted
the charges. It's sure not for you if I have to explain the Brit term "local."

And neither is Charlie B's, a bar so precious to its patrons that none
of them has ever complained that the bar has an unlisted telephone and
no sign on the front door. (Not even a neon beer sign winkling in the front
window; Charlie says it attracts the wrong sort of clientele.) And you
couldn't pry the address out of this writer with fire ants, Chinese water
torture—real torture for a drinking man, indeed—burning bamboo
splints soaked in tequila, or lite beer.

It's somewhere in Western Montana. Sitting in the same holy space
once occupied by Eddie's Club, legendary watering hole of the sixties.
That's all you get. If you don't know somebody who already knows
where it is, then you can't find it. It's better that way. Trust me.

One of the things that makes Charlie B's beloved by those of us who
drink there is that the clientele is smarter and more widely read than most
university faculty clubs and this place may be the last place where the
American Dream of a Melting Pot still breathes.

On a typical Friday afternoon—Charlie doesn't have a happy hour;
nor does he insist that his patrons be happy; just polite—the bar fills with
a lot of people who've known each other a long time.

Like a gift, the unexpected spring sunlight covers the afternoon
crowd with golden shafts, bars of light you don't care to break with hands

or heart because they blind you to old friends and memories. The gray, leaden fist of winter has stopped slamming you in the face, and it's time to gather the tribes again, gnaw on rib bones and chicken wings, sip a beer, chew on a whiskey, choke down another schnapps. Time to party.

The guest list, forged by time and written by years of friendship, money loaned, drinks bought, troubles shared, gossip forwarded and other unsavory matters, looks a little like this: Native American, Mexican Americans, redneck Americans, Afro-Americans and just plain-brown-wrapper Americans; smokejumpers, electricians, ex-cons, ecologists and eco-terrorists; broken-down cowboys, busted-out drunks, undercover cops and house painters; wildlife photographers, wild life, bear hunters and working artists; wordsmiths and want-to-bes, environmentalists, musicians and trust fund hippies; tea merchants to the world, silk-screeners, the best sheetrocker in the state and the last of the great street poets; Vietnam vets, carpenters, car-collectors, interior designers, drama majors, short-order cooks, truck drivers, bikers and lawyers. Even the occasional liberal politician.

It's as if you gave a party and everybody you ever knew, or wanted to know, came, and they all got along nicely, nobody too dumb or seriously mean, as they talked about the inane—sports, weather, gun laws and the invasion of Montana—and the serious: Whitewater and Clinton's sex life; Bosnia and South Africa; tax revolts and school bond elections; ex-spouses, jobs and our children.

That's right: We have children, some raised, who join us, and some still working on it, and we go to PTA meetings and Little League games, take them fishing and hunting, and try to pass on the verities as we learned them: respect for animals and the land and for each other; a sense that we all have to live in this world and have no right to judge each other; and a strong disrespect for organized religion, bureaucracy, and needless stupid laws. Sort of a Montana ethic, one might suppose.

A pretty heavy load to bear for this dim, smokey bar, where the supposedly decent people never come and can't even begin to belong, surrounded by laughter and loud music, smart talk and politically incorrect jokes, playful intelligence at work. And cocktails. The liquid refreshment of the gods, stolen like fire, thus condemned by angry gods, who never meant for mere mortals to have this much fun.

Some of us are even hanging around on the walls, and have been for years: portraits by Lee Nye. Gold stars cornered for the dead and missing, the grizzled, grinning faces still alive in the stories, immortality for the price of a round. To misquote a famous Missoula writer: We are in this together.

Another thing also unites the crowd: Nobody wants me to write this piece. "We'll be overrun by tourists and amateurs," one old friend complains. "Never," I pray to the Church of What's Happening Now, Daddy-O.

Down at the end of the bar, residing and occasionally buying a round for the bar, stands the man: Charlie Baumgartner himself. But he never stands there long. Charlie believes that the bar business is work, so he's always working: helping the two lady bartenders, pouring drinks, packing ice and dumping garbage like a peon; fielding telephone calls, unlocking the cigarette machine for a disgruntled customer; and buying drinks. Charlie B's upholds the Montana tradition of occasionally buying a drink for the customers. All of them. Not just his regulars.

And this is just the middle of his work day, which starts long before daylight when he and his faithful dog, Hootch, climb in the truck and start working the bar business. There's beer to be stocked, food and whiskey to be bought, cooking and cleaning to be finished, day-drinkers to be consoled, deposits to be made and a million other chores to make sure that his customers come back like tattered homing pigeons to their coop.

Lee Nye, photographer, who once stood behind the stick at great length at Eddie's Club through the turbulent sixties, says Charlie is just about the perfect bar owner: he really cares more about his customers than making money. Charlie's version of this is that if you treat people decently, they'll answer in kind. (Sounds a little bit like the Golden Rule, eh?) Anybody can sell drinks, he says, but damn few bother to provide an extra living room, complete with holiday dinners. Charlie lays out a great spread on Thanksgiving, Christmas, St. Paddy's Day, Super Bowl Sunday and Veteran's Day. You don't have to be a turkey, a Christian, Irish, a football fan or a vet. Just show up. Make yourself at home.

Charlie seems to have been successful with his approach. He has a solid clientele in the day, some of them old hands who have followed him from the beginning, old men and women who he cares for, makes sure they eat every day and don't drink more than their aged livers can handle. Then he has a five o'clock crowd, working folks who stop in for a couple every day. Then about eight the kids show up, filling the sidewalk in front with mountain bikes and the bar with sweet-faced youth and raging hormones. They may not be big whiskey drinkers, but they sip enough imported beer to make Charlie B's the largest purveyor of imports in the area. He sells more than even the grocery stores.

Charlie's doing something right: He just bought the building that houses his bar. Not bad for a guy who got into the bar business when he came back at twenty from thirteen months in Vietnam, a tour that included a gruesome hitch with Graves Registration. No wonder Charlie loves hanging around with happy, live bodies.

And no wonder that Charlie B's is world-famous. Certainly in the UK, Germany and France. The French seem to have adopted Charlie B's as their home away from home. The bar has been profiled in a dozen French magazines and was recently featured on French television. Again. And the seven million French who watched the show on Channel Seven can't be wrong.

When asked how he feels about this continuing fame—the bar was also featured in an Alarm music video directed by Tim Hunter of River's Edge fame—Charlie's answer is typically ingenuous: Well, I don't think about it much.

Violence. An issue that must always be addressed when people and alcohol are gathered in close quarters. Charlie B's looks like a tough, working-class bar. Some people—you know those people, who wouldn't say shit if their mouth was full of it—who treasure their middle-class illusions are afraid to come in Charlie B's. Maybe they're right to fear for their immortal souls. But more likely it's themselves of which they're afraid, afraid of being seduced by drink, a proven snake, by rake-hell laughter, a known addiction, and by disobedience, a sure mark of the Beast.

We aren't saints, and Charlie B's is not a chapel. But it's not the World Wrestling Federation, either.

So after fourteen years of hanging out in the bar, I can only count six or eight moments of violence, and only two involving me. Once, I was strangled briefly by a stranger when I agreed with him about the deadly threat of nuclear waste, a reaction never completely explained. But he turned me loose when I suggested he might be engaging in inappropriate behavior. He must have been raised by early yuppies because he took his hands off my neck. The other time I was standing between two angry guys who both grabbed me by the throat, but they each thought I was the other guy. When they discovered their mistake, they were so embarrassed they both left the bar.

Because it feels so much like a place you live, the customers usually take care of the violence before it gets out of hand. Years ago, as I was explaining to a French news-magazine journalist what a copacetic place Charlie B's could be, a fight broke out down the bar. Two little guys punching the bejeesus crap out of each other. But a local writer tossed the instigator out the front door so fast he didn't even have a chance to bleed on the hardwood floor.

So, gut it up, partner. Take a chance. If you can find us, come on in. We haven't barbecued a tourist in years. The help won't let us.

Speaking of the help. Western women bartenders are the best, and in Montana, which always has turned out the best of the West, Charlie has gathered about him a crew of Angels. To get to know them outside the bar, I took most of them to a long, boozy, laughing lunch. Lynn, Daphne, Liberty, Elizabeth, Amy, Chrissy, Alexis, Heather and Little Mary. CC, Jennifer and Mary Place couldn't make it. But I can guess. They range in age and type from early twenties to mid-thirties and from professional bartenders or old Missoula hands to college students, but they share Charlie's sense of fun and his vision of what a bar can be, and they have become a living metaphor for that vision. Plus, they are sweet, smart, funny and tougher than hammered shit. And they love and respect ol' Charlie, their mother-hen.

When Daphne's house catches fire, Charlie is the first person there to help the next morning. When Little Mary needs a pickup and a strong back to bring a new recliner home, Charlie's there. When Lynn's fellow students find out how she pays for law school, they curl their lips. But she's had two tours behind the bar and knows that what she's learned about life there will probably serve her well when she stands in front of the legal one.

It's not just the customers who benefit from Charlie's notorious generosity. We are all better people for it.

So this is fare-thee-well from our corner of space and time. May the road rise to your feet, the wind be at your back and you be in hell before the Devil knows you're dead. I still won't tell you how to find Charlie B's, but I'll raise a glass to the hope that some day Charlie Baumgartner will buy you one.

A SHOT AND ABUSE

By Tim Cahill

IT IS EARLY ON A MONDAY AFTERNOON and I am sitting in Livingston's Owl Lounge, with my portable word processor, writing an article about the Owl Lounge. We journalists do things like this for what we call verisimilitude. Write about a bar in the bar itself. Drink some beer. Hey, someone's got do it. I'm supposed to figure out why I like and patronize the place, which is something I have frankly never thought about.

Charm and decor certainly don't enter the equation. The Owl is a long narrow bar with red carpeting and red walls. The walls are not precisely the same shade as the carpeting, or the drapes for that matter, but all the various reds are abstruse in a bad steak house or seedy brothel sort of way, and when there's hardly anyone in here, like now, you can look around and get this awful claustrophobic sense that you are, in fact, drinking inside a dinosaur.

The place is owned by two hirsute brothers, Dana and David Latch. Together they look like the cough drop Smith Brothers or two-thirds of ZZ Top. David would like me to say that he's a rotten blood sucking weasel who ought to be drowned in a vat of toads, but the true fact is that, despite all appearances to the contrary, he's a nice guy and a gentleman. His brother, Dana, on the other hand, can sometimes be, oh, just slightly acerbic. The Latch brothers are the Lennon and McCartney of bartending.

Social interactions in the Owl are influenced largely by Dana's quaint personality, which is to say they are characterized by various levels of defamation and scurrility. Dana, widely known, as "Mr. Warmth," dispenses curative wisdom in the form of abuse.

The theory behind abuse therapy is that it forms an emotional callus over some sensitive spot. Got a bad haircut? Stop off at the Owl. Two hours of serious denigration and you're ready for anything the world at large can throw at you. A man comes to depend on this treatment by mistreatment.

At present, for instance, I am wearing new "cowboy cut" jeans, a new cowboy shirt, new cowboy boots, and a new 4x Stetson I won in some raffle. I am not a cowboy. I seldom ride horses. The fact is, however, that in one more week I have to go down to Utah where a magazine I work for has asked me to learn "cowboy" skills, at a "cowboy skills ranch." Never mind that half my neighbors do this sort of thing for a living. The magazine wants me to go to freaking Utah. Where, I might add, the residents' religious convictions have resulted in the lack of any decent bars. There aren't even any bars like the Owl there.

I'm wearing the clothes now so they won't be brand new in Utah. In an hour or so, when the after-work crowd gets here, people are fairly certain to comment on these sartorial pretensions in relation to my nearly complete lack of experience in the field of animal husbandry. I anticipate a large ration of abuse therapy. Get the embarrassment phase of this cowboy deal over right now. Then, later, what the hell, let 'em laugh in Utah. I'll be the Callused Kid.

Here's the good news: You don't even have to be a regular to endure a session of therapy at the Owl. Try to order a drink from Dana during a televised NBA game. Good luck. What you see is the back of his black Harley-Davidson T-shirt, featuring a large drawing of a hand, one finger extended in a gesture medieval residents of Italy called "digitas imputatis." The back of Dana's shirt reads, "This bird's for you."

Who would put up with such abuse? Everyone, it seems.

Livingston is a small town, and doesn't afford residents opportunities for social, economic and occupational segregation. Hence, the real charm of the Owl: You meet ranchers from the Shields Valley, shop owners, artists, lawyers, writers, salesmen, bikers, construction workers, journalists, everyone. In a larger town, the various elements form their own cliques, some people drink at the Cafes des Artistes, or the Lone Star or Porkies or Hog Heaven, what have you.

In the Owl, however, environmental activists co-exist and even chat amiably with folks who work in and support the timber industry. The mix includes folks of all ages—from the barely legal to the barely alive—as well as dinosaur hippies, musicians, gallery owners, fishing guides, photographers, real estate salesmen and the Odd Archaeologist. No arm wrestling.

I believe it was the Odd Archaeologist himself who asked me not to write about the Owl because then a lot of rich Yuppies would come in and spoil the atmosphere which, he insists, generally consists of a lot of people sitting around talking about their outstanding warrants and felony arrests and most recent shooting sprees.

In fact, there are plenty of perfectly ordinary reasons why a thoughtful person might want to avoid the place. Over the past dozen years, for instance, the Owl has suffered a minor infestation of writers. Their books are arranged in a place of some small honor behind the bar: Bill Latch on the national parks of South America, Walter Kirn's fiction, Peter Bowen's Yellowstone Kelly novels. Up there behind the bar, there are books about fishing and practical demon keeping and sex in America and one guy who claims to have been Pecked to Death by Ducks.

The only altercation I remember in the Owl involved writers and was one rather of my own making. A fellow from a New York magazine was in town, doing a story on Livingston. We were talking. This visiting writer commented that people here were entirely too sensitive to recent changes, even if those changes tended to degrade the aesthetic and environmental values of the place. "So what," they guy said, "lots of little towns get messed up all over America. Messed up bad. It happens all the time. So what?"

This was, I should point out, a rather small writer, short and very slender. You could pick him up real easy, by the neck, which is what I did. Arguing by analogy, I suggested that "lots of little guys get messed up in bars all over America. Messed up bad. It happens all the time." I'm afraid I may have shaken the individual somewhat at this point in what I saw as an attempt to personalize the issue. "Now you tell me, pal: So what?"

And then there were a lot of people standing around saying, "hey, hey, hey," in a placating manner and I realized they were saying "hey, hey, hey," to me and that what most of the hey sayers had in mind was a situation in which I let go of this writer's neck and stopped causing a disturbance because there were a couple of dozen other people in the place trying to talk about their felony warrants and shooting sprees in peace.

This was not a good thing for me to do. People who cause a ruckus are invariably ejected from the Owl. Can you imagine what it would be like to be 86ed from such a place? It would be like being asked to leave the black hole of Calcutta.

Men who don't understand some part of the meaning of the word "no," are asked to leave as well, because this sort of behavior drives out female clientele, without which a place becomes fairly humdrum.

Some people, I've seen, have been asked to leave the bar because they've been drunk, and obnoxious, but most people are drunk and obnoxious in about the same way, and after a while it gets monotonous. Boring.

The Owl, in fact, is the only bar I know where an otherwise inoffensive individual was asked to take his patronage elsewhere because he was incredibly mind-numbingly boring. Not obnoxious, mind you, or aggressive in any way. Just boring.

This was a man I liked, a fellow whose heart, I think, was good. He had several fine qualities worth discussing—he was, for instance, an avid fly-fisherman, a former collegiate wrestler and a good chili chef—but some complicated synapse, some hideous fault at the core of his being, caused the man, after a single drink, to talk exclusively about, well, about welding. Welding is not bad conversation fodder, at least for the first ten minutes or so. An hour of welding talk gets tiring. Three hours of welding is too much for anyone, professional welders included. The man was driving customers away. I believe it was David Latch who asked the guy to modify his behavior in regard to conversations about welding. Or else. He was, sadly, unable to comply.

Something to think about as five o'clock rolls around. Pretty soon the afterwork crowd will begin to arrive, and I'm gearing up for my ration of therapy. In a few more minutes the door will open and Dan or Bev or Zug or Scott or Al or Terry or Rozzy, someone will be standing there, haloed in the late afternoon light. Someone who, undoubtedly, will have something to say.

So no, it probably won't be boring tonight inside the dinosaur, and yes, I suppose that's why I like it.

THE NEW ATLAS BAR

By Toby Thompson

ON EASTER SATURDAY, there is sparse traffic in Columbus. Though the sun shines, Itch-Kep-Pe Park, where William Clark camped in 1806 near the confluence of the Yellowstone and Stillwater rivers, is deserted. Businesses that support this town of fifteen hundred—Flowers by George, Gaden Rule Lumberyard, Stoney Butte Saddlery, Branding Iron Cafe— are emptying, and the lone building on Pike Street with vehicles out front is granite block with a scarlet sign: The New Atlas Saloon.

Forty miles west of Billings, Columbus was a stagecoach stop on the Yellowstone Trail in 1906 when New Atlas was founded. Its narrow entranceway, guarded by heads of two enormous elk, is like a portal to the underworld. The foyer is dark and lined with ancient photographs cobwebbed by shadowy antlers. Two back bars with opposing mirrors frame the patrons doubly. A cowboy leans across one counter and pecks a barmaid on her cheek.

"Happy Easter darlin'," he purrs, "I hope your rabbit dies."

The bartender, Cheryl, has opened at eight, "Still tight." She nurses a headache. "Go'n home," she urges, "please." Darkhaired and thirtyish, she's diplomatic with regulars. As is the management: a sign overhead warns, "Watch for Falling Drunks." Another demands, "Take Care of Your Children, or Take Them Home." Yet another, beneath an intricate sketch of the Atlas, reads, "See 'em Dead Zoo."

"Petting zoos advertise, 'See 'em Live,'" Cheryl says, laughing. "Here you can see 'em dead."

There are sixty-eight stuffed animals in the New Atlas, faces contorted with a taxidermist's snarl or bodies anticipating combat. Heads of deer, boar, bear, moose, buffalo, mountain goats and steers, join whole carcasses of coyotes in a melange the antithesis of a peaceable kingdom. The room is a mortuary of static rage. Near its poker area hangs a grotesque two-headed calf that an employee says, "Lived ten days. It couldn't eat. Food went in one mouth, came out the other."

What one seeks in a great saloon is form to frame or isolate chaos.

One wants chaos, but a proper framework is needed to contain it. The same holds true for interior landscape. One wants to hold chaos at arm's length and in a kind of check. Front and back bars, paintings and gaming tables are the primary artifacts of an interior landscape. One shakes that landscape hard as the mood dictates, or another something, faceless and edgy, shakes it for one.

New Atlas is stout as a mahogany coffin, its high ceiling of delicately embossed tin lending the feel of an undertaker's display room. The back bars are transplanted from Butte, product of Brunswick-Balke-Collender. Stately wooden booths line the saloon's rear. A melange of artifacts remain from pre-Prohibition years: poker tables, a nineteenth century piano, gaming chairs, and a keno table with attached wooden stools. "Gents'" sports a sizable trough urinal. Atlas's kibitzers today are youngish sheep and cattle ranchers, tradesmen or wheat farmers, but several retired men—one with a dowager's hump plunking quarters into a Montana Superstar machine, the other straight spined at the bar in a ball cap proclaiming, JUNK—PICKED UP FREE—are tippling alone.

"Vic Gee," Cheryl says, "you been here 'bout as long as these heads."

He looks up. "Tire's being fixed."

She serves him a draw.

"My father," Vic exclaims, "came here every morning to play solo— that's a poker hand—and brought me from the time I could walk. I was born in nineteen. Being Prohibition, the Atlas sold beer and wine. But they had a speakeasy serving everything, with hotel rooms upstairs for questionable ladies. After Prohibition they opened as the 'New' Atlas. I was born in Columbus but moved north to Rapelje. Hoppers ate us out."

Vic points at a photograph behind the bar. "That's T.P. Mulvihill. Old Tom, his dad, was a wool buyer who stole a carload of sheep to buy this saloon, they say. He collected the heads. People'd bring one in if it was interesting. T.P. took over during the forties. A cocky little twerp. Drank pretty good. Was a navy pilot, then sprayed crops, but never learned to live in society. He's eighty-five, in a rest home at Big Timber. Hell, I'm seventy-four. Sell a few vegetables from my green house in Rapelje."

Drinks are affordable to retirees at the New Atlas: seventy-five cents for a draft, a buck-fifty for bottled beer, two-twenty-five for top shelf bourbon. And the hours are convenient: eight a.m. to two a.m., all week. Cheryl pulls Vic another draft.

He grins. The country channel's tinkling and for a second I expect him and the stuffed heads to dance. Until the early eighties, a Butte saloon called Luigi's, featured, "The World's Largest One Man Band and His House of Dancing Dolls." Circus artifacts and mobiles dangled from the ceiling: plastic cows, wriggling snakes, fighter planes. At first glance everything appeared stable. But with the movement of fixtures (drawers, ice chests) figures were set in motion: a huge plastic hammer dropped toward the bar as if to crown a customer, a spider lowered over the men's room door. When Luigi struck his first chord, every mechanical creature began hopping and shuffling to the music. Even the bar shivered with Luigi's beat. "Go to Helena!" he'd scream. "You're so dumb!"

Back at the Atlas, Vic and I stare into the huge back mirror, its arched frame like the altar screen of a French cathedral. Something dwells there in ancient mahogany, polished brass, hardwood ice chests, front bar, paintings, stuffings and paneling. Something like stability.

I spent four years searching for the Great American Bar, and know the classic saloon to be of nineteenth-century invention. While the agrarianism of eighteenth century America allowed for tavern service at specific hours, the more hurried schedules of nineteenth century Americans, with their split and staggered shifts, their drink-now-for-tomorrow-we-work attitude toward the still limitless possibilities of the continent, called for more flexible service. Why bother with food and entertainment if what a person wanted was a beer between shifts or a snort of rotgut after roundup? Give him a stylish room with a back bar done in the spirit of an industrial Gilded Age, where he might gaze at the image of his prosperity and drink standing up as someone in forward motion should.

Like the Renaissance parlors they aped, nineteenth-century bar interiors were created as testament to the permanence and all-power of money. The miner standing in a saloon in Virginia City might not articulate this, but sensed that the back bar shipped today overland from St. Louis meant class and high style, that his camp was prosperous, that he'd be shoveling gold tomorrow if his determination held.

The same was true for Columbus.

Named Sheep Dip for its whiskey, then Stillwater for its lesser river, by 1906 it had mining, ranching, the railroad, a quarry that cut granite for Montana's state capitol, the Crow reservation nearby, but especially commerce. Atlas's two back bars were an embarrassment of riches. Few saloons could match them. The room's artifacts, its heads (like gargoyles on the great cathedrals), its photographs of trout and coyote kills, and its implements were the media of their day. They said, *this* is what's important in Columbus. Now they spell history.

New Atlas remains one of Montana's finest saloons. The state is lavish with them: the M&M in Butte, the Old Saloon in Emigrant, the Cort in Big Timber and numerous others. Pilgrims travel from round the nation to drink in Big Sky country. They pay fealty to Atlas, its murky netherworld, miniscule fear factor, and cheer in the face of death. But today it's the regulars who're prayerful.

"Hell no, I don't vacuum," Cheryl says of the heads. "Afraid they'd come out *bare*."

Vic shrugs. "Was a hanging next door," he says, apropos of nothing, "they never figured why." He sips. "T.P. had two liquor licenses. Eventually he took his second to the bowling alley. Had another bar downstairs, where they danced."

"It's a mess," Cheryl interjects.

Could I see it.

"Lord, no," she barks. "Took one fellow down and it like to broke his heart."

I contemplate this. Vic senses my frustration. "Got a Stockman's at Rapelje," he offers.

I brighten.

"Head for the graveyard," he declares. "Then cut north."

THE JERSEY LILLY

By Allen Jones

COMING FROM THE WESTERN HALF OF THE STATE—fast food, strip malls and stop lights—Roundup is some sort of edge. On the way to Forsyth, Highway 12 passes through phases of stockyards and riverbottom, irrigated hay fields and, finally, dry grassland. Halfway between Roundup and Forsyth, Ingomar sits waiting for something to happen.

In most ways, it's an unremarkable town. A few dogs on porches (more dogs than people), a few houses and horse trailers, a couple of campers and old pickups. To find the Jersey Lilly, you turn in past the toothless shell of a hotel and the empty railcar that used to bring water to the town. A UPS van might be parked in front, a ranch truck, not much else. Carrying the private histories and proud idiosyncrasies of most small western towns—sheepshearing, railheads and old banks— Ingomar's most distinguished feature is, in the winter, it's only working business.

The Jersey Lilly is a place you come to. There's no reason to already be there.

I drove from Roundup with some trepidation. I had heard about the Jersey Lilly for most of my life, but had never found a chance to visit. My father still talks about dropping in before an antelope hunt twenty-five years ago; at 5:30 in the morning, there was already a guy in a navy cap drying glasses behind the bar. Writers and photographers I have admired—Jim Harrison, John Smart, Kurt Markus—have devoted time and lines to the bar and its beans. This is only a small, rectangular saloon out in the middle of nowhere, one of hundreds in the West, that has nevertheless managed to distinguish itself from the average. Somehow.

And I was afraid that I was too late. Bill Seward, the man with the navy cap, had had bypass heart surgery a year or so ago, selling the bar in August. If the bar hadn't sold, it would have had to shut its doors. Nevertheless, the exposure of the sale had been negative. Before making the drive—four hours from Bozeman—I called both Bill and Johnna Newman, the current manager of the Jersey Lilly, asking to meet with them.

Bill was living just down the street, and Johnna made the trip into town most days anyway, driving in from a ranch where she and her husband had lived for twenty-three years.

At a table in the bar, I sat talking first with Johnna—slim and short-haired, quick with the confidence of ranch work—and then with Bill, asking each about the bar. Three barmaids went on and off shift while we talked: Anna, Patti and Helen. Each has worked for the bar for five, seven and one year, respectively.

There's nothing excessive about the Jersey Lilly. It's a good place to sit and eat and drink a little. The lights aren't too dim—no low bulbs to give suspicion of stale cigarette smoke in the corners—but they aren't too bright, either, the floor too clean. For somebody with muddy boots and just-washed hands, it sits with every other fine saloon at the exact point of balance. For identities that are perhaps a bit lonely, a bit anxious at the thought of the world, it could be the place to hinge a life.

"We've tried not to change too much," Johnna said, lighting a cigarette. "Mostly, we've just cleaned the place up. We did put a new grill in the kitchen. And I changed the old rotary phone in the booth to a touch-tone. Everybody has phone cards now."

I looked around at the Seward paraphernalia still caught on the walls. A yellowed, cracking poster with pictures of every heavyweight champ, right up to Ali. A boxing glove still hanging from the door of a bank safe. (The safe is now used as a walk-in storage closet.) A moose head with a cigarette hanging out of its mouth. (Bill said, "If he hadn't stopped to light that cigarette, I never would have been able to shoot him.") Perhaps most importantly, there were the soup bowl and cook-pot of beans sitting on the table, an accompanying plate of crackers and croutons beside them, the small jar of homemade hotsauce.

"Oh," Johnna said, "and we took out the old coal stove and put in a propane heater." She turned back to Anna, leaning toward us with her elbows on the bar. "Have you noticed that everybody wants to sit at the table beside the jukebox? They used to sit here, next to the heating register, but now they all move over to the vent."

When Bill came in, Johnna politely moved back to the bar to talk with Patti, the latest barmaid to come on shift. I sat at the same table with Bill, listening while he talked back and forth over his own history.

He bought the Jersey Lilly from his father in 1958. For the next thirty-five years or so, he ran the place mostly by himself, living in the basement and getting up at three most winter mornings to fire the coal heater. Prior to the Jersey Lilly, he had variously worked as a professional boxer, served in the Navy in the south Pacific, and put in a bit of training as a vet.

He is a small man, small enough that he used to have to put on weight in order to fight as a lightweight. (He won 38 of his 45 fights by TKO.) Now, almost sixty years away from his last fight, his fingers are knotted and shiny with age, and he takes his time walking across the room. His most notable feature, the thing you notice right away, is a string tied to the bridge of his glasses that runs up under his cap. "I was fixing an old crank engine in 1958," he said, taking off his cap and running his hands over his head, the baldness and stiff, gray bristles. The string circles around the crown of his head. "And the crank came back and flattened my nose for me. I didn't want to always be pushing my glasses back up, so I came up with this thing."

If personality is any reflection at all of the place it lives (or perhaps the place a reflection of personality), Bill Seward is still very much a part of the Jersey Lilly.

If nothing else, there are the beans: a spiced-up combination of garlic, onions, bacon, cumin, sweet peppers and jalapeños. "My wife and I," Bill said, "when we bought the place, decided to have something that would bring people back. Now when I was in Chicago, there was this place that would serve these real good little crocks of beans. So we just toyed around and toyed around until we came up with this recipe. It got to where people knew they could get these beans here. We used to tell 'em, fill up on the beans and then you can just take your steak home with you."

Under the same philosophy, Bill worked up what he calls "Sheepherder's hors d'oeuvres"—a saltine cracker, a slice of orange, a slice of onion. It is a real surprise that the combination somehow works, the sweet orange cutting out the sharpness of the onion. "We named it that way because we figured they're so good they'd make a sheepherder hungry enough to eat his own cooking."

Bill sat folded in his chair, a little lost in his coat, a little slow about looking to see who was coming in the door. He's a comfortable man, and what used to be his bar is still a comfortable place. Families coming and going. Yesterday's newspaper lying on the end of the bar. The kind of place where you can sit down between the fifteen-year-old grandson of the bartender and the forty-year-old son and catch up on the latest.

Jerry Brown, the new owner, lives in Ingomar, although he spends part of his time in Minnesota running his other business interests. He has known Bill and the bar for almost twenty years, and he's known Johnna and her husband even longer. Bill has nothing but good things to say about him. Brown's most visible passion is hunting, and so he's brought in a collection of incongruous African heads: kudu, gemsbok, eland. Beneath them, he installed bronze plaques, detailing what kind of animals they are and where they were taken. Uncomfortable with the out-of-town heads, some of the locals ended up taping their own versions over the plaques. Under the kudu, there's *Bearded Longhorn Prairie Goat,* roped on main street of Ingomar. Under the gemsbok, there's *Longhorn Bull, struck by lightning on Froze to Death Creek.* Under the eland, there's *Roadkill Mulie, flattened on U.S. 12 near Ahles.*

Seward stands at the bar by himself, posing a bit for magazine photographs. A couple of hired hands from a nearby Galt ranch come in, nod to Bill, and walk past him to sit at the bar with Cokes. Johnna and Helen, the last of the three barmaids, stand behind the bar and pass the time.

Without its people, the Jersey Lilly is mostly just a collection of drying boards and a painted sign out front. Inside are the last pieces of Seward and a slow, small collection of new pieces, new ways of approaching Ingomar and the Jersey Lilly. Just as good, somehow, but different. Everything moves. Everything changes.

Half the wall above the kitchen is white, the other a dirty tan. It's as far as the cleaning's gotten on that part of the bar. Beneath the wall, Helen serves up a pot of beans, not quite as spicy, maybe, as Bill would have made them, but still about the best you'd find anywhere. Bill climbs back into a van that will take him a hundred yards down the road to his small cot and books. "To me," he says as I shake his hand, "this is the hub of the universe. In the south Pacific, you could see so far, you could see the curvature of the earth. But here, on a clear day, you can see the steam over Colstrip, seventy miles away."

Outside, the Jersey Lilly is the brightest set of lights for twenty miles. A dog barks. The wind blows a door shut. Past that, there's just the road back to Roundup.

EDIE'S PLACE

By Scott McMillion

YOU'RE CAMPED IN THE MISSOURI BREAKS, down by the river with the elk and the geese in the thick stands of red willow. Chasing antelope all day, northern lights streaking up at night. A little whiskey by the fire. You've been waiting all year for this.

Then comes the rain.

At first it's not so bad, curled up in the tent with a book. But after a day or two, when you're mired in gumbo so slippery you can barely stand and so sticky you're afraid to fall down, when your camp mate is the kind of artist who sees liquor bottles in the stars, who eats raw garlic all day and likes to talk, well, the situation starts to lose its shine.

And then you run out of beer.

In a desperate mood, you tune in the Christian radio station from Havre, which tells you, hallelujah, there's a cold snap coming.

True enough, praise God, about midnight the drizzle takes on a little texture, and at first light there's a half inch of snow over a frozen crust on the gumbo. You break camp, cross your fingers and head for the ridgetop, six miles uphill.

By the time you get there the sun is strong, and the prairie looks so white and pure you know it can't last. The snow is melting and the crust isn't doing much good any more. Drive another mile and chubby stalactites of gumbo hang from your mirrors. Gumbo clogs your wheel wells; you can't even slide a hand between the tire and the fender and you're thinking about tie rods and flat tires and wheel bearings and hoping everything holds up. But you don't want to pitch camp again. The paved road is forty miles away, and that makes you pretty unhappy, but not as unhappy as you would be spending another beerless night in the tent with the garlic eater.

So you look down the road, wonder for a moment if Edie is open, and the choice is made. You point it toward the highway and punch it through the slop, going sideways about half the time.

Somehow you make it. You always do.

You hit the highway and turn toward Edie's place. It's still early, but it's been a long time getting this far and it's time for a drink. *Please*, you say, *please let the sign be on.*

Edie's place is the Mobridge Bar, which is all there is to Mobridge, Montana. Edie Komarek has been running the place for thirty-nine years, long enough that she opens up when she feels like it and closes when it suits her mood. If she's ready for business, she'll turn on the red Rainier sign. You can see it from the highway.

"If the sign's on, I'm open," she says. "If the door's locked, it means I'm in the trailer or in the barn or somewhere, but I'm open."

So you wait. You don't honk, but you might get out and stretch, walk in the yard among the fuel cans and railroad ties, the rusty El Dorado, the frayed horsewhip and the elk bones. Soon enough, Edie will come and unlock.

But before you can do all this, you have to find Mobridge, which takes a little work. I'd driven past the place for years before I realized it was anything but a cow camp.

You won't find it on a state highway map or in the Rand McNally road atlas. It's halfway between Landusky and Bohemian Corners, forty miles north of Grass Range, an hour east of Winifred on dirt and gravel roads. It's sixty-five miles from Lewistown, seventy miles from Malta and forty-five miles from an antelope camp the artist and I call Dogtown, which puts it just about in the middle of Montana.

To get there, head for a spot about three miles south of the Missouri River on Highway 191. Halfway up the steep climb that takes you out of the Breaks and on to prairie, look for a green sign that says Mobridge and points west to the hardscrabble ranch a half mile away in the coulee bottom. That's the place.

Back in the fifties, people had high hopes for Mobridge, thinking it might turn into a town. But it has never been more than Edie and her husband George, a baseball team of stray children they took in over the years, and the cows and the elk and the coyotes.

Surrounded by the Charles M. Russell National Wildlife Refuge ("It's the only licensed bar I know of on a federal game reserve," says Edie), Mobridge reflects the Breaks country that surrounds it: isolated and tough, with no frills. People who live in the Breaks—and there aren't many of them—know the land has rules you follow if you want to get along. It's the same thing in Edie's place.

Thou shalt not curse, thou shalt not disrespect thy wife or women in general, thou shalt not praise the federal government and thou shalt not sympathize with a coyote.

Thou shalt keep thy spurs off the furniture, thou shalt leave thy gun in the car and thou shalt call Edie ma'am.

And thou shalt not get cute. If Edie hands you a free drink in a go cup, it's time to wise up; you've just been tossed.

And you will be referred to as cornbread, Edie's all purpose oath.

"How in the cornbread he thought he could get away with that in here I will never know," she might explain later, after she's tossed somebody. "He knows I won't put up with that cornbread."

Edie and George are working on fifty years together. They hooked up in 1949 and they both got quite a catch. George was a tough, good looking cowboy, the kind of guy who could talk the town of Lewistown into sponsoring a big rodeo and then win the top money. Edie was a beauty from southern Idaho. George found her in Great Falls, where she was going to hairdresser school, and talked her into giving it up for life as a ranch wife in the Missouri Breaks.

"I didn't even know how to drive, let alone tell a cow from a horse," Edie said. All that came fast enough, though. Pulling calves and hauling water. Heat and ice and gumbo. Edie learned these things.

Then George looked at his patch of bottom land along Armells Creek one day and saw money sprouting in the alkali deposits.

It was 1956 and work had started on the Fred Robinson Bridge over the Missouri, breaking up the longest unbridged span of big river in the country. Paved roads were still a distant dream and, after work, the men found nothing but forty miles of prickly pear and gumbo between them and the nearest saloon. And George owned the closest piece of private land.

A state liquor commissioner winked and told George he ought to build an oasis down there. George liked the idea. The Fergus County Sheriff didn't like it a bit, and Edie thought he was crazy.

But George won, a log cabin arose from the gumbo, and for years the place hopped.

Edie opened up every morning at seven, cashed $5,000 worth of $151 paychecks once a week, sold drinks and charmed the construction crews as a good looking blonde in desolate country can always do. ("I never thought I was good looking until I looked back at the old pictures," Edie said last summer. "I always thought my nose was crooked or my butt was too big. You know how women are.")

George's enthusiasm spread. The Chambers of Commerce in Lewistown and Malta got real excited about the bridge that linked their towns.

They even had a contest to name Edie's bar and the town they hoped would flourish around it. Governor J. Hugo Aronson—The Galloping Swede—chose the winner: Mobridge.

"I didn't have a preference," Edie said. "I couldn't care less."

The town never happened, of course, and business slowed down after the crews left, but George and Edie made the place work anyway. George put on rodeos in the corral, there were dances in the bar, and people came from all over. Germans and Bohemians from south of the river, Sioux and Métis from north of the river. Pretty much everybody was connected somehow to the cow business in those days, and they all met at Edie's place.

Then things started to peter out. The liability got too high to have rodeos any more. Cars got faster and more comfortable, which meant bankers from Malta didn't stop for Bloody Marys on the way home from Billings. DUI laws got tougher. And the unforgiving Breaks country, the part of Montana where a new trailer house signifies pretty high living, just gets emptier and emptier.

But Edie stuck it out and she stayed in character.

"Cornbread on you," she'll tell a wiseguy.

Look around her bar and you can tell how long it's been there and how little the place gets used these days. Bits of tin foil on the pour spouts keep dust out of the liquor bottles. On the bar lies a wooden muddling stick, crucial for crushing fruit and sugar in a proper Old Fashioned. But Edie has run out of bitters and she won't cheat, she won't make an Old Fashioned without it. Decorations advertise products that don't exist any more: Great Falls Select beer, three types of Chesterfield, Oasis cigarettes.

You've got to wonder. Can Edie's oasis last much longer?

George is poorly these days. A stroke has slowed him down considerable, and the log building that houses the bar has seen better days. For some reason, a lawn mower is stored next to the pool table, right under the photograph of George's World War II Seventh Calvary platoon, eighty men on horseback in a snappy formation. The pool balls all roll southwest, and the jukebox doesn't get plugged in much. Edie says it gives her a case of the nerves. While the beer truck still delivers, the man with the frozen pizzas drops Edie's order at Roy, thirty-six miles away.

George is seventy-seven. I knew better than to ask Edie's age.

People aren't as friendly as they used to be, Edie laments, and it's obvious that not as many of them stop by anymore. Too many days bring no customers at all.

But as for me, I'm going to stop and see Edie every time I'm in the country, and she's got the sign on. I'll wipe my shoes on the mat and I'll watch my cornbread mouth, unless I'm talking about coyotes or the government. I'll call her ma'am and I will make my friends do the same. I will not complain about the pool table and I will always leave a tip.

And the next time I'm stuck in the Breaks with the artist, mired in mud, devoid of beer and steeped in garlic, we will turn on the radio and listen for good weather news. And when we finally hit the pavement, I know which way we'll turn, hoping and hoping that the sign is still on.

THE LOWEST BAR IN MONTANA

By Denis Johnson

WITH MIXED FEELINGS, I HAVE TO SAY that the Club Bar of Troy, Montana, though still owned and run by "Downtown" Tony Brown, isn't quite the region of danger and chaos it once was. I used to describe the Club as a patchwork homemade-feeling saloon with a barrel stove and a fight every night and dogs and orphans wandering in and out. The stove and the feeling remain, but Tony has repainted and refurbished— even the bathrooms are downright hospitable—and he insists there were never any orphans around in the first place, but I claim some of the dogs probably were. It's nice for Tony and for the saner patrons that the establishment hasn't seen a fist-fight or a drawn firearm in quite some time. But it's kind of depressing for those (admittedly few) of us who enjoyed dropping in at the Club in pretty much the same spirit that Elizabethan Londoners used to visit the Bear Pits.

Troy is a little town in Montana's northwest corner, up near the Yaak River. For a while, Tony Brown was the mayor of Troy—I think during that brief period in the seventies when American politics went way off the tracks. He bought the Club in '73, lost it ten years later, got it back in '89.

The Club sits across from the railroad tracks on Yaak Avenue, also known as Bar Street. I visited recently during the regular Thursday Open Mike Night, when local talent assemble and entertain a few folks, mainly each other. The joint was crowded, and while several really gifted and a few astonishingly awful musicians had at it, Tony Brown showed me photos taken in the bar and pointed out memorabilia on the wall, much of whose origins he can't seem to remember. He's hung the environs with bric-a-brac and posters of James Dean, Marilyn Monroe, John Wayne. There's a six-foot-long blue marlin caught by a friend whose living room was too small for it. "Actually," Tony said, "his wife caught it. If he'd caught it, they'd have found room." Above it hangs a rod and reel, but it's got nothing to do with the fish. It was hocked by one of the gamblers to stay in the poker game.

I think you could describe Tony most briefly as a small man with a big face. Somewhat elfin. This night, he was all slicked up in dress pants, dress shirt and fancy suspenders decorated with musical notation, as if he intended to MC, but he didn't get on stage except occasionally, and then just to blow his trumpet until physically restrained by some of the other musicians.

Tony's very proud of his postcard collection, messages from loyal patrons who have wandered into the unlikeliest places—I was surprised to find that one from me had reached here all the way from Afghanistan, a land without a postal service. I'd only sent it so I could say I'd tried. Tony said, "Hey, the mail service is great around here. My mom told me she got one this morning just addressed to 'Betty'—no last name, no zip code, no nuthin. Came right directly to her. Didn't even say 'Troy, Montana' on it."

He showed me several pictures, kind of photographic studies, actually, of this one bald guy who passed out at the bar and then someone drew a face on his shiny head with a blue magic marker and red lipstick. Apparently this man never woke up, never noticed. Joy, the barmaid, told me he stumbled later to the john, where he tilted forward while doing his business and left the imprint of his cartoon eyes on the wall.

Tony is also inordinately impressed with the Elvis-theme thank-you card he got from the Junior High basketball team he coached last spring. He insisted strongly that I put something down about it in my notebook.

I asked if my coffin was still around, and Tony took me back to the storeroom to see it, a cheap one made of half-inch plywood that looks like a big man would fall through the bottom when his pallbearers gave it a heave. I have always believed the coffin will be mine when I die, so I can be buried in it in my back yard next to my wife Cindy and my dog Harold (Cindy's not there yet; Harold is), with Tony Brown saying a few words in farewell (Tony performed the service at our wedding, too), but I believe he's sold my coffin to, or promised it to, or used it for collateral on small loans from, a great many people. I haven't actually paid for it yet myself. Generally he says it's "for the next guy who dies in here." He's got a lot of other stuff piled around it—old beer signs and unidentifiable junk. His storeroom's half the size of the barroom itself.

The Club is the only place where I ever witnessed an actual barroom brawl. This was on a Friday night five or six years ago. Everyone in the place was up and fighting except for me and one old veteran of WWII, both of us hanging onto the poker table for dear life and hoping we'd have enough uninjured players to get the game going again when this was over. It wasn't the choreographed, stool-slinging slugfest you see in

movies. There was just this squabble that everyone kept attaching themselves to until a kind of mass or glob of Montanan animosity heaved itself
this way and that, shoving into the pool-table and knocking over stools
and repositioning the booths. Every time they got near the plate-glass
window I thought they'd go through it, but they didn't; not that time;
sometime later it got busted and was boarded over for several months, if
I remember right.

I was in there one slow night when the assembled clientele—about
a dozen winter-weary Trojans (half a dozen gamblers and not many more
drinkers)—were entertained by a couple who went into the ladies room
to consummate some unholy wine-illumined dalliance. For five minutes
there wasn't a sound in the place but their cries of abandon, until they
came out smiling shyly, smoothing their garb, and everybody applauded.

Plenty of the old spirit remains. It's just that you don't need twenty-
four-hour life insurance and a big dog to go inside and feel
comfortable—though dogs are still allowed. "Not all dogs," Tony advis-
es me—"some dogs."

Tonight the atmosphere is loud and happy, and the patrons are certainly enjoying themselves. Tony introduces me around, going in
particular for the respectable citizens: high school teachers, a hospital ad-
ministrator. Tony says he managed to bring peace to his domain by
instituting a lengthy "86" list. Though the new policy means a cut in the
establishment's income, he says his clientele is down to "friends only."
Anybody's a friend until proven otherwise, of course. But any trouble and
you go right to The List.

Tony still runs his poker game three nights a week. Often the Club
hosts professional bands, and occasionally a comedian. Last February,
Tony put on a Poetry Slam that brought more than two dozen versifiers
in from the woods around Troy to read to an enthusiastic audience. For
all such events Tony makes dinner—sandwiches, stews, things like that.
Tonight it's enchiladas and beans and chips and salsa. You get it on a paper plate, and if you don't like it, well, then don't pay—the jar labeled
"Dinner Donations" sits next to the register.

I stayed in town overnight, two blocks from the Club at Tony's residence, which used to be a boarding house and still boasts a sink in every
room and numbers over the doors. I got Number Seven, and Tony, his
wife Valerie and their three kids were lost somewhere else inside the
place. Part of the film *The River Wild* was shot in this house, but was ultimately cut out of the movie. Tony didn't mind—they remodelled the
downstairs for free.

The next morning, I got up early to observe Charlie, a retired iron-worker from the Southwest, who starts the fire in the barrel stove and gets things opened up in the morning at the Club. There's a morning coffee crowd which shows up about seven thirty every weekday.

Charlie counts last night's Dinner Donations while Uncle Jack comes in with Uncle Jim, both men well into their eighties. They admire last night's dinner take—about ten bucks—and start in guzzling java and swapping jokes, really old jokes, jokes that were ancient when these guys were young.

They introduce me to a younger couple, Cindy and Darryl—"Cindy keeps the language halfway clean around here," Uncle Jack assures me. Darryl's a big guy, and Cindy's a tiny blond. Behind the bar, Tony Brown keeps a photo of Cindy out front of the Club with a seven-foot-long mountain lion she'd just shot dead in the hills outside town. This morning they're heading back home to set sixty muskrat traps before lunch. Cindy's been skinning muskrats all the previous day.

Uncle Jack likes that idea—"I'd love to see that. And stirring gravy. Stirring gravy. I could sit on the couch all day and watch a woman stirring gravy." Uncle Jim agrees it's one of the most erotic sights on earth.

They've all been here for decades, for close to a century in the case of the Uncles, but nobody present can remember when the Club was founded or can guess how old it is. They all agree on one series of statistics, however, that distinguish this tavern from all others:

The point in Montana closest to sea level lies twenty-some-odd miles away, where the Kootenai River flows across the state boundary into Idaho—elevation 1,826 feet. The morning patrons guess Bar Street to sit at 1,877 feet above sea level. And since the Club has a basement, it goes down to 1,860 or so, making it "the lowest bar in the state."

In celebration of this distinction, Charlie puts a shot of something in each of the Uncle's coffee. I'm not sure that's a good idea at all. But I guess he knows what he's doing.

Just as I'm leaving, a guy out front in a big gold Buick with Washington plates wakes up with a dead battery. I recognize him as one of last night's patrons as he rolls out and looks at his car. "I been sleeping in it all night," he says—maybe with the door cracked open or his head on the horn, and that would explain his lack of power. He studies the whole situation and delivers his own conclusion: "You can have one hell of a good time in that place."

TRIPS

SUMMER IN THE BEARTOOTHS

By Gary Ferguson

LYING AWAKE IN THE WEE HOURS, on a night thick with moon. The mountain goats have come again, glowing lumps of ivory pouring down the benches like so many ghosts, hurrying to graze in the meadows beside the tent, eager to lick salt from the traces of urine lying at the edge of camp. They whine and shove at one another, arguing over patches of grass, filling the air with a sound like whimpering dogs. I slip on my glasses and peer out the door of the tent, not quite believing how different things look at this hour. The lunar light has transformed this sprawl of rubble—by day as fierce and Promethean as any landscape in Montana—into something seductive, a place more silk than granite. From sunrise to sunset there's little to these barren reaches but stone and snow—a twist of meadow here and there, perhaps, a pinch or two of buttercup and monkeyflower. But now the harshness is gone. Melted. Like candles in the sun.

We left Kersey Lake two days ago, fly rods and flasks of rum stuffed into our packs, bound for the big, steely waters of the western Beartooths. There are four of us: a marketing professor/fishing wizard from Montana State University and two transplants from New England. One is a young technical writer from the suburbs of Boston (this is his first backpacking trip), the other an ex-advertising man from Connecticut. And of course yours truly, who wakes up most days feeling joined heart and hip to these mountains. When I made invitations for this trip I thought that at best one or two people would actually come. I should have known better. Suggesting a Beartooth trip to anyone who climbs or fishes is like inviting a preacher to a screening of the hereafter.

The wilderness has revealed itself to us slowly, in stages, each one more amazing than the last. Our early miles were through ordinary timberlands—workaday woods of lodgepole and Douglas fir, and clean, spare gardens of whortleberry. But by the first afternoon the forest had fallen back, torn open by spires and abrupt ravines. House-sized chunks of granite lay on the bottoms; fir trees hung by their toes from cracks in the canyon walls. The higher we climbed, the more there was a sense of earth yielding to sky. At Bald Knob Lake, I recall not so much the basin where we camped, but the way the evening hung on in a wash of alpenglow; and long after that, returning from a fishing trip to find the lake's granite islands looking timorous, withering under a plate of stars.

From there the world has been one of high plateaus strewn with boulders and escarpments, rolling on mile after mile, as if the entire continent had been baked to stone and thrown to the clouds by some grand explosion. I recall some years back studying topo maps of this area and concluding that crossing the landscape would be a mellow, even cordial affair, like wandering the swells of the high prairie. Now I know that ninety-nine steps out of a hundred land not on soil, but on canted boulders. Though brief, inclines at the head of drainages and along the edges of lakes are remarkably steep; in truth there's no route that doesn't require grunting up and down countless rocky bluffs and pitches of talus and scree.

Taken as a whole, of course, the Beartooths wear many faces. From the windswept plains far to the north the range appears as a vast, dusky slab of green and gray eating up the southern horizon. Venturing closer, stark tongues of rock begin to appear—limestone, tilted into parapets by the uplift of the mountains. And then hints of the great valleys—Rock Creek, the Rosebuds, Stillwater, Boulder—each framed by long sweeps of treeless tundra. In the short blink of summer the highlands erupt in carpets of buttercup and mountain heath; alpine avens, cotton grass, and forget-me-not; pussy-toes, bluebells, and paintbrush. Though the soul of the range is granite, in a few places there are also fantastic islands of sedimentary rock. Like 1,200-foot Beartooth Butte, rich in the fossils of bony-plated fish, floating like a battleship on a bed of basement crystalline rock many times its age. Curiously, all record of the intervening years has vanished, making it possible to cross two billion years of history in a single step.

There are few moments when we're not aware of the fact that the Beartooths are a fierce generator of weather. On most afternoons the sky tends to evolve to match the terrain; clouds build into great cumulus mountains, or rush into view as broken, tattered shards of cirrus. Here one is never free for long from great stabs of lightning and fits of sleet, snow, wind or biting rain. And yet so far our weather has been utterly clear and calm. Flawless. It's peculiar, unsettling in the way that an absence of earthquakes might finally intimidate someone in Southern California; the longer you go without incident, the more you worry that when something does hit it will knock you senseless.

Given this frenzied stew pot of weather and the severe terrain, it's easy to see why the Beartooths remained largely unexplored well into the twentieth century. The not altogether unfriendly summit of Granite Peak, which at 12,799 feet is the highest point in Montana, wasn't scaled until 1923; five more years would pass before the second ascent. Maps of the region, even those compiled in the late 1950s, seem remarkably incomplete. Lakes and streams are misnamed or misplaced. There are huge blank spots tossed across the page, as if the cartographer got called away in the middle of the job.

We take our breakfast with the goats. For the better part of an hour they've been coasting back and forth across the fifty or so yards that separate our tents, staring at us between bites of dwarf clover, perhaps hoping that we'll have the courtesy to pee again before breaking camp. At one point a yearling passes by close enough to touch. She's curious, but nervous too, her black eyes flashing, the heavy muscles of her forequarters tense, ready to fling her back to safety. It seems incredible that in mid-August these gnarly climbers are still some three months from the breeding season. The thought of them being up here in the thick of a November squall, furiously rutting away on some crag at the edge of oblivion—well, it's hard not to admire the sheer fever of it.

By mid-morning we're off again, cross-country, heading toward the south flank of Granite Peak. Lakes the color of cobalt rest between the rocks. Rough-legged hawks peel the air with black-tipped wings. From boulder-strewn ridgetops we can look west to the crown of Mount Wilse, and southeast into a shimmer of uplands, rising like breakers from the Beartooth Plateau. In those few moments when I'm not looking where to put my feet my eyes are roving, searching for patterns in the jumbles: the graceful curve of glaciers, thin smears of ice wedged into the crack of distant coulees, egg-shaped rocks stained with lichen, cracked by the cold into perfect halves.

Though the Absaroka-Beartooth Wilderness is in summer a busy place, much of the use is concentrated along the few trails that ascend dramatic alpine valleys. On these remote plateaus visitors are fewer and farther between; fishermen and climbers, mostly, driven by the promise of summits, or rumors of portly brook trout, and cutthroats, thick as forearms and full of fight.

The vast majority of people who touch this range aren't on foot at all, but in cars with heaters running, parked at the edge of any of a hundred choice curves along the Beartooth Highway. This unlikeliest of roads was conceived by a mining camp physician in Red Lodge, who saw it as a means of bolstering a faltering coal-mining industry with tourism by connecting Red Lodge to Yellowstone Park. It was truly a "build it and they will come" sort of thing; to many it must have seemed every bit as bizarre as hacking out a baseball diamond for ghosts in the middle of an Iowa cornfield. But the god of pork-barrel projects smiled down, and in 1936 the road was completed. And suddenly the locals had to figure out just how one goes about flirting with tourists. In that sense it was a fresh, whimsical time, towns behaving like an old bachelor farmer who suddenly decides to court the widow down the lane. Early travel brochures were home-brewed in the best sense, less like commercials than family movies. Unlike other places in the West seeking tourism at the time, Beartooth communities didn't get into spitting matches over how much better their mountains were than those of Europe; by and large they were more concerned with simply sharing the gems that made them what they were.

A Red Lodge brochure from 1936, for example, showcases the "Top-of-the-World Bar"—at that time a colossal outdoor saloon along the Beartooth Highway at 10,000 feet, chiseled out of twelve-foot-high snowbanks. One photo shows bartenders in fedoras and cowboy hats pouring beer and whiskey to some two dozen visitors, hearty souls who would hopefully sober up enough to sail their Fords back down five thousand feet of switchbacks. In the same brochure is a rather stark photo of a stout, 80-year-old Finnish woman. She stands slumped under a heavy wool coat, scarf bound like a bandage on a face round as a China moon, cradling a two-foot-long fish in her arms. "Yes sir," says the caption, "There's big ones here and Grandma can catch 'em."

Tonight we'll rendezvous with photographer Tom Ferris and his friend John at Skytop Lakes, trade car keys, and tomorrow morning each group will wander off in opposite directions. Several times today Wynn and I have pulled out the topo map and tried to convince ourselves that we might be able to climb out of the Skytop Lakes basin, edge around the southeast flank of Granite Peak, maintaining elevation, and from there scramble northeastward onto the top of Froze-to-Death Plateau. But it's a ludicrous idea, and we know it—wishful thinking in thin air. One would not cross that shoulder of Granite Peak so much as hang from it, picking and poking in an out of a thousand dead ends, at the same time running the risk of slipping down the mountain on ice fields into piles of stone. The final dose of reality comes when Tom and John walk into camp late in the evening, bedraggled, worn down and out by their own trek from Froze-to-Death Plateau—a trip that by air is barely three miles. No, they say, the southeast flank is impassable. Reaching Froze-to-Death will mean climbing a thousand feet out of this basin, dropping down an equal distance into Granite Creek Lakes, and then climbing 1,700 feet up to the plateau. Nearly all of the route is on clutters of talus and scree, most of it so steep you can blow your nose in the hillside. "It's not fun," Tom says soberly. "It's an endurance contest."

The morning sun hits the top of Granite Peak and Mount Villard nearly two hours before it slides over the basin's east ridge, allowing us to finally shed our hats and felt jackets. A flock of cormorants is floating in the glass of the lake, half-sunk, as if their bellies were full of ballast. Friends have long assured me that there are no fish in Skytop Lakes. And yet these are definitely fishing birds. Oriental cultures still tie ropes around the necks of cormorants, set them off boats to dive for fish, then hurriedly reel them in to squeeze the catch from their necks.

Between bites of oatmeal we chew on a conversation started last night, about whether to head for Froze-to-Death Plateau, as originally planned, or opt for a lower route, rich in opportunities for fishing. Personally, it's hard to give up the high road. After three days I'm hooked on these heights of land, and there are moments when it seems insane not to opt for that last, long crawl up to the roof of the world. But in the end fly-fishing wins out. In truth all of us are hearing the siren song of a certain distant lake—a call that begins with a quiet pondering of trout, and ends with us climbing ridges with barely a word to one another, wired with thoughts of the first cast. No doubt the choice is also inspired by the fact that each of us came on this trip to unwind. Untangle. Eric is not only suffering the usual stresses of building a house, but stinging from a fit of insanity in which he hired two girlfriends and his mother as laborers. John's been writing navigation manuals for the worker's comp system, and Wynn is wading with sharks, campaigning for the Legislature. As for me, my body and soul are rusted a bit from having just spent ten weeks rolling down ten thousand miles of road. Given all this there seems less value in pushing up summits than in simply casting a line here and there, soaking up a little sun, launching late-night, rum-laden rambles under the stars.

Our choice proves to be a good one. Three hours after breaking camp in the Skytop Basin we're standing on the shore of Acme Lake, silly with bliss from having watched our rods bow time and again against a remarkable bouquet of hulking, shrimp-fed brook trout. For my part I end up acting almost possessed, going back to the water time and time again until Eric and John practically have to carry me drooling from the lakeshore. I don't fully shake the craving until thirty minutes later, on a crumbling, precarious climb up and over a three-hundred-foot cliff. The rest of the day is long and sweet—a fast skinny dip in a puddle of ice water, then a slow drop through a glacier-scoured valley, the four of us spilling across meadows and over plugs of talus back to the East Rosebud Trail.

My last best memory of the trip is sitting on the shore of Ramble Lake in the moonlight, a belly full of fish, trading sips of hot chocolate from a Nalgene bottle. I recall at one point staring up at a distant thumb of the Beartooth Plateau, some four thousand feet above me, wondering at the night falling on that blasted landscape; whether goats would be there, nibbling on kobresia, cavorting beside lakes with names like Gravel, Rubble, and Till. Almost as long as I've lived next to these mountains my imagination has tended to skip over the nearly perfect alpine valleys to roam these more stern, forbidding upper plateaus. I like the fact that the sheer chaos of those places turns even brief visits into whacks on the side of the head. Radical boulder therapy—making independent the codependent, hitching up the hearts of the down and out.

The evening of the day we walk out finds us huddled on my back porch around a grill full of steaks. Over the tops of the aspen I can see a small piece of Town Mountain, at the northern edge of the Beartooths, and past that, a trace of the Silver Run Plateau. There's already talk of another trip. This time, we swear, it'll be a journey given over to rambling without thought of destinations. It's going to be even more steeped in fishing. And from now until the time we leave we'll take comfort from the mere thought of it. We've got this fresh haul of memory in our pockets now, understand—something to cut and paste into daydreams, something to squeeze like a fidget stone through the long months of winter.

BIG WATER, BIG FISH

By Allen Jones

THROUGH THE BEARTRAP CANYON, the Madison river drops seventy-five feet in less than a quarter mile. It falls away from Ennis Lake a couple of degrees warmer and ten degrees rougher. The river immediately below the dam twists into some of the roughest whitewater in Montana, tightening down until the cliffs on either side press together like a thumb over a hose. The water shoots out in often graceful arcs. People have died here.

But on either side of the whitewater there's all this great fishing.

If you have ever bought a very good rod, something so expensive that the money really should have gone to the kids' education; if you have ever lied to your friends about what you've been using—if you are one of those people—then you will eventually find yourself faced with a certain, embarrassing question: How far will I really go for big fish? In the worst manifestations, wallets, egos and rods all break under the strain.

Of course, the next significant question, a week or a month or a year later, is this: What am I doing here?

The Beartrap is a tough deal. You can hire someone to float you through it and you can hike into it from the north but there's only a handful of guys that can float it and fish it. There are three distinct stretches of whitewater: Whitehorse, The Kitchen Sink and Greenwave. The Kitchen Sink...a singular hydraulic tough enough to have a name to itself. It needs a careful setup and a true education behind the oars. Miss the setup or a turn and you will be in trouble. Daunting by itself, it sits in the middle of two hundred yards of boulders and quick turns and scrotumtightening drops.

I was fishing with Randy and Jeff. Randy runs a fly-shop in Ennis. He grew up there: fishing, hunting, floating. He's been guiding since 1979, and even now, fifteen years and a divorce away from high school, he still maintains a kind of fish-crazy energy. He's one of those rare individuals that just knows how to do stuff. Tying flies, fixing lunches, getting an elk for his freezer damned near every year, he makes a living off knowing how to do stuff. Johnny France, an outfitter in Ennis, floated Randy

131

down through the Beartrap the first time in 1980. They had two boats, with Randy following behind until they came to the Kitchen Sink. Johnny floated Randy through in the first boat. They put in and Johnny told Randy to go back and give it a try himself. He'd watch from the bank. Randy guided for him for the next six years. Although this would be my first time down, Randy had taken Jeff nearly a dozen times before.

We put in off a rip-rap bank, just below a sign that said only rafts over 14 feet should float this water. I eyed the raft, which seemed small. It was a self-bailer, with a line of canvassed holes around the inside edge, just higher than the water, just lower than the inflated bottom. In the water, we worked to find our seats on the slick bulge of the raft. Randy pulled twice with the oars, enough to get us out into the fast water, and said, "What're you waiting for," nodding unspecifically to the river.

In front, Jeff had already unlimbered his rod and was slinging a streamer back and forth, working line out.

In October, Hebgen and Ennis lakes were letting out water, preparing for runoff in the spring. Familiar boulders were underwater and higher ones were taking on a new look. On October 21st the Madison dam was letting out 2,485 cubic feet per second. This, versus something like 1,500 feet in December. The water temperature was 47 degrees; versus 70-something in August. But it didn't feel like 47 degrees. It felt like ice, colder than flowing water had any right to be.

This isn't the Madison around the Varney bridge, braided and polite. It's not even the Madison another click closer to the Gallatin Valley, the luxury sport vehicles parked on the road, the thousand dollar rods fishing the wide water. The Beartrap carries a tougher cast—knuckles under a glove—and even where it's not dangerous you can feel the potential of it all. The speed and the scattering of boulders and the banks rising up fast. You look down at the Vs behind the biggest boulders, white at the edges, so deep you know you would never be able to find the bottom, and you catch yourself thinking: How big are the fish down there?

Jeff pulled in his rig and clipped off his streamer, working on a big bug-little bug combination: a Yuk Bug with a smaller one tied directly to it from the hook. "The big meal deal," he said, holding it up.

I stayed with the streamer under simple reasoning: big fly, big fish. Then I looked over just as Jeff's strike indicator shot down at an odd angle. The reel whirred off line and we were all suddenly grinning. Randy brought the raft over onto the shore and stepped out with his net. There was a flash of something brown and gold and enormous under the water. The fish, cagey enough to have grown old, went deep, trying to find something to wrap the line around, to beat the hook against. Jeff gave it right full rudder and brought it back up a bit, closer to the bank, pulling with the luxury of a 2X leader. In ten minutes, it came to the bank, side lolling up.

Jeff has taught me most of what I know about fishing. Randy, whom I know less well, taught Jeff. It would be harder to find a boat of unrelated individuals more closely tied to each other's history of accomplishment. There is no pretense or dissembling involved. The fish wasn't the largest Jeff has caught, and it wasn't the smallest. It would, however, be the best that any of us caught that day: a beautiful, twenty inch brown, patterns of fall color spectrumed across its side in wide strokes. He held it up and the camera was brought out and the fish was eased back down into the water and we all kind of looked around.

We both hooked onto a few more good fish in the upper stretches. A decent rainbow for me and another good brown for Jeff and smaller rainbows for each of us in a river where small rainbows are supposed to be whirling themselves out. Randy rowed, mostly watching Jeff's indicator, nodding to a corner or two that he thought Jeff might miss, and it was all great and good with only a vague idea of anything unusual ahead.

True to every story I have ever read, we heard the whitewater before we saw it. We came around a corner and Randy began pulling the boat into shore. Ahead of us, the rocks arrowed down into a tight geometry of dark water. From somewhere up ahead we could hear the faint, continuous sound of tires over gravel.

On shore, Jeff jumped out and tied off the raft. Taking their cue, I began breaking down my rod. Everything loose was strapped down. Our wader belts were tightened, our rain coats were zipped to the chin, and our life vests were strapped up until they almost restricted our breathing.

Randy dumped it in '83 in the Kitchen Sink, almost dying. The river held him under for nearly a minute, tucked up in a ball, spinning. His hands were over his head when he came up, and he shot out fast enough to break three fingers against the rowing frame. He crawled out of the river a half mile downstream, cold and battered. That was in June. The river was running 5,400 feet per second. Randy being Randy, he went and ran it again three days later at 5,800 feet and made it.

Through the first stretch of water, Whitehorse, we were laughing back and forth. I snapped off a couple of pictures with a waterproof camera. We stopped again before the Kitchen Sink. Jeff and I were both sitting in the front, giving weight to the nose. Randy said, "If I say go high, Allen, jump over Jeff's lap. If we go down, it'll be on your side." I nodded.

We saw hikers on the trail above the river, just beside the whitewater. They flew past as we dropped into the rapids, faster than I would have thought possible. How fast? Twelve miles an hour? Fifteen? Probably not twenty. One of the hikers was pointing at us. The first waves splashed in, soaking our faces and dripping off our raincoats and waders. My hat shed off a screen of drops. I looked ahead into a quick, steep turn.

Then we were down into the Kitchen Sink and it wasn't like we were dropping into it so much as it was coming up to meet us. The nose dug down into the water and then back up before any of us had left our seats. Half a boat of water splashed in and out through the bailer. We turned once, twice. The boat jigged around under us, caught by the strength of the river. *This*, I thought, *is why you need a good setup*. Once into the line, there wasn't much you could do. You were entirely in the hands of your guide and the river.

The energy of water and speed passed up through the rubber of the raft, conducting itself into the palms of our hands. The river had opened itself up, twisting out to show us its teeth. The raft jerked down and immediately back up, confused by competing forces.

Then we were in the flats as quickly as we had begun and Jeff and I were looking at each other, grinning, weighing down the nose. Randy was rowing back to the shore. "There's a good hole coming up," he said. "Might as well unstrap the rods."

Randy handed Jeff the oars after the last bit of whitewater and we fished for another two hours. As good as the fishing was above the rapids, it should have been better below, but things were slow. Randy caught fish in the back of the raft—one every now and then—but nothing like what he would normally do. I had hold of only one, unseen brown that took my line down to the bottom and kept it there until I pulled the hook.

It got dark very fast and none of us spoke. I reeled in my line and took a turn around the butt to hook it into a guide. Behind me, Randy switched to a streamer and began stripping it in, depending on the feel of any strike. The wind had died. There was the sound of water dripping off Jeff's oars and Randy stripping line.

The edges of the Madison Range saucered up around us, cracking in the west in front of the last of the sun. A car drove past on the road just down from the landing, its lights on. We put in at the ramp—a slice of gray in the dark—and pulled the car around to unpack by the headlights.

The day had been the closest thing Randy had come to a vacation for the last month: having a good friend in the boat who could row. He had a paying client lined up for the next day and would be putting in at the same ramp where we were taking out. Jeff and I each had our own jobs. Around us, the dark pastels of hillside and water and sky were running together like hands through hair.

The familiar thank yous were exchanged, waders were peeled off and rods were slid back into their cases. There was the kind of wind-burned happiness that comes from accomplishing not much but a few fish out of good water; no real point to the day just spent beyond the simple fact of its new existence. Behind us, the Beartrap roared on.

HEADWATERS

By Doug Peacock

THE MONTANA SUMMER DAY EASED towards the coolness of evening. As the shadows crawled across the river, swarms of caddis and mayflies churned above the shaded water along the bank. Trout rose along the rocks and at the current's edge. I grabbed my fly rod hoping to get a cast off as I floated past. The drift boat slammed into a rock. I dropped the rod and picked up the oars. Fly-fishing the Big Hole River while rowing in low water was next to impossible.

It was the first of July, and I had just entered a time in my life when I needed to disappear for a while. No vehicle or boat trailer remained behind to mark my departure at the launch site near Divide, Montana. Jim Crumley—after dropping me and my gear off below the bridge—had towed the old trailer to Livingston where he left it in front of a friend's house. My own pickup had gone away with my ex-wife.

It had been one hell of a year. My close friend, the writer Edward Abbey, had died; tribal loyalty dictated I be there to attend his death and see to his requested illegal burial deep in the desert wilderness. These duties I executed. Then there were the wakes and memorials—hard on the health of the living. Two months later, the FBI busted the radical environmental group Earth First!. Since Earth First! was loosely conceived around a book Abbey had written, these events were linked. The problem was that on the same morning that the group's leader, Dave Foreman, was popped, the FBI showed up at my home in Tucson. By then I was in Montana, but I was still concerned. Though I was too old and antisocial to have played a significant role in Earth First! or any other group, subpoenas for Grand Jury appearances had been served to people I knew and I had places—wild places—on my spring and summer schedule and didn't want any mandatory appearances to interfere with my trips. I figured the Feds would eventually back off; I wasn't that important and rumors had surfaced that legendary lawyer Gerry Spence would, if necessary, defend me. I did nothing to discourage them.

The *Los Angeles Times Magazine* said this:

"Spence, who has taken on Foreman's case pro bono, became involved when his good friend Doug Peacock called to ask for help. Peacock happens to be the man Edward Abbey modeled his rabble-rousing character Hayduke after in The Monkeywrench Gang.*"*

The first part about Peacock happened to be massively incorrect: a mutual, good friend did indeed call Gerry to ask him to help, but it wasn't me. I chose to let the misinformation stand. The truth could marinate for a while. This may have been a tad chickenshit of me, but it certainly didn't hurt in keeping the feds at bay.

Seeing myself as on the lam from the feds wasn't the only thing on my mind; I'd call it merely a significant distraction. Much worse, I had let unfounded reports that the FBI was after me sour my mood. The cornered-ferret aspect of my otherwise charming personality had surfaced and my marriage came apart. So here I was, stuck on this damned river, up the proverbial creek with no paddle, getting ready to put my life on the currents of a stream that was rapidly drying up in one of the worst droughts of the decade.

No one besides Crumley knew I was here, and no one knew how fast or how far I might travel downstream. I didn't know myself. Since I had no way to get off the river—no truck or trailer waiting down river—I just had to keep on going downstream. I had some rudimentary maps but no details showing what awaited me on the rivers below. The Big Hole ran another fifty miles south and east, hooking into the Beaverhead near Twin Bridges, after which it was called the Jefferson. The Jefferson meandered over another 100 miles back to the northeast where it joined two other great rivers, the Gallatin and the Madison, to create the headwaters of the Missouri River. No matter how long it took or how difficult the obstacles, I wanted to reach the headwaters.

My boat was a thirty year old plywood dory someone had dubbed "the Green Queen." The name stuck. My biggest concern was that the heavy boat wouldn't make it through the low water. It was already scraping over rocks in the riffles and shallows of the tail-outs. Ranchers diverted an incredible amount of water out of this river to irrigate alfalfa fields for cattle. Diversion dams blocked the river in numerous places to channel the flow into irrigation canals. Since the three-hundred pound craft was too heavy to carry, I'd either have to lower it with ropes through the dams or push it along the bank on log rollers. I'd figure it out as I went.

I maneuvered the boat around bucket-sized boulders into the main tongue of the river, scraping bottom in the shallows. Trout were rising with regularity, but I kept at the oars for another half hour; I wanted to get a few miles away from the bridge and out of sight of any road or ranch by dark.

The river meandered left and disappeared against the dim light of a bank of cliffs about two hundred yards downstream. On the right was a strip of cottonwoods separating the river from a fallow pasture beyond. I pulled hard on the wooden oars and drove the bow of the heavy boat up on the muddy bank next to the big trees. I'd make camp here.

Mosquitoes buzzed around my ears. I slapped Vietnam War-surplus "jungle juice" on my neck, face and balding head. The bugs would disappear as the temperature dropped after dark. I'd work with the tent then; putting the sucker up in the darkness was no big deal. Now I wanted to fish.

I waded out into the cool river in long pants and rubber sandals. In addition to the caddis, a few olive-colored mayflies were flying around. In the fading light, the bugs looked as small as dust. My blunt calloused fingers stabbed the fine 5x leader tip blindly at the microscopic fly.

I waded upstream, casting to rising fish. The first four casts were ignored, but on the next, a ten-inch brown nailed the imitation. I quickly landed and released it; I wanted his bigger brothers at the edge of the fast water.

I hadn't experienced a night like this in a long time; sometime after Vietnam I had lost, without ever having been aware of the precise moment, the enjoyment of night fishing. This evening was like my boyhood in northern Michigan. I remembered three nights in the 1950s at my grandfather's cabin when fish—hundreds more than you ever imagined lived there—fed voraciously on the surface. I remembered standing on the bridge by Grandpa's cabin in the dark, the moon not yet up, hearing several dozen splashes every minute. Thirty years later, standing on the edge of the current of the Big Hole River, I felt all the old magic.

I halted forty feet below the top of the run. Two beer-keg-sized rocks framed the gateway to the long tongue of the run. Below the closest rock and just at the edge of the current a good sized fish was rising. My fly was meant to imitate a mayfly spinner. It was the final, beautiful stage of the mayfly's life; death and beauty lived close to my heart these days. The big fish rose again. I tried a cast, but the fly dragged just at the point of the rise. The trout quit feeding.

It was too late and dark enough that I was ready to call it a day. Just as I turned to set up my tent, the big fish below the rock splashed again.

Just one more cast. Returning upstream, I dropped the fly smack on the spot of the rise. Nothing happened. My guess was that the fish was feeding on the emerging nymphs that were floating near the surface. I recast the spinner hitting the rock above the feeding fish. I tugged the fly slightly, letting it sink below the surface. When it reached the big trout there was a splash and I set the hook. An eighteen or nineteen-inch rainbow leaped between the surge of current and the eddy. My fly was lodged in his jaw. The leader had broken. I had struck too hard. It had been a long time since I had caught a big fish on a tiny dry fly.

Night was coming on and my camp still wasn't made. A little panic ran across my shoulders and gripped my chest. This fear of dark defiles had been a lot worse twenty years ago when I had just returned from Vietnam. Tonight it wasn't as bad, but it wasn't nothing either; it was enough to take the edge off the pleasure of fishing. Actually, to kill it altogether.

I broke camp and pushed off just after daybreak, hoping to avoid being spotted by early boat fisherman, still shaking off the previous night's uneasy mood. Though no one would think twice about someone in a boat here, a person camping guerrilla-style might draw attention. I wanted total anonymity for a few weeks. I needed some down-time to check into what was going on with my daily operation, maybe make a few changes. Nothing I knew could serve that purpose as well as a river: the simple, almost mechanical exercise of keeping the boat in the river, the total solitude, the stark, clean living far from the temptations of whiskey bars and foie gras.

A fine mist lingered over the more turbulent sections of river. In the stillness of morning, the cry of a hermit thrush hung over the woodland. I rowed into the current and pointed the stern downstream. I knew this section of the Big Hole was where I would run into the most people during the approaching 4th of July weekend. I wanted to get through it as quickly as possible.

Framed by the Bitterroot, Pioneer, Anaconda and Pintler mountains, the Big Hole runs north some fifty miles before it cuts east to the Divide bridge and begins a more southerly run to the tiny town of Glen. After Glen, it meanders through braided channels to the bigger town of Twin Bridges, where it joins the Ruby and Beaverhead to become the Jefferson.

A bridge loomed ahead and, beyond it, an outcrop called Maidenrock. There were a few fishermen and a couple rubber rafts getting ready to push off. I pulled hard on the oars, propelling the boat by as quickly as possible, rowing around their fishing lies, trying not to disturb them. I nodded as I passed. It was already about nine o'clock in the morning, and the commercial guides were active. I decided to wait out the heat of the day and all the boats it promised, snoozing under the shade of a juniper tree. In the lengthening shadows of mid-afternoon, I pushed off once again.

That night I camped in another thicket, then pushed off at first light, aiming the boat downstream, eager to pass by the few houses and the tiny village of Glen. Drifting past the few buildings, I saw no one. I was leaving civilization behind; there wasn't anything downstream until you hit the Beaverhead. I began to breathe easier; I was home free.

It was clear running all the way to Twin Bridges. There were no roads along the river and scarcely a human structure, unless you counted the diversion dams. I passed another of these barriers, about the fifth major one since putting in at Divide. Here a bulldozed wall of alluvial gravel blocked two-thirds of the river and diverted part of it into a canal to irrigate nearby alfalfa fields.

It was a fine, mild day, not hot, just a hint of breeze; a few clouds decorated an immaculate Montana sky. I found pleasure—even exhilaration—in the simple, repetitive act of rowing. Along the south bank under the trees, I could smell the sun on the hawthorne, chokecherries and rose hips, the rich redolence of fruit awaiting ripeness. On the larger boulders—at least two feet above the present water level—thousands of empty stonefly cases clung to the rock.

Everything was in transition—bugs and plants, the river itself, always moving, changing. I thought about my own appetite for metamorphosis, the image of dying a little death, shedding the old skin, scratching the itch for a change.

By late afternoon, I passed another major dam diverting a big hunk of the river. The Green Queen banged over rocks. I had to get out every third of a mile, tie the bow line around my waist, lift a bit and drag the dory over the shallow heads of narrow chutes.

I began to wonder if there was going to be enough water in the river to float me down to the headwaters. The combination of consecutive drought years and anachronistic water laws promised to kill the Big Hole. It looked like half the river water was repeatedly diverted every five or so miles. How long would it be before the entire river dried up?

That evening I made camp in a tiny, lovely clearing in the middle of a magical little island. A grove of cottonwoods walled in an enchanted, lilliputian glade. On most years, this little meadow would have been silted up, but with two years of serious drought and more of low water, a rich soil had developed, allowing for a mossy carpet of lupine and paintbrush.

I had a bottle of Montana Riesling I'd picked up at the bar in Montrose, the only wine available with a cork in the bottle. I wanted to use the white wine to poach a Big Hole trout.

It was about two hours before dark, and caddis had been spreading across the quieter water for a couple of hours. I walked up the south channel. I watched a trout rise with great regularity. I watched until I could finally make out the seventeen inch body. A really good fly-fisherman would try to match the hatch. But I didn't have flies small enough, and couldn't have tied them on with my fading near-distant eyesight if I had. I did have one fly on a #14 hook; a ratty old Red Quill. In it's dishevelled condition, it could pass for a smaller-sized fly. I was hungry and needed a fish for dinner.

I cast the scraggly imitation five feet above the fish and let it drift down with no discernable drag. Nothing happened. I tried for the chunky brown for ten minutes, finally giving up to walk down the beach. Several fish were feeding toward the tail of the island. In the fast, smooth water, I could see the backs of fish bulging in the current. I flipped the Red Quill upstream and across the channel, gave it a tug to pull it under the surface, then mended my line. As it reached the feeding trout, there was a boil, and I was on to a nice rainbow about a foot long. I guided it into the shallows and beached it on the shore, whacking it on the head and quickly cleaning it. I wanted this one for dinner.

I picked mint from the river's edge, pulled up a few wild onion plants from the marshy end of the island, and grabbed a handful of sage from the higher bank. Back in the clearing, I kindled a small fire. I pulled out four new potatoes from my food bag and wrapped them in squares of aluminum foil, placing them on the periphery of the fire to roast. I balanced a small skillet between two rocks and kept a small fire burning with dead twigs of willow. I popped the cork on the white wine with my Swiss Army knife, poured a tin cup of Riesling for the cook and dumped a half-inch into the skillet. I dropped crushed wild mint leaves into the wine and chopped up the corm of wild onion. I mixed the onion with a few leaves of native sage and stuffed the trout with the mixture. When the wine began to steam, I carefully laid sections of trout into the pan, finally fashioning a tent of aluminum foil over the pan and leaning back to sip on the sweet but cold and reasonably crisp wine and look up at the window of sky. The brighter stars were coming out. Camp was made, the tent was up, and dinner was cooking.

My muscles were sore from rowing, but I felt good, content to listen to the soft murmur of water gurgling around the little island. Somewhere downstream, I could hear the cry of a great horned owl beginning a night of hunting. I hooked a spud with a cottonwood stick and poked it with a knife to test for doneness. Condiments were salt for the potatoes and a squeeze of lemon for the rainbow trout, which just flaked with the knife. I could smell hints of mint, chives and sage on the trout. A fabulous meal.

I awoke to the sound of heron wings. The sun was on the trees; it was later than I was accustomed to getting started. No matter, I had no schedule or any destination. I was merely on the river; on the lam, on the river.

Just before midday, the light softened. I became aware of a huge looming cloud edging into the southwestern sky. The cumulus thunderhead dominated the entire southern sky, its slow, steady movement was unyielding. I moved along in the Green Queen, enjoying the gusty air, drifting with the current and feeling like I was the river—travelling slowly through the country, smelling the earthy fetor of the Big Hole, feeling the afternoon breeze rise in advance of the thunderheads, anticipating a hard wind in the cottonwoods, turning the leaves upside down, white against the distance of darkening sky, imagining the first splash of rain on the water, the deluge quickening into a brief but heavy downpour, the sound of the storm abating, the willow and alder dripping into the quiet water along the bank, and birds singing, thrush and vireos and jays and a killdeer's piercing cry below a red-tail hawk, screaming.

Ahead, the river divided into two braided channels. I didn't know which one to take. I didn't want to end up blocked by a downfall or logjam, especially, with a storm blowing in. It occurred to me that I should probably find a spot to get out of the river and wait out the weather.

In my boat, I carried enough rain gear and plastic garbage bags to sit out a little rain, but the approaching storm looked big enough to generate considerable wind and lightning, maybe even hail. I needed to find a place to erect the tent where a tree wouldn't blow down on it and where I could sit on an insulating pad in case the lightning got close.

Off to the right, an overhanging snag afforded a little place to securely tie up the boat. Hurriedly, I carried tent, pad and sleeping bag into the trees. I picked a site in the lee of a big tree that had been hit by lightning and pruned of the hazard of dead branches which might blow off in the wind. I quickly put the tent up and tied it to the tree. I stuffed my pad and sleeping bag inside and ran back to the boat to get more gear—enough to wait out the duration of the storm. The first whipped drops of rain stung my face. The storm had arrived.

I dove into the tent just as the deluge abruptly turned into hail. I zipped up the rain fly and huddled in the center of the dome. Hail pounded the tent, the tempo thunderous and growing louder. I wondered if it would hold up to the force of the hail. I peeked out with the dim instinct of an animal trapped in a collapsing den and could see the full rage of the rare summer ice storm now. The size of the hail ranged between big marbles and small golf balls.

Ten minutes later, I stepped out into the white summer landscape. Two inches of hail lay on the ground. I could hear the painful bellowing of cattle in every direction and magpies complained loudly; perhaps their colonial nests had been damaged. The wounded cows sounded pitiful and comic and, for a moment, forgetting my real beef was with the ranchers, I chuckled thoughtlessly.

I gathered up an ice-chest full of hail. How I wished I had a few beers to ice down. Once more I packed my gear. The hail in the Green Queen had melted, and I bailed out most of the water with a plastic gallon milk container with the top cut off. The river had some color in it and seemed to be growing milkier by the minute. I pushed off and aimed the boat at the right channel, where most of the water flowed. The river divided again, and by now the channel was only about fifteen feet wide. The narrow river snaked through trees and bushes; I couldn't see the bottom through the chalky clay in the river. A dark brown mink surfaced on the water and scampered up on a log, watching me as I drifted close. He disappeared into the brush.

A quarter of a mile downstream, I came to a huge cottonwood log that spanned the entire channel. It was three feet across and a foot above the water. There was no way I could get over or through the obstruction.

I stripped off my clothes and re-dressed only in tennis shoes and a tee-shirt to protect me from rope burn. I tied a bowline loop in the bow rope and draped it over shoulder and under the opposite arm. I tried to haul the boat directly upstream but it was too heavily laden; if the water was more than knee deep, I couldn't get enough leverage to pull the Green Queen against the swift current. I tied on another twenty feet of rope and went upstream to the bank, braced against a log and pulled the dory hand over hand through the deep channel. I repeated this technique whenever the water was too deep. Two hours later, exhausted and breathing heavily, I had moved the boat back upstream to where the river had divided. Despite the cold water, sweat ran into my eyes. I peeled off my shirt and submerged in the milky river. I air-dried for five minutes and got dressed.

Past Notch Bottom, the river continued to rise, though not at an alarming rate, and the color lightened to marl white. There would be no fishing until the river began to clear, and that could take days. At the High Road bridge, I hid the boat in a willow thicket and walked a mile east into Twin Bridges to buy bread, apples and a pint of Canadian whiskey that I sipped on as I walked along the road back to the boat. An osprey sat in a snag above the Green Queen. I shoved off back on the river. I poured VO into a tin cup and added a little water, keeping the cup on the floor boards of the drift boat when I had to use the oars. Seven herons perched in a dead tree ahead, looking like vultures. I toasted the long legged water birds, finishing the cup of whiskey. By now, I was a little bit loaded.

The river pulled me steadily away from the pleasant, though crowded, cloister of buildings. Ahead, the Beaverhead joined the Big Hole from the northeast. Right where they met, a large beaver slapped the water. There were two wide channels now, and I couldn't decide which one to take. At the last moment, I chose the right one. I pivoted the boat and stupidly missed a stroke with the oar. The river was swift and muscular and drove the Green Queen into a dead-head log and stove in the side. Water poured through the hole in the side of the boat.

I tried bailing the boat but water was coming in too fast. The collision was dumb but not critical, although I would have to patch the hole. I started looking for a campsite. Past the confluence with the Ruby and Beaverhead, the Big Hole ended. The river was now known as the Jefferson.

Most of the land along the Jefferson was private and posted. I consulted my Interagency map; there was a small piece of state land just around the bend. Since I had to sand, glue and dry the area where I stove in the side of the boat, I wanted to know I would be on public land.

I camped on a sand clearing separated from the river by low willows, hammering the shattered plywood hull back into position with a flat rock and scraping it clean with a knife; the break wasn't as bad as I thought. I kindled a little fire near the boat to dry the wood so the glue and duct tape would stick. Snipe winnowed and darted in the evening sky. Most of the milky silt had settled out and the river began to clear to the color of dark whiskey.

Speaking of whiskey, there was some left in the pint of VO. But I wasn't in the mood. Ed Abbey had died of complications from an alcohol-related disease. I'd pay honor to an old friend and quit drinking for the rest of the trip. I uncapped what was left of the blended whiskey and added its contents to the booze-colored Jefferson.

The next morning, I tested my patch and added an extra layer of heavy-duty camouflage duct tape to each side of the hole. It would be two more years before the tape would be replaced with a proper patch. Ahead loomed a trident-shaped voodoo heron tree; six of them perched in the lightning-struck tree and ten more flew by overhead.

The Jefferson and upper Missouri were neither popular floats nor electrifying white water areas. This was sparsely populated ranch country. I didn't expect to see any other boats or many fishermen on the hundred-mile run of river. Each night I would camp hidden in a grove of cottonwoods or a thicket of willow, guerrilla camping, like Huck Finn, something I never got to do as a boy. I would rarely be seen—only when passing towns or bridges—and no one would pay any attention to me then. It dawned on me that I could keep going down the river, down to the Missouri, past the Yellowstone, into the Mississippi, past towns and cities, all the way to the Gulf of Mexico if I wanted to and was willing to portage around the dams. I could continue to row during the days, forage for food, hunt, fish and camp hidden by timber or nightfall all the way to New Orleans—an ancient, neglected, but tested path for a renegade to stay on the lam in America.

This vague notion of being on the lam, of being on the run from some variety or abstraction of trouble or authority or danger, was actually generic to my life; it had been my companion throughout the years of war and peace, both in Vietnam and in grizzly country. I had always felt more comfortable hidden in thick vegetation, crawling into the brush, walking just inside the tree line, faceless in the easy blanket of night or even in a crowd.

By now the river was dropping, clearing and the barometer stabilizing. I rigged up to fish again. I had lost almost all of my small stash of tiny mayfly and caddis imitations upstream, snapping them off on feisty rainbows when I first got on the river. I tied on a big black stone fly nymph, wading out in my tennis shoes to fling the graceless but effective fly upstream and across. When it reached the lie of the feeding fish furthest downstream, I raised the tip of my fly rod to take the slack out of the line. The line hesitated and I struck. I was fast to a good fish.

The trout made a run downstream, bulldogging on the bottom for two minutes at the tail of the pool, then bolting upstream. I eased the heavy fish to the edge of the current; a hook-jawed male rose to the surface. The brown trout was about twenty inches long and not very heavy in the body. I had my son Colin's landing net with me, but this fish was too large for the net. No matter; the net was to keep me company, to remind of the little boy I loved, not necessarily for netting trout.

I gently beached the brown trout, holding him very lightly with a wet hand. I reached and twisted out the barbless hook with a pair of hemostats and freed the trout.

I moved on down the river in the Green Queen, stopping often to fish. Just short of the Ironrod bridge, I made a late camp in a small, thick grove of trees. There was a diversion dam just below the bridge that I wanted to time my passage through, around or over; I figured I might have to get wet and wanted the sun to be up.

The next morning, I beached the Green Queen just above the bridge and walked up to the road to have a look. The river was broad and shallow here, and the current had slowed. The diversion dam was just below the high iron bridge. I walked out on the bridge and leaned over a steel beam, checking the dam with my binoculars.

It was made of big slabs of concrete dropped or bulldozed into position. In the middle of the raw slabs, water surged through a line of debris. This break was about eight or ten feet wide, and there was a concrete slab in the middle. The river dropped perhaps six or eight feet in the twenty-foot cascade of water. There wasn't a straight shot or clean run through the gap. There was no way the boat could pass through without smashing to bits on the concrete slabs.

I took everything out of the boat and left it on the bank next to the dam. Enough water moved through the gap to provide a cushion against the biggest slab below. If I could ease the boat over the drop-off into the first big boulder, the water would carry it off to the side and down a ten-foot cascade into another slab. As long as the boat wasn't moving too fast, smashing against the rock shouldn't damage it too badly. I figured I'd use my body, pulling against the bow line, as a break.

A slick of water rushed through a ten-foot break in the diversion dam then split into two white tongues of current surging around a half dozen big hunks of cement. The entire drop was only ten feet or less over a thirty foot course, but there was no clean run through the debris. The right channel was better, but neither was good.

I could belay the heavy boat until it started down the tongue of water. Then I'd have to let it go and grab the rope and belay again just before it smashed into the second big boulder. I was aiming for a soft smash. The Green Queen was also tied to a second longer line to keep it from floating off down the river once it bounced off the second rock.

The boat sat poised at the top of the slick. I held the bowline in a belay around my waist, letting out line an inch at a time. When the stern eased into heavy flow, I let go. The boat roared down the slick into the first boulder. I grabbed the line and braced myself. The dory pulled me off my feet and glanced off the rock to the right. I lost my footing and went under. When I re-emerged, the Green Queen was about to smash into the second slab. I seized the line again and hung on as hard as I could. The force of the river against the boat snatched me off my belay and tossed me into the rocks, ripping my pants and tearing the skin off a shin and forearm. I went under again but fortunately missed knocking my teeth out on the rocks.

I looked downriver. The Green Queen floated in quiet water at the end of the line.

I was on the river again. I didn't want to beach the boat every time I wanted to fish, so I rigged up a heavy leader with a big, expendable fly, an "experimental" pattern tied on a salt water hook with long saddle hackles, dyed brown, tied on the hood with coarse hackle next to the eye. It looked like a half-butchered chicken.

I pinched on a big split shot and flung the thing side-arm across the river, the huge lure sounding like a ruffed grouse barrelling over my head. I stripped in the fly as rapidly as I could in fifteen-inch movements,. Between the fourth and fifth strip, a good fish struck the fly. I played the fish with one hand and pulled on an oar with the other until I could beach the Green Queen. I held the fish out of the run and finally released a seventeen-inch brown. Further downstream, I whipped the monstrous fly across the run, allowing it to settle deep before stripping it in as fast as I could. A fifteen-inch rainbow shot up in the air with the fly in its mouth. I was onto something. In the agricultural valley of the Jefferson, irrigation ditches and diversion dams had silted up much of the stonefly habitat. The giant nymphs were rare. Common big fish food were crayfish and muddlers. The half-butchered chicken fly, retrieved in jerks, imitated both.

That afternoon and the next morning, I caught seventeen fish between fifteen and twenty-two inches. Three quarters of them were brown trout; the few rainbows were always at the head of the runs in the faster water.

I caught so many fish that I quit fishing altogether for a while. The bloom of excitement upon first hitting the river had faded with seventy miles of fishing. The "catch and release" fishing which had drawn me here no longer sufficed. I had become a big softy. My eight-year-old son Colin would sometimes remind others that"grasshoppers (or trout) have families too."

Beginning with my little boy, I tried to think about the lives of other creatures. I was, by this stage of my life, beyond any notion of "sport" as a sustaining practice of the wild. For me, wilderness fishing, hunting and gathering—at their best—are utilitarian uses, activities that count, endeavors that get something as real as food or practical knowledge out of the wild, a purpose for going there more vital than scenery, recreation or diversion. Here on the Missouri headwaters, seeing myself as "hunter" was a swollen exaggeration of the fact that I was living off the land— gathering mushrooms, catching fish and crawfish for dinner.

But the perception was the same and bound to the point of view of the animal pursued. You pay attention and enhance your alertness by shrinking from view, scenting the air and remaining silent. It means to get outside yourself, to see anew, to make new combinations of the things you already know. As a "hunter" on the Jefferson River, I was a washout, and could now imagine myself weeping over a gut-snagged whitefish. Still, the notion of vitality lingered. It was empowered by curiosity, attentiveness, by an utterly open mind. My autumnal passion, like old Abbey's, was increasingly sensate. Being alive here was the shared inhabiting of other creatures, heron dreaming, the green empathy of the forest, reflecting like a river.

During the night, a gentle rain beat against the tent for half an hour. Coyotes cried out across the river. At daybreak, I was awakened by whitetail deer splashing nosily across the river. I made coffee, packed up and pushed off into the current.

The river drew me towards a grove of huge cottonwood trees set back from the river on the right bank. The trees towered above the willow scrub-field. I could see many stick nests in the upper branches. I held the oars motionless above the water, drifting like a great green leaf on the skin of river. The glade opened, and I stared at a hundred stick nests in four big trees, a third or more of them occupied. I didn't twitch an eyelid.

The current pushed me out and down, slowly turning the stern towards the rookery, which was the biggest by a factor of four I had ever seen. I drifted past, eye to eye with dozens of herons, two or three to a nest, young birds standing on stick nests, a scene I might have expected in the Serengetti.

The Green Queen and I floated in and out of days. The river buoyed us up and down. I rowed on, the flake of boat and man. Though my hands were calloused with furrows of thick skin, my body felt hypersensitive to the world around it. I remembered the time a bark scorpion, a little desert arachnid packing a nasty wallop, stung me on the little finger and how the nerves were sensitized for weeks, and even running lukewarm tap water over the finger felt unbearable and like fire.

Now it was less painful, less tactile, yet otherwise much the same. I could feel through my skin the minuscule changes of temperature manifested by passing changes in vegetation reflecting the heat. I heard the faint silicious rustle of fine sediment suspended in the current grazing the green side of the boat, a fine rustling alongside the rocks. With my eyes closed, I could sense the changing currents and navigate sightless into the main channels. I had quit killing fish and crayfish. I became a total vegetarian. The lack of booze gave me an uncommonly clear head. Modern living had numbed me to the audible, olfactory universe of birds and insects whose messages arrived on every breath of breeze. The river was bringing them back.

Below the great colonial rookery, the river took me under another bridge, past alfalfa fields irrigated by noisy pumps sucking up the dwindling water flow through big rubber hoses, past ugly levees and open wounds on the land made by bulldozers and backhoes. The bottomland here had been held in private ownership for several generations and it was assumed—a canon of modern real estate practice and the central illusion of our age—that the land was the property of the owner to be used in any manner they saw fit, conveniently forgetting that we are only the most recent of arrivals on this continent of immigrants, that the land was procured from others who stole it from native people who never owned it to begin with. The heron, the deer, the bear and wolf were here long before any of us. And the river, which took its character from the land, ran through only as a still pool in summer, reflecting the churning thunderhead; beneath its mirrored surface the water was everything it had seen before and all that it had always been, the same recycled molecules of water had been mixing since the creation everywhere on the earth.

Warmer-water fish now occupied the slower holes and the tail outs of longer runs. Schools of whitefish, suckers and an occasional big squaw fish darted away from the shadow of the Queen passing over. The river pushed past the towns of Whitehall and Cardwell and drove easterly slicing a canyon through a little range of limestone mountains. The grassy slopes rolled up into the wedges of timber lodged in draws and on north slopes. The caves of Lewis and Clark Caverns lay on the north shore just ahead.

Downstream of the caverns, the river bent away from the road and sliced a gentle gorge through the hills south before dumping out onto the valley of the confluence of the Jefferson, the Madison and the Gallatin rivers—the Missouri headwaters. An old homestead stood on a bench above the river next to an abandoned railroad. I put in early in the day wanting to linger here up-river in the last roadless section of the Jefferson. I basked in the last embrace of sun. I got out a bar of soap and took a bath. Lolling naked on the gravel bar, I listened to the river, the faint buzz of insect, the hatches, the swoop of swallows and nighthawks, the soft murmur of water.

Later, I pitched my tent in the deserted orchard. A great horned owl hooted me to sleep. The audible song of river beckons me downstream. In my sleep, I resist. The anchor of dreams holds me firm to the cobble terrace, drawing me deeper into the moist womb of alluvial earth. The owl returned.

Then it was daylight. The dream loitered. I wanted the meditative mood to hang on forever. It wouldn't last but I could make it linger: the inexorable pull of the river, the relentless tug of gravity, that counterwind of entropy ballasting down even our most imaginative flights, the endless flow and ebb of water, now eddying up below a narrow tongue of rapids along a slow hole where I beached the boat for the night. The last night out.

Sixteen days after launching at Divide, I landed just below a bridge near Three Folks, fifteen pounds lighter—the result of no booze, a trout and crayfish diet and lots of rowing. I hid the Green Queen in the willows, hitched into Three Forks, and found a phone. I called my friend David Quammen, who lived upstream on the fork called the Gallatin.

"Please come pick me up," I implored. "I'm at the headwaters."

FIVE RIVERS, FIVE DAYS

By Brian Baise

THE BOAT ITSELF IS SIMPLE: two plastic pontoons, two steel bars and a plastic seat. My legs ride in the water and, with a pair of kick-fins, provide all my navigation and propulsion. Ostensibly, this is a boat built for rivers, although, on the left pontoon, there's a half-legible warning against whitewater.

I'm barely into my float down the Big Hole River when my right fin falls off. I need that fin, especially with the river funneling into the outside edge of a turn. Broadside to the current, in water just below my waist, I stand up; the boat, however, keeps going, knocking me off my feet. I go down, both legs hooked over one pontoon. The boat rides on its side, half-tipped over and coming into another turn.

My mind alternates between not wanting to drown and hoping nobody is watching. My fly rod points somewhere upstream with line pouring out, the woolly bugger lodged into the flank of some sunken tree. Quiet water. I need quiet, slow water where I can dry off, have a meeting with myself and consider matters. I dog-paddle pathetically, dragging the boat and trying to keep my head up.

Standing, safe for the moment, the legs of my waders ballooned with water, I watch a guided trip float by. "Any luck?" I ask them. They don't answer, but stare, half-concerned, half-amused. "Just taking her out for a spin," I tell them. "Seeing how she handles." They keep staring. "Water's not too cold today. Comfortable actually."

From where I stand, I can still see the bridge where my car is parked. Downstream, there are seven more miles of the Big Hole before my planned take-out. Without too much trouble, I could haul the gear back to my car and start again later, maybe tomorrow. But looking back upstream, I don't feel like carrying the boat through the heavy brush. It is largely out of laziness that I sit down in the seat, lash the laces of my remaining fin through the metal buckles on my boots, and kick out into the current.

And so begins the fishing trip, my tour of a few trout rivers in Montana. I have five days to kill, and it seems appropriate to kill them on a series of rivers with a fly rod in my hand. It's not intended to be any sort of soul search and no struggle for survival: I have a car, a credit card, a fly rod and a few spinning lures in case things get desperate. I want to float down a few rivers, fish for trout and barbecue a couple of them over an open fire. Then I want to get up and do the same thing the next day and then again the next. It's September, the rivers are low, and I wouldn't want to be anywhere else in the world.

I'm fishing the Big Hole just below Melrose. This late in the season, it's low and fast, shallow and slippery. The current pushes you along like any piece of driftwood, and fishing becomes less a science than a free-for-all. There are so many fish in so many places that you can catch them almost any way you want. I've had success on streamers in a caddis hatch and on dry flies in dead, summer heat. Where's the trick? Whatever you're using, use it well. These fish see lots of fishermen and don't like any of them.

I lift my legs through a shallow riffle section. With my fin out of the water, I'm essentially helpless, caroming off small standing waves and spinning in circles down the river. These spots are common at this time of year on the Big Hole, and tend to come immediately before the wrenching turns where the river pushes out onto the rocks. I fly through this first section, and, as it drops off along the edge, I lurch and kick frantically to avoid the bank.

Just out of this turn, I start preparing for the next one.

An hour later, my time has been spent kicking back and forth between safe sides of the river, keeping myself on the inside edge of the bends. Fishing has become secondary, reduced to an occasional troll.

It's maddening to float the Big Hole this way—out of control, trying only to keep afloat. This stretch alone could afford years of fishing, and I'm giving it one mad dash. In some ways, I just want to get it over with and start again tomorrow.

As the afternoon passes, I manage to fish a few holes, but usually at such a speed that it isn't worth it. With one fin, I can barely keep off the banks, let alone stall long enough to float my fly over any holes.

Evening comes, and I take out at the first sign of a road; somewhere, I think, near Glen. With this boat, light enough to carry by myself, I'm able to put in and take out wherever I can hitchhike back to my car. Tonight, I'm picked up by a man with a load of hay in the back of his truck. I embarrassingly admit to not having had much luck—any luck, actually. He can't understand how anyone could float the Big Hole and not catch fish. I regret not lying to him.

At my car, I throw a few casts from the bank, hoping to pick up dinner and a little pride. On the third cast, I catch a cottonwood, twenty-feet up, and leave the fly in the tree.

South on 15, North on 41. It's a short drive to the Jefferson, and I set up camp near Parson's Bridge in the dark. My fire is the only light on the river bank, and I wish I had caught a couple of fish, if only for dinner. My cooler holds what's left over from the last trip: peanut butter, two cans of beans, a stale loaf of bread, rice and noodles, tortillas, water, an onion, green pepper and a lemon.

The morning comes with rain, and I'm up early to work on the boat: I adjust the seat, tighten the backrest and duct tape a board across the back of the pontoons to keep my day-pack dry. I light a small fire, eat noodles for breakfast, and then drive into Twin Bridges for a pair of fins.

I've fished the Jefferson before, but never with much devotion. This river takes the curls and pivots of its source rivers and flattens them out, becoming a paced, plodding fishery given to gradual, steady bends. It's not an obvious river: you need to be able to read water and fish wet flies well. With it's black, sinking runs, it holds mostly brown trout, and they keep in places that aren't always easy to see.

The cloud cover has brought *baetis* to the surface, and fish rise along the banks and in the seams. Within an hour, I've caught almost ten trout, two of which fill my dinner sack. Heads rise and roll, and in the still parts of the river, it's almost like fishing a lake. I use a size 16 Adams until I run out, and then I switch to a small, dark-bodied Wulff pattern that does almost as well. The trout are sipping flies from the surface, lazy and slow, making slight, guttural sounds as they inhale. As the morning moves on, the fog sinks lower, and the Jefferson rolls out of the mist before me like a line drawing.

From this kind of boat, where the fisherman is the pilot, landing fish is as much the challenge as catching them. If I'm in the middle of a quick run when I hook into a fish, there's little I can do besides keep floating, dragging the fish with me. Today, I hook into a rainbow trout that darts upstream just as I am floating around a sharp turn. At one point, I can't see the end of my line, but the fish is still there, shaking and fighting for its life. By the time I'm able to land it, a couple of hundred yards downstream, the sixteen inch rainbow is exhausted. After I release it, it rests behind my leg; minutes pass before it finally kicks back into the current.

I take out near a secondary road. The fog has lifted, but the mountains are still covered. I stand with my thumb out for an hour before I have any luck.

Up 55, West on 90, North on 287. I find a camp on the west bank of the Missouri above Townsend. It's just after sunset and everything but the edge of the West is dark. I walk down to the river to gather wood. Whitefish rise in the shallows.

Back in camp, I season the trout with lemon juice, salt, pepper and chopped onion, and wrap them in tin foil to lay in the coals of the fire.

An old Mustang pulls into my campsite, circles once, and parks. Two high school kids—letterman's jackets, snoose cans, caps backwards—climb out and roll a couple of beer kegs out of the back seat. One of them turns up the car stereo, while the other one turns and notices my camp. He walks over, introduces himself politely and asks if I would mind their small party. Small? I eye the two kegs.

"Go right ahead," I tell them. They are pleased and return to tapping and icing their beer. Within an hour, there are a hundred people at my campsite. Car headlights face inward, and it's blinding to look anywhere but up or down. My campfire has become a bonfire, and my tent has somehow been elected as the place to go and smoke pot. A two-man tent, it's holding six, their silhouettes and shadows exposed every few seconds by the flick of a lighter. *Kids.*

Morning. I walk down to the water and see a hatch of pale morning duns on the surface. The fish are feeding, and I skip breakfast. Not thinking, I launch the boat into a swirling eddy and break into a sweat trying to kick out of it.

So close to its headwaters, this part of the Missouri is a trout river, and it's trout are telling. Heavy, thick and bright, they are bullish: heads like anvils. Hooked, the brown trout rush, dive and sit on the dark bottom, banging their heads back and forth; when they finally relent, you feel like you're lifting the entire bottom of the river. The rainbow trout try to tear the rod from your hand; they want to survive, and their feral instincts are almost intimidating. On the Missouri, a sixteen or seventeen-inch fish looks small, mostly because of what else lives in the deep holes of this river. You hear about these fish being caught at fifteen pounds or greater. In this boat, I wouldn't know what to do.

Floating the Missouri with half my body actually in the river, I think about the water I'm immersed in—this water that's traced itself through the Jefferson, the Madison and the Gallatin; and before that, the Big Hole, the Ruby, the Beaverhead, the Gibbon and the Firehole. The genetic lineage in the Missouri River is, as far as trout fishing is concerned, perfect: inimitable. No other river in the West is the product of such major and significant trout water. For a trout fisherman, the Missouri is the grand finale, the crescendo.

The morning produces action on small mayflies. The fish aren't rising much, but they're active and willing to take a fly within reach. It's not hot today, but with the sparse cover, it's easy to imagine the heat in the summer. Predictably, the dry flies thin out by noon and the afternoon is spent dragging streamers off the banks. The biggest fish of the day is a twenty-inch brown trout. I stop on an island to land it, but it runs, and I get back in my boat to follow it downstream. Eventually, I'm able to pull it into the shallows—it has a flaring yellow belly and a slight, dark blue cast around the edges of its gill plate.

Before dark, I take out near the highway above Deepdale and catch a ride in the back of another pickup truck. A hitchhiker is already back there, heading for Florida from Vancouver. It occurs to me that a better man would go with him and finish this story fishing for tarpon in the Keys.

South on 287, East on 90. It's been three days since I started, and for the first time, I feel tired. It's almost midnight when I arrive in Livingston. I want to fish the Yellowstone below town tomorrow, so I drive almost to Springdale and sleep on a small gravel pullout close to the river. Of the waters fished in this trip, the Yellowstone is the one I know best.

Early in the morning, there are large pale morning duns on the water as well as a very small, white mayfly. I fish the larger dun first, but to no avail, and switch to a size twenty comparadun. I stop on one corner, fishing my way up a section of riffles. Nothing happens until I cast into the top of the run, farther than I would have normally gone. I pull a good fish out, and then another; they seem to be stacked up in the teeth of the rapid, holding as if in formation. My eyes burn trying to see the tiny fly in the chop, and my time is spent watching for the flash of a fish rolling on the surface.

The next hour is sporadic, and I stop for lunch on a sandy island. The wind has slowly gained momentum all morning. In my boat, light and exposed, a strong, upstream Yellowstone breeze would make my trip nearly impossible. It isn't until I'm sitting under a cottonwood tree, watching the branches blow hard to the west, that I become fully aware of the burgeoning windstorm.

Back in the river, I turn around and begin to kick my way down-stream. My seat is enough to catch the wind, and I have to kick constantly to make any headway. In the slow parts of the river, the wind actually pushes me upstream. It's two steps forward and one step back.

The sun is almost down. The wind is a fall wind, cold and wet, and picks up dirt from the fields in sheets. In the increasing darkness, I crash hard against a boulder, convincing me to beach the boat and hike to the highway. It's dark, and I have trouble seeing barbed wire fences. I cross one fence and walk through somebody's hay field; I cross another fence and walk through somebody's herd of sheep. I reach a small state road, cracked and potholed, and start walking west, hoping for a ride. Four cars pass and don't stop, and I have to practically jump in front of the fifth to get them to stop.

It turns out, as I drive back to get my boat, that I was just a quarter mile short of the Grey Bear takeout. From there, I walk upstream for my boat and gear, hurrying a bit. I still want to reach the Bighorn tonight.

East on 90. After the Laurel exit, I run over a skunk. Billings comes and goes, and everything grows darker in its absence. There is a sign for an all night cafe at the next exit, and I am suddenly hungry. The cafe is just the bottom floor of a house, complete with couches and television. The only employee, a large, ruddy woman, is noticeably unsurprised when I walk in. She is the waitress, the cook and the cashier, and she tells me they do a fair amount of business, almost all of it at night. I order a sandwich, a large coffee and a piece of pie. We talk, but she never asks what I'm doing or where I'm going at that hour.

South on 47. Nothing moves in Hardin. There is no wind, and it seems like the town might have been still for years. I drive almost to Fort Smith and exit onto a fishing access road, and then up along a bad road that follows the river upstream. I can't sleep, and so I tie on the biggest streamer in my box and cast it from the bank. It's too dark to see the end of my rod. One fish grabs the fly on my second strip, but it dives and wraps the line around the bottom, and I break it off.

I've always thought of the Bighorn as a serious river. It emerges from the dam and immediately begins its slow trip north towards the Yel-lowstone, as if every mile was a dreaded one. The fish exude the same air, and their elusiveness seems to come not from their instinctive quickness but from a careful analysis of every fly they see. These fish are patient, al-most calculating: they think, they consider, and then they eat. Fooling them is no easy affair. Fishing wet-flies here is easier, but coming to the Bighorn to fish wet flies is a little like going to Beverly Hills to shop at K-Mart.

The best way to fish the Bighorn is to float it, stopping frequently to cast to rising pods of fish. You get one chance per fish, and if you screw it up, you might as well throw your fly at another one. The opportunity to catch large trout on dry-flies is as good as anywhere, spring creeks included, and that's what keeps people coming around every year.

The Bighorn sets your nerves on edge. It's not a relaxing day of fishing. You grit your teeth, you concentrate, you tighten every muscle in your body trying to get the fly to land softly, drag-free on the water; then the fish ignores you, and you cuss. I've sworn to quit fishing after a day on the Bighorn.

I put in around Three Mile. Throughout the day, I fish various dry-flies, everything from attractors to soft-hackles, creating some luck between frustrations. I try nymphs in the heat of the day, but with weed beds so long at this time of year, I spend more time cleaning algae off my fly than fishing with it.

The biggest fish of the day is a nineteen-inch rainbow trout caught unexpectedly, right before the takeout. I was floating an ant pattern along an unremarkable bank, only half-paying attention. The fly passed under a log and was sucked down in what I thought was the current. Then a fish jumped and ran straight at me as if it wanted to take a bite out of my leg. I noticed then that the fish had my fly in its mouth, and I manically began to grab at my line for some sort of control. It jumped three more times, and then dove, held and held, until it loosened and came. Who needs skill anyway?

It's late in the evening on a Friday, and I've been off the water for an hour. I should return to Bozeman in the morning, but, I don't kid myself: no self-respecting fisherman has ever woken up with the Bighorn ten feet from his ear and driven away from it. My problem does not end there, though. On the way home, I'll pass the Boulder River and the Yellowstone. Driving past these rivers without stopping to fish for a few hours, maybe a day…it wouldn't make sense. If nothing else, it's a question of looking at myself in the mirror.

I drive into Hardin. It's night now, and the town has come to life; traffic is pacing the streets and the bars are full. I step into The Branding Iron for a beer. A few later, I think that I could just as easily be in Dillon, beginning again.

Montana could afford a lifetime of these trips. It's at once frustrating and heartening. I want to fish it all, to see and fish and float every river. I want to know all of it.

Perhaps this is why we love our home water: because we do know it. We freeze with it and thaw with it, flood and dry with it. It's a friendship, albeit a one-sided one. But it doesn't stop us: We imagine the river cares for us, too, respects us for respecting it.

These fishing trips are necessary. They air us out a bit, widen our periphery, and, ultimately, make us want to go home again. They remind us why we chose our homes in the first place, the reasons for it. And so sitting on a barstool in Hardin, after five days of fishing new water, I'm thinking about fishing that corner above Livingston that I've fished a hundred times before, the one holding a handful of long brown trout I have begun to recognize.

RIDIN' WITH RAY

By Jon Jackson

IN, I GUESS IT WAS THE SUMMER OF 1972, Ray Carver suggested that he and I should drive to Iowa together. Ray was living in Cupertino, California, near Stanford, and wanted to come up to Montana for a few days before assuming a teaching job at the Writers Workshop, where I was starting my second year as a student. This was fine with me. I'd known Ray for a short time; we'd been introduced by Bill Kittredge, at whose house Ray would be staying. I was working up on the Blackfoot River on Dave and Annick Smith's house. Shortly after I heard about Ray's proposal, Dave and I had an unfortunate but not too serious falling out, so it seemed a good time to take off.

Ray was a tall, pudgy man with thick curly hair. He was a habitual smiler and chuckler, absolutely charming and a wonderful story teller. Everything seemed copasetic in Ray's world. He was also a severe alcoholic. In fact, Bill Kittredge told me after he'd first met Ray, at a conference in Seattle, "I like to drink and I know you like to drink, but I never met anyone who likes to drink as much as Carver likes to drink."

Ray arrived in Missoula driving a 1964 Falcon convertible. It was in decent shape, but he wasn't. I think he'd had a difficult summer coping with his wife and two kids. He was laughing, but it was clear that he was looking forward to teaching at Iowa while his family stayed in Cupertino. My situation was exactly the opposite: after a summer away from wife and daughter, I was going back to them as well as to Iowa—a textbook example of mixed feelings: I missed Ruth and Buzzy, but I hated to leave Montana.

When I got to Bill's, Ray was ready to ride. I spent at least one night there. I don't know if this was the time when Ray hurled chicken at Bill and me, at the Double Front Cafe, but it may have been. Anyway, the next morning we departed. I was considerably hung over and I'm sure Ray was. Since it was clear that I was going to drive, I told Ray that we could have no drinking while we were on the road. With great round eyes and a look of absolute innocence, he assured me that he agreed. He proudly

showed me, however, a handy little plastic drink caddy that he'd purchased. It sat on the seat between us.

I shook my head. "No, Ray, we've got to cool it." Nonetheless, he insisted that we stop at the Eastgate Lounge, on the way out of town, for
some essential supplies.

"Just ice and grapefruit juice," Ray claimed. The grapefruit juice
came in little six-ounce cans, and he bought two six-packs of them.

About fifteen miles down Interstate 90, he delved into the back seat
and brought out a half-gallon of vodka.

"We better just have a wee drinky, to kill this hangover," Ray said.
We had the top down on the convertible, and it was hot and dry in the
brilliant September sun. All my reservations went by the board. By the
time we bypassed Butte, two hours later, we were both fairly drunk.

This beautiful highway sweeps up and down the mountains for another hundred miles, and we stopped in Three Forks, the headwaters of
the Missouri River, to visit with our old pal Rick DeMarinis, who was
closing out the summer there. We had a couple of drinks with Rick at the
hotel, then raced on toward Billings, where I expected we'd get a hotel
room.

By the time we got to Billings I had already sobered up (perhaps one
could say, sobered down), but Ray was blissing out. We had been talking
more or less non-stop about life and literature, and Ray didn't want to
stop for dinner. He urged me to press on to Hardin. When we got to this
little town on the edge of the Crow reservation, Ray was disappointed
that there wasn't a Denny's or some other chain restaurant. He didn't
trust small town cafes. It was getting quite late by now, and I was hungry,
but I couldn't convince Ray that eating at the local "Eat" cafe was a good
idea. He insisted that we should drive on. I drove around the cafe in
Hardin a couple of times, hoping that he would capitulate.

It was after two in the morning when we reached Sheridan, Wyoming. We booked into the cowboy hotel without even being able to get a
drink in the local bars, not that we needed one. Nothing was open in
town. We went to bed on vendor machine crackers and peanuts, along
with a final drenching of vodka—straight now, all the juice long gone.

This was one of the great cowboy hotels in my experience. Neat and
clean. The beds were single beds, double mattresses, high and tight. The
heat in the room was steam radiator, and we needed it in the chilly mountain air. We were on the third floor.

About six o'clock, I woke up. The sun was just up, another bright
day and it was already starting to warm up. The steam heat was still hiss-

ing, however. My fingers felt like sausages and my head was pounding. My eyes felt like…well, they didn't feel like my eyes—more like a couple of gritty marbles.

I looked over at Ray, whose bed was next to the window. Ray was lying on his back on top of the bedspread, wearing only his Y-front briefs. His mouth was open and his tongue was visibly furry. His breathing sounded like low strangling. Moby Dick came to mind.

I got up and went to the sink. It was full of vomit. In the mirror my eyes looked like two bloody hen turds in a bowl of milk. I went out without waking Ray.

It was beautiful and cool on the streets of Sheridan at six o'clock. I walked down the street to the Stockman's Bar and Cafe. I ordered a shot of George Dickel sour mash bourbon, then a chilled schooner of Lucky Lager with tomato juice and hot sauce, then another shot of Dickel, then breakfast.

I was starving. I decided on the "Wrangler" breakfast, which featured a small sirloin steak, home fried potatoes with gravy, and two eggs over easy, with toast and jam and coffee. I was eating this and sipping coffee, alternated with red beer, and reading the Wyoming newspaper when the phone rang in the saloon. There was not one other person in this saloon. When the bartender called out, "Jon Jackson?" I was surprised, even a little alarmed.

Ray said, in a husky voice, "I feel like a hired killer."

"A hired killer, Ray?" I said.

"I'm looking down onto an empty western street and I don't know what town I'm in," Ray said.

"Well, you must know what town you're in," I said "because you just called me on the phone in the bar."

"I opened the yellow pages to 'Taverns,'" Ray said. I heard a noise; perhaps he was turning the phone book over. "Sheridan!" he said. "What happened to Hardin?"

"You called every bar until you got to the Stockman's?" I said. I took a sip of red beer.

"I called about three bars, then I saw the Stockman's and I knew you'd be there," Ray said.

"I'll wait for you," I said.

"Do you know," Ray said, "that when a cat dies, it is often just within hours of the wife, or husband, walking out?"

I had no idea what this meant and perhaps I've gotten it wrong. Maybe he said "if a cat dies." I thought it had something to do with the problems that men and women have living together. It was only later, when I'd actually been to Ray's home, in Cupertino, that I understood the true nature of his stories about the precariousness of domestic lives. But I didn't know enough about Ray, yet.

Later that same day we left a bar in Cheyenne on a dead run with two or three cowboys racing out onto the street shouting at us. I don't know what it was all about. We stayed in a huge hotel in North Platte, Nebraska. In the morning, Ray insisted on walking the bill at Howard Johnson's (he loved walking the bill in restaurants, I soon learned, which may account for his preference for these miserable chain outlets— Denny's, Sambo's, etc.—because they were large, busy and one didn't feel guilty about stiffing a huge corporation, I suppose.)

It was a blazing hot day on Interstate 80, cruising across Nebraska. We had put the top up on the convertible for the shade. There was no reason, or any likelihood, for sobriety so I tried to restrict myself to just an occasional vodka and grapefruit juice while Ray told me stories about his mentor, John Gardner, whom he'd known at Chico State, or rhapsodized about Isaac Babel or Chekhov.

About an hour down the freeway I noticed with some uneasiness that a highway patrol car had taken up position about two hundred yards back. My speed was all right. I thought I was driving carefully enough. I wondered if the restaurant in North Platte had notified the cops that we'd absconded without paying our bill. For some reason I didn't mention this cop to Ray. He seemed a little shaky, and I guess I felt that it wasn't worth mentioning. He wasn't waving a bottle around or anything, just occasionally sipping from a large plastic cup filled with innocent looking liquid and, anyway, the top was up, as a shade against the brutal sun. I guessed that the cop was just cruising and probably checking out the California license plates on this ratty old convertible. I hoped that they were current.

Then, all of a sudden, the cop car accelerated and sizzled past us. Ray literally whooped and threw his cup into the air in fright, spilling it over the front seat.

"Oh shit!" he yelled and began frantically sweeping ice cubes off his lap and trying to hide the half-gallon of vodka. It wouldn't fit under the seat, so he rammed it under some clothes in the back.

But the cop turned off a mile or so ahead and went streaking back westward, obviously in pursuit of someone else. "Thank God," Ray cried and almost immediately began building us fortifying refills after our close brush with the law.

I didn't tell him that the cop turned again, crossing the median and coming right back to take up station behind us, two hundred yards back. I had on very dark glasses and I was sure Ray couldn't see me constantly checking the speed and the rearview mirror. Ray soon settled and resumed his tales of literary gossip. To my unspeakable belief, the cop trailed us for only a few miles before drifting off at the next exit and I didn't see him again.

By the time we rolled into Iowa City that evening we were both completely drunk. I drove by the Iowa House, a campus residence for visiting professors and the like, where we dropped off his gear and checked him in; then we drove to my house where he met my family briefly and left with the car. My wife was happy to see me, as was my little daughter, after a summer away, and they didn't seem to mind my condition. I suppose they put it down to the rigorous drive.

About four o' clock that morning, however, I heard a noise on the stairs and my wife woke up. "There's someone in the house," she whispered, frightened.

"Jon? Jon?" said a voice, calling softly. I got up. It was Ray. I thought he must have gotten lost and had somehow found my house, but it turned out that it was more complicated. He had met an amiable young fellow at a bar that evening and the fellow was now sleeping in Ray's bed, at the Iowa House, and Ray wanted me to get rid of him. I urged Ray to go to sleep on my couch, but he wouldn't do it. "My typewriter, Jon. What if he steals my typewriter?"

I had to go back to the Iowa House with him. The young man in the bed turned out to be good looking and black. He was also fairly drunk and tired. He didn't want to leave. He said he was an actor and was leaving in the morning on a bus and he had to get some sleep. He said Ray had offered him a place to sleep. Ray said it wasn't true. Ray said he'd come back to the room and gotten ready for bed; then he'd remembered there was a vending machine down the hall and he wanted a carton of milk before bed, so he went to get it, in his pajamas, leaving the door open, and when he came back this guy was in his bed. Ray said he remembered him from the bar, but he hadn't offered him a room. Ray insisted that I throw him out.

I couldn't throw the guy out. It would require a kind of violence that I wasn't up to at the moment. I said we should call the campus police. Ray was against it, but when I threatened the visitor—whose name, I believe, was Rodney, or something like that—with the cops, he just huffed and rolled over to sleep. So I called the cops.

While we waited for the cops, Ray and I paced about the room in a surly way, and Rodney refused to pay any attention to our entreaties. Either he didn't believe that we'd actually called the cops or he really figured he was on safe legal grounds. The cops were young and old and they seemed to have difficulty fathoming the situation. In the course of their questioning of Ray and Rodney, two wildly conflicting stories that made any listener's mind reel, I looked down and noticed a jar of Vaseline next to the bed on which Rodney still reclined, looking rather fetching in his leopard-pattern briefs. I sauntered over casually and kicked the jar under the bed.

The older cop beckoned to me and we went out in the hall. "What the hell's going on?" he said.

"Well," I said, "Professor Carver wants this guy out of his room. I think he may have innocently, but drunkenly, offered the guy a place to sleep, but once they got up here, Professor Carver decided he didn't want him around...for reasons that probably only became apparent at the last moment. So...maybe it's unfair, but he wants him out. I'm sure he doesn't want to cause the young man any trouble," I added.

The cop understood. He went back in the room and said, "Rodney, get up. I'm gonna buy you breakfast and then you're gonna go to the bus station, to catch your bus."

And that was that. Ray never could quite recollect the sequence of events leading to the incident, but some time later, he conceded that maybe he had offered Rodney a place on his couch. "But he didn't want to sleep on the couch," Ray said. It seems that Ray may have ordered the guy out, but then he returned while Ray was down the hall at the vending machine. About the Vaseline...well, it wasn't Ray's, and it may have been its appearance from, say, Rodney's bag that precipitated his ejection.

A day or two later I met Ray in the hall of the English-Philosophy Building, and he invited me over to the Iowa House for a drink. We were chatting away amiably, sipping the usual vodka and grapefruit juice when there was a knock on the door. I answered it. A very pleasant little man in a tweed jacket, flannel trousers and penny loafers said, "Pardon me. I'm John Cheever." He held out a hotel glass. "Could I borrow some Scotch?"

"Ray," I said over my shoulder, "do you have any Scotch?"

Ray hurried forward, his lips and eyes all "o" with awe. "John Cheever," he said. "No, I'm so sorry. I don't have any Scotch. Would you like some vodka?" He hurried back to the dresser to retrieve the huge bottle of Smirnoff's. Mr. Cheever smiled sadly and deigned to join us in vodka. Straight. No ice, no grapefruit juice.

He was wonderfully urbane. He smoked a cigarette, I believe, and expressed his admiration of Ray's stories. He even seemed to know who I was, although I'm sure he didn't. Ray confessed his devotion to Cheever's stories. I tried to top him with a more erudite, witty appreciation, but I don't think Cheever bought it. In fact, I had met Cheever before. Tracy Kidder, Stuart Dybek and I had been instrumental in getting the Writers Workshop to hire Fred Exley, the semester before, and Exley had audaciously prevailed upon Cheever to come read at Iowa, after which he consented to return to teach a semester. So Exley had introduced us, briefly, but Cheever would not have recollected the meeting.

After another drink, Cheever said, "Where does one get Scotch around here? Is this a dry state?"

Oh no, we assured him. The Iowa State Liquor Store was fully stocked and had reasonable hours. If he liked, I volunteered, I'd be glad to take him to the store in the morning. It opened at nine. Should I stop by for him at, say, ten?

"What's wrong with nine?" Cheever said. "Or a quarter to?"

I picked John up at the curb of the Iowa House the next morning at 8:45. He was dressed in the Ivy League manner. A nice fall day in the Midwest. I was driving Ray's Falcon convertible. Ray didn't need it, and we were engaged in private negotiations about me purchasing it. I drove John to the liquor store, and once inside, I became entranced, as usual, with the spectacle of extraordinary wines that some over-zealous but well-informed state functionary had purchased for the stores. I bumped into John Irving, a very knowledgeable lover of German and Alsatian wines, Moselles too, who was greedily pondering the Spatleses. He gave me a brief discourse on the incredible value of the collection, then frowned and said, "What are you doing here so early?"

I told him about Cheever. John didn't know John, but he was eager to meet him. We went to look for him. He wasn't in the store. We went out to the car and there John sat, secure with a half-gallon of, I think, something as poor as Cutty Sark. When we approached the car he was actually having a hit from the jug. When he caught sight of us he embarrassedly lowered the bottle and the window, extending his hand to Irving. They admired one another's work.

In the car on the way back to the Iowa House, he gently reproached me for not having glasses in the car. I pointed out a package of plastic glasses that Ray had provided.

Sometime later I bought the car from Ray for fifty dollars. But Ray was never able to provide a title. My little daughter loved the car. She loved driving around Iowa City in a convertible. She liked John Cheever, too, and on at least one occasion, at one of those ur-Deutsch restaurants in Amana, John cheerfully and graciously tolerated her clambering about on him.

I believe it was in the same restaurant that one evening Ray came to grief with his walking the bill act. He had invited me to dinner at Amana—I think we went to see John O'Brien first, had a few drinks, then drove on. It was just Ray and me in this ersatz bier keller, eating quite a bit of gravy sodden kalbfleish. Finally, Ray says, "I'm going to the john. You wait five minutes, then you go to the john. I'll get our coats, in the meantime, and I'll be waiting out by the car." Now I understood why he wanted to park so far away from the restaurant.

I'd already endured a number of these "dinner bolts," as our friend Chuck Kindler called them. I hated them. It wasn't so much the dishonesty, the inanity and juvenility of walking the bill, but the unspoken assumption that I would be complicit in this act without being consulted; I mean, obviously he knew when he walked into the place that he wasn't going to pay, probably didn't have the money to pay, but yet he had invited me to dinner. Shortly after Ray left for the bathroom, I got up and walked up front, past the register. My coat was still hanging among others on a rack along the wall. I picked it up and went to the car. I drove back on a side street and parked a little ways above the restaurant. I could see the large parking lot. It was November or December. Cold and raw. A hefty woman in a dirndl came out and stood there, looking around. I was trying to spot Ray. Surely he had escaped. But where was he? I waited for a long time, then decided he must have been drunker than I'd thought. Perhaps he couldn't find the car, wandered down into the little town. I drove around the streets for awhile, looking for him. Finally, I cruised back past the restaurant.

Ray was waiting outside the restaurant, standing disconsolately in his overcoat. Fearful that he was simply a staked goat, I drifted past him and turned at the end of the block. In the mirror, I could see Ray glance around for a second or two, then set off in the opposite direction, toward the center of town.

I drove down to pick him up. He didn't reproach me for abandoning him. He apologized for having taken so long. It turned out that once he'd gotten to the john he'd had to take a shit. In his eyes I had prudently left in time. The repercussions were unpleasant, because he had taken his coat with him into the john (clearly he had not intended to give me any leeway at all, any more than I did him), and when he came out they grabbed him. He had no money. He gave them his address at Iowa House, and his position, and I'm almost certain that the bill was finally paid by the University of Iowa, with a scolding for Ray. At any rate, by the time we were halfway back to Iowa City we were laughing about it.

The following summer I drove the Falcon back to Montana. I was again living up on the Smith Ranch, up the Blackfoot, writing a novel. One day I drove the Falcon down to Bonner, to the Post Office. When I came down out of the P.O., a Missoula County Sheriff was parked behind the car. The cop beckoned me over. "Is this your car?" he asked.

"Yeah," I said.

"Do you have any registration?"

I didn't have any. I knew the California plates had long expired. But through great good luck this sheriff's deputy was my younger brother, Larry.

"Drive this car back up the Blackfoot," he advised, "and park it behind Annick's barn. I'm not sure, but I think it's probably stolen."

Later, the Smiths used the car as a horse feeder, dumping hay into its compartments. Eventually, the county came and hauled it away for junk.

HUNTING
AND
FISHING

IN A PERCH'S EYE

By Greg Keeler

TIME TO GET THE TIP UPS OUT OF THE GARAGE and replace the diminutive Mr. Twisters and Sassy Shads; time to tie on the Dicky Pearls and polish off the Swedish Pimples; time to string up some new line.

On Canyon Ferry, they let you fish six lines through the ice, so winter can be a real meat-fest, especially if you like perch. Vern Troxel does. Vern and I have haunted that first major reservoir on the Missouri near Townsend for about twenty years, ever since he first showed me how to pop a perch's eye from its head, poke it on a barb, and catch another perch with it. In the fifties, Vern moved to Townsend from Wisconsin for the logging. In Wisconsin, they know a lot about perch. Vern can wander out to a spot on a vast plane of ice, say "here," drill a hole, and catch perch until his styrofoam cooler cracks.

I've watched him closely to see what he does. There's a dance involved—having to do with the auger—where he takes his time drilling and stares off toward Mount Baldy while humming some obscure song from the fifties. There are also certain subtle movements, but since Vern is a small man and since his legs have been mangled so badly over the years by broken saw chains and fallen trees, the subtleties are hard to pick out from his normal stance. There is also the elixir of his home brew that adds communion to the dance with a dark rich flavor, a mood of color and temperature that seems distilled from an essence lying deep under the ice. Somewhere in this process he points his rod to a spot two and a half inches above the hole; then, as if charged by some small voltage below, his arm will go up, the wand will bend and he will add another fish to the flopping pile which has materialized beside him.

Sometimes, after the ice is thick enough to drive on, a pickup will pass and Vern will decipher the primitive code of its bellowing driver: "Vince says they're takin' hawgs near the dikes." This means we will soon be at the shallow end of the lake, lifting perch the size of acorn squash from three feet of water, building small bunkers around ourselves with their bodies. I'm always rather astounded that so many huge perch would rush to a single spot where they've just seen several colleagues jerked into oblivion. Vern just takes it as a matter of course as he heads and guts them with a couple of strokes of his knife, pops a few of their eyes out and baits up again.

At this point, squeamish readers may be flinching from the carnage, but I must beg your indulgence. There's a point. Perch taste good.

If there were a Norman Rockwell painting of a gawking, bug-eyed, flat-topped boy scarfing down fried fish, I would be that boy, and perch fillets would be that fish. A fellow from Fish and Game who lives down the street from me will drive straight home from the lake and single-handedly eat his whole catch in one evening. Vern goes into a Wisconsin lilt when he talks of preparing them for the table—flour dusted, beer-battered, blackened, broiled or boiled and buttered; close to but better than walleye. He'll fillet fifty to a hundred in a night, zipping the knife down the skin—as if he's conducting a little meat symphony, parceling out every flake of flesh like an expensive, illicit drug.

Sometimes Vern can't go with me and my perching trips devolve into tawdriness. The ritual dancing, singing and bellowing vanish and I'm left in an existential void. Instead of heading straight through a blizzard for the ice, sixty-five miles from Bozeman, I'll let the snow distract me and pull in at a truck stop in Belgrade. There I'll order "the brain eater," a combination of biscuits and gravy which resembles a chunky viscous fluid from an old science fiction movie of the same title.

When I arrive at the lake I'll let various local phenomena distract me from the ritual at hand. Instead of singing and staring at Mount Baldy, I'll watch snow-suited East Helenans whizzing across the ice on ATVs, pink-cheeked toddlers perched on their gas tanks, serving as windbreaks, while I drink Old Milwaukee tall boys. I will slip and hit my head on the ice so that the afternoon becomes an odd dream—not a nightmare, but more of a quandary: there used to be perch here. I saw them. Vern showed them to me.

I will imagine how, in Vern's presence, a cloud of perch the size and shape of a '56 Buick will pull up under his feet and debark through the hole before him. Without Vern, the Buick never arrives. By two or three o'clock, the "brain eater" and the tall boys will make me question whether the five perch I've caught are real or just reminiscences.

I will also enter a sort of surreal realm where perch are replaced by an Oriental dragon fish called ling or burbot, a fish designed to eat things larger than its head with a mouth that expands into an aquatic hoover, a hoover that vacuums up perch. Years ago, Vern used to describe ling as a vague possibility, something that lived in Clark Canyon Reservoir near Dillon and tasted like rattlesnake, something that could be caught at night with treble hooks buried in balls of dog food. But in recent years they have exponentialized in Canyon Ferry. Without Vern beside me, the ling creep up like gothic chimeras, chasing and eating all the prettier fish and then gulping the eye dangling on my Swedish Pimple so that I have to snake-ease them up through the hole and watch them vomit small schools of perch on the ice before me.

It seems that the less Vern is able to accompany me, the more the ling reproduce and diminish the perch. I've grown to view this conflict in terms of Star Wars with Vern as Yoda, the ling as Darth Vader and Vern's home brew as "the Force." When one of their horrid devil's heads breaches in the hole before me, I feel Vern materializing over my shoulder chanting, "Use the brew, Greg. Don't give in to the ling side." Thus, graphite light saber in one hand and dusky brown bottle in the other, I quaff the elixir and do battle with the forces of darkness.

MONTANA, MAGDALENA AND FRIENDS THAT FISH

By Stephen J. Bodio

> *"Hunting in your own back yard becomes*
> *with time, if you love hunting,*
> *less and less expeditionary."*
> — TOM MCGUANE

TOM'S BACK YARD, OF COURSE, IS THE BOULDER RIVER. Mine, for many years, was the vast, dry Big Empty of the Gila country in New Mexico. It's a magnificent, hairy chunk of land that ranges from about 4,000 feet above sea level to nearly 11,000 at its highest peak. The bottoms have a flora and fauna influenced by the Sierra Madre—vermilion fly catchers, red-faced warblers, Scott's orioles, javelina, walnuts, agave. The peak's inhabitants would be familiar to any Montanan—elk, mule deer, black bears, Steller's jays, ravens, Clarke's nutcrackers. If I picked my route, I could theoretically hike for 140 miles in one direction without crossing any pavement.

Living where the Rockies blend into the Sierra—or, if you prefer, where Montana meets Mexico—has abundant charms, but blue-ribbon trout water has never been one of them. I've always found it a bit odd that New Mexico's most famous fishery (about six hours from my little Magdalena rock house) is the tailwater of a dam. No matter how good the fishing is, I find it impossible to get excited about driving six hours to fish under a dam, with anglers standing side-by-side as far as I can see.

The Gila does have trout. High up in the cold, wet forests of Willow Creek, you step carefully. It's hard to believe that there are no grizzlies, but the last one was killed here in the late twenties. A smaller native remains—jewel-like Gila goldens, little, nearly extinct relatives of the cutthroat. They shouldn't be bothered. Lower down in the western drainages you begin to pick up other species. New Mexico writer Dutch Salmon has written eloquently of the Middle Gila River box, where you can catch big browns, smallmouth bass and channel cats on three consecutive casts of the same streamer.

But the Gila, four hours away on winding backwoods roads, is still too far away to count as home water. The tall mountains south of Magdalena have streams that run high in spring runoff, if the snowpack was decent, and again after the summer rains. All but one, several hours south, go completely dry in between, and even that one sinks into the desert and disappears. Real local fishing around Magdalena (other than one experiment fishing for big goldfish in a cattle tank, using a 4-weight Orvis rod—a little too silly and desperate) came to mean fishing in the Rio Grande.

Which was, in retrospect, a Good Thing. The years between 1979 and the present saw the rise of modern, high-tech, obsessive fly-fishing, not to mention the rise of fly-fishing as the chic pursuit for boomer-yuppies—a bloodless, expensive blood sport. With my New England background, cane rod, father's Hardy, and an impeccable tradition of brook trout, salters and striped bass, I might have become an insufferable snob. Fortunately (for many reasons other than fly-fishing) I was too poor to travel much for many years, and so had to learn how to be a local.

In fishing, being a local meant unlearning years of fancy fishing prejudice and learning that stalking monster catfish can be just as artful, nature-friendly and difficult as casting a perfect dry fly. I came to love the drowned jungles along the Big River's ditchbanks for their sounds and smells and sights and inhabitants, from eagles to herons to huge rattlers. I ate small catfish and returned the few very large ones to the river to grow even bigger. I read about catfish and carp in English magazines. I read Bozeman's own Greg Keeler and his "Ode to Rough Fish." I found that the carp would take a wet fly, and sometimes even a dry, and that they were as beautiful as Chinese paintings. Every so often I'd venture down to the Gila with Dutch or Omar, Magdalena's hardest-core trout fanatic, to chase trout. But now it was just another facet, not The Way.

And then five years ago I fell in love with a woman who lived in Montana, who was a life-long fly-fisher rather than a nouvelle purist. (She even knew what wet flies were!) I began commuting, for lack of a better word. I loved New Mexico, but I had been coming to Montana since 1971 (no, not for fishing) and knew I could enjoy time there. My work was portable, and Libby wasn't.

For the first few years, I didn't have much time to fish, nor was I in town for the best parts of the trout season. But this year, the expense and craziness of constant traveling overwhelmed us, and I decided to make my base in Bozeman, using Magdalena as a hideout and writing retreat. I looked forward to a rediscovery of trout.

I was not entirely naive about the last fifteen years' developments. Among my other laughably-titled "jobs," I review books for what I think is the best of the fly-fishing mags. But the transition from Magdalena to spitting distance from every famous trout stream in North America other than the Battenkill—I only exaggerate slightly—could be daunting.

Some of it was just fine. Two friends who were former guides, and patient, respectively, introduced me to float-fishing and the real art of the nymph, something I had never bothered with in New England. I have never been a remotely organized fisherman, and I have a childish delight in seeing a surface take. When they weren't taking on the surface, my father's tutelage in wets and streamers had usually sufficed. But now Larry had me making short casts upstream, watching a tiny orange float indicator, and catching fish that I didn't know were there. It was fun, as fishing is supposed to be.

Still, many other facets of Montana trout continued to bother me. Every kid in every fly shop knew, or pretended to know, more about everything than I ever wanted to clutter my head with. The number of anglers on the big rivers was almost scary. I am ashamed to admit that I felt a certain pressure to perform; being what one friend, facetiously I hope, called a semi-famous fishing writer made me feel that I should know more trivia than the kids in the shops, not less.

The low point might have been when I got in a discussion about fishing with two wealthy, fat, well-traveled businessmen who had just come back from a private spring creek. One of them first dismissed the micro-hatch matching there as "fairy fishing." But when his friend, an apparent employee, countered with a defense of tiny flies and long leaders, his boss immediately boasted to me that he had in fact caught and released fifty more fish than his companion had. Fifty? I went home depressed; this was no fun at all.

So what did I want? I decided I wanted several things, not necessarily all at the same time. First, I wanted to catch fish in places where I didn't have to be aware of other anglers. I wanted solitude so that I could be aware of the river, and maybe a bit so that I could practice my technique without strangers looking over my shoulder.

I wanted to, well, catch fish. I was not up to the expensive anality of matching hatches on private creeks; I didn't know if I ever would be.

And I wanted these places to become part of my home, to be places I visited over and over again. I even wanted to eat an occasional fish, something I'd best not admit in certain circles. In short, I wanted Montana trout fishing to be as enjoyable as the more elemental New Mexico version had become.

I am a peculiarly book-minded person despite the amount of time I spend outdoors, and it was two of this year's books that helped me start on a new road (and not incidentally reminded me, the jaded reviewer, that new things can be said in fish lit, too!) One was by a native Montanan who now lives near Boston, M.R. Montgomery. In *Many Rivers to Cross*, Monty goes on a pilgrimage in search of native trout. He is as tired of famous rivers as I am, and a lot funnier. He says: "The out-of-place rainbows and brook trout and brown trout are modern improvements in the land above the plains, on a par with ski lifts, interstate highway truck stops, restaurants with wine lists, and motels with cable television...Anytime it's hard to catch trout, you are not in the real West; you are on some river stocked with alien trout and freighted with eastern anglers who have taught the trout painful lessons and then put them back." He has advice, too; "...it doesn't matter whether you go looking for rare birds or odd trout or mountain lions. Choose your own grail and head uphill."

The other book is by Lewistown internist and mad sporting fanatic E. Donnall Thomas. (Don does some things even stranger than write or deliberately catch whitefish. He stalks mountain lions with a longbow. And eats them.) His book, *Whitefish Can't Jump*, is both lyrical and hilarious. Dr. Thomas has fished for salmon in Siberia and bonefish off Christmas Island; he's also pursued whitefish near Livingston, and devotes chapters to pike and even crappie. He sums up his philosophy in a passage that should be burned onto the walls of every fly shop in the world, not just in Montana: "It's time to lighten up. Fly-fishing (or any other outdoor activity) should never become an excuse to lose one's sense of wonder at the natural world. From mountain stream to ocean flats, water is the source of most of the world's great mysteries, from wayward flounder to Loch Ness monsters. There should be room in the curious fly-fishing heart for all of them."

Which is exactly how I feel. Next year will be my first full year in the state, and I have some plans. Libby knows the tiny local streams, the ones that run uphill, to the kind of places that Monty recommends. John Holt knows, I sometimes think, every backwoods pond in the state that is nearly impossible to bushwhack into.

Datus Proper, famed for his work on difficult spring-creek trout, hunts birds with me. He confides he likes the backwoods fish, too, "especially to eat." Better watch that admission, Datus. But then he has already admitted, in the pages of this magazine, that he fishes for carp. John

Barsness, my oldest Montana friend, is another carp fan. He and I are planning some carp safaris, and to travel to Fort Peck reservoir for pike. I suspect we may find some cats there, too. Flatheads should take a big, dark, soft-hackled fly, about the size of a small trout...

Hell, I've been invited to go fishing by my retired neighbor Neil, who brings fish back to keep in his eight-foot-deep backyard lily pond. He's a Montana native who uses bait. But when in Rome...

And one of these days, maybe I'll even get around to those number 22 drys on that spring creek. Montana, after all, is a pretty big back yard.

PROMISED LAND

By Charles F. Waterman

ON JULY 1, 1957, WE DROVE INTO MONTANA, parked our 1952 Oldsmobile, rented a furnished apartment for less than thirty dollars a month and went fishing. When we left that fall, I chiseled a little two-inch "W" on a round boulder near the Madison River—the only graffiti of my lifetime. I wasn't sure we'd be back. The initial was still there almost forty years later. Boulders don't wear away very fast.

Montana had the best trout fishing in the United States, Joe Brooks said. He said it in his living room in the Florida Keys, and when he spoke of Montana, it looked as if he might leave for there at any moment. But we were about as far away from Montana as we could get without a passport. Brooks, whose headstone overlooks the Yellowstone River, was a beloved angling missionary of Montana trout fishing and the best-known fly caster of his time. When we headed for Montana, he wrote us a two-page outline of people and places there. All Montana people and places were wonderful, he said.

At Dan Bailey's Fly Shop in Livingston, we learned the Yellowstone was muddy, but Dan said the Madison would be fine over at Ennis. He said something about a salmon fly hatch coming up, but to us, hatches meant little insects to be matched after a magnifying glass classification. That is not quite the way it goes with salmon flies.

We went to Ennis and moved into Bud Baker's Riverside Motel, then we went upstream a piece and began using dry flies on some eager rainbows that weren't very big. The other side of the river looked better, and I waded across, moving with the assurance of a heron because I had a brand new non-slip setup of carborundum chips stuck to my wader soles. We'd gotten the chips and stickum in Denver, along with some other fishing supplies, in the misguided attitude that Denver would be the place to prepare for Montana trout fishing. When I headed back across the Madison, my carborundum chips had worn off, and I had to swim through one really deep part. My wife Debie laughed raucously.

This is not merely a shopping note for people intending to wade on slippery rocks. I had forgotten a Leica in the back of my vest. The Leica repair genius in San Francisco did his best, but it wasn't much. We didn't have very many Leicas.

Somebody told us the salmon fly hatch was just a little upstream, and we jockeyed the Oldsmobile through a field of boulders near Cameron. When we approached the river, we noted the weeds and willows were bending over, but it was not a grasshopper plague. It was salmon flies. The peak of it lasted for four days, and we saw one other person as a distant silhouette. I guess he was a fisherman.

With a big salmon fly (that's really a stonefly) crouched on the rim of my sunglasses and another crawling across the back of my neck, I waded into fast Madison water and was glad to get downstream from a boulder higher than my head. We had two flies especially recommended for such an occasion—a Sofa Pillow and a Muddler Minnow. (Remember the Sofa Pillow because it's what holds this yarn together.) I made casts to the shoreline willows where most of the big flies seemed to be, and only an ambitious nine inch rainbow charged the squirrel hair and fuzz. Then, wondering if this salmon fly thing was what it was cracked up to be, I made a long cast to near the river's middle, reaching a relatively smooth spot bordered by boiling currents with jutting rocks. There was a glug I imagined I could hear over the river's roar, and I headed for shore, following a 3-pound brown trout. After I reached dry ground, I chased along the bank and won somewhere downstream in a tiny backwater. For days, we called that shoreline "Stumble Alley."

Our best fish were out in the middle, ignoring the rule that they should be against the deeper banks where the flies congregated. A lot of them, mostly browns, weighed around three pounds.

That night in the motel, Debie announced that the fish were prepared to strike anything they could whip, and that she was going to tie a super-fly she could see in foam, rapids and river splatter.

"It doesn't need to look like a salmon fly," Debie said. "It needs to look bigger and better for a fish that is making a pig of himself."

Her fly began with a Sofa Pillow and grew from there with a big, fuzzy silhouette. It caught a lot of big trout, but we never quite made the mark needed for the Dan Bailey Wall of Fame (4-pound stream trout on a fly), which was a consuming passion at the time. We missed it by a couple of ounces once and by one ounce another time. We called Debie's production the Haystack Fly, and I sold the story to *Outdoor Life*, although the editor asked me if all this really happened or if we had just whomped up a gimmick. The fish sounded too big, and he never did quite trust me.

It developed that there had been a Haystack Fly (completely different in appearance) built by someone else somewhere else at another time, so we apologized, but much later there were tackle shops advertising the "Madison River Haystack."

Debie always said she made it by releasing the squirrel and keeping the hair, but a man with a tweed jacket and English waders (a social statement of the time) did not smile.

I have two stories I have worn out, but they are completely true and they define our early Montana years. I asked a filling station operator in Clyde Park if it was true there were mountain goats in the Crazy Mountains. He said there were, but we'd need horses to get where we could see them. When I laughed that we were a little short on horses, he said we could use his, no charge, and that we could use his stock truck to haul them for free. All of this happened while he filled our gas tank and wiped our windshield.

And on our second year—that would be 1958—a filling station man in Bozeman looked over our GM Carryall (by then, we were prepared for the back-country) and invited us to elk hunt with him from his camp on Freezeout Mountain—no charge. He invited us while he filled our gas tank, and it was the only time he had seen us. He said his camp was a pretty comfortable layout.

In the fifties, trout anglers from other parts of the country seemed to come to Montana primarily for *big* trout in *big* rivers, and they began to use big rods that could throw big flies into big water, especially in the late fall when the browns were spawning. Even the native anglers weren't quite ready for that approach, and fly-fishing a river the size of the Missouri or Yellowstone the way Joe Brooks did, with big streamers and the same rod he might use for bonefish, didn't quite fit the traditional pattern.

Jason Lucas, world-famous and for many years representing *Sports Afield* as fishing editor, sought some of the smaller creeks. The Yellowstone, for example, he explained, was too big for fly-fishing, and he used other tackle there. At the same time, eager fly casters trying to make the Bailey Wall of Fame stood deep in heavy water and recorded their longest casts, using Atlantic salmon tackle.

The Wall of Fame was a curse to me, for I was the wretch who missed it for years, long after my wife had a fish there, the first woman to make it with a stream trout. Other fishermen comforted me with their hands on my shoulder, and strangers watched me furtively in lunchrooms. After all, my wife had tied the accursed Haystack Fly.

When we first fished Montana in the fall, no one was using what was to become the "shooting head," although the rods were powerful. The Woolly Worm, not yet dignified by the name "nymph," was a great standby of the native anglers, generally fished along the edges on the big rivers. Joe Brooks stood on a high bank, looked down at some "flop casting" of small flies and shook his head in sympathy. "The good fish are out in the big water," he said. "Those people don't know what fall fishing is!"

He and others of the long-line clan were happiest with cloudy days, late evenings and fall chill. The boom of a big game rifle far up a river valley went with the territory.

For the long throws, the favorite had become the burr-headed Muddler Minnow and its variations, even though it wasn't a Montana invention. Young John Bailey, son of Dan Bailey, was a tow-headed grade-schooler with a crew cut, and his mother laughingly called him "Muddler," but he doesn't remember it.

The Spruce Fly was another big winner in the early big-fish chasing, with most of the outsized flies worked at mid-depth. Then came huge nymphs, generally dark-colored specters. I recall the late Ray Donnersberger was a master with them, working the very bottom. Even more than the Sofa Pillow, some of those creepy-crawly things looked as if they should be stepped on.

In the sixties, big-streamer throwing may have reached some kind of peak, and big-trout chasers had their own underground of information. Most famous of all, I suppose, was the Beaver Creek pool on the Missouri, not far from Helena, where we stood in pushy, cold water and watched for that magic moment when mountain shadow would reach it on chilly October evenings. My Wall Fish curse evaporated immediately, and I double-hauled earnestly in hope of a 10-pounder, which I didn't miss by far. Everybody caught big fish.

Tourist anglers began to be counted, and fisheries management brought violent disagreement. For a time, there were the foot-long rainbows dumped at bridges by hatchery trucks, fish that would strike on every cast. "Tourist fish" were what we needed, promoters insisted. When the numbers of serious trout followers began to be counted, it was an unpleasant shock for the hatchery lover to learn that introduced fish were actually harmful in the long run.

We once made a movie of the hatchery rainbows striking on every cast. We learned that one foot-long rainbow striking a photogenic Royal Wulff is very similar to the next foot-long rainbow striking a Royal Wulff. We junked the film, and I don't even know what became of the camera. Movies weren't our game anyway.

The running skirmishes over river dams were with us from the time we first splashed into the Madison. What we've called "underground tourism" came into the open when the perennial plans for damming the Yellowstone reached a high point. Aside from other effects, big-water recreation with big boats and yachting caps has long appealed to promoters in inland states. The "underground tourists" were serious trout anglers who spent much of the year in the state, hardly noticed among the other residents, but at the threat of a dam on one of their favorite rivers, they helped fill the auditoriums.

The pro-dam people had their reasons, and some of them were outspoken. Here we bring in Joe Brooks again, in what became a rather unusual but effective appearance. Brooks, the one "tourist" well-known and much-liked by natives, was speaking of the values of free-running trout water. I guess he made his case a little too strong for one youthful dam promoter, who probably didn't know him at all. When Brooks mentioned the cash-spending visitors attracted by trout, his critic spoke up. "Go home! We don't need ya!" he yelled.

There was an embarrassed hush, followed by excited mumblings. "That did it!" said the man next to me. "That hothead wrecked the dam for the time being! Montana has better manners than that!"

There had always been the truly scientific anglers with their little flies and nymphs and their true love for small and "technical" streams. Many of them had been the same people who threw big streamers across big rivers, but they'd had no problem getting access to places like Armstrong's Spring Creek. Suddenly, there were a great many of them, reading and writing of technical angling and learning more about insects than most professional entomologists. The result was paid fishing in some cases, a condition reached after all sorts of temporary arrangements by Trout Unlimited and stream owners. And while many natives refused to fish in such waters, it was paid angling that saved most of them, and actually allowed them to improve.

"The trouble with Armstrong Creek," said Dan Bailey when I first met him, "is that the hatch always runs from 10 a.m. to 2 p.m., and is always matched by a number 16 Light Cahill."

That has indeed changed as have many other things about the "technical" streams. But then, I saw only two or three parties drifting Montana rivers the first year we were here. With each new party, came a new view of the place, and soon it belonged to so many others.

SEEING THE PRAIRIE

By E. Donnall Thomas, Jr.

WHEN I FIRST CAME INTO THIS COUNTRY to stay twenty-five years ago, we drove south out of Canada after a two day non-stop run from Montreal where I had just finished a medical internship. We had been on the road all night—Susan and I in our old Landcruiser, Dick and Annie in their truck behind us—and by the time we had crossed the border into northeastern Montana, we were all flush with the feeling of a new country and the exuberance that escape from any form of confinement implies. Then the sun began to rise behind us, and, with the light at our backs, we could look forward into a new definition of emptiness. It is simply impossible to record those first impressions except by virtue of what was not there: towns, traffic, vertical terrain; the hurly-burly of life as almost everyone of us knows it. The sense of isolation was so complete that I felt as if I could lie down and go to sleep in the middle of the road in total safety.

Despite the regard for wild places that all of us shared, a general sinking of the spirits swept through both vehicles as the dawn let us appreciate the extent of our sudden isolation, the magnitude of the nothingness we had entered. We sped on across the open landscape searching for something in which to ground the senses—a hill, perhaps, or a tree—but there was only more sagebrush and more grass, and finally more sky than any of us could ever remember seeing before. By the time the new morning light had burned the shadows out of the road, I knew that I had to stop and get out and look, and I did. None of it was any easier face to face. We can do this, I said to Susan. We can do this. Then we drove on down the road to our new home and did it.

We went on to learn all kinds of things in the year that followed, about subject matter as diverse as our marriages, our professions and ourselves. That's not unusual, I've subsequently learned; one of the prairie's favorite tricks is to foster a rich sense of introspection among its inhabitants. None of the year's lessons, however, were any more striking than our new environment's resounding contradiction of our own first impressions. The apparent emptiness that left us stunned upon arrival was an illusion born of our own false expectations. Needless to say, the mistake was ours rather than the prairie's.

The varied natural history we discovered all around us really should have come as no surprise. Savannah habitat is the richest in the world, and the combination of temperate climate and wide open spaces is responsible for the genesis of a remarkable number of the world's vertebrate species, including, for better or for worse, our own. The grasslands and broken coulees of eastern Montana are no exception to this pattern of biodiversity. The prairie's charms are no less real for being less than obvious. Out here, it just takes people awhile to see what lies around them, and, consequently, many never do. I suppose that's what we get for living in an age of easy gratification.

But *why* don't we see? What is it about this country that makes people hurry right on by with their eyes fixed straight ahead like urban commuters trying to ignore a homeless panhandler on the street? The answer to this question will probably tell us all kinds of things about ourselves, but before we pursue it, I would suggest that we take a look at what there is out here to miss.

Dawn is always the prairie's finest hour. The flat, clear light rising in the east emphasizes the country's subtle texture, and, on the best mornings, the sunrise stretches far enough away along the horizon to suggest the essential curvature of the earth. There are no intrusions here. The nearest town is twenty-five miles away, and even though it is the county seat, an outfielder with a good arm could throw a baseball from one end of it to the other. What is really absent here is people; what we see and hear and smell this morning is what we have left behind. It is shocking to realize that our greatest accomplishment as a species may be to escape all traces of ourselves, but if that realization is what it takes, so be it.

It is early May. I am curled up inside a crude blind made of sagebrush and camouflage netting. A tripod and a camera with a 300 mm lens rest between my knees. I discovered this sage hen lek several years ago when I was living out of the back of my truck during the course of a divorce. The birds' joyous appearance suggested the possibility of renewal at a time when I badly needed to be reminded of that possibility. I've come back here every spring since then, and I have yet to be disappointed.

As usual though, there is apprehension at first light; the sagebrush seems so barren, the anticipated event so unlikely. But suddenly the players begin to materialize as if by magic, heavy, gallinaceous birds whose plumage so perfectly matches the terrain that it is obvious no one would ever see them unless the birds chose to be seen. Then a low, booming woodwind note sounds somewhere behind the blind, and the dance begins. As always, the experience is so dramatic that I cannot begin to think about the camera and its technical demands until I have absorbed some of the sights and sounds around me.

Boreal game bird species—ruffed grouse, for example—depend predominantly on auditory cues to advertise themselves during mating season. Because of the open terrain they inhabit, all prairie grouse offer a striking visual display to supplement the sound effects during their springtime rituals, and none is more spectacular than the sage hens'. Viewed from a distance, this assembly of sixty males would look like a handful of cotton balls blowing about in an erratic wind, a phenomenon that is visible for miles. The white spots represent the under-plumage of the males' inflated throat sacs; the somewhat hysterical sense of motion derives from their up-and-down rhythm as each cock dances to the beat of an unseen drummer.

But that is all impressionism. The reward for getting up early and crawling into the blind before sunrise is an appreciation of the details: the splendid yellow of the naked throat sacs glowing in the morning light, the delicate coif of black hackles on top of the nearest cock's head, the fearful symmetry of the displayed tails, with every feather groomed to a perfect point. This is choreography, not an accident; an event as crisp and precise as a production by the Bolshoi Ballet. The functional view is that there is nothing going on here but the propagation of the species, but, even as a naturalist, I'm skeptical. The simple manufacture of sage hens shouldn't have to be so involved, so intricate, so beautiful.

The light rising behind me climbs at a measured pace toward the necessary f-stop, but by the time it reaches the critical level, the birds are already losing interest in their own performance. I snap a few quick frames, and then it is over, for reasons known only to the sage hens. The cocks stop dancing, the inflated throat sacs disappear, and the roar of wings fills the air and subsides, leaving me alone once again in the middle of the empty prairie with nothing objective to show for my trouble but a few exposures that will never do me any good. No doubt there is a lesson here about the futility of trying to capture and possess what should be left alone, but I am beyond all that by this time.

What matters now is this: the prairie looks barren once again, but I am fortunate enough to know better.

To some degree, all remote country is destined to be defined by its earliest chroniclers, in which respect the plains of eastern Montana really couldn't have done much better for themselves if they had tried. The trained eyes of Lewis and Clark saw what few have seen with equal clarity in the nearly two centuries since their original Voyage of Discovery. Even though they came from the unspoiled, pre-industrial version of the eastern seaboard, they were clearly astounded by the natural bounty they encountered, and the most remarkable element of their journals may be just how little they missed.

The waves of entrepreneurial pioneers who followed were driven by the material promise of furs, gold and business, most of which lay in wait on the distant Pacific coast. Those are the sort of concerns that introduce the element of time into the algebra of travel, and as soon as that happened, the prairie became, above all else, an inconvenience, a vast source of tedium eating away relentlessly at human spirits and the bottom line. I suspect that this is how we first developed the insidious cultural notion that the midsection of America is something of an embarrassment, an ordeal intended to make us suck up our guts and get on to the good stuff as expeditiously as possible. That bias persists to this day, and it helps explain the uneasiness my friends and I felt when we stopped beside that lonely road and asked just what the hell we had got ourselves into.

For nearly a century after Lewis and Clark's original exploration, eastern Montana remained largely unsettled. Then a combination of forces made the prairie impossible to ignore any longer: new waves of immigrants with agrarian backgrounds needing somewhere to go; the development of hardy strains of wheat suitable to the prairie's harsh winters; a worldwide shortage of grain brought about by the First World War; and some world-class false advertising by railroad interests that realized what an economic boon a settled prairie would mean to them. The homesteaders' view of the prairie was a functional one: they saw what they needed to see to keep themselves alive. In the end, that wasn't enough for many of them, but at least they tried.

In fact, much of what we expect to find appealing about the outdoors is culturally determined, a simple fact that has never served the prairie well in the public relations department. There is no intrinsic reason why pine trees should be prettier than sagebrush, or mountain peaks more inspiring than badlands and coulees, although most visitors to this state certainly seem to think so. And why not? A generation's worth of coffee table picture books and unimaginative writers have enforced this idea so relentlessly that most of us have unwittingly come to believe it.

In this visually oriented age, much of the prairie's emotional distance derives from the difficulties it causes the photographer. There's nothing wrong with the light out here, but the overreaching sky often allows nothing but a brief window of expression at the edges of the day. What comes in between is often served harshly. And the country doesn't offer much of itself through the viewfinder either. The flat terrain out here seems to be lying down all the time, like a pouting model. No wonder the prairie has so much trouble competing with the western half of the state in the public imagination.

The fact is that we come programmed to believe in looking up for our inspiration. The mountains and the trees, whose absence from the prairie so many observers lament, appeal to the same instinct as the church steeple. They draw our attention upwards, where western cultural influences from Michelangelo to Christopher Wren have insisted that God resides.

Leave it to the prairie to remind us of the limitations of that point of view.

It is February, and I am hunting coyotes. The coulee's rim winds back and forth in front of me until it disappears in an amorphous white sea of clouds and snow. There is no horizon today, and it is impossible to tell where the world ends and the sky begins. If I were the last person alive on earth, I could not feel any more alone.

Today the coyotes are more an excuse than a quarry. If it were really important that I kill one, I would be carrying the .243, but I've got the longbow with me instead. Every half mile or so, I ease my way out to the edge of the coulee, set up behind a bush, and cry like a dying rabbit. The noise is so ridiculous that it's hard to keep from laughing. That's one reason why I do my coyote calling in remote places: there is hardly any chance that anyone I know will ever see or hear me.

All right, I'm not here for the coyotes. I'm here for the exercise and the feel of the weather against my face and the release from the tedium of cabin fever. I'm here to remind myself where I live and why. You can fall for any place on earth when the going is easy. Belonging requires that you feel at home during the hard times, and out here that means winter. The easy thing to do is to run away from it like the tourists and the songbirds, but once you've ruled out that option you either learn to embrace the winter or you go mad. And coyote calling is more than an embrace, it's total immersion.

Today, the absolute lack of color is even more striking than the lone-
liness. The landscape stretching away into the distance looks like the
background for an old black and white movie. Figure-ground relation-
ships are hopelessly distorted by the snow. A raptor appears below me,
riding a wind current through the maze of twisted terrain, and I reach out
to grab it like a bug before I realize it is a hundred yards away. Across the
coulee, stunted junipers materialize like darkened ghosts, defying the
eyes to make sense of them. This is getting spooky. It's time to call one last
time and go home.

I hike across to the next point, crawl out to a pathetic windblown
bush that will have to pass for cover, and call down into the yawning gap
in the earth before me. Nothing moves, but that doesn't matter; nothing
has moved all day. There are so few distractions here. I settle in and wait,
and finally I see.

A bow's length away lies the dynamic imprint of a bird's two wings,
each primary recorded perfectly in the snow's powdered texture. There
are no footprints. Whatever made these marks came by air intent on landing but changed its mind at the last instant, leaving this simple record of
its indecision before it climbed back up into the sky and disappeared. I
pride myself in my tracking ability, but this is uncharted territory and I
have no idea what species of bird left these wingprints. On the basis of
size alone I guess the visitor might have been a magpie, but that is only
speculation. The amazing thing is the utter delicacy of the impression, the
certain capture of the detail left by every feather. This is just the sort of
thing an inquisitive person should be willing to walk a few cold miles to
see.

Which is why there are no regrets when the coyotes once again
refuse to be bamboozled by my predator calling. They're all just excuses
in the end, the coyotes and the pheasants and the elk and the trout, excuses to be where others cannot invent reasons to go. And that is how you
learn to see the prairie in the end: by looking for it.

MOVING TO MONTANA

By Stephen J. Bodio

MY FIRST SIGHT OF MONTANA was through the window of a Greyhound bus.

It was 1971. I was, incredibly, divorced, though barely old enough to vote. I was headed on impulse to Washington state, to hang out with an old friend in the biology department at Pullman. There were practical aspects to that visit that have no place here, but I had another agenda, hidden even to myself except at the edge of sleep. Montana, even then, looked to be a place were I could invent myself out of a handful of contradictory fascinations I could not resolve in Massachusetts.

For instance, I was in many ways a conventional rebel of those times: hair past my shoulders, a taste for illegal substances and rock and roll, and a devotion to Jack Kerouac and Ken Kesey and Richard Brautigan.

But I also loved fishing and hunting with an unholy passion, despite the disapproval of my friends in Cambridge and Boston. I loved all of it, all the time, with a fire that burned hotter then than it ever can again. In the summer, I crawled up streams under thick alder tangles just to hold, for a moment, five-inch native brook trout with colors better than any trout ever painted. I froze on winter sand bars within earshot of the surf for a chance at scoters, shooting an Iver Johnson double so worn that it doubled about every third shot; I haunted cemeteries and golf courses for rabbits and gray squirrels with my faithful redtail; I cast immense, awkward eelskin rigs from eleven-foot, revolving spool surf-casting rods into the Cape Cod canal, trying for the last of the big cow stripers.

Deer hunting meant taking a stand in cedar swamps where visibility might be only fifty feet. Rifles weren't allowed; my deer gun was a humpbacked Browning autoloader I still own, a "sweet sixteen" loaded with slugs ahead of buckshot. I used the same gun for grouse in even denser cover; it was choked too tight, but it was what I had. I remember the astonishment in the eyes of two proper Yankees who toted a Parker and what I now think was a Purdey when I emerged from their covert in blue jeans and a denim shirt, my long hair held back with a blue and white bandanna and that evil gun over my arm. They were polite, but I suspect I embodied their nightmares.

I had other dreams. Ernest Thompson Seton had fed my childhood on Lobo and the Pacing Mustang and various western dogs, on the tale of the jackrabbit he called the Little Warrior. Even as I wept over the fate of his heroes (most Seton protagonists die miserable deaths), I was also devouring hunting stories by Russell Annabel and Elmer Keith, Ernest Hemingway and Jack O'Connor. I knew there were other ways to do things. There were trout out there more than sixteen inches long, in rivers where you could cast without hitting a tree with your rod. Deer and antelope stood belly-deep in sage (whatever that was); you had to be careful not to silhouette yourself on the skyline. You shot a .270, of course, a pre-'64 Winchester Model 70 with a classic stock.

There were more contemporary temptations, as well. western falconers were alleged to be training Arctic gyrfalcons to attack mighty sage grouse on the plains of Wyoming and Montana. There were stories about Jim Weaver, a falconry legend even before he ran the Peregrine recovery project at Cornell, walking into the Charles M. Russell with a gyrfalcon on his fist, a daypack, a bedroll, matches and a German shorthair, to appear a week later as well-fed and rested as an active falconer could be.

And, the grapevine had it, there were strange activities near Livingston. A bunch of young sportsmen as crazy as I was were camped there, writing and drinking and talking and helling around, fishing and shooting birds and dreaming big dreams. It seemed there might be a place for me in the West, where you could be young and wild but also a gentleman of literature, where you could appreciate a Parker and an Adams, a 7x57 and a Leonard rod, not to mention both Turgenev and Edward Abbey.

I didn't find any of this on my first trip; I was too distracted to make new friends in any case. My moods ran more to solitary drinking and chain-smoking unfiltered Camels. What I found was something more important: the sheer physical and sensory impact of the West. Our first stop, somewhere east of Miles City, was before dawn. As a shaft of light pierced a black horizon bigger than the ocean, I felt my lungs expand for what felt like the first time in months, then relax. Tears sprang to my eyes; I felt that the world was bigger than I ever realized back in New England. I turned to see a juniper and a white-faced steer glowing in the impossibly clear air. A magpie leaped from the tree and started the world again, trailing its shining ribbon of tail, and I knew with absolute certainty I'd be back.

Other epiphanies were to come. My first sight of real mountains (forget forever New England's hills) lit at the top like icebergs, with a light that I had never seen before but that I would remember with a sort of Proustian flood of senses twenty-five years later in front of a little Bierstadt in the Nygard Gallery in Bozeman. A brilliant cinnamon teal drake curving to drop into a pond near Butte. A herd of whitetailed deer feeding out into a meadow west of Billings at dusk. (I doubt I ever saw one that far from a tree in Massachusetts.) They all confirmed my first decision, which became "west," but not Montana.

Ten years after my first sight and decision found me in the Gila-Mogollon country of New Mexico, one of my childhood realms of escape, writing for a living. Some of those Livingston-ites became long-distance friends in the way writers do, mostly by mail, as did some of those falconers. All of us were writing about the West and sport and other passions, living lives we had fantasized when we were kids reading the magazines and books that formed us more than our parents did.

And then my partner Betsy died. My life turned to chaos. After a year of roaming and drinking and attempting to bring some kind of order to my life, I wrote the story of our New Mexico home, our birds and dogs and hunting, our life, her death. The New York publisher who commissioned it got cold feet, feeling the book was too odd and too western, and I feared I was going down the drain. In a last desperate act I asked Jamie Harrison, then working for Russell Chatham's brand-new Clark City Press, if she might show the manuscript to her father, Jim Harrison, who might tell me if it was worth a damn. I thought Clark City was to be a fine-art press for Russ, and was shocked when she called back a week later with a generous offer that included the painting which now graces the cover of that book, *Querencia.*

Montana, and Montana sport, became a door back into sanity for the second time. Russ Chatham lent me a Suburban when I flew up, a suite at the Murray, a shotgun, sometimes the whole house at Deep Creek. There were ruffed grouse in the willows in little drainages that led up into the Absarokas, blue grouse in the willows in little drainages that led up north toward the Crazies, brook trout as brilliant as the ones of my youth (but three times bigger) in a little pond somewhere up above Chico.

Russ introduced me to a woman he knew, a widow, a professional cook and a mail-order executive, who could drop a cast of wet flies exactly where she wanted, who knew where the wild ("not yuppie") trout were. For my part, I taught her about bird hunting and falconry, and bought her a lady's gun from another Montana writer. I began to commute, if driving every few months between houses twelve hundred miles apart can be called commuting. I vacillated between twenty-eight bore quail guns and big twelves for sage birds, settling on a little English side-by-side sixteen. We learned how to be together in both places.

This month, September, Libby Frishman and I are marrying, in the little Episcopal church in Bozeman, marrying each other and joining our two communities. In a sense, we're marrying two states, two states of mind, two sets of friends, two still-magnificent ecosystems. The separate pulls and sports, of New Mexico and Montana, might be the subject of another column, but that's for later. Right now, we're headed south. We'll be back in November. Montana, if not just Montana, feels like home.

TED TRUEBLOOD

By Russell Chatham

WHEN I FIRST ENCOUNTERED the name Ted Trueblood, the name itself—unusual, theatrical even, especially in context—suggested
reliability. In those days there was a popular men's adventure magazine
called *True*. It was not a fishing and hunting magazine, but each issue
usually carried a story or two about one or the other. Many were by Trueblood. Trueblood tells the truth in *True*.

To be an outdoor writer in those days, it was also necessary to be
a photographer. A story about muskie fishing in Leech Lake would necessarily feature a dozen pictures of various aspects of the trip, not the
least of which would be the writer holding up his biggest dead muskie.
Trueblood's articles with their requisite illustrations never seemed to picture the author. Twelve or thirteen years old at the time, eyes and ears
peeled for possible stuff of mythology, my friends and I talked about
whether or not there actually was a Ted Trueblood, or whether the name
was dreamed up by someone at *True* just because it sounded good.

Then one day he arrived at the Russian River just north of San Francisco. We never actually saw him, but word had it that he was shad
fishing, which was what we were learning to do. And he was fishing with
all the local experts, people like world casting champions Myron Gregory and Jon Tarantino, Doug Merrick from the Winston Rod Company and
Bill Schaadt, who, even in 1952 was already a legend based on his inten-
sity and consummate skill.

The following spring, Trueblood published his story, and it was
about Schaadt the man, and shad the fish, both pronounced exactly the
same. There were pictures of fishermen wading in the Fife Creek pool,
shots of jumping shad, of Bill casting. But again, not a glimpse of the author. I was sufficiently convinced the man now existed, but I wanted to
see what he looked like.

A few years later, we had the first of what was to become a succes-
sion of dry years in California, a phenomenon which created a new wave
of dam building in the state, including the one which doomed the Russ-

194

ian. It was the winter of 1955, and all through the fall and into the winter it didn't rain. The steelhead came in, starting much earlier than normal. On my birthday, October 27, the day I got my first driver's license, I left home before dawn, arriving in my first car at Duncan Mills shortly after dawn hoping to find a grilse or two in the riffle above the bridge. Instead, I found the river loaded with big steelhead. Although I hooked several, they tore me to pieces, and I never even came close to catching one.

At that time, there was a character around the Bay area who started the first *Fishing News*, a weekly tabloid. He also had a short radio program on which he would announce in the staccato style of Walter Winchell where all the various fish were biting. His name was Al Accardi, and he billed himself as "The Fishfinder."

I was still in high school, so I could only get to the river on weekends. On one of his midweek shows, he was raving on about the thousands of steelhead fishermen were catching. We knew for a fact that some hardcore locals like our neighbor Earl Crawford, known on the river as "The Snake," were catching three or four limits a day on flies, a limit being three fish. And Earl wasn't even a fly-fisherman. Accardi went on at length about how Bill Schaadt had one on almost continuously from dawn until dark, day after day. He added that the fishing was so hot that it had brought Ted Trueblood out from his home in Idaho to fish with Bill.

On Friday night, I left for the river as usual, only this time my anticipation was fueled by the fact that the next day I was going to see Ted Trueblood with my own eyes.

In the morning, I drove into the secret little road to the north of Watson's Log Hole where Schaadt's 1937 Dodge was already hidden in the trees. I waded the riffle and walked upstream. I could see Bill even at a distance because he was wearing a very visible red and black checkered coat. He was rowing his beautiful ten foot flat-bottom wooden river boat to shore with one hand while his other held a curved, living fly rod.

As I approached, he reached shore and jumped out to play his steelhead. A small group of men were standing by a fire drinking coffee, warming themselves and watching Bill. I, too, wanted to watch the master of masters, the expert's expert. At the same time, I looked for Trueblood. He couldn't be among this crew of slouching duds watching instead of fishing, but though there were several boats still out in the pool, I could see all were bait or lure fishing.

"That damn Schaadt," one of the men said. "How the hell does he do it? He brings one fish in, lets it go, then rows out and, two casts later, he's got another one."

Another added, "And that Trueblood who was here all week fishing with him was close to keeping up. You never seen anything like it."

I barged in, "Where is Trueblood?"

To which one of the men answered, "Heard he went home yesterday on account of he didn't want to fight the weekend crowds."

Cecil Whitaker Trueblood was born in Boise, Idaho, in 1913 and was raised on a farm nearby. The nickname, Ted, was probably a family habit that stuck. Early on, he must have been drawn to the craft of writing because he sold his first story to *National Sportsman Magazine* in 1931, the year he graduated from high school. It was called "A Certain Idaho Trout."

The editor of the magazine, Edmund Ware Smith, himself a popular outdoor writer, published it under the byline, "J.W. Wintring," insisting that Ted Trueblood "was a nom de plume, and not a very good one at that."

Throughout his career, succeeding generations of readers would continue to question the reality of his very existence. He continually placed his ego in the shadows and maintained the habit of only rarely allowing a picture of himself to get into print; even then, it was usually at some odd angle or, more often, from the back.

A legend grew up around Trueblood's writing, and it was not uncommon for readers to write to *True* or to *Field & Stream*, where he wrote a column each month for forty-one years, suggesting that a team of ghost writers was responsible for his work. Ted did have a well developed sense of humor, and at one point he wrote a column denying his own existence.

In the very best sense of the word, Ted Trueblood was an expert. He was an expert hunter, fisherman, woodsman, conservationist and writer. The outdoors relative to the press have always spawned experts, only a small handful of whom have been genuine. For instance, during Trueblood's career there were a number of other popular hunters and fisherman such as Jack O'Connor, Fred Bear, Robert Ruark, Ernest Hemingway, Lee Wulff, Jason Lucas, A.J. McClane and Joe Brooks. Among this crew, however, one is routinely overwhelmed with posturing, braggadocio, glamour, social position and self-importance. And, with the exception of Hemingway, a decided lack of interest in literary style or grace.

Trueblood was unglamorous, had little money, lived modestly, and took his work seriously. At the same time, he never took himself too seriously, and always maintained a sense of playfulness and a sense of humor.

Although from quite different backgrounds, you can define some real similarities between the life and work of Trueblood and that of Roderick Haig-Brown. Both viewed the practice of writing with appropriate respect and humility. Both lived full, whole lives in locales where the environment was wild and intact, where, in those saner pre-jet set times, they mostly stayed close to home; if they drove someplace, it was only for a reasonable distance. And while enjoying the sporting fruits of their respective home grounds—Trueblood in Idaho, Haig-Brown in British Columbia—throughout their lives they built an abiding understanding of their local creatures and habitat, in the process becoming what we call environmentalists at a time when this concept enjoyed no popularity whatsoever.

Trueblood lacked the formal, classical training Haig-Brown received in England, but nonetheless he esteemed the craft of writing and was concerned with clarity, grammatical correctness, formal essay structure, vividness, rhythm and pacing. He also understood the emotional building which leads the reader line by line, paragraph by paragraph, toward an inevitable conclusion.

Not long ago I read through a large part of Trueblood's oeuvre— over a thousand stories. One I came across was about a deer hunt during which Trueblood follows the movements of a deer herd—and one big buck in particular—over a period of several days. The story is about the essence of hunting which is looking, hearing, following, waiting, anticipating and understanding. At the very end, the buck steps out of the aspens right where Trueblood figured he would, and the story ends with him lining up the crosshairs.

I vaguely remembered reading this when I was a teenager, and it occurred to me that a story I wrote about tarpon fishing in the Keys was unconsciously patterned after it. In my work, everything revolved around what led up to the fish biting the fly, at which point the story ended.

Trueblood frequently said he did his best work while in the field. He wrote in a notebook, sometimes in a hunting tent, sometimes sitting out under a tree. This way, if it was a story about something that just happened, events were at their freshest. But if he was writing a philosophical rather than instructional, practical or narrative essay, he still maintained he was most focused and at peace in the wild, and that a pencil was a more appropriate tool than a typewriter.

After high school, Trueblood attended the College of Idaho, and then the University of Idaho in Moscow. Following that, he returned to Boise and began working as a reporter for the *Boise Capitol News*. While there, he met his future wife, Ellen, who was also a reporter for the paper. In 1936, while still in Boise, he played a major role in organizing the Idaho Wildlife Federation, the start of a lifelong interest in conservation.

In 1937, he went to work for the *Deseret News* in Salt Lake City, and at the same time began selling articles to *Field & Stream*. He and Ellen were married in 1939, and for the next two years Ted tried earning his living solely by freelance writing. Even coming out of the Depression, this was a tough assignment. He and Ellen were on a first-name basis with hand-to-mouth living, and he wrote about it in a story wherein he discussed wild duck recipes. Things were so close to the bone, they were eating the ducks Ted shot in the morning for dinner every night until they could hardly bear to look at another. Still, late in life, Trueblood was quoted as saying, "If I had my life to live over again, I'd spend more time hunting and fishing and less struggling around for low wages."

In the early forties, Trueblood was asked to become the fishing editor of *Field & Stream*. Tired of just scraping by, he accepted. Of course, this meant moving to New York where he and Ellen lived just outside the city for several years. The story is that one day the Truebloods' neighbor keeled over and died of a heart attack while shoveling the snow off his driveway. He had been a hardworking man who had been saving all his life for retirement.

At that, Trueblood immediately reassessed his life, then announced he was going back to Idaho where he was going to do nothing but fish, hunt and write about it. The publishers urged him to stay on, but he refused, so they made him an associate editor, and from 1947 until his death in 1982, he wrote a monthly column for the magazine from his home in Nampa, Idaho.

As time passed and the population of the country grew larger and larger, Trueblood recognized that when he wrote about a particular place, the immediate effect was to send in a crowd. Unlike so many of his contemporaries, he was sensitive to this, recognizing that his own explicit enthusiasm could literally devastate the quality of a particular hunting or fishing locale. Back in the early sixties, Trueblood discovered a little known run of huge steelhead. This time, there were in-your-face pictures galore, the most impressive and astonishing of which featured Trueblood himself in full Kodachrome, holding a twenty-pound fish. In the story, he refused to divulge the locale, creating somewhat of a flap in the angling community. And although *True* was deluged with letters and phone calls,

Trueblood never did reveal the vital information.

In the arena of gear, Trueblood was spare and sensible. In our era where goods have become the point, Ted's things were the bare bones of practicality, a gleaming example of how simplicity shines the brightest. Yet he knew the quality. His camera was a Leica, his shotgun a Remington pump, his rifle a Winchester model 70, his fly rod a Winston, his reel a Hardy Perfect.

He who would be an expert must first know that other experts before him have important information. Trueblood knew this, and when he developed a serious interest in fly casting, he went to San Francisco where it had been raised to its highest level. He got an assignment to do a story about Lew Stoner and the R.L. Winston Rod Co. for *True* magazine, knowing that every casting record in the world was set with a Winston Rod.

The kind of steelhead and salmon fishing practiced on the Russian, Gualala and Eel Rivers in northern California was entirely a matter of distance casting. Trueblood understood that he who casts farthest casts best. At first glance, this may seem a rather crass concept, especially to a spring creek fisherman used to presenting small flies at twenty feet with great accuracy. But the fact is as speed and power increase, as they do in distance casting, mistakes in trajectory and timing are magnified. Every world champion distance caster has always held all the accuracy records as well. The often heard remark that most fish are caught on short, accurate casts has validity, but is irrelevant to what constitutes world class fly-fishing.

Trueblood gravitated toward Stoner, who many considered the best rod builder ever, and toward the champions who set the phenomenal records, foremost of whom was Jon Tarantino. He also befriended Myron Gregory, a world champion and the man who devised the system of numbering fly lines according to weight rather than diameter, which is universally used today.

Along with his tangible expertise, Trueblood maintained a lifelong enthusiasm for environmentally sound ideas, groups and projects. It would require a page just to list his distinguished service awards. In the end, what matters is that he was a man who cared and then acted upon those cares.

In 1973, the year after I moved from California to Montana, several friends drove up for a summer visit. They were Grant King, Bob Nauheim, Frank Berraina and Bill Schaadt. We fished all around the area for a month or so, ending up at Henry's Lake. It turned out that Trueblood and Barrett were there fishing too. Bill was anxious to see his old friend and somehow arrangements were made for all of us to meet for dinner in West Yellowstone.

As the hour neared, I tried to remain casual, but the years of intense admiration would not allow it. Bill Schaadt, who Trueblood said taught him more about fishing than anyone he'd ever known, had by this time literally become my surrogate father, and he was about to introduce me to the man I next admired most, someone I once thought didn't exist.

But exist he did, and in his devotion to the craft of writing—applied to the natural world which he lived, breathed and loved with all his heart—he elevated what we have come to call "outdoor writing" to the highest, cleanest level to which it has ever been taken. He gave his craft a simple dignity and honesty, which brought him the respect, love and admiration of all his following.

When the two men entered the far end of the room, I remember thinking they seemed somewhat smaller than they should be. As they approached, I looked hard at Trueblood. There was a calmness there, along with the slightest smile. Tears tend to blur things, but I could still see his red wool coat as I heard Bill deliver an introduction. When I felt his hand close around mine I looked up, but his face was completely indistinct.

CATCH & EAT

By Alan Kesselheim

I KNOW THAT WRITING THIS WILL ESTABLISH ME as a heretic in the Church of Latter Day Fly-Fishing. The title alone is enough to cast me into the netherworld of those-who-bait-with-Vienna-all-meat-wieners, those who recline along muddy river banks on flood buried sofas, whose fishing poles are propped against forked willow sticks, and whose red-and-white bobbers laze in tepid, silt-rich, greasy green waters. So be it.

Among the more enduring (though not exhaustively investigated) of my family's stories is one set in the murky yesteryear of my parents' youth, shortly after the second World War. In this tale, they are newly married, unburdened by children or the responsibilities of careers. They have taken a rustic cabin somewhere in the West—California, Montana, Wyoming. The state doesn't matter, but there is a small, clear stream purling by behind the log building, a stream fairly aromatic with the presence of trout. It is nearing dinner time.

In the gloaming, my father dons a pair of swimming trunks and goes around back. He is a lean and fit young man, with a full head of dark hair. He pauses to assess an upstream bend, then slips, gasping, into the snowmelt current. Slowly he works his way, breasting the flow, toward a particular shadowy stretch of mossy, overhung bank. Here the details blur somewhat in the retelling, and we skip ahead to the point where my father emerges from the water, hands firmly grasping the struggling evening's meal, a muscular trout plucked from its dark lair, where my father knew all along it would be.

There is more to the story. Something about an awkward meeting with the groundskeeper, my father dripping wet, fish still flopping. Some discussion of fines and rules of conduct, then forgiveness. At no point, however, is there any equivocation as to the trout's fate. The story ends with sizzling butter in a fry pan, a squeeze of lemon, the fragrance of delicate meat wafting on the evening breeze.

Apparently, this savage hunting ability was a skill my father developed growing up in Montana and which he employed from time to time as a young man. As with so many of the stories that rise from the prehistory of parents' lives before children, the characters and events bear little resemblance to the people we know as youngsters, or to actions we can imagine for them.

Nevertheless, it is an alluring, even thrilling tale, especially to the ears of a young boy. I loved the idea of stripping away every artifice and feeling toward physical contact: an implacable ambush of strong hands. Even now, it appears to me a feat roughly analogous to stalking to within arm's reach of a bull elk and dispatching it with a sharp stick.

Around the age of ten or twelve, I questioned my father closely on the issue of his trout-catching prowess, along with other veiled regions of curiosity. We even once went on a weekend fishing trip, Dad and I, with an eye toward passing along this attractive familial bit of outdoor lore. As I remember, there was a fair amount of talk about tickling fish bellys, and of propitious methods of approach. We scouted more than one likely stretch of stream bank. As it happened, things kept getting in the way of ever actually getting into the water...a relief, I think, for all parties.

Most of my fishing, as a youth and currently, has employed a variety of Mepps spinners, red-and-white daredevils, jars of pastel-orange salmon eggs, and styrofoam cups writhing with earthworms. Most of my fishing has been—and here's where I get into deep water—with dinner in mind. In fact, I think I can safely claim that I have pretty well never gone fishing without having dinner in mind.

My allegiance to the catch and release creed has been limited to turning back those victims either too small or too large for the fry pan. What this means, nowadays, is that I hardly go fishing at all.

Yes, I fully understand the catch and release doctrine. Fishing is yet another in the lengthening list of outdoor pursuits so many of us enjoy that we are in danger of loving it right over the brink of extinction. It has become necessary to think and act in ways that leave a few fish in the water, even if they are a tad scarred and traumatized by repeated lessons in the catch and release catechism. What I don't understand, frankly, is, when you remove dinner from the equation, why anyone would bother!

I hear, now, the collective sharp intake of breath from the readership. Fly-fishing has, after all, transcended the mundane business of slapping food on the table. It has achieved the status of art form, aesthetic pursuit for its own sake, therapy for the relief of everyday stress and strain. Cheaper and more enjoyable by far to wade off into the willows for a day or two, graphite rod aloft, than to pay a shrink's salary or enter whatever is the New Age shrine du jour. Besides, there is the self-righteous joy that comes from returning the day's take. What other hunt gives so much and removes so little?

So the elite of the angling world (a class that has grown to the point that elite might be stretching it a little) gussy up in fancy regalia—fishing vestments, if you will. They travel far in the quest for waters blessed with certain, ordained, finned life forms. They lavish entire vacations and wholesale hunks of their savings accounts in the pursuit of this piscatory grail. They stalk, they scheme, they lay in wait, they employ skills built up through hours of video viewing, front-lawn casting workshops, guide's tips, and the inevitable accumulation of tree-climbing, snarl-snipping humility that is the lot of budding fly-fishers. In season, they are daily aquiver with that predatory hunting thrill.

Then, at the end of the day—ruddy from exposure, whipped by shrubbery, senses tingling with the memories of glinting swirls and jarring strikes and whiffs of trouty bank—they go home and grill up a slab of cow! What's wrong with this picture?

For me, at least, it doesn't cut it. It's like a frustrating dream. Just when your mouth is all set for some elevating achievement, some seduction, some success, you are jarred awake to find yourself in the same place you woke up in yesterday. Call me small-minded, unprogressive, retrograde, but in my house it's catch-and-eat, or nothing. Maybe it's a genetic thing.

ENCOUNTER AT THE SUMMIT

By Robert F. Jones

A HUNTING TRIP CAN BE A SERIES OF FLASHES, the least important of which is the one that grows from the barrel of a gun.

We are blasting down U.S. 93 from Missoula to Hamilton in Mel's broad-shouldered Ford van. November in Montana. The Bitterroot Mountains rise to the right of us, tall and impersonal, so unlike the humanized mountains of the East or even the West Coast. These are hard mountains, black-faced with fir and pine, that don't give a damn who dies on them. Lewis and Clark's men had to tighten their belts here in the fall of 1805; the roots they gnawed to supplement their jerky supplies were bitter. These are not the sort of mountains you want to stare at for any length of time. They are too complex in their geology and history, too big in every dimension to soothe the soul.

It's snug in the van, though. Mel has the heater turned up high, and over the radio Loretta Lynn is singing *Don't Come Home a-Drinkin'*. Her voice has that special timbre, somewhere between a sneer and snivel, common to roadhouse cocktail waitresses and lady country singers. Mel opens a fresh tin of Copenhagen. I tuck a hefty pinch in my lower lip and the juices start to flow. It's a nicotine hit unlike any other—a small, warm, friendly explosion in the chilly caverns of the skull.

"Nope," says Mel, "they ain't come down off the peaks yet. They're still on top, lyin' up by day in the lodgepole tangles and feedin' at night. Plenty of sign, though, up in the Skalkaho Country." He rolls down the window and squirts a shot of snuff juice into the slipstream; the left side of his van bears a ragged, tan racing stripe. "Me and Harold, we was up there just yesterday. Deer sign lower down, but all the elk sign was way up near the top. We'll have to climb for 'em, I fear." He closes the window and the cold, clean mountain air disappears in a blast of heat and song and Bull Durham smoke.

Melvin McNeal, strawberry rancher. A strange, almost sissified occupation for a mountain man, but then the times have changed drastically since the firm of Bridger, Beckwourth & Broken Hand, Unltd. closed shop. Put Mel on a mountainside, though, and his true nature shines like a beaver pelt. The swift, shuffling gait that never varies, uphill or down. The quick, sneaky, game-seeking eyes common to muggers and born hunters. Bent-shouldered, big-knuckled, as spare of words as he is of flesh, Mel McNeal would not have been out of place 150 years ago, riding down in the Great Basin on the back of a raddled mule with a Hawken over his pommel and Jedediah Strong Smith leading the way. His scruffy, rust-colored beard underscores the image. "I won't shave again until I've got a bull elk in the meat shed," he says.

Already two deer are hanging there, glazed almost black in the dim, sweet, frigid air of the shed behind his house. The smell of hanging game has always seemed exciting to me—a ranker, wilder smell than that of the beeves and swine we used to whiff in the butcher shops before the supermarkets took over and hid all meat from the senses, under plastic. I suppose that in the smell of slow putrefaction there resides some arcane folk memory, the promise of full bellies for the tribe. Mel's two deer, young and tender but pathetically small without their heads, hides and guts, dangle from the roof beam by their ankles. I lay a hand on one of them: smooth, hard, cold. Like the Bitterroots, where he killed them earlier in the season.

Mel's yard is a bit of a zoo. Peacocks and guinea fowl scamper around, kicking the gravel and nattering at one another in the incessant warfare of the bird world. Domestic mallards waddle up blatting for a handout. These are the Godzillas of duckdom: twice the size of the few wild mallards that have dropped in, uninvited, to spend the winter with Mel's pen-raised flock. "Aw, I like having birds around," he explains. "Not just for the eggs and the meat, either. It's more the idea—peacocks in Montana. They're a tough bird, though. They hold their own pretty good against the foxes and the hawks and the coyotes. And the neighbor dogs are flat *skeered* of 'em!"

Out beyond the yard is a pond full of icy water and Kamloops rainbow trout. Mel calls them "cannaloops," confusing their real name, which comes from the distant Pacific Northwest, with "cantaloupes," and in a way they *are* like melons to him: starved for trout, all he needs to do is pick up a rod, hike through the yard, flip a spinner into the pond and come home with a couple of three-pounders. For his serious fishing he heads for the mountains.

Deer stew and home-baked bread for dinner. Mel's wife Jan is a shy, plump woman who blushes readily at compliments about her cooking ("Nothin' much," she says). Like so many mountain women she takes her skills for granted, makes little of them, unaware of their natural beauty and her own. Instead, she affects an air of weariness and worthlessness, tempered with flashes of desperate independence which she has probably learned from the huge face of the color television set that dominates the McNeals' small living room. The only book in the house is a Bible. Now and then she flares angrily at her two sons, Sean and Max, themselves shy boys still under the tutelage of women, but her rages are perfunctory, ritualistic and immediately followed by a lot of loving. The boys will be O.K. once they are allowed to think of themselves as men.

In the bedroom hang Mel's trophies. A royal elk of seven points, a wide-racked whitetail deer, a solemn mountain goat, a pronghorn antelope, a pair of black bear hides and the heavy, glowering, bug-eyed head of an elderly bull bison that Mel tracked down and killed in Yellowstone country years ago. The presence of the dead animals in the bedroom is at once awesome and ridiculous. It would be like making love in a wing of the Museum of Natural History. I am put in mind of a remark my daughter made when she was three years old and saw her first mounted deer head. She stared at it for a long time, then said firmly, "The rest of him lives in the wall."

That night we take a run up the mountain in Mel's jeep, heading for a salt lick that the elk sometimes visit on their way down from the peaks to their wintering grounds in the high valleys. The idea is not to kill, but to see if they are moving, and if so, just who is doing the moving—cows and yearling calves, or the big bulls we are seeking. Though the autumn has been a strange one, fraught with warm weather and unrelieved by snow, the bulls should be finished with the rut by now. If so, they will be banding together again in their bachelor gangs and replacing the meat and muscle they lost over the past month during their titanic battles and their long-winded, randy chases after the cows. If the bulls are moving down the mountain it will make our hunt that much easier. The closer to the valley, the handier the roads, the shorter the distance we will have to drag our kill. A bull elk can weigh 600 pounds, gutted. If we kill one at the top of the mountain, we will have to cache it somewhere and then return for Mel's donkey, Jenny, to pack the meat and the trophy out. "We can do 'er," Mel says, "but it ain't no fun."

At the foot of the mountain we rendezvous with Mel's hunting partner, Harold Nelson. He, too, is slumped and bearded in the image of the mountain men, but in contrast to Mel's dour demeanor, Harold is a mountain wit. The eyes behind his granny glasses squint and sparkle. We can almost hear him creak as he climbs into the jeep—he suffers from emphysema and a spinal fusion, he announces, the result of too many smokes and a fall from a cliff some years back. He was once shot by another hunter, over in Idaho where he was born, and now refuses to wear red or Day-Glo orange clothing in the field for fear that he will make an easy target. He has a low opinion of most hunters, including Mel.

"Your average hunter," he says, "is like a dog chasin' a car. Even if he catches it, he don't know how to drive."

Winding up the mountain in the dark, Mel asks Harold how his love life is.

"Waal," says Harold, lighting up a cigarette to feed his emphysema, "it used to be wine, women and song. Now it's Metrecal, the old gal and *Sing Along with Mitch.*"

They call him Count Nelson down in the valley, one of those negative nick-names, like a fat boy known as Skinny. Yet he is an authentic American original, tough and human, a man whose only lies are told at the expense of the world's cruelty and for the amusement of his friends. He damns all citybound ecologists as "flower sniffers," and cuts Christmas trees for a winter's living, yet in the days I walked the mountains with him I discovered that he knew the names of all the birds, beasts, trees, mosses, rocks, lichens, clouds and peaks much better than the field guides I had brought with me. He kills meat to feed his family. "You know," he said one afternoon as we rested on the sunnyside slope of a frozen peak, "there really ought to be only one man hunting in this country. That way it wouldn't get drained of meat so quick, and all the flowers wouldn't get tromped down. I hate to see it goin'. But I'll tell you who that man oughta be. Harold Nelson."

"How old do you reckon Harold is?" Mel asks.

"Oh," after a long pause, "about 139."

"He's thirty-nine."

At the salt lick, nothing but deer sign. The elk are still up high. Winding back down the mountain we pick up the brassy flash of eyes in the headlights. "Coyote," says Mel. "Kill the bastard!" says Harold. Mel stops the jeep. He opens the driver-side door and steps out with his .243 Browning lever-action rifle, takes a rest on the door and shoots. The eyes wink out and we see a long, yellow shape skipping away through the night. Mel shoots again. "Nailed him!" Harold walks up the road and comes back holding the coyote by the brush. It is a bitch, a young one. The first bullet shattered her right front leg, which dangles by a shredded tendon. The second bullet took her through the chest. Her tongue lolls and her eyes are not yet glazed. Harold cuts off her tail with a clasp knife and slings the carcass back into the woods—"for the magpies."

Fortuitous killing offends me. A man should know what he intends to kill, should seek out the particular object of his murderous instincts, seek it out as an individual, know its habits and its track, how they differ from others of its kind, and understand the meaning of his own heart as the gun fires. Otherwise killing is gluttony. God knows I have killed animals indiscriminately in my life, but their deaths haunt me. Those acts were far more grievous sins than any lies, cruelties or infidelities I have perpetrated on my human victims. A lie, a putdown or an infidelity is a calculated act; roadhunting is simply gratuitous. I seethe silently for a while, then bluntly ask Mel and Harold why they gunned down the coyote. After all, a coyote eats mainly mice and carrion; Mel and Harold themselves are not sheepherders; the coyote is misunderstood in that regard; studies prove they don't kill that many domestic animals, and even if they did….

"That's how we *do* around here," says Harold.

"Shoot," says Mel, injured, "it's just a coyote…."

I flash, and it's as brief, as bright as the muzzle blast from Mel's rifle…the people I've hurt too often. Then Mel passes the snuff tin around. We load our lips and head for the barn, talking normally again.

The next day we leave before dawn to hunt Deer Mountain, a peak to the southeast of Hamilton. The sun, when it finally arrives, reveals a terrifying aspect. The roads that climb these mountains are little better than the tracks of a snail climbing a beanstalk. Slick, thin, the merest translucence on a steep surface, they wind around and around, aimlessly following the line of least gravitational resistance. To look down from the passenger side of the jeep is to court instant vertigo. Mel drives loosely, turning his head to talk. Thank God he is no chatterbox!

The best approach is to study the distant mountains. Trapper Peak and Sleeping Child, Lost Horse and The Lonesome Bachelor: my Forest Service map dispels acrophobia as effectively as a tranquilizer might paranoia. I sink back into the gray dust of geography and history, adrift and happy in a world of long-dead trappers and distant, sleeping children. Harold peels an orange from his lunch pail and the sharp romanticism of citrus fills the jeep. Then he curses the fibers that stick between his teeth. At the top, Mel parks the jeep and we dismount, stiff and groggy, to check our rifles.

"Colder'n a mother-in-law's heart," says Harold, his orange-scented breath pluming in the early light. We're up in the snow, more than 7,000 feet at this point, and the air bites the jaws like a dentist's drill. Still, it's not much snow—three inches at the most—and the only sign we have crossed on the road has been that of deer.

"We'll poke around for a while up here," says Mel, "and if we don't jump any elk we may find deer. Take 'em if you see 'em—in this district you're allowed two on your license, either sex. Kill any grouse that you see. They're good lunch meat for tomorrow. We don't hunt 'em up here like you do back East. These are fool hens, won't flush worth diddly. They either stand and squawk at you or else jump up into the trees and figger they're safe. Shoot their heads off. If you see an elk or a deer, shoot for the heart—well, you know that anyway. I don't hold with these gut-shootin' fellers or these dudes that take what they call 'haunch shots' on a running meat critter. Waste a lot of time that way, tracking them out." He spits his quid of snuff. "Meet back here by noon."

It was the longest speech he ever made.

In terms of big game the day is a wash out. But in terms of coming to an understanding with this vast, cold-hearted country it could not be more successful. Mel and Harold shoulder their "crowbars"—a rifle is a workman's tool in these parts—and amble downhill into the snowy pines. Their footfalls and voices fade even before they are out of sight. Lesson No. 1: sound travels vertically in this vertical country. A man with a broken leg could shout his head off, empty his rifle with distress shots and not be heard by his partner a few hundred years away. I head uphill with my own partner, a lean Californian named Roger Ferry who is also my brother-in-law. Roger is tall, soft-spoken, bespectacled, a consummate woodsman who grew up as a deer hunter in the flat, tamarack and muskeg country of northern Wisconsin. Like so many of us from that land of waning opportunity—"America's Drearyland," some embittered ex-Badgers call it—he went West. Though he majored in French literature at Marquette University and had ambitions to write when he was younger, he now runs a small home-improvements business in Sacramento. Being his own boss, he has plenty of time for the pursuit of his true vocation: hunting and fishing.

We pause at the crest of Deer Mountain, Roger to glass the country for game, I to catch my breath. My knees have turned to water with the climb and, despite the cold, most of it is squirting out through my sweat glands. In this thin air, not yet acclimated to the altitude, I stand about as much chance of catching my breath as I would of catching Frank Shorter in the marathon. Roger, by contrast, is fresh as a sprig of alpine rue. He quit smoking years ago for just this reason.

"Nothing moving but an eagle," he says, putting down the glasses. "Away over there, across the valley. You know, if you hammered Montana flat and crimped it down a bit around the edges, you'd have a perfect lid for the whole Pacific Ocean."

We split up and swing across the shoulder of the mountain, hoping that one of us will push a deer, or maybe even an elk, out of its bed and into range of the other. The wind up here groans like a god with a bellyache. The pines and firs—some of them mature giants, uncut during the big logging boom of the 1890s because of their remote locations—sway and clatter and yowl under the push of the north wind, but at ground level the air is still. Except for a few ravens that croak their ragged way overhead, bitching at the wind that keeps pushing them off course, and an occasional camp robber, the mountain seems empty of life. I see some old deer sign and the tracks of a coyote that came through the previous afternoon when the snow was still wet with the afternoon's relative warmth; the doglike prints look as big as a wolf's, but are blurred and splashy around the edges.

Then I catch a flicker of movement in the lodgepoles below me. Sitting, I glass the thicket with my scope. The gray twitch resolves itself into an ear. Than a wet brown eye leaps out of the neutrality of the background. Then I see the animal whole: a mule deer doe. It always amazes me when they snap into focus that way, and I wonder how many I have passed, and how close, that I never did see.

Mel said to take 'em—either sex. My mind does its quick rationalization number: I sure could use the meat. I bring the crosshairs down the crease behind her shoulder, a nervous optical caress. She is at least 300 yards away. The scope is jumping rhythmically, just the faintest of up-and-down movements, but enough to ruin my shot if I take it. I expel my breath, but the jumping continues. My heartbeat. I start the squeeze anyway, and just as the trigger reaches the breaking point I see out of the corner of the scope another muley behind her—a buck, only a crotch-horn, a two-pointer but a buck—and in that instant the rifle goes bang. The snow jumps. The two deer disappear.

A clean miss. My hands are shaking.

There is no blood in the snow where she stood, and I see where the bullet dug a trench in the dirt beneath it. It's a deep hole, like the kind we used to shoot marbles at in the schoolyard. Marbles and murder: I'm glad

I missed her.

Back at the jeep, Mel and Harold are building a fire. They drag up a few snow-sodden pine logs, drench them with gasoline from the spare jerrican and flip a bonfire. I wonder what Bridger would think of the technique, as opposed to flint and steel. He'd probably approve. Those men were nothing if not pragmatic. Later, Roger tails in with two blue grouse dangling from his belt. He surprised them in a break down the mountain, and when they flew up into a nearby ponderosa he headed them, one, two, just like that. Just like Mel said.

That night, skunked, we hit the saloons of Hamilton to recharge our depleted spirits. Most of the patrons are ranchers and drovers. They shake their heads solemnly at Mel's account of our failure, offering suggestions for the morrow. "Use to be a lot of big old bulls down there on Hog Trough Creek, on the back side of Black Bear Point." Too durn early for that country. "How about Water Sign Meadows, or farther on down by the One Tooth Cabin?" Too durn far. White Stallion, Two Bear, Sawdust Gulch, Railroad Creek—all have their drawbacks. We sulk over our beers, listening to Merle Haggard on the juke. "I'm a lonesome fugitive...."

The light in the bar is warm and minimal, the colors from the jukebox paint rainbows on the walls. I get a kick out of the signs on the walls of backcountry saloons—a form of Americana that has largely disappeared from the cities:

"No Shirts, No Shoes, No Service! (Bras Optional.)"

"My heart ees yours, but my ass is zee government's."

"Of all the purebred strains, the Herefords and Black Angus have attained the greatest popularity in Montana."

"Yea, though I walk through the Valley of the Shadow of Death, I shall fear no evil...'Cause I'm the MEANEST SON OF A BITCH IN THE VALLEY!"

Harold cocks his white cowboy hat back on his brow and shrugs his sheepskin jacket higher on his shoulders—he'd duded up, clotheswise, here in town. He even smells pretty good, having gone home for a shower. His glasses catch the glint of light from the jukebox and he stares at us like the sunset of a rainy day, after the clouds have passed.

"All right, you 'tater-ass sissies," he says to us, "tomorrow we'll hit the Skalkaho Country. She's a mean 'un, so cold up there you could milk a cow in chunks. But that's where the noble wapiti is right now, and that's where we'll get 'em."

The morning, still hours before dawn, is not black but rather a dirty gray. The vaulting sky suffers from ring around the collar. It snowed during the night, and walking out into the cold we feel a sudden surge of hope. The new snow has to help us. Mel's ducks and guineas and peacocks seem to sense our good spirits: they cluster around, even though it's long before their usual wake-up hour, yammering for breakfast. So what—our own breakfasts are still warm and heavy in our bellies— scrambled eggs, beans, venison steaks cooked up by a sleepy Jan in her housecoat, in that rich, warm kitchen. "Good luck," she says, then scurries back to bed, to nod off under the glowering glass eyes of the big gone bison. We climb into the jeep and head for the Skalkaho Country.

The climb is not nearly so fearsome this morning, despite the fresh snow that slicks the tracks. Mel has the same faith in the surefootedness of his jeep as the oldtimers had in their ponies, and it is faith more than anything that makes for good driving. Roger even dozes off during some of the steeper stretches, with the jeep swooping down horse trails like a World War II Stuka with its divebrakes extended. Harold chatters on and on about his eldest son, a seventeen-year-old who has broken his back three times in car crashes. In the most recent one he hit a tree at ninety miles an hour. "He's a hell-raiser like his old man," Harold self-congratulates. "Like they say, only the good die young." Another son, fifteen years old, is a nationally ranked high school wrestler. Harold is proud of him, too.

We top out on the mountain with the dawn. Mel eases the jeep in four-wheel drive and low-low, and with the brakes virtually locked, down what he claims is a trail but which looks more like a cliff. We cross a creek, red in the light of the sunrise. Then we follow a logging trail beside it. Deer and elk tracks spot the fresh snow; we may be pushing them ahead of us. At the end of the logging trail Mel parks his jeep. To our left the mountain rises higher still, straight up it seems, its slope (if such it was) studded with ponderosas.

"At the top she levels off," says Mel. "It's fairly open along the ridge line, but there's thick lodgepole tangles on either side the shoulder. The elk are lyin' up in them jungles there. You and Roger climb on up there and then split up and work down along the ridge line toward the east. Me and Harold'll go back down to the end of the ridge and come up slow, in case you push anything ahead of you."

"And if you don't know which way's east," adds Harold, "I can loan you my North Dakotian compass." He pulls out a woman's powder compact and opens the mirrored lid. "It don't show you where to go, but it shore shows you who's lost!" Haw, Haw.

The climb is a killer, but thanks to the new snow there is inspiration at every halt. Elk sign galore. Vast stretches of raw dirt mixed in with pine needles where the bulls have been tussling. Mounds of fresh droppings, some of them still warm at the core. Saplings rubbed raw earlier in the autumn when the bulls were polishing their antlers for the rutting battles, the red bark of the skinny trees dangling like a teen-ager's braids. At the top we halt. The sun is just coming visible over the rolling rock ahead of us. The big red ball again.

"I'll drop down here to the right," Roger whispers, "just over the crest of the ridge. You stay just on this side of the crest. Let's move along real slow and easy, like you'd still-hunt the swamps up near Eagle River in Wisconsin. Stay about a couple hundred yards apart. I'll whistle every now and then to let you know where I am, and you whistle back."

I push out along the ridge, pausing five counts for every five steps I've taken. The old angst rises along the back of my neck—air prickles, my skin as sensitive to sound as a fever victim's to the touch of a breeze. All the senses peak in moments like this, all the tastes come flooding back to distill themselves on the tongue, blood and breakfast. My eyes seem to widen and deepen in my head, huge light-suckers, vacuums that draw in every color, every shadow, every movement. The tension on the nerves and muscles—latent death—rises with every step and redoubles with every pause. If a man were to live his whole life with the taut sense of a hunter at the end of a stalk, he would die at the age of three....

The first crashing sound hits me like a truck coming around a blind corner. I wonder for an instant if Roger has fallen off a cliff. Then the bull elk tops the rise, galloping like a horse, and swings his huge head to look at me. I stare into his big brown eye and he keeps right on going, watching me watch him go, the wide rack steady over his hammerlike head, his neck low—and I don't even get the rifle to my shoulder before he's gone. Damn, I'm thinking, they don't run like deer at all.

And then the second bull appears, half a second behind the first one. He's smaller by a bit, and he pauses in his gallop to look at me, slowing to a trot. I snap off a shot and kick dirt under his belly. Off he goes, and I start to curse myself—what kind of hunter am I, stupid no good....

And then the *third* bull appears. The third bull! Someone loves me! Unconsciously I have moved up the ridge toward the spot where the animals are crossing, and now as this bull slows to stare at me I have dropped to one knee and the rifle is steady and the crosshairs touch the spot behind his shoulder and as he moves I swing with him and the rifle goes bang. I see the guard hairs fly over his heart. He leaps ahead, down the mountain, out of sight, and I can hear his jumps—one, two, three, four, five, six then a pause—and then a heavy thud that seems to shake the earth....

Over the knoll ahead of me, snow hazes down from a pair of quivering spruce trees. I move up quickly and quietly and look downhill. The elk is down. In his dying flight, out of control, he crashed through a dead tree and somehow twisted his way through two others—the ones that produced the snow shower. He lies on his left side, his legs flexing. He is big as a horse, umber-colored, touched with cream and dark brown, dying. As I stand there watching him die, the big feeling washes over me again: bigger than guilt and pride, though akin to them, bigger even than love and loss, though their brothers, and I flash on down through time to the men who crawled deep into the earth to paint their prey by torchlight on the wet, cold walls, and then crawled out again to kill meat, their god.

Roger comes over the rise and looks at the dead elk.

"Hey!" he says. "You got one!"

The rest of a day like that goes slow, gutting the game, dragging it down through a mile of stumps and gullies and fallen timber. A creature that size takes its own small revenge for its murder, in the form of barked shins and skinned knuckles, and you start to wonder if the oldtimers weren't right in their meat-hungry philosophy: eat it as it lays. But all of that is the malaise of anticlimax. At the bottom of the mountain I stopped and laid on my belly in the snow and drank from the stream—the water clean and brassy cold. I walked back up to where the bull lay. Steam rose from his open body cavity, sweet in the cold. Mel looked at him, deadpan behind his rusty beard. Harold stroked his own scruffy chin.

"Couldn't have picked a nicer bull if you tried," he said. "He ain't the biggest, but the rack is perfectly even. You don't find that too often in a young bull. And the meat will be good eatin', which you don't find in the Boone and Crockett class. You'll have the head mounted, of course?"

Of course. And now, with the head on my wall and the meat in my freezer, the Montana elk hunt is complete. My neighbors think of me as the meanest son of a bitch in the valley, but I still have my flashes intact: Mel, Harold, Jan, Roger, and a country even meaner than I. A country that, if hammered flat, could cover the whole Pacific Ocean. I hope it never happens.

RIVERS
OF THE
BIG SKY

THE RIVER THAT RUNS THROUGH IT: THE BIG BLACKFOOT

By Annick Smith

ON SUMMER EVENINGS I LOOK NORTH from the deck outside my log kitchen and watch night crawl up the Bear Creek drainage from the blue-black valley of the Big Blackfoot. The humped mountains all around are scarred by clearcuts and slashed with logging roads. Owls cry. Ghosts of old forests rise in dusky light. I imagine the deep woods as they were before Anaconda, before Champion and Plum Creek. A long-billed snipe dives from the clouds, wind chiming through his feathers in a trilling, whistling mating call.

Some nights the northern sky pulses green—green waves and luminous stripes passing over the eaves of my shake roof. After fireworks one Fourth of July in our Wild-West days of the 1970s, a bunch of good-old boys and gals were passing the Jack Daniels around a fire burned down to coals. A visiting writer stood by the tailgate of his pickup, stoned on acid. He looked up to the sky, then at us. "You seeing the same thing I am?"

I cannot fathom what my friend saw in his altered state, but the rest of us were craning our heads toward the light show on the Milky Way. We studied the northern lights with the fascination of Neanderthals gawking outside their caves. Remembering that night I think of light flowing like a river; I think of blood and sap—the common, recurrent, and fluid patterns of life.

There is an idyllic morning I carry around with me like a lucky rubbing stone. It is 1971, our first summer at the ranch, and my husband Dave and I and our four boys have gone fishing on the Big Blackfoot. We drive our sand-colored Land Rover to the edge of a high bank upstream from the mouth of Belmont Creek. Dave and the older boys scramble down to the rocky shore. It is cool in the morning shade of great branched ponderosas. The salmonfly hatch is about over, but a few of the heavy, or-ange-bodied insects hang onto willow branches in the dewy air. When their wings dry, they will beat suicidally over riffles where lunker rain-bows are waiting for breakfast.

"Use live ones for bait," shouts Dave, knee-deep in green water. Dave moves toward the head of a fishing hole. The boys and I hop through willows, service-berry and chokecherry brush. We snatch the sluggish salmonflies. Within the hour Dave hooks and nets two twenty-inch rainbows. Eric and Steve with their squiggling live flies catch smaller trout. Even I get a good bite. The fishing is hot, and then it's over.

I bring out tuna sandwiches, peaches and chocolate-chip cookies. A thermos of coffee. A jar of lemonade. After lunch, with the sun high and the water cool, I am happy to lie on damp sand, the older guys gone downriver in search of elusive big ones, the four-year-old twins making dams out of colored river stones—aquamarine, rose, jade green.

Norman Maclean would soon memorialize such precambrian "rocks from the basement of time" in the title story of *A River Runs Through It*. He would describe the Big Blackfoot's deep patterns: the unity of a three-part fishing hole, the river's billion-year geologic history. Maclean would con-nect the river and the act of fishing to a Presbyterian brand of theology, and to an aesthetic of craft and art. He would articulate universal feelings of helplessness in the face of self-born destiny and death.

But on that faraway summer morning I had no idea that my Hu-manities professor from the University of Chicago lived just up the road at Seeley Lake. I did not know that his wife had recently died, or that he had retired from teaching. I would never have guessed that twenty miles upriver, at the age of seventy-three, Norman Maclean was beginning to write a great book about family and fishing and love. Or that the book's culminating scene would take place exactly where I sat day-dreaming in the midday Blackfoot breeze.

My husband Dave grew up along the Mississippi in Hastings, Min-nesota, and loved to skate. He read the boys *Hans Brinker and the Silver Skates* so they would get the idea of his life on the river. "We'd skate the backwaters," he said. "Make fires, tease the girls." His words created a Brueghel world, a nostalgic etching by Currier & Ives.

In winter, at our favorite swimming hole a quarter mile above the mouth of Bear Creek, the Blackfoot freezes two feet thick and two-thirds of the way to its northern shore. Twenty yards downstream the riffles run year round. The beach we call ours is a gravel pocket bounded by high cliffs embroidered orange and chartreuse with lichen. I have skied down to the river in January, played tag on the ice with little boys and puppies, followed tracks of deer, rabbits and mice.

We never skated on Blackfoot pools because there was too much snow those winters of the early seventies, snow four feet deep in our field. And Dave was too ill to skate. A hereditary metabolic disease had caused his arteries to become clogged with the yellow cholesterol we could see in patches under his deep-circled blue eyes. Dave did not have the energy to clear an ice rink on the river, and I didn't care enough to do it myself.

"I want Annick and the kids to have something after I'm gone," Dave told a dear friend, knowing he could die any day. We had discovered a hundred-year-old hand-hewn log house abandoned along the Blackfoot, across from Ovando. We tore it apart, then rebuilt it on our 163 acres. The house and the land would be our hedge against mortality.

Dave died of a heart attack in May of 1974, and we spent the next two Christmas holidays at our friend's house in Seattle. By 1976 we were healed enough to stay home. My oldest sons, Eric and Steve, came back from college. The twins, Alex and Andrew, who were in the fourth grade at the Potomac school, tore into the presents under the tree. We feasted on ham scored with mustard and brown sugar, then gathered around the red-brick fireplace that I had designed and Steve had helped build. It was our first addition to the house since Dave died, and we knew he would be proud of us for creating such a beautiful thing

There was a book I had intended to give to Eric or Steve as a present, but once I started reading it, I could not let it go. The slim volume had a powder-blue dust jacket. It was the first edition of *A River Runs Through It*.

"Your father would have loved this book." I told the boys. I read the ending aloud. "Eventually, all things merge into one, and a river runs through it..."

Seven years later, in September of 1983, Norman Maclean inscribed my dog-eared copy: "To Annick Smith—who lives where it is more beautiful but so tough the Finns and Serbs lined their fields with rock-piles and then gave up." We had become partners—Norman, Bill Kittredge and me—in the development of a dramatic film based on that book

Eventually Bill wrote a script under Norman's exacting tutelage and I began the long and painful process of raising production money. But Norman became ill and Robert Redford became interested in directing and producing the film, and Norman sold him the rights because he believed that in Redford's hands the film would be made soon, and right.

The result was a new script by a professional screenwriter and an Academy Award-winning movie that Norman did not live to see.

The final irony of *A River Runs Through It* is that the film was not shot on the Big Blackfoot. If any story is wedded to place, that one is, but logged-off hillsides make disturbing pictures. The river had become too degraded for Redford's idyllic vision.

The Big Blackfoot is degraded. It is number twelve in the nation on the American Rivers Group 1994 listing of threatened watersheds. Above Lincoln, the Blackfoot's upper reaches are barren, poisoned by arsenic and other hard metals leached into the waters from a century of mining for gold, silver and other precious metals. The area has become one of Montana's beleaguered Superfund sites, with lawsuits and studies and cleanup beginning, but having no end in sight.

The mining danger is far from over. Phelps Dodge is planning an immense cyanide heap-leach gold-mining operation upstream from the Lander's Fork that will run along the Blackfoot for over a mile. The company intends to dig a pit 1,200 feet deep—700 feet below groundwater level. They plan to stack the rock from their pit 600 feet high along Highway 200, adjoining the riverbed. Phelps Dodge plans to take care of the environment as best they can, but those of us who love the river are worried. We are more than worried, we're scared shitless.

Downstream, near Ovando, a fisherperson will find trout. Fishing the Big Blackfoot has been tricky for at least the thirty years I've lived in proximity to it, but now it is stingy and erratic for even the skilled old-timers. The Department of Fish, Wildlife & Parks has often stocked the river, and in the riffle near our swimming hole I have caught eight-inch hatchery rainbows with notched fins. Recently, catch-and-release regulations have been instituted to encourage regeneration in some of the popular stretches along the Blackfoot corridor, but to hook a big native cutthroat trout is nearly impossible.

A fisheries expert told me the Big Blackfoot has the best large-river bull trout population in the nation. But that is not saying much, because bull trout are more threatened than the river. If they make the endangered list, and if the Endangered Species Act survives the lobbyists who are planning to gut it, federal laws may help protect the Blackfoot ecosystem. There might be restrictions on logging and mining on public lands. Even private holdings could be affected, although a recent court decision makes this scenario less plausible. In any case, we would have funds to restore spawning beds choked with sediment, and to help ranches repair overgrazed tributaries and ditches that cattle have stripped of brush.

Without shade to cool running water, streams run warm. Native trout cannot live in warm water.

Bull trout are an indicator species. If they go, the western slope cutts will soon follow, and the rainbows, the owls, the elk, bear, and cougar. You can go to the Department of State Lands and see GIS Landsat photographs of the region. What you will see is a land denuded. Yet the pillage continues, most of the profits going to out-of-state corporations for short-term profits. It seems we never learn. We are determined to repeat the old boom-and-bust story of the West until nothing is left.

We need more than a plan to save the Blackfoot bio-region. We need immediate action. There is an association on the job called the Blackfoot Challenge. Its mission is "to enhance, conserve and protect the natural resources and rural lifestyle of the Blackfoot River Valley for present and future generations." Along with a steering committee headed by Land Lindbergh, and chairman Jim Stone of the Rolling Stone Ranch, the Challenge works cooperatively with ranchers, state and federal natural resource managers, environmental groups, biologists, and small landholders like me.

The Blackfoot Challenge has hosted informational field trips about weed control and riparian management. It brought Senator Baucus to Dick Creek for a day of work. He helped install off-stream watering holes for livestock; skidded logs into the stream to provide overhead cover for fish; and planted willow shoots to stabilize the stream banks. The Challenge has initiated public meetings at community centers and rural schools in Potomac, Ovando/Helmville, Lincoln, and Seeley Lake. At the first Potomac meeting, I joined with my logger, rancher and commuter neighbors to discuss concerns about preserving rural ways of life and work in the face of development, recreation, and conservation.

If local residents, who are snake-bit by any threat of government interference in their lives or livelihoods, can be convinced that the Blackfoot Challenge will speak and work for them rather than against them, it might become a model for regional self-help.

Recreation may not be as poisonous as cyanide, but it poses another danger to the river. In Norman Maclean's youth an occasional canoeist might have driven his Model-T up a gravel road through the narrow, twisting slit of the Big Blackfoot's canyon to shoot Thibodeau Rapids. He would have enjoyed his day in wild solitude. This July, while the water is high enough for floating, a horde of sweaty tourists will spend half an hour to drive the same route up the newly enlarged Highway 200. They will parade down the Blackfoot in dayglo orange rubber rafts, drink beer and pop from floating coolers, and trail strings of children in inner-tubes. In his last years, Maclean would not fish below Sperry Grade because people he called "Moorish invaders from California" had desecrated his sacred places.

I, too, have felt outraged at strangers tramping on what seems a private preserve. But I am not on firm moral ground. I have rafted the river with my own cooler and kids in inner-tubes. We shoot the rapids for the fun of it.

Speaking of shooting, sometimes I am witness to events in the Blackfoot Valley that make me wonder if everyone's gone pure loco, even the elk. Elk close-up are larger than horses; their long necks and tawny colors remind me of camels. In prehistoric times, elk roamed the prairies, but in our times they have survived by hiding from predatory humans in remote mountain ranges. The herd of elk that lives in the logged-over hills around my place has reverted to the instinctual pull of prairie grass, perhaps because their highland cover is gone. They come down to graze on the Potomac valley's hay meadows when they should be in the high country; lowland elk, a rancher friend calls them.

Several years ago, on the opening morning of hunting season, about fifty lowland elk grazed in a stubble field just off Highway 200. One jeepload of hunters screeched to a halt. Soon there were cars and pickups lined up on the road. Guns exploded from every fence corner. A rancher in his barn ran for his rifle and joined in the blood-lust slaughter of more than thirty elk. Luckily, no person died in the crossfire. During the following weeks, local people would stumble across the decaying carcasses of eleven more elk that had been wounded, got away, but did not survive. The coyotes rejoiced; so did the vultures; the rest of us grieved.

When old ways of living on the land area are abandoned along with ancient rules of hunting and responsibility to natural life, we must invent new ways appropriate to our new values and technologies. If the river is important, so is the wild country that it runs through, and so are the people who live off the country. Families who have inhabited the Blackfoot valleys for generations are puzzled. "You can barely make a living raising cattle any more, or farming," one neighbor says. "The only thing worth a nickel is real estate."

For over a century the economy along the Blackfoot has depended on its trees: logging; mill work; driving log trucks; packaging log homes; making posts and poles. Several of my sawyer neighbors were employed by Anaconda and Champion until company crews were disbanded.

These days they work as gyppo outfits and are paid by the piece. They receive no health benefits, no security, and have little economic motive to care for the land because they know it has been logged beyond sustainability in their lifetimes. There is no place for such men in the new economy of tourism, golf courses, and condos.

Last winter I wandered into a favorite bar in Missoula. The saloon was full of young people garbed in synchilla and decrying development. "Isn't it terrible, the way they've widened the Blackfoot road so RV's can get over it?" said one activist.

"I'm glad they've improved the road," I said. I drive Highway 200 almost every day and have known too many valley kids who lost their lives on the dangerous old curves of Rainbow Bend. The activist's Pavlovian response against development was no more exalted than the anti-environmental dogma of "Wise-Use" junkies. Polarized attitudes have put people who share basic values at each others' throats. It's crazy.

Every year forest cover for wild animal decreases. Erosion increases. Silt chokes creeks and settles in the river. More and more folks log their woodlots and consider subdividing their land because they are out of work and need the income. Every year you can witness the transformation of country to suburb, of wild woods to industrial ugliness. I wonder if we are making a wasteland, if Norman's book and the work of historians, artists, photographers, and journalists will be the only ways our inheritors will come to know the natural diversity and beauty of this land. I wonder if humans can survive the spiritual blight of a world stripped of wild animals, trees, and pure running water.

Pilgrims are needed to save the sacred. Once, as part of our plan to make a film based on *A River Runs Through It,* Bill Kittredge and I took producer Michael Hausman and director Richard Pearce on a location-scouting expedition with Norman Maclean. We came to where the Clearwater River flows into the Big Blackfoot and were snapping photos of a great rock, the clear water swirling around it. We were picturing Paul shadow-casting.

A young couple came striding up the bank, wicker creels over their shoulders, rods in hand. In the woman's fishing vest was a familiar paperback. "What's that book?" Mike asked.

The young people were high school teachers in Colorado. They were retracing the fishing spots in Norman's story.

"Would you like to meet the author?" asked Mike.

Some pilgrims are not so literate. One July evening I decided to try my hand with the new fly rod my fisherman son, Eric, gave me for my birthday. My companion, Bill Kittredge, and I headed for the fishing spot where Norman Maclean once described his last expedition with Paul. Bill had fished that water with his own brother, and it was the salmonfly hole where my young family had picnicked nearly twenty years before.

We walked through the woods toward a sand bar. Long-stemmed daisies and yellow buttercups glowed in the leafy light. At the head of the hole a young man stood with his left arm around a woman. His right arm moved rhythmically forward and back as he cast a line into the river. Both figures were buck naked.

I wanted to stand in the shadows and watch, wanted to see if a red coffee can of worms lay at the man's feet. Bill pulled me away. The sweet acrid odor of decaying cottonwood leaves reminded me of days when I walked the Blackfoot with David Smith and the poet Dick Hugo, and Norman Maclean—all of them gone. Bill stooped to pick up a soggy wallet with a driver's license and a man's picture dated three years before. We had visions of death on the river, and love, at the same moment.

Connecting with a river means learning to float. You think you know where you're going, and then you encounter an unexpected turn, a current or flood; you are swept under; you emerge transformed. The river hides rocks and deep snags and downed creatures, and it is this secrecy that draws me—the tension between what's on the surface and what lies beneath. I believe we are more like rivers than we are like meadows.

Floating on my back down the Blackfoot on a dog-day in August, I like to point my toes downstream and look up to cliffs and clouds. A redtail hawk sails above me. I float past silver-plumed willows. Blue dragonflies hover above a riffle. A kingfisher with his crested, outsized head dives for a minnow. Immersed in liquid light, I find relief from self and time.

Each of us has memories we sing over and over again like a song in our inner ear. If your place of memory and connection is the Big Blackfoot River, you are blessed, as I am. You will want to do what you can to save the river so your grandchildren can float its green waters and fish its native cutthroats and bull trout. You will teach them to dive into deep pools, touch stones that go back to the beginnings of time. The river is not dead yet. Boys and girls should make love on its banks.

ETERNAL WIND AND WILDNESS: THE MISSOURI

By John Barsness

IN THE WINTER OF 1843 some Blood Indians killed a black man at the American Fur Company trading post called Fort McKenzie, located just up the Missouri River from the mouth of the Marias. This was in the days when human beings legally owned each other, and the black man belonged to Francis Chardon, the man in charge of McKenzie. According to one early historian, Chardon was " an able but unscrupulous man, and something of a desperate character when his evil nature was once aroused. " Together with his partner Alexander Harvey, "one of the most abandoned desperadoes known to the fur trade," Chardon plotted revenge.

Chardon and Harvey loaded the fort's cannon with rifle balls and pointed it at the gates. When a group of Bloods approached the fort to trade, the gates were thrown open and Harvey lit the cannon's slow-burning fuse. But before it could fire, the impatient Chardon shot one of the Indians with his rifle. They scattered just as the cannon sent its load of shot through the winter air, and only two Bloods were killed.

Shooting customers didn't do business any good and eleven-year-old Fort McKenzie was abandoned, then burned by the Bloods. Chardon relocated seventy miles downstream, building another post on a flat opposite the mouth of the Judith River in the fall of 1843, named Fort Chardon in honor of his exemplary self. But Chardon's reputation as a total son-of-a-bitch followed him, and no Indians came to trade. Fort Chardon lasted only a winter before it too was burned, possibly by Chardon himself to deny the Indians any remaining loot.

Fort Chardon was only a blip at the tail end of the Missouri River fur trade, but in some ways it was a seminal one. After that, very few Indians along the Missouri trusted anybody with a white face, a distrust that would culminate on the Little Big Horn three decades later. So some interest was taken when a highway road crew, working on the Missouri bridge just below the Judith River in the fall of 1980, bulldozed up chunks

of old wood and a few blue beads. At the time I was working as the cartographer for an archaeological research firm in Missoula, and the next
spring we were told to go investigate.

The old palisade was still intact under the sandy loam of the Missouri bottoms, though the wood had rotted away to almost precisely the
same consistency of the dirt. We file-sharpened shovels and started scraping gently at the traces that showed in the bulldozed ground, and after
two days uncovered the outlines of a typical fur trade fort: about eighty
feet square, with blockhouses at the northeast and southwest corners,
where intrepid traders and other abandoned desperadoes could fire
along the length of the palisades at attackers. We dug test pits, finding lots
of trade beads, pieces of clay pipestem, square nails and flat-tipped wood
screws, which definitely placed the time of the fort before 1859. It seems
that the technology to put points on mass-produced screws wasn't in-
vented until the Civil War; before that each screw had to be started into a
hole made by an awl.

It was late April when we scraped up the remains of Fort Chardon,
the spring wind blowing the dust into our eyes as we screened the dirt for
traces of 1843. The fort itself wasn't much, the fur trade equivalent of a
Fourth of July firecracker stand, the palisade posts made out of split
saplings only a few inches in diameter. One good cannon blast, even of rifle balls, would have blown down any of the walls. On several occasions
local ranchers parked on the gravel road above the leveled site and looked
down as we dug in the dirt. There was nothing there—just some faint
ocher lines in tan soil—and after a few minutes they'd shrug and leave.

But we could feel something there, down in the test pits that eventually covered the site like squared craters in the moon. We felt it as we
dug up a rusted knife, wondering if Chardon himself had cut into roast-
ed buffalo hump with this piece of steel. We felt it again when we crossed
the bridge that had replaced one of the old Missouri River ferries, and
walked up the prickly-pear hill above the mouth of the Judith to find tipi
rings, small and large. The smaller rings, some archaeologists say, were
made before 1730, when tipis were hauled with pack dogs instead of horses.

On top of the dry-grass bench we turned our shoulders into the
spring wind. The same wind once carried the scent of dead buffalo,
drowned when they fell through river ice during the spring thaw; the
people living inside these rings of stone smelled the wind, and went
down to the river to butcher the carcasses. It was all the hard Missouri

wind: it ripped the dusty baseball caps from our heads, drowned the cattle of homesteaders in the whitecapped river, sent the old ferry whirling downstream, and fanned the burning of Fort Chardon.

It has been my odd fortune to spend most of my life living along various parts of the Missouri. I grew up in Bozeman on a street near Sourdough Creek, one of the highest tributaries of the river, and looked for arrowheads along its banks. There was still a stump, just upstream from where our street ended, supposedly carved by William Clark's men when his half of the Corps of Discovery—know to most as the Lewis and Clark Expedition—passed through on their return to St. Louis.

Our family would sometimes drive down to the Three Forks to see where the big river began, and while my father had all the children captive around the picnic table, he would describe how the Hidatsa had raided Sacajawea's Shoshone camp when she was not much older than us, chasing her band across the shallow summer riffles and up the Jefferson. He was the grandson of Montana homesteaders, an English professor with a Ph.D. in that conglomeration of history, literature and philosophy called American Studies, who never quite knew what he was looking for. We listened to his story, and to his theory that the Missouri was the artery of Montana history, but we were really there to throw sticks in the river so we could throw rocks at the floating sticks. Now I visit the Forks on a July day and can see the way the sun-edged water splashed from the hooves of the Hidatsa horses, can feel the weight of buckskin soaked in the Missouri, a buckskin dress too heavy to let a young girl run from horses.

I have chased cows on horseback and hunted elk up in the high semi-arctic basin we call Horse Prairie, along the trickling creek where one of Lewis and Clark's men placed his feet on either side and claimed he "bestrode the heretofore deemed endless Missouri," the same valley where Sacajawea's long-lost family was found through one of their loose horses, so starved they ate raw deer guts, chewing one end while pressing the contents from the other.

Along the upper Missouri itself, I've rowed drift boats, catching brown and rainbow trout introduced by the same generation who dammed the most memorable scenery of Lewis and Clark's journey, the Great Falls. As soon as the Corps of Discovery mapped paradise, we commenced to "improve" it, as if there could be any improvement on cutthroat trout, Montana grayling and the Great Falls of the Missouri.

Down near North Dakota the river was formed by ice-melt along the edge of the last glacier. I've followed the sand-barred channel there, be-

tween the glacier-leveled fields of the north bank and the untouched badlands of the south, in an open outboard piloted by a seventy-five-year-old
Dakota Indian: hunting ducks and beaver, bending buffalo-berry bushes
over a tarp spread across the gunwales of the boat, beating the orange
berries from their thorny stems with sticks cut from diamond willow.

From the forks to Dakota it is all the Missouri, but if the river is our
essential artery, then its heart is the Breaks, wilder now than at any time
since Lewis and Clark. Shortly after they dragged their pirogues and keel-
boats upstream, steamboats started pushing their way into the current, at
one time setting a record that turned Fort Benton into the world's most inland seaport, some 3500 miles from the Gulf of Mexico. But in low water,
boats could only navigate as far upstream as Cow Island, where Chief
Joseph on his run to Canada once surprised a whiskeyed-up poker game
at the small trading post. Above the cottonwood flats where the post once
stood, occasional .44-40 cases still show up below the shallow trenches
where the traders dug in to shoot at Indians who only wanted to eat.

If you visit on the right sort of day, with nobody else around (quite
common at Cow Island, even yet) you can know the way the silent appearance of half a thousand Indians might completely disconnect the
synapses of a bored whiskey mind. It is also not hard to imagine the puz-
zlement of the Indians, carefully ransacking the post for flour and buffalo
jerky, as the traders popped away at them from artillery range with their
impotent Winchesters. Below the rifle pits there stands a single foot-thick
wooden post, a long Winchester shot from the river, where steamboats
tied up before the river changed course decades ago.

In the cliffs near Cow Island, people have found dinosaur femurs as
big as railroad ties; yellowed buffalo bones still erode from gullies. The
shacks of the woodhawks who cut firewood for the steamboats, and the
old homestead cabins that once lined the river, are all abandoned now.
Some are so decrepit that unless you find a chunk of broad-axed timber
you'd never know anything was built there, though one log homestead
still has a galvanized funnel embedded through its wall, for bladder relief
during blizzards that must have seemed very damned long. On hard cliffs
there are occasional petroglyphs, simple stick-carvings of the sun and an
antelope and a hunter. Once, searching under an overhang for a rattlesnake to tickle and photograph, we found a pile of human bones. It
turned out to be a genuine Indian burial, though already discovered a few
weeks before, the reason the skull was not in there with the snakes, but
resting on some university desk-top, waiting the pronouncements of
learned elders.

A friend and I canoe down there every couple of years or three, because it is so empty, a wilderness contained along a narrow river, the
steep sandstone now housing animals once long-gone from the plains, elk
and bighorn sheep and mountain lions and who knows? One old rancher, now dead, told me he shot a wolf in the mid-1970s near the mouth of
the Judith.

Our excuse for floating the October river in hand-driven canoes is
mule deer, with antlers so large even a stylized petroglyph might not imitate them. You could call us trophy hunters, that often malignant term,
except for the fact that we have never killed a deer down there. We have
looked at them, a buck or a herd standing at the head of a coulee rough
enough to kill a Himalayan climber, not seen anything resembling a petroglyph, and let them be. We camp on Lewis and Clark's river bars and
read from their journals, or in the shade of a yellow-leaved cottonwood
near an old homestead, or at the mouth of a draw filled with buffalo
bones, a bighorn ram standing and watching us as innocently as others
watched the Corps of Discovery.

We get as alone and lost as anyone can in the last decade of the twentieth century, in these contiguous and disintegrating Lower 48. One year
my friend's mother had a stroke and his wife called all the available au-
thorities—the local sheriff's department, the Fish Wildlife & Parks, and
the Bureau of Land Management—to try to get word to us down in the
deepest Breaks. Four days later we were waved into the bank by some
hunters who had walked in, who relayed a garbled message that made it
seem that either or both our wives were dead. Four days, when people
who knew the river were looking for us pretty hard. The news was not exactly heartening but some months afterward, knowing we could
disappear sure was.

At the end of the digging of Fort Chardon I had to stand in the wind
and plot all the little treasures on my field map, where we'd found beads
and knives, where the outlines of the palisade ran. I borrowed a transit
from one of the highway crew, rather than use my usual Brunston compass, and found something odd: the walls of the palisade were exactly
square, but only ran almost north and south. They were off six degrees,
tilted to the east. This puzzled us no end, because any official rectangle
built by white men is almost always laid out along the axis of the earth,
rather than facing the sun like any sensible tipi.

And then I remembered something we don't often encounter in
Montana because our white architecture is so new. The magnetic pole
moves. "True" north shifts around in an erratic pattern like the worm

holes in the logs of a woodhawk's cabin. Back in Missoula I found that in 1843, magnetic north was just about six degrees different than in 1980.

And that is what always happens every time I think my Missouri has been finally laid out and defined, forged into some historical memory like the maps of the Louisiana Purchase the Corps of Discovery was sent to explore. Each time the river gets nailed to the earth it decides to shift channels, switching part of someone's ranch to the north side of the river, eating into another buffalo jump, or leaving big gaps like the Shonkin Sag in the middle of the Highwood Mountains. Each time someone decides to build a bridge they hit a mammoth tusk, or dig up the bones of an Indian woman with copper thimbles on all her fingers. Every day the wind blows downriver you can smell cottonwoods or asphalt , or hear the Great Falls or the rumble of wheat trucks. Each time I look the current shifts, a sandstone cliff crumbles over an old stagecoach road, there are elk in the Breaks again, the world is six degrees off truth, and I have to start all over, up where the Three Forks come together and the Missouri River begins.

THIS SAVAGE LAND:
THE YAAK

By Rick Bass

YOU CAN SEE THE GUYS FROM THE EAST getting a bit funny-eyed, when Tim and I walk down to the put-in carrying a chain saw. It's raining hard, pouring off the brims of our caps, and they think it's a practical joke—the four-weight fly rod in one hand and the Stihl 034 Super (with extended bar) in the other. They're so polite, these guys from the East—famous writers, famous fishermen and world travelers—that they don't know whether they're being had or not, but they don't want to risk hurting Tim's or my feelings, so they just kind of huddle in the rain and puff cheerily on their cigars and look up into the drizzle—the damp green woods, with infinite shades of blues, spruce, fir, cedar, pressing in from that riverside wall of green—and they look out at the mist rising from the river. Even the name itself sounds somehow terrible and sharp, Yaak, like the sound a hatchet might make, cleaving flesh and then bone, and per- haps they think, well, why not a chain saw? I am not a fisherman but I love the woods, and the guide, Tim, my friend, has invited me along. They are all dressed elegantly, ready for a bit of sport, and I am wearing my old-stained overalls, ragged steel-toed boots, and I'm acutely aware of being half a foot shorter than any of these lanky, graceful gents—Tim, Tom, Charles, Dan and Chris. Actually Chris is from Utah, Dan's from South Dakota, and Tom's from Jackson Hole, Wyoming, but from a Yaak standpoint, this qualifies them as Easterners. Charles is from Nova Scotia. We have two drift boats and a raft with us, and when I climb in one of the boats with my chain saw, I think they are also acutely aware of my stumpiness, and with the saw, and climbing awkwardly—not knowing much about boats—I do not feel like a fellow fly-fisherman, but like a pi- rate.

How gentlemanly are they? Dan hunts gyrfalcons in Saudi Arabia with princes. Charles and Tom and Chris own more bird dogs than I have empty aluminum cans in the plastic bag behind my barn. They hunt red deer in Mongolia, wild boar in Europe, and now they've come to the Yaak to fish in the rain for tadpole-sized brook trout while some troll rides along with them, scouting for firewood.

"Got enough gas?" Tim asks me. "Got your saw tool?"

I nod. Now Tim goes over to the fishermen and asks them what kind of flies they have, and what size. Charles, Dan and Chris answer him dutifully; only Tom thinks to question authority. "Does it really matter?" he asks, and Tim looks surprised, then says, "No, they'll probably hit anything."

There is so much about fly-fishing that I do not understand, but I know that Tim is a great guide, so great that he does not have to be a snob. The river doesn't get too much traffic, for reasons of the multitude of tiny unsophisticated fish that will never be anything other than tiny, as well as for the long winding flat stretches of river, and also because, as the gentlemen visitors who've come into the valley are beginning to see, there is throughout the valley the vague and uncomfortable sense that the locals—us—may be watching you from behind the bushes, and that they—we, the locals—have some other-ness that is not easily defined, but which is not relaxing to visitors.

We didn't move up here to be around crowds, which may bring up the question of why I am then mentioning this river in the first place, this slow-moving water of dull-witted fingerlings. (I am tempted to tell you that Yaak is the Kootenai word for carp, or leech, or "place of certain diarrhea." It truthfully means *arrow*, but could also double to mean *rain*.)

Tim and I spend a good amount of time at other periods of the year hiking in the mountains, looking for antlers, looking for bear dens, looking for huckleberries, and in the fall hunting for grouse, and later in the winter, rattling deer and chasing elk—and then after that, grouse again, in the snow, in December, with our beautiful, talented dogs, and after that, ducks...

On these trips, year in and year out, Tim and I go round and round in our anguish: do we keep silent about this hard-logged valley, or do we pipe up plaintively, make little cheepings, like killdeer skittering along the shore? We really don't care for the tourist hordes to come gawk at the clearcuts, or come feel the blue wet winds—to eat a cheeseburger at either of the local bars, to stand in the parking lot and marvel at the menagerie of woods-hermit-come-to-town-on-Saturday, as if a circus is parading past: gentle hippies, savage government-lothers, angry misanthropes, romantic anarchists, and a few normal people who in their normalcy appear somehow odd. Surely they are masking some great aberration. And those are the ones who come to town—who venture out in the light of day! The rest of us like to hide.

There is a certain duct-tape of the spirit that pervades up here. I'm not sure why, unless it's simply that things break a lot. It hasn't infected Tim yet and I guess after seven years if it were going to, it would have. He's neat and precise and does his job, finding fish and wild game in an orderly, calculated fashion. But many of the rest of us tie socks over our broken windshield wipers, for instance, rather than venturing into town to get new wiper blades. We try to keep three of everything: one that runs, one for parts, and one for a backup, if there's not time to switch our parts. But usually there's time.

We get our food, our meat and berries, from the land, and our produce from our gardens: root crops, which can stand the eternal cold. Blue smoke rises from chimneys year round. The scent carries far in the humidity, in the drizzle.

The grizzlies aren't any problem up here; what will get you are the leeches, blackflies, mosquito hordes, and eight species of horseflies (including one the size of the head of a railroad spike, whose bite is like being nipped by a fencing tool).

I don't mean to be falling over myself so much, rolling out the welcome mat. The logging trucks just keep on rolling out of the valley (the Yaak gives up more timber than any other valley in the Lower Forty-Eight; of late, up to two-thirds of it has been big mixed conifers, rather than the readily available beetle-killed lodgepole). They drive hard and fast, leaving the valley, leaving the country with their cargoes, and they will run your tourist-ass off the cliffs in a minute, then laugh about it.

Tim's livelihood depends, more or less, on bringing people into the valley. But like most of us, he thinks it would be nice to keep Yaak the way it is, or even better, the way it was five or ten or twenty years ago. (Twenty-eight years ago, there was only one road through the valley. Now there are over a thousand miles of road, and counting. And still not one acre of protected wilderness.)

Relax. I'm not going to lay the enviro eco-rap on you. Or will try not to. I'm trying to kind of place you in Tim's position.

He needs people to ride in his boat and cast flies, for him to keep living up here; just as some must keep building roads, or cutting trees, to keep living up here. But when there are no fish, and no more trees, and when every last mountain has a road onto it...then what? Then do we learn Russian or Swahili or Chinese, and start a community college in the Yaak, and teach semiconductor manufacturing in the evenings?

Tim's already gotten a bad reputation, a bad rap, as not really wanting to guide. There's very little telephone service or electricity in the Yaak, and it's a long damn way to any airport—over three hours to Kalispell, four to Spokane, five to Missoula, one way—and so many other sweeter places are so much closer, in this state.

Phone service and electricity are erratic up here. Tim's answering machine has some electronic glitch—some pulse of the wild, perhaps, that it has picked up from the soil itself, as the coils and cables snake just beneath the skin of the earth—which causes it to shut off on the incoming message after your first six words, so you'd better choose them well.

Other guides joke (though I get the sense they really believe it, too) that it's something Tim does on purpose—that not so deep down, he doesn't want new clients. Or maybe that he wants them, but then feels guilty about wanting them. The way I feel guilty, about writing about this wet buggy valley.

So Tim gambles that the people he introduces to the slow snag-infested water will fall in love with the valley and work to keep it from being further abused, and I make the same gamble, continuing to write about it.

That's what the chain saw's for, on this trip: snags. It's a little river, and trees fall down across it regularly, blocking your passage. In other places, the deep river suddenly splits into four braids, each only a few inches deep, so that you may have to portage if you don't pick the right one. Also, there is a guy up here who lives along the river and hunts with a blow dart. He likes to hide in the bushes and shoot tourists. At first you think it's just another horsefly. But then you develop a headache, and then you grow sleepy. You put the oars down and lie down in the boat for a minute, just to nap, you think...

If you did come all the way up to this last tiny river, it could be deadly not to use Tim for a guide. And if you did come, there'd be that vow of undying commitment we'd ask you to sign: to fight forever, hard and passionately for this wet people-less place, on behalf of all wildness—to keep it as it is, at least.

Of course, we're asking you to take that vow anyway, whether you come or not. For the grizzlies, wolves, woodland caribou, elk, and wolverines that live back in what remains of the wet jungle, and which you would never see anyway, if you were to come up here, as they've all become almost totally nocturnal. And for those eight species of horseflies, which have not.

I guess you're waiting to hear about the river, and about fish, and here I am yowling about wilderness like I've got my teat caught in a wringer. But it seems so simple. We have only three Congressmen for the whole state. There is no designated, protected wilderness in the valley. If everyone who liked or favored clean water and the notion of a dark secret place, with feisty little fish and tame moose and great blue heron rookeries and dense spruce jungles—if everyone who liked these things would begin a correspondence with the three gentlemen concerning the Yaak, I think they would finally come to understand that, timber budget or not, the remaining roadless acres in the Yaak should be protected.

Back to the gents. It's an honor to be in their company. They don't care if they catch fish or not. They just enjoy being out-of-doors, and in a new land. Since childhood they've probably caught seven million fish, cumulatively. Every fish mouth in the world is sore from their hooks. Today they're just enjoying being alive. They're just standing in the rain.

I'm in Tom's raft, to begin with. Dan and Charles are in their own boat, and Tim's ranging ahead of them in his boat, with Chris, like a bird dog. The guys stop at the first gravel bar and get out and wade near the line where some fast water meets some slow water, and begin casting pretty casts into the line.

But nothing. Tim rows on, as if knowing there aren't any fish there. Tom watches Tim disappear around the bend and starts to say something, but doesn't. We lean back and watch Charles and Dan cast. If they catch something, maybe we'll rig up. Charles, Dan, Chris and Tom have been on a road trip across Montana—they've fished nine rivers in nine days. This is the tenth, and Charles (from Nova Scotia, and formerly, New England, and before that, the South), is raving about what a beautiful, perfect little trout stream it is: how it reminds him of when he was a child, and was first learning how to fish on tiny little brook trout rivers.

He's tired of all the muscle rivers of the past nine days and, believe it or not, tired of all the muscle fish. He's content to drift, and smoke his cigar in the rain, and cast.

The Yaak is a tiny river but an important one, especially with the loss of the upper Kootenai River (and the now-extinct Ural Valley) to the wretched dam that formed Lake Koocanusa, in order to send more juice to California. The Yaak flows from four forks down into what remains of the Kootenai, a river that reminds one of the Mississippi. And the Kootenai then flows, Yaak-laden, into the Columbia. And we know where the Columbia goes, and what happens to it.

It boggles my mind to stand in one of the cedar forests high in the mountains of Yaak, and watch that creek—say, Fix Creek—go trickling down through the forest, a foot wide and a foot deep—and to picture it being received by the Yaak, and then by the Kootenai, and then by the Columbia, and then by the ocean.

This is my home. I love it. It is in danger.

I know that in writing about a river, you're supposed to concentrate on the fish—and then, narrowing the focus further, upon the catching of them.

Tim's a good guide, a great guide. He can find you a big deer. It's not real good elk country—too many roads, not enough security areas, according to biologists—but he can give it the best shot of anybody. He's ruining me, corrupting me with his maniacal sense of sportsmanship. We shoot only about every tenth grouse, now. *Too slow!* we'll cry to each other when a bird crosses the other's path, or *Young bird!* or *Old bird! Let'er go!*—year by year increasing our ridiculous standards, out of our love for this savage place, until a grouse just about has to be going ninety miles an hour downhill through doghair lodgepole in the rain for us to get the green light

I wonder sometimes if I will corrupt Tim with my duct-tape-ness. While hunting with him, I carry plastic Ziploc bags and collect bear scat to give to the biologists for DNA testing of genetic vigor. While drifting the Yaak we stop and search for pretty river rocks. We collect water samples. Corrupting each other, we do just about everything but fish. Tim tells me the names of the insects, teaches me to cast, but time and time again I skew the subject, and talk about baseball, or football—about his moribund, erratic Patriots, or my choke-bound Oilers.

If it's spring, we discuss the autumn; if it's fall, we discuss the spring. In the summer and fall, when it rains, we talk about how nice it is to be dry.

I jabber a mile a minute, and never about fishing, and rarely about hunting, but always, it seems, about the valley.

Tim rows in closer to shore to examine the skeleton of a bull moose that has drowned in one of the deep holes, and tells me about the time he caught an eight-inch rainbow by dragging a nymph through the moose's algae-hued skeleton, ten feet down—the fish rising from the pelvis to take the nymph and then trying to turn back to the sanctuary of the vertebrae, but no luck, Tim horsed him in, released him gently...

I know you're not going to travel this far to catch an eight-inch rainbow. But maybe you can travel over to your desk and pick up a pen. Sort through the papers 'til you find a stray postcard. And write the three gentlemen.

The five gentlemen and myself drift. It's a pleasure to watch them cast. The word Tim uses to describe the river is "intimate." The Kootenai is where he makes his money (as much as any guide ever makes, which is to say, not much), and the Yaak is what he saves for a few special lazy days of the year.

It's still raining, but slants of light are coming down in shafts and beams through the fog-like clouds along the river, fog hanging in the tops of the giant spruce and cedar and fir trees that remain. These trees are a function of the thin soil, tight gray clay over glacial cobble, and the soil is a function of the bedrock, which is in turn a function of the earth's belly, the earth's anatomy—what she desires to belch up here in this spongy, lush river country.

At times it is more of a creek than a river, like a child's ride in a raft through an amusement park, with the theme of "jungle." You can reach out and touch either bank, in places. Deer rise from the tall grass to peer at you, only their heads visible over the banks: big-eyed does, wide-ribbed in pregnancy, and bucks in velvet nubs.

"Short casts," Tim tells the occasional wanderer who inquires about fishing the Yaak with him. "Short casts. Intimate. You can see everything. You can see the moss growing on the rocks. You can see the caddis nymphs, the stonefly nymphs, crawling under their rocks. You can see the fish. Intimate," he says.

Purple anvil-shaped thunderheads tower behind us, rising between the forested mountains all the way to the outer arc of the atmosphere, and perhaps beyond: we are so wet, so drenched, and it is still raining so steadily, that perhaps it is raining on the moon. Still, that's behind us, to the north, crossed over into Canada's great reservoir of roadlessness, and perhaps some brief clearing lies ahead of us.

We pass beneath an old wooden covered bridge. Soon we will be out in the riffles, in which we have all been catching tiny leaping rainbow trout, black and silver, like anchovies.

We trade off riding in different boats and rafts, to chat; to get to know one another. It's not about fishing. It's about being in the Yaak. It's about feeling the magic of all the little feeder creeks, cedar-streams, not so rich in nutrients, but rich in magic, emptying into the Yaak's little belly. Later in the summer there will be a drought, whose only saving grace will be that the temperatures never get too hot; though the river will drop drastically, lower than it's ever been measured in white man's history; and in August, fires will move through on the south-facing slopes, cleaning out the underbrush, the dried-up buffalo berry that has grown up following old logging operation, and cleansing some of the lodgepole stands up high of pine beetles. And in September, on Labor Day, as on every Labor Day, the rains will return, extinguishing the fires, and beginning to give ease to the suffering creeks, and the fish, all fish, will begin gathering at their mouths, readying to spawn in the fall rains, as they have almost every year through the millennia.

(Tim, a lover of waters, has moved up and down almost every creek in this country, every backwater beaver-slough he can find, taking pictures of the occasional freak brook trout, or the incredibly rare, lingering-on giant West Slope cutthroat trout—and the creeks which haven't been streamside or headwaters-logged, no surprise, tolerate the droughts much better, each year, than the clearcut stretches...)

We pass beneath giant cedars. A few more fish. I hook a ten-inch rainbow which will be the heavy of the day. Wild rainbows, and wild West Slope cutthroats, and the gorgeous little brook trout. It's not unusual, Tim says, to catch all three; while just below, in the Kootenai, the bull trout line up, stack up at the mouths of feeder creeks in the early autumn, the last handful of bull trout in this drainage, bull trout breathing water breathed by sturgeon, and each year these little creeks get filled in with more and more sediment, lower and lower, and each year the bulls wait to make their heroic runs one more time.

We talk about books, we talk about politics, we talk about dogs and food and friends and assholes. We talk about the ocean and about Africa and about childhood. Charlie is smoking a pipe now, and the smoke mixes with the fog. These damn little fish keep hooking themselves on our casts. Some of us put our rods down and just ride. The water turns dark, deep. Like any small river, the Yaak can be overfished by a single meat-guy, and has been. The days of big fish in big holes are no longer with us, but because the river's small, the little fish still hide behind almost every rock.

Later on, at supper, we'll hit our friends up for letters to save this wild green place—this place which has never been saved. We'll tell them how, in all the years, there's never been a single acre of wilderness protected; how the international timber companies have long had their way in this forgotten, hidden place. We tell them that it's time to hold the Montana delegation responsible. Tim will discuss the Kootenai, and the

Libby Dam operations, at length. The sign-up sheet will be passed, the new letter writers recruited, before dessert's passed out—if they want any dessert. A trade; the army, the small battalion, growing by four.

All that will come later. Right now it's time only for intimacy. Green drakes begin to rise from the water, and Tim is overjoyed: in seven years, he's never seen them on the Yaak. He wants to believe that the river is recovering. We're drifting through a meadow now, where every year before cattle had grazed, but this year the cattle are gone, and the willows have grown at least a foot, and the green drakes are swarming, landing on our arms as if trying to tell us things.

A purple thundercloud drifts up the river to meet us—lashes us with stinging rain. We laugh like school kids walking home in a storm. We come around one corner—aspens, white pine, alder, ash, all clinging to a rock outcrop—and turn into a cool dark tunnel of cedar and spruce. Another bend, and now an old spruce stretches across the little river, spiny limbs splayed everywhere, resting a few inches above the river and spanning it completely. It's so big that it had to have long been a giant even before the whites first moved into the valley in the early 1900's. It's probably fifty inches across; it's too low to go under, but too high to drag our boats up over it.

The current has quickened, here in this dark tunnel, and we back-paddle to avoid being drawn into the limbs and turned sideways. We're all aware of the furious, silent power of water, even relatively mild water—the strength of its mass—and the way things can turn bad quickly.

Carefully, I climb up on top of the tree—thrashing through the maw of branches—and Tim anchors, and hands the saw to me.

The saw's wet, and won't start, at first. We're a long way from anywhere. It's raining harder still.

Finally the saw coughs, then ignites, with a belch of blue smoke and a roar, and I choke it back to a purr, then start blipping off branches to clear a working area. Sawdust showers all three boats, and all five fishermen. The rain beating down quickly mixes with the sawdust to coat them all in a sodden paste. A bit of bar oil drips into the river, sends a heartbreaking iridescent rainbow downcurrent. So much for the pious talk of the afternoon.

I begin making my crosscuts in the huge tree. The roar is deafening. How will I be able to hear grouse flush, this fall?

So much for intimate. The green wood sags. Our worst fear is binding the saw, and I'm careful, but can't get beneath the log with the blade—not unless I put it underwater.

There's a creaking, and the log drops an inch, pinches the saw tight. Now we're screwed. We take turns clambering onto the log and pulling, wrenching and twisting—a fly-fisherman's version of *The Sword in the Stone*. A fly-fishing guide's nightmare. Surely he's wondering why he brought me.

The rain lashes at us. Finally Tim, in the strength of desperation, is able to free the saw. I start it back up. Nothing runs like a Stihl.

I'm standing in the bow of his new boat, now, making a new cut, and making good progress, when a new sound begins to emanate from the saw, a splintery sound, accompanied by a certain bucking and vibrating feeling within the boat. *Ahh*, I think, *we're into the heartwood, now.*

Out of the corner of my eye, I notice a new color of sawdust beginning to appear in the pile around our ankles: a cream-colored sawdust, a sawdust that is the same color as Tim's boat.

He's such a gentleman! "That's okay," he says, when I lift the saw and stare, aghast, at the cut in the gunwale: as if I aimed to sink us! "Just a ding," he says.

He doesn't belong up here, really. He's like those four other gents. He's too courteous, and too *professional*. I'm afraid of giving him my virus, the one that makes you fond of duct tape; afraid of infecting him somehow with a woods-priggishness, a kind of savagery that is not uncommon in Yaak. I want him to be immune from it: and so far, he is. His New England heritage, etc. I've already torn up his truck; he parked it behind my old beater one day, and I backed into it. "Ah, that's okay," he said then, too, "just a ding."

It's a different place, up here. A certain roughness of spirit; a wildness. You can see it in the old cars and trucks, in all the old rotting things. A certain endurance, a willingness to go on, even when a bit crippled up by hard times, by deep snows, or whatever. But Tim's a pro, and such a nice guy: I feel guilty, as if my looseness, my Yaakness, might cramp his style. As if the valley might cramp his style.

He loves it, too. At least as much as I do. I guess if he were going to turn into a savage, it would have already happened.

I finish the cut, avoiding the boat this time. The log drops with a crash, swings free; the current surges. New structure—a new hole for the worm fishermen. We pull up anchor and release ourselves through the slot, like salmon through a gate. The rain finally lets up, and sunlight comes pouring down out of the mountains. We're into the long, slow water, now—flat water, and lots of rowing. We're cold, chilled to the deep bone. Fresh sawdust floats downriver with us, preceding us for a mile or so.

Shadows deepen. There's one touchy moment when we come to a spot in the river where a man has draped a 220-volt electrical line across the river at neck level, as if to electro-shock us; but it turns out he's only doing some welding over on the other side of the river. In the dimness like that, we might not have seen it, but Tim knows the man, is friendly with him, as he is with everyone, and he gives the magic password, and the man lifts his cable high enough for us to pass through unelectrocuted.

We take out in deepening, buggy twilight, slapping mosquitoes, and go up to the tavern to catch one of the basketball playoffs. Later that night, we feast on a wild game supper, wine and cigars and stories past midnight.

Driving home that night, Tim will tell me, he saw a lynx cross the road, with only three paws; the fourth paw was raw and stumpy, Tim said, probably from a trap, but it seemed like the lynx was going to make it, just by the way it went across the road. Tim could tell it was still wanting to go on, he said, and he said he got the feeling that it was going to be all right: that it would be able to rest up, and recover.

WALKING THE BOULDER

By William Hjortsberg

AS A SPECIES, WE SEEM INEXORABLY DRAWN toward water. Rivers run through our lives and our literature. Human bodies are largely composed of H20. Perhaps this explains the mysterious attraction. The river that runs through us is saline, the chemical composition of plasma so close to sea water our very blood duplicates the ocean which once nourished our single-celled ancestors. A solitary walk along any beach reconfirms this connection. Our ancient mother's soft lullaby is the sound of rushing water.

When I was a child, I spent my summers in a stately turn-of-the-century shingle-style house in a part of the Catskill Mountains that did not have comedians or singing waiters. Screened by billowing maples, elms and white oak, Woodland Brook ran below the house on its way to join the Esopus near the town of Phoenicia. The creek's constant purling pervaded my early life.

I learned to swim and fish in its chill pools. The smell of rain drying on sun-warmed river rock forever recalls faraway summertime afternoons: shivering and gooseflesh after skinny-dipping, searching the creek bank for flat round skipping stones, tickling the cold bellies of brown trout lurking in the watery shadows beneath cushion-sized boulders. Looking back, it seems Woodland Brook's early seductive whisper has influenced just about every geographic choice I've made in my life.

One winter, my parents took me by train to St. Petersburg, Florida. I was almost six. Snapshots show me having a swell time at the beach and I'm sure if I'd spent my entire youth at the shore instead of just a month or so, I'd be living someplace in the Caribbean now, rather than in a log cabin overlooking the Boulder River, south of Big Timber in Sweet Grass County. I've been here more than ten years and have learned to be unfailingly precise about my location because there's another Boulder River in Montana, which flows out of the Boulder Range and joins the Jefferson near Cardwell. This can cause some confusion.

When I tell people I live "on the Boulder," they always assume I'm talking about the town of Boulder on the banks of that other river. Presumably, Montana's pioneers were so busy chopping down trees and scratching ore out of the ground there was time for only the most limited lexicon when they finally got around to bestowing place names on their new surroundings. Our landscape is littered with a plethora of Pine, Deer and Deep creeks, almost every county boasts a Jewel or Lost lake, and we are blessed with not one, but two, Boulder rivers.

The one I live on forms high in the Absaroka-Beartooth Wilderness, near Boulder Pass to the northeast of Sheepherder Peak, at an elevation of 9,500 feet. It runs north, being joined along the way by East and West forks before, in turn, flowing into the Yellowstone at Big Timber. (This distinguishes it from the other Boulder River, which flows in a southerly direction and gets to the Missouri a whole lot sooner.)

From my deck, I look down into a small glacially rounded mountain valley where the Main Boulder meanders in great looping ox-bows. The stern, looming facade of the Lion Head, a two-hundred-foot rust-colored limestone cliff, dominated the scene like some improbable mountaintop sphinx. Golden eagles nest here, conveniently above a resident population of ducks and Canada geese, gabbling far below at every willow-fringed sandbar bend.

The slow water lazes between vast boulders and pools deep enough to drown a moose. One big hole, the bottom lost in dark implacable green, is the site of an unfinished pioneer bridge. I can just make out the blunt, blackened ranks of weathered pilings jutting from the shallows along the opposite bank. A beaver lives in the jumbled driftwood thicket piled against several large stranded logs on the gravel bar tailing below the hole. The resident rodent resents any intrusions, unobtrusive anglers no exception. When I fish here, often as not the beaver makes an angry appearance, paddling around in circles and slapping his tail on the surface like a canoe paddle. This dude is an expert when it come to spooking rising trout.

Just across the gravel road from my cabin, the tranquil stream abruptly plunges into a steep canyon. The sudden rapids stood in for the Blackfoot River, providing a portion of the "shooting the chutes" sequence in Robert Redford's film of *A River Runs Through It*. Tumbling toward Boulder River falls, which at 110 feet is entirely more lethal than its cinematic equivalent, the river I walk along plunges from pool to pool, a terraced cascade of angling possibilities. Sandpipers skitter along the gravel banks. Ouzels bob and dip beneath the turbulent surface. In season, a profusion of wildflowers bejewels the mossy walls framing the start of the canyon.

Back when I first moved to the Boulder more than a decade ago, the Natural Bridge was still among the standing, although most of the year it stood beneath the surface, covered by a huge pool just upstream from the brink of the falls. Not that it mattered; the incredible waterfall was the main attraction.

That first winter, in the spirit of my Woodland Brook boyhood, I took many exploratory hikes, up and down the river, learning the local terrain. Carved over the eons by rushing water, the dramatic canyon below the falls divides the landscape for half a mile like the ultimate Christo project. Vertical limestone cliffs drop a hundred feet deep into the earth, cleaving the gentle grass-covered hills. I soon found my way to the bottom, following fissures where blocks of the 315 million-year-old sedimentary rock shelved away from the canyon wall. The strata is Mississippian, an ancient ocean floor studded with tiny fossilized shells.

Those first few seasons, the upper falls flowed all year long. In winter, encased in a towering icicle, the falling water formed frozen crystalline tubes tall as a skyscraper, magic as the minarets of Oz. Wintertime transforms the vast pool at the base of the waterfall into a landlocked pond. During periods of low water, the Boulder River flows underground for the length of the canyon and I clambered over the whitened boulders, enclosed on either side by sheer cliffs, an environment so seemingly extra-terrestrial that pretending to be Flash Gordon required a minimum of imagination.

I searched for fossils on the gravel bar skirting the long, narrow pool where the river emerged at the canyon's abrupt end. Half-buried in the sand, the grotesque mummified remains of a dog lay frozen on its side. It looked to be an Airedale and no doubt far more friendly in life than the skeletal snarl suggested. A thick leather collar encircled the cadaverous neck. I had no trouble making out an embossed phone number on the dangling brass tag.

When I called the number, I got a veterinarian's office. They knew all about the unfortunate Airedale. The previous spring, the dog had been playing fetch with his mistress, an elderly widow, who accidentally threw a stick into the rushing Boulder River. To her horror, the animal leapt after it and was swept over the falls. The vet allowed he probably wouldn't inform the woman of my recent discovery.

Encountering something so emblematic of mortality on my initial expedition proved oddly prophetic. Within the next couple years, dramatic changes occurred on the stretch of river near my home, the first a bit of magic worthy of Merlin. Just back from a trip to London one March, I went for my usual stroll, across the road into the National Forest for a look at the waterfall. From the wooden footbridge arching over the Boulder, I made an astonishing discovery; the falls had vanished.

The final hundred yards of streambed leading to the precipice were bare, bleached and lunar; dry as a boneyard. All the water in the river now swirled down into a large hole beneath the Natural Bridge. It was an astonishing sight. As close to the parting of the Red Sea as I'll ever come.

I wondered if a logjam had clogged the hole. Did it suddenly break free? Whatever the reason, the Boulder River now flows over the upper falls for only brief periods during spring runoff. The lower falls still cascade mightily, itself a thing of wonder, but it can't compare with staring down through multiple mist rainbows as an entire river drops off an overhang ten stories high.

The second big change came the summer the Natural Bridge fell down. I wasn't around when it happened, having spent the night in Bozeman, but people still ask me if I heard it go. There was initial talk of vandalism, some wacko with dynamite, but no evidence backed this up and in the end, the finger of blame pointed at an earth tremor. Forest Service signs still proudly announce: NATURAL BRIDGE FALLS. There's even a parking lot for visitors. Not that the spectacular view from the canyon rim isn't worth a stop, but it does seem as if the headliners have died and gone to heaven.

Modest proposal: Why not chunk a couple of school bus bodies down into the big hole? Get some water flowing over the falls again. Surely this is no more insulting to the environment than the asphalt walkways snaking through clustered fir trees to the lookouts at the canyon's edge. Since all the king's horses and all the king's men can't put the Natural Bridge back together again, isn't having a working waterfall better than nothing at all?

Of course, this nothing comprises everything worth saving on earth. The Boulder Valley retains an integrity of place quite rare in our frantic age of constant change. The large ranches on the lower river and the church camps above the falls look much the same today as they did thirty years ago. Few subdivisions intrude on the way things always were.

A distressing amount of media attention has focused on the handful of celebrity residents on the Boulder and West Boulder without taking into account what is truly beneficial about their presence. Not much mention is ever made of the conservation easements many have placed on their property, thereby perpetuating permanence, that rarest of legacies.

I've heard this form of land preservation decried as "elitist," a position with which I strongly disagree. There are numbers of public campgrounds and trailheads along the upper river. I ask myself, if I lived in the city and hauled my pickup camper up the Boulder for a week of hunting or fishing, would I rather drive through an untouched valley that still looked the same as it did in my childhood, or would I prefer confronting wall-to-wall aluminum doublewides?

Land developers like to dignify their profession by describing such destruction of pristine rural areas as "progress." Surely, George Orwell warned us of the dire consequences inherent in accepting such insidious example of Newspeak into the language. Only a nightmarish dystopia would consider a trailer park more progressive than a mountain meadow.

Time to climb down off my soapbox and take another stroll along the riverbank. I walk beside the Boulder as often as I fish her inviting pools. There are said to be no whitefish above the falls and indeed I've never caught one in the upper river. Brook trout, rainbow and cutthroat all share this water. The wily German brown is here as well, but can be found in greater numbers in the slow meanderings downriver or over on the beautiful West Boulder, as perfect a trout stream as the mind can imagine.

Game abounds. It's rare not to encounter whitetail and mule deer. I've also spotted elk, moose and black bear while rambling under the floodplain cottonwoods. Small animals are everywhere. Beaver, muskrat, skunk, mink, marten and marmot all frequent the shoreline. In winter, bald eagles hunt along the Boulder and are a common sight, hunched in the bare treetops like arboreal Capuchin monks with their stark white cowls.

Aimless walks are mainly my pleasure, simply maundering along without motive, delighting in whatever wonders serendipity happens to provide. Sometimes, though, it's nice to have a destination, an actual goal to provide my goofing-off with a sense of purpose, however incidental or far-fetched. On the southern slope of the Lion Head are several large caves which can be reached by starting up the Grouse Creek trail. This is a hike that actually goes somewhere.

As I ascend, the Boulder diminishes to a twisted silver ribbon decorating the valley far below. The largest of the caves frames this view like a gigantic picture window, but scenery alone is not what makes the climb worthwhile. Five ancient red pictographs embellish the rough cave walls, daubed crudely onto the uneven rock. Two are sun symbols (or perhaps represent stretched bear hides), two are stick-figure hunters (one holding a shield), and the fifth depicts a small tethered animal.

I heard a rumor once in the McLeod Bar that these were actually painted back in the '30s by the foreman of a local dude ranch who wanted the tenderfeet to have something to write home about. This might well have been the way it happened, but I prefer to believe the pictographs are over a thousand years old, the work of shamans seeking to give form to the inexplicable. As such, they provide a fitting decor for a cave where the rock shelves in back are piled thick with pine boughs, soft beds for the cougars who litter the sloping sandy floor with the gnawed vertebrae of deer and elk.

Not everyone gets to live in ShangriLa. I know I'm a privileged character and never a day goes by that I don't thank whatever benevolent fate brought me to the Boulder River. So much that is fragile and beautiful on our benighted planet is threatened with oblivion. It is the duty of those lucky enough to live in paradise to protect what we have left.

Recent attempts to weaken the state's clean water standards are but one threat to the pristine beauty we perhaps take for granted. The Stillwater Mining Company has gained approval for a new underground platinum and palladium mine on a site up the East Boulder. The planned tailing pond will have earthen walls three hundred feet high within a shadow's length of the river. It doesn't take much prescience to foresee potential disaster in this plan.

Edward Abbey, wise curmudgeon guru, once counseled us all to defend our drainages. This is sage advice. Think globally, act locally. Whenever I walk along the unblemished banks of the Boulder, the soft murmuring voice of running water reminds me of my proprieties. I hear the comforting echo of Woodland Brook, feel the pull of every trout stream I've waded in a lifetime of fishing. A river pulses through me, profound, compassionate, as vital as blood. Only a fool would fail to heed its eternal call.

VISIONS OF A RIVER: THE HENRY'S FORK

By Geoff Norman

IT WAS NOT LOVE AT FIRST SIGHT, which was unusual for someone who had never met a river he did not love. But I was an angler who lived in the East and this was my first trip to the West to fish the rivers that I had read and heard so much about. Rivers that had become mythic in my imagination. And the Henry's Forks, when I first saw it from the highway, was disappointing.

Its surface was wide, flat and the color of lead. There was no cascading white water and there were no boulders in the middle of the stream. No majestic trees along its banks. Instead, there were pullouts where pickups and a few RVs were parked. The usual gas stations, motels, bars and laundromats—as well as a couple of fly shops—along the side of the road. An empty, monotonous country covered in grass and brush that was a tawny yellow in the middle of a dry summer. Except for the sense of epic space and a line of mountains off in the distance, the scene had a familiar, pedestrian feel. I could have been back in the East or the Midwest.

Feeling slightly cheated, I went into one of the fly shops to buy a license and get some advice on the fishing. I'd give it a day, I thought sourly, then move on to something better.

That first impression turned out, like so many, to be not just deceptive but flatly wrong. Since that day, twenty years ago, I have tried to get out to fish the Henry's Fork at least once every year. I haven't always made it, but each time that I have, my ardor for the river has grown. If there is a paradise after this life, and I slip through the screening process, I could happily spend eternity wading the water around the Railroad Ranch, in a state of sublime and perfect bliss.

My love affair with the river began tentatively that first day. I did not know, yet, about the Ranch, downstream from Last Chance, Idaho, (a name which I found immediately irresistible) or the Box Canyon, upstream. I simply fished the water across the highway from the Henry's

Fork Angler which, if it looked uninspired from the road, was a wonderful surprise when I stepped into it.

Instead of the surging currents and slick rocks that I had found in other streams on my (often literal) baptism into the world of big stream western fly-fishing, I was walking on a firm bottom covered with sand and gravel. Much of the bottom was covered with a fecund growth of weed. The Henry's Fork was, I realized, actually a much larger version of the spring creeks I had fished back in Pennsylvania. Later, as my education progressed, I learned that the Henry's Fork is, in fact, largely spring fed with temperatures and flows that are more or less constant, though the needs of the potato farmers downstream sometimes come into conflict with the desires of the anglers, and the river is occasionally low because water that is necessary for good trout habitat has been released for irrigation. In paradise, there will not be these kinds of conflicts. But in Idaho, anglers have had to learn to organize and exercise some political muscle.

But, as I say, I learned all that later. On my first day, I was content to wade effortlessly and to marvel at the weed growth that spawned mayflies, thousands of which were hatching all around me. They were small flies: pale morning duns. I hastily tied one on and began casting. Several trout were rising around me. They were all what I would have considered, back east, "nice fish," and a couple of them were a lot better than that.

Within a few minutes, I had put that inauspicious first impression behind me. I fished and kept fishing until there was not enough light left to see my fly and I realized it was time to quit, chiefly because I hadn't done anything about finding a place to spend the night. This became a pattern. When I get near the Henry's Fork, I tend to forget the small stuff: sleeping, eating, that sort of thing.

This is not, decisively, because I catch a lot of fish there. The Henry's Fork is, as even the good angler will tell you, a tough stream. Perhaps because the flow is gentle and the water is clear, the Henry's Fork rainbows are exceedingly wary and selective. You frequently use very small flies and you almost always fish very long, delicate leaders. My memories, especially from those first days, do not include big numbers, which accounts, in part, for the attraction. This is elementary angling logic. The harder the fishing, the better.

So I was quickly beguiled by this river. Changed my plans and decided to stay a few more days. Which is how I came to learn about the Ranch and the Box and some of the water that inhabits my dreams during the long, fishless times back east.

I'd met a man in the Henry's Fork Angler, a doctor, whose feeling for the river was touching and infectious. When I told him I liked the river but I'd only fished the water we could see from the shop, he grew agitated. This was, he said, like saying you liked the Sistine Chapel even though you'd never been inside.

He arranged a float trip for us, down through the Ranch, for the next morning. And our guide would be the owner of the shop, Mike Lawson.

Your memories of days on the water tend to merge into a kind of soft-focus blur, but I can still recall that day with absolute clarity. The fishing was very good, and I can still picture a few of the rainbows, when they took and when they jumped and when I brought them to the net. But the river was the forceful element in this little drama. We got away from the road, from the traffic sounds and the profiles of the RVs parked on the pull-outs, and the river widened and made a sweeping turn. It never picked up speed or got any deeper but it became, now, a much more imposing stream, and I imagined that I could feel the connection to the Pacific, where this water would end up, a couple of thousand miles from here, after it had merged with the water from the South Fork and the Columbia. This was, unquestionably, a big western river. But quiet; not a brawler.

The day was achingly clear with the looming blue profile of the Tetons distinctly visible as you looked downstream and beyond. Between casts, when the fishing was slow, I would look back at the mountains. For some reason, I had a hard time taking my eyes off them—the way they rose, so abruptly and cleanly, above the plain of the land—it was the most compelling view I could remember.

The day got hot. I fished a couple of bank feeders for two or three hours. Crawled up on the bank and slept for an hour. Then watched an eagle riding the thermals and looking for something to kill. It was a long way from the rivers, and the world, I knew.

We floated down into the water adjacent to the actual Railroad Ranch. It was later in the day, and the air had turned cool. The banks and the distant hills glowed orange. The Ranch buildings were not occupied, though these were still the days before the Harrimans had turned the buildings and the land over to the state of Idaho for a park.

It was, I thought, about as fine a spot as you would find on this earth. You know the way that young girls can look at a castle or a big, old mansion and think that it would be impossible to live there and be unhappy. That's the way I felt, on the clear, cool evening about the Railroad Ranch. With half the West to choose from, the Harrimans had picked this spot, and it must have seemed like a no-brainer. High up over Million-aire's Pool with a clear view of the Tetons one way and the wide sweep of the river the other...of course, absolutely, build the ranch right here.

We fished on down past the ranch, and at one point I shared a stretch of water with a moose that stood about hip deep and fed serenely on vegetation. I tried to distinguish the rise of a whitefish from that of a trout. I floated a big, down-winged brown drake over a very nice rainbow and caught the fish, the best I had taken all day. I listened to the alien sound of the sand hill cranes coming in. I was transported. You go to the river to fish, but also because—not to put to fine a point on it—there is something cleansing about it. I felt that way. Reborn...almost.

Mike Lawson, who had known the river all his life, told me stories about the rivers as we floated and fished. I got to know Mike, a little, that day and a lot in the years after that day. I was back when the new Harri-man State Park was dedicated, which Mike considered a sad occasion, even though it would certainly be good for his business. I think he felt it made something that had been private and special into something public and common. On another occasion, I took my wife out to the Henry's Fork and we fished with Mike. He took us back up from the river, into a big stand of lodgepole, where we watched a herd of elk move through, the big bulls bugling. For a couple of Easterners, it was like a revelation.

I went back, on another occasion, with my daughters. They were young and had trouble with the small flies and long leaders, but they could see that the old man was a little weird about this river, so they in-dulged me. And just last summer, when my boss said he wanted to learn how to fly fish and that it seemed like I was the right person to teach him, I took him to the Henry's Fork. I booked a couple of backup days on the South Fork, where I knew we could catch fish, but I wanted him to see the Henry's Fork. He was curious about my passion for trout fishing, and I decided that he needed to see the source. We had a very tough day. It was cold and there were not many flies hatching. But when we speak about going again, he talks about that river and the elegant water we fished right at sunset when he broke off the biggest fish either of us hooked on that trip.

I have not fished—or even seen—it all. Which seems appropriate, somehow. But I have seen a lot of it, from the Box Canyon which I fished during the stone fly hatch one year, to the junction with the South Fork. And I can see, again, what I have already seen without even trying very hard. Back east, on a bad day in March (when they are pretty much all bad) I can see, looking downstream, the wide sweep of the river, the tidy buildings of the ranch, and the angular face of the Tetons, their peaks as white as the occasional soft cumulus cloud that drifts overhead.

I do not know if what I see is, technically, a vision. But I do know this: it will surely do until something better comes along.

THE CLARK FORK: RIVER OF AWE

By Caroline Patterson

AS IT FLOWS FIVE HUNDRED MILES WEST from Montana's Silver Bow Creek to Idaho's Lake Pend Oreille, the Clark Fork is many rivers. Called at various times the In Mis sou let ka, the Spetlum, the Southern Branch of the Flathead and the Missoula River, the Clark Fork is ponderous as it divides the naked hills around Warm Springs, Montana. Furious as it squeezes through the Alberton Gorge. Swift and mysterious as it cuts through the high banks at Superior. But the part of the river I know best is the watery vein that flows through Missoula. Broad, slow, brown in spring and green in late summer, the Clark Fork is a river I have always thought of as civic.

On its north shore, Missoula's downtown rises above the muscled water—the grey, mysterious Wilma Building, a catacomb of apartments and theaters where Marian Anderson once sang and Houdini escaped from a locked trunk, the brick bank buildings and hotels and the ramshackle houses that were the town's first red light district. I have looked at this downtown for thirty-nine years and the sight still fills me with longing for new dresses at the Mercantile, for lunches at the linen-covered tables at the Florence Hotel, for the childhood those names conjure up.

If rivers tell stories, and who's to say they don't, the Clark Fork would gather around a campfire with the other tributaries of the Columbia and tell a story something like this: Nearly 70 million years ago, there was a lake stretching from Drummond to Dillon until the first Rocky Mountains rose up to divide its waters into streams and lakes and rivers.

What comes next and many years later, the Clark Fork would say in a hushed voice, is ice. Thick masses of ice oozing down the broad Purcell Valley of British Columbia to dam the Clark Fork River. The river swelled into Lake Missoula. Back then, a man could swim from Trapper's Peak to Mount Jumbo in waters deep as the Andaman Sea.

Then the dam broke. And in the five days it took to empty the lake, the Clark Fork's drainage carried more water than all the rivers of the world combined. Imagine the wall of water, the scream of it, churning west nearly sixty miles an hour, scrubbing canyon walls bare in the Clark Fork and Flathead rivers, sculpting Rainbow Lake out of solid bedrock and clawing out streambeds in southeastern Washington. The lake filled and drained at least thirty-six times, each time engraving its story in the earth and necklacing Mount Jumbo with a new shoreline.

Up this river—that the Salish crossed to dig bitterroots and the Pend d'Oreilles plied with birch bark canoes and fished with hemp nets strung bank to bank—came the curious, the disaffected, the rebellious and the desperate. It was a highway of wonder, an interstate of grief.

There was Meriwether Lewis. On July 3, 1806, Lewis attempted to cross the river at a "rapid and difficult part of it crouded (sic) with several small Islands and willow bars which were...overflown." His raft sank and he had to swim to shore—wetting his chronometer, he notes with irritation. In 1809, David Thompson, the man the Salish called Koo-Koo-Sint or Man Who Looks at Stars, established the "Saleesh House" trading post above present-day Thompson Falls and mapped the area from the "brown knowl" of Mount Jumbo.

Settlers arrived in the 1850s. Chasing after the settlers came the railroad, snaking alongside the Clark Fork River in canyons so narrow the locals said dogs had to wag their tails up and down. Huge camps of railroad workers—with thousands of Chinese and many fewer white men—crawled east and west until they met at a Gold Creek in 1883.

There were also the fugitives. Take the Lee family on Trout Creek, a tributary of the Clark Fork west of Missoula. The Lees escaped from Utah after Grandpa Lee was executed for leading the September 1857 massacre of non-Mormon immigrants. They were a tough bunch. The grandmother had been partially scalped, the women carried six-shooters and one of the family members was a preacher, who married and buried them and shot them if they got out of line.

My great-grandfather was the most unlikely pioneer of them all. A sturdy, industrious Scotsman in round-rimmed glasses and wool suits, he set up a law practice in the old Florence Hotel and was not particularly unhappy, not particularly bold. "I am delighted with Missoula," he wrote in his formal script May 11, 1900. "Even if it seems as if all the nice pleasant sociable fellows I meet go to cockfights, etc."

As a child, I turned my back on the river. So did my father and his father and his father before him, for my great-grandfather built our prairie-style brown house in 1903 so that it turned away from the river to face the street—the opposite of the way people build homes today. This difference has everything to do with what people deem precious: in a sparsely populated town newly scratched into the dirt, what my great-grandfather chose to look at were other humans. Perhaps it was habit—he had just left the crowded streets of Chicago—or an instinctive huddling for warmth against the wilderness. Perhaps he needed assurance, right out his window, that he wasn't alone.

Nevertheless, when he wrote his son about his prospective home, the Clark Fork River was its principal attraction. "My dear boy," he wrote on June 28, 1900. "Right near where you are going to live when you come is a nice river. Won't we have fun fishing, though? And we can throw stones in the water, and when we get tired doing that we will hitch up the horse and take a buggy ride."

Imagine him, a young father at the crack of a new century, in search of a new home where the water is clear and the air is clean, where his frail, five-year-old son will thrive.

The train churns west across the hot prairies, over the Continental Divide and into Missoula, a wide valley surrounded by mountains and divided by rivers drunk with snow melt, and as he steps off the train that giddy day in May, he knows this is home. "My dear sweet wife. My darling Cad," my great-grandfather wrote to his wife on May 6, 1900, "Missoula is the place you can expect to settle…The business portion is very well built, several nice 4-story brick buildings with elevators, steam heat, etc., and the residences are pretty… And there are plenty of lovely drives along the river for us and Johnnie and *waa*" (the child my great-grandmother was carrying).

The possibilities of the place infected him with an uncharacteristic and slightly defensive zeal. "My darling wife and boy," he wrote June 4, 1900. "There are great opportunities here for raising fruit, principally apples…A person for $1500 can put out an orchard that in six years will begin to pay from $2000 a year. To tell you what apples and pears will do here, you'd think I was daffy."

His exuberance builds as he concludes the letter. "I'll make enough money here in a few years so both of you and Grandma and Kate and Abby will have more than they no (sic) how to spend. This is the place for the whole crowd to come and *cut out* all worrying."

Eight years after my great-grandfather arrived in Missoula, it rained for thirty-three days and thirty-three nights and the town held its breath as the Clark Fork River rose to the twelve-foot mark on the post of the old mill. Wagon bridges washed out, the Milltown Dam nearly overflowed, the Northern Pacific depot had the only working telegraph in town and railroad tracks flooded, stranding the Missoula baseball team in Helena. The Higgins Street bridge collapsed June 6, 1908, and businessmen, like my great-grandfather, who walked across the river to their offices that morning, were unable to go home. To deliver the Sunday *Missoulian*, carriers shot an arrow attached to a rope from one side of the bridge to the other, then hauled papers across the river.

I'm sure the flood's religious significance was not lost on my grandfather, for it seemed the water's fury wanted to wash his new home away, wash the land clean of anything manmade. "Everything imaginable almost came down the Missoula river yesterday," started a *Missoulian* story wittily subtitled, *Houses that Pass in the Day*, "including many houses, three railroad stations and one section house."

When the sun shone on June 8, its heat was dizzying—especially for one reporter. In *Flood Waters Fall Fast* and *Old Sol Reigns Again*, the writer proclaimed, "Yesterday was the first of the long series of days that will see the spirit of Missoula arise and correct the wrong done by the might of the waters. Western pluck has brought Missoula through the time of storm and stress. Western energy will restore her to conditions that will be so much better than those of a week ago that, a year hence, people will rise up to call the high water of 1908 blessed."

There have been many floods since then, but in February 1996, it seemed as if the water was again trying to purge the land of humans and their detritus. Floodwaters washed out deer and trees and houses and took the lives of several young men. Heavy metals—the mine tailings that have spilled downriver from Butte to Bonner's Milltown Dam for nearly a century—tipped over the dam and headed west. Those old ghosts of excess, the arsenic and copper and zinc and cadmium inheritance of our fathers, killed thousands of fish in their wake.

As a child, when I stood in the alley behind our house and looked down the bluff at the ditch bordering the river, this is what I saw: dirt-clouded bottles, tin cans, old stoves, car seats punctuated with rusty springs like errant corkscrews, and an old refrigerator. Across the river was an ice house where, for a quarter, the proprietor would allow a truckload of garbage to be dumped into the river. Further east was another garbage dump. The University and the local hospital discharged untreated sewage into the river.

The river disgusted me. The water was grey and oily-looking and occasionally ran red as blood. The fish that we caught were sluggish and sick-looking. Once, to the horror of my mother, I actually swam in the river and afterward developed a terrible itch. The river was something we turned away from, we dumped our waste in, we hated.

The Salish, who dug bitterroots and battled the Blackfeet Indians on its shores, called it the River of Awe.

I was told I could play in the yard or the neighborhood, I could even walk downtown, but I was never, ever to play by the river. This wasn't just because of the danger of drowning. The Milwaukee Railroad ran alongside the river, a world apart from my protected life. A world of hobos, those men who slipped around the edges of things and left mysterious symbols (cat's paws some say) so the others knew to show up at my great-grandmother's door for a loaf of bread or one of my great-grandfather's old overcoats. I like to think of these wilder versions of him, riding the rails out of town.

The tracks have long since been pulled up, the railroad station converted to a national hunting club. Old-fashioned lights now line the paths crowded by joggers and dogs with lolling tongues and windmilling tails. While these paths have opened up the river front for me, part of me yearns for that old sense of danger and foreboding. We have tamed our riverbanks into a land of bark-covered paths, but we have lost that sense of mystery, of life on the periphery, the hoboes drifting here and there, the trains whinnying their way out of town. The morning I found several empty bottles of Old English malt liquor near a blackened fire circle in Hellgate Canyon, I was oddly comforted.

I walk along the river in fall, winter, spring and summer. It is where I go to watch the clouds roll into our valley, it is where I go to watch them roll out. A friend once compared this walk to going to the Lincoln Memorial in Washington, D.C.—this is where we go to touch the heart of the town.

It is high spring and the sun is bright, the air is soft and all is a riot of color and sound and smell. The river is brown and muscular and fast, crawling up the banks and spilling out of the ditches—even its sound is dangerous. It floods the island in the middle of the river where, I once heard, society matrons proposed putting a whorehouse so they could keep track of who rowed out to it. "There is a whole island in the river," my great-grandfather wrote his son in May 1900, "by the bridge within 200 feet of my office and a deer was on the island eating grass. A lot of men and boys tried to catch and lasso it and nearly did, but it got away from them by swimming down the river."

From the tangle of budding mountain alder and willow, come the high staccato of chickadees, the braying of blackbirds, the liquid arpeggios of robins. Pink blossoms flock the stray apple tree in front of the *Missoulian* building and I wonder who planted it and why they left. There is the sweet smell of wet earth and of cottonwood, its leaves curled in sticky syrup.

As I walk, I feel inextricably linked to this place that filled my great-grandfather with such longing and surreptitious excitement that he had to reassure himself and his worried wife that he was constant in his affections: "If I could only go to sleep with you (and Johnnie) in my arms and *soothe* little *waa* to sleep how happy we would both be. Don't think for a moment I don't miss you just because I am in a new place with new scenes, they don't take your place for a minute."

But of course it did take their place—and why wouldn't it? Here he was in a place that was all possibility. Everything: earth, river, mountain, sky, some kind of clay he could mold in the shape of his dreams. Isn't that what happened to all of our grandfathers? At first, before the Indians were killed and the rivers were ruined and the air darkened with smoke, wasn't the West all about the intoxication of what could be? Possibility that, in the end, was destroyed because it was simply too pleasurable?

An osprey flies straight down the river, dipping down and down, threading water and sky. As I stand on the bank, four generations later with a baby of my own, I wonder if my great-grandfather would sorrow for what his generation did to the river and if he would still bring an ailing child to a country where the water is laden with heavy metals. I wonder what happened to the innocent and high hopes he brought to this raw country where he settled forever: "My dear sweet wife, I am so anxious to make a nice home for you so we can all live together and have all we want and not have to worry." Great-grandfather, I want to say as I stand on the brink of life with a new child, this river—with its beauty and its danger—is the mystery between us.

AUTHOR BIOGRAPHIES

Brian Baise is a 1995 graduate of Princeton University. A writer of both fiction and nonfiction, his work has appeared in a variety of magazines. Formerly the managing editor of *Big Sky Journal*, he is now a contributing editor and author of their Books column.

John Barsness has written on the outdoors and western history for a number of national magazines, including *Field & Stream*, *National Geographic*, *Sports Illustrated*, and *Gray's Sporting Journal*, where he also served as editor. His *Montana Time* was chosen as one of the ten best flyfishing books of the 1990s by Trout Unlimited. In 1996, he received the Excellence in Craft Award for lifetime achievement by the Outdoor Writers Association of America. He lives in Townsend, Montana, with his wife, the writer Eileen Clarke, and two Labrador retrievers.

Rick Bass is the author of fourteen books of fiction and nonfiction, including *The Book of Yaak* (essays) and *Where the Sea Used to Be* (a novel). He lives in Montana's Yaak Valley, which still does not have a single acre of protected wilderness.

Ralph Beer is the author of the Spur Award–winning novel, *The Blind Corral*. His essays and stories have appeared in *Harper's* magazine, *Modern Maturity*, and *Big Sky Journal*.

Stephen J. Bodio is a full-time writer, an old-fashioned naturalist, and a sportsman. He is the author of many highly respected books, including *On the Edge of the Wild*, *A Rage for Falcons*, *Querencia*, and *Aloft*. Bodio has been a book-review editor for *Gray's Sporting Journal* ("Bodio's Review") and a resident member at Sterling College's Wildbranch Writing Workshop. His essays and articles have appeared in *Smithsonian*, *Big Sky Journal*, *Men's Journal*, and elsewhere. Born and educated in Boston, he has lived in Magdalena, New Mexico, for seventeen years.

Tim Cahill is the author of six books, including *A Wolverine Is Eating My Leg*, *Buried Dreams*, *Pecked to Death by Ducks*, and *Pass the Butterworms*. Cahill is currently an editor-at-large for *Outside* magazine and a contributing editor to *Rolling Stone* and *Sports Afield*. He lives in Livingston, Montana.

Russell Chatham is a painter and author living in Livingston. Since 1958, he has had more than three hundred one-man exhibitions of his art. His writings include the books *The Angler's Coast*, *Silent*

Seasons, and *Dark Waters.*

Jim Crumley was born and raised in South Texas in 1939, educated at Georgia Tech, Texas A & I, and the writer's workshop at the University of Iowa. He is the author of six novels, all of which are in print and have been translated into a number of foreign languages. His books include *One to Count Cadence, The Wrong Case, The Last Good Kiss, Dancing Bear, The Mexican Tree Duck,* and *Bordersnakes.* His stories and articles have been collected in *The Muddy Fork.* He has lived in Montana since 1966.

Gary Ferguson has been a full-time, free-lance writer for seventeen years. His science and nature articles have appeared in more than one hundred national magazines, including *Outside, Sierra, American Forests, Big Sky Journal, Travel Holiday,* and productions of New York's Children's Television Workshop. He is also the author of thirteen books on nature and science. *The Sylvan Path: A Journey Through America's Forests* was a starred selection in the prestigious *Kirkus Reviews,* while *Spirits of the Wild: The World's Great Nature Myths* was selected by the New York City Public Library as one of the best books of 1996. He lives in Red Lodge, Montana, with his wife, Jane.

Dan Flores holds the endowed chair in the history of the American West at the University of Montana, Missoula. His sixth book, *Horizontal Yellow,* will be published by the University of New Mexico Press in 1999, while his book *The Natural West* will be published by the University of Oklahoma Press in the same year.

Winner of the Pacific Northwest Boooksellers awards for both his short story collection *Dry Rain* and his memoir *Indian Creek Chronicles,* **Pete Fromm**'s latest books are the collections *Blood Knot* and the *Tall Uncut.* He lives in Great Falls, Montana.

Fred Haefele's fiction and essays have appeared in publications such as *Missouri Review, Epoch, The New York Times Magazine,* and *Newsday.* His memoir, *Rebuilding the Indian,* will be published in June by Riverhead/Putnam. His novel, *City of Trees,* will be published later this summer. He lives in Missoula with his wife and daughter.

William Hjortsberg has lived in Montana for more than twenty-five years. He has published seven works of fiction, including *Alp* and *Gray Matters* and, most recently, *Nevermore.* His novel, *Falling Angel,* has been translated into twelve languages and was filmed by Allan Parker as *Angel Heart.* Screenwriting credits include *Thunder and Lightning* and *Legend* (directed by Ridley Scott). He is currently working on a biography of Richard Brautigan.

Jon Jackson is the author of the acclaimed Fang Mulheisen mystery series, most recently including *Dead Folks* and *Man with an Axe.* He lives in Missoula.

Denis Johnson's fifth novel, *Already Dead*, was published by HarperCollins in 1997.

Allen Jones moved to Montana with his family at the age of twelve, publishing his first short story two years later. Having graduated from the University of Montana with highest honors, backpacked through Europe and hunted in Africa, he became editor of *Big Sky Journal* at the age of twenty-five. His book, *A Quiet Place of Violence: Hunting and Ethics in the Missouri River Breaks*, is available through *Big Sky Journal* in Bozeman, Montana.

Robert F. Jones is the author of twelve books, most recently *The Buffalo Runners* and *Deadville*. His short stories and essays are included in twenty-one anthologies, among them *Seasons of the Hunter* and *Where We Live*. Currently a contributing editor of *Sports Afield* and *Men's Journal*, he lives on a mountain in Vermont with his wife, dogs, guns, and flyrods, but travels the badlands whenever he can.

Greg Keeler has published five collections of poetry: *American Falls, Poetryman, The Far Bank, Spring Catch*, and *Epiphany at Goofy's Gas*. He has also written three musical comedies that tour the Northwest and several collections of satirical songs.

Alan Kesselheim lives with his family in Bozeman, Montana. He balances a career as a freelance writer with a passion for adventure. When he's lucky, the two ambitions feed each other. His latest book is *Threading the Currents* (Island Press).

William Kittredge recently retired from the creative writing program at the University of Montana. His most recent books are *Hole in the Sky, Who Owns the West*, and *The Portable Western Reader*. He has books in progress for Knopf and University of California Press.

After living in places as varied as New York City, South Korea, and Antarctica, **Scott McMillion** returned in 1988 to his native Montana, where his family has lived for four generations. His writing appears in major newspapers around the nation and has won many awards for investigative and environmental reporting. He is the author of the recent *Mark of the Grizzly* (1998, Falcon Press). He lives in Livingston, Montana, with his wife and daughter.

Wally McRae is a rancher, a poet, and an entertainer...in that order. Wally and his family operate the Rocker Six Cattle Co., a cow/calf livestock ranch, just north of the Northern Cheyenne Reservation, and between the Rosebud and Tongue River. In 1989, he received the Governor's Award for the Arts and was the first Montanan to be granted a National Heritage Award by the NEA. He has been writing poetry for more than twenty-five years.

Geoffrey Norman is editor-at-large of *Forbes FYI*, the author of nine books, and has written for a number of magazines, including *Esquire, Outside, Sports Illustrated,* and *Men's Journal.*

Caroline Patterson has published fiction and nonfiction in *Epoch, Alaska Quarterly Review, Newsday, Seventeen,* and *Southwest Review.* A former Stegner fellow in fiction, she lives in her hometown, Missoula, with her husband and daughter.

Doug Peacock champions wild causes from an abandoned cathouse south of Livingston, Montana. He is the author of a highly respected book, *Grizzly Years.*

Annick Smith is a writer of essays, short fiction, and a filmmaker whose feature films include *A River Runs Through It* and *Heartland.* She was coeditor with William Kittredge of *The Last Best Place: A Montana Anthology.* Her books include *Homestead* and *Big Blue Stem: Journey into the Tall Grass.* Born in Paris, raised in Chicago, Smith is a widow who has lived for twenty-five years on her homestead ranch in Western Montana where she raised her four sons.

E. Donnall Thomas, Jr., writes regularly about bowhunting, wingshooting, fishing and wildlife for a number of magazines, including *Traditional Bowhunter, Bowhunter, Gray's Sporting Journal, Alaska, Fly Rod & Reel, Shooting Sportsman,* and *Outdoor Life.* He has published two bowhunting books, *Longbows in the Far North* and *Longbow Country,* two volumes of fly-fishing stories and a book on western wingshooting, *Fool Hen Blues.* His most recent book is *To All Things a Season.* A practicing physician when he's not outdoors, he also edits a section of the *Journal of Wilderness Medicine* dealing with the value of the outdoor experience. A former Alaska resident, Thomas now lives in a rural Montana community with his wife and children.

Toby Thompson is the author of three books of nonfiction, most recently *The Sixties Report.* He contributes frequently to many leading magazines, including *Outside, Vanity Fair, Esquire,* and *Sports Afield.* He teaches nonfiction writing at Penn State University and lives in New York City. He has been visiting Montana regularly for thirty-five years and considers Livingston his second home. He is currently writing a memoir about growing up in Washington, D.C.

Charles F. Waterman has written about the outdoors for more than sixty years and is the author of more than a dozen books on hunting and fishing.

Kim Zupan grew up and worked ranches on the eastside of the Continental Divide and spent a decade as a professional rough-stock rider. He is writing a novel from his home in Missoula.